Total Jihad

To Mayor Smith,
Thanks not just for the candy,
but for your example.

Eric Rozenman

3/03

Total Jihad

By Eric L. Rozenman

RavensYard Publishing, Ltd.
Fairfax County, Virginia USA

ISBN 1-928928-09-9

Published by
RavensYard Publishing, Ltd.
P. O. Box 176
Oakton VA, 22124 USA

www.ravensyard.com

Dedicated to
Jordana and Mikal
"From generation to generation"

Part I

> *"Thus says the Lord: 'I will return unto Zion and will dwell in the midst of Jerusalem. There shall yet old men and old women sit in the broad places of Jerusalem and the broad places of the city shall be full of boys and girls playing.'"*
>
> —Zechariah 8:4-5.

Washington, D.C. (April 20, 2007)—A killing in the White House—specifically in the Old Executive Office Building next door—was impossible to conceal, even for the president and Secret Service. But in a city whose news media functioned as its central nervous system, and an ever-excitable one at that, details of the White House shoot-out were scarce. The lid was on; neither Col. Abner Samuels' name, nor his rank or position with the National Security Council had surfaced. The fact that he died carrying a fistful of contingency plans for U.S. involvement in a Middle East war likewise remained suppressed. But the Capitol Hill grapevine—rabbit-like, prone to exaggeration, driven by e-mail—did better. It fleshed out the skeleton of official details into an entertaining, inciting melange of truth, half-truths, and falsehoods, stepbrother to television news. Still, not good enough to suit Congressman Jonathan Marcus.

Less than twenty-four hours earlier, Col Samuels, in a private briefing that violated Pentagon regulations, had delivered ominous information to him and two colleagues. A few hours later the officer, half mad and completely drunk, had set off for the White House. As far as Marcus could see, members of Congress needed to know exactly why—even if President Johnston and his artificially enhanced first lady refused to tell them....

* * *

Washington, D.C. (April 19, 2007)—A congressman in Bullfeathers at mid-afternoon was not unusual. But a congressman with an officer in uniform, decorations on his chest and well into his third drink, was. At Bullfeathers, on the House side of Capitol Hill at First and D Streets Southeast, congressional staffers and their bosses, lobbyists, reporters and consultants of every stripe preyed on each other and, thanks to deductible business luncheons, on the taxpayers.

"Another Manhattan for the colonel, another decafe for you?" the waitress asked Marcus. A provocation in designer slacks and low heels, she could have been a starlet-in-waiting in Los Angeles, Representative Jonathan Marcus thought. Here, she went to graduate school at night, studying international relations and law, and ached for a congressional committee staff job. Washington brimmed with young men and women like her, drawn by the aphrodisiac of power and the potential for money that followed. Especially young women, including some like Monica Lewinsky and Chandra Levy, for example, feminist offspring too clever to know better.

It was, he thought again, the opposite of New York, which drew people by the possibilities of money, which then would bring power—and at a tangent from L.A., where notoriety, often built on little more than bad behavior, commanded attention, which became power and perhaps ultimately, money. In New York a profile too public sometimes impeded gain; in Washington, adulation often preceded destruction.

"Ah, I'm getting too old for this," Marcus muttered, nodding at the waitress as she strode back toward the bar, her flanks high and firm against her beige slacks.

The waitress, meanwhile, wondered who the suit was with the colonel. He looked like a congressman, in the standard-issue navy blue suit, well-made, well-tailored—with the obligatory off-red tie—subtle, sharp but not flashy enough to put voters off. The officer, not a general, might be of marginal utility to her; a congressman, particularly if he turned out to be a committee chairman or ranking minority member, now that was something else. She continued attentive.

"No, you're not," Samuels slurred. "Just too cautious. Too hesitant."

The man's mind was still working, even if his tongue wasn't, Marcus thought. "And you'd better pay attention to what I'm telling you!" Samuels snapped.

Marcus glared at him, but listened, just as he had the day before, when the colonel asked to speak with him and two other pro-Israel members after a hearing at which the assistant secretary of defense for international assistance had testified. A be-ribboned colonel, in the slate blue full dress uniform of the Air Force, had been sitting near the assistant secretary at the witness table. Except for whispering some advice before the latter answered a military question, he had said nothing. Now the man—tall, lithe, with fiery eyes—approached Marcus.

"Congressman? I'm Colonel Abner Samuels, Middle East specialist on the National Security Council. Can we talk? Somewhere private?"

"Sure," Marcus replied. He had met Samuels before, at the Israeli Embassy's annual gala Independence Day reception, when the Israelis insisted on behaving as if theirs were a country like any other, established, equal, sovereign. The sliding scale of diplomatic representation each year—a full complement of European and Asian ambassadors when the Palestinians were happy, a handful of deputy chiefs of missions and the odd Balkan or central Asian military attaché when Israel cracked down on Arab terrorism—argued otherwise. Marcus suspected that the officer was Ambassador Tarbitsky's source at the N.S.C. The colonel's reputation as something of a maverick preceded him. "The chairman has a small, private office right around the corner. Staff can open it for us."

"We'll join you," said Larry Levinson, with Mel Bernstein at his side. The pair, Democrats like Marcus, fell in without an invitation. Marcus, eyebrows arched, looked at Samuels. The colonel shrugged.

The four of them marched out of the hearing room, Rayburn 2270, past the portraits of the present and former chairmen, portraits which grew larger and more florid the closer their subjects' tenures were to the present, out under the two-story high ceiling with its strong indirect lighting—meant to give this arena of policy a glow from on high, as if sanctified—and off the rich bottle green rug, decorated with leaves of gold laurel. At one of the two heavy wooden double doors Marcus hesitated, glancing at a glass-encased display box mounted on the wall.

Inside was a medal, a shard of pavement, and a small plaque. The pavement was a piece of runway from the airstrip at Jonestown, Guyana, gathered after the murder of committee member Leo Ryan in 1978. The medal was Congress' posthumous award to Ryan, and the plaque tersely recounted his selfless, relentless quest to do his job and protect his constituents. Marcus often stared at the little shrine, measuring himself and his colleagues against the example it commemorated, measuring himself and doubting.

In the chairman's small, well-appointed sitting room, a hide-out really, behind a door that carried no identification other than a number, no legend informing passers-by which committee or member worked beyond the threshold, Col. Samuels unzipped his black leather portfolio. He withdrew several photographs, eleven-by-fourteen black-and-white enlargements. Propping them on an elegantly upholstered love-seat, he pulled his Pentagon standard pen-like laser pointer from his shirt pocket and gestured authoritatively.

"Gentlemen," he said, "these satellite photographs clearly indicate the deployment of Jordanian, Iraqi and Saudi armor just east of the Jordan River, on the eastern lip of the rift valley. They highlight a similar concentration of Syrian armor on the Golan Heights and, with Lebanese markings, in the Bekaa Valley. These are large deployments. That they were there during the Thirty-Six Hour War is not news. That they remain—and have been reinforced—would be, if it were not highly classified. To keep it out of the news and off the Internet we've taken the unusual step of disabling the commercial surveillance satellites. NASA has put out a story about electro-magnetic storms in the upper atmosphere.

"And although I could not bring the photos to back up this next assertion—taking too much that would not be displayed in open session might have raised eyebrows at N.S.C.—the concentration of Iraqi and Saudi warplanes at Jordanian airfields also continues. I believe the Arabs will attempt to finish off Israel in the near future. The very near future. And that's regardless of how many more concessions the Jews make."

"So this briefing is unauthorized?" Marcus asked.

The colonel shot him a withering look, one that declared Samuels could not abide simpletons, especially not now. Marcus, unfazed, was nearly as concerned about the wild gleam in the officer's eyes as about the information the latter was leaking.

"Look, colonel," Bernstein said. "We all know these intelligence photos are subject to interpretation, let alone computer manipulation. And even when the data are clear, pictures alone can't determine intent. Otherwise, we and the Kuwaitis would not have been surprised by Iraq in 1990, the Israelis would not have been surprised by the Syrians and the Egyptians in 1973...."

Samuels cut him off. "Congressman, there's nothing ambiguous about these particular photographs. I told you what they show–thousands of enemy tanks positioned to go over to offensive operations immediately, only miles from Israeli forces, forces depleted and not resupplied after the latest fighting. As for interpretation, today's technology is a generation better than that used for the Persian Gulf in '90, half a generation ahead of that used in Afghanistan a few years back. And failure in interpreting intelligence data–like the Israelis in '73, or the Pentagon regarding China during the Clinton years–usually is a matter of political denial or wishful thinking, not technical inadequacies.

"As for intent, in the Middle East military planners rarely err by preparing for worst-case scenarios. That was the secret of Israeli success–in 1956, '67, at Entebbe in '76, Osirak in '81, even Lebanon in '82, at least early on. It was all about preemption to prevent the worst case and even winning. But beginning with the first Palestinian intifada in late '87, and Oslo in '93, war-weary and demoralized, they began betting on best-case scenarios and lost their freedom of maneuver."

"Lost it to whom?" Levinson asked.

"To themselves, to their own yearning for peace. And, in a logistical sense, to us, Congressman, to us. That was the lesson of the forced cancellation of the Lavi fighter-bomber project, of the suppressed Phalcon command-and-control plane deal with China–after which we immediately began selling the Chinese supercomputers, as if that weren't a bigger security risk." Samuels spoke as a teacher might to a sluggish class. "When we forced Sharon to withdraw from Beit Jala after just two days in 2001, leaving the residents of Gilo in Jerusalem no safer from snipers and mortars than before, when we insisted Israel let Yasir Arafat walk out his shattered offices in Ramallah five years ago, when we oversaw the stationing of international monitors in the West Bank and on the Golan Heights, we not only 'protected' Israel from international condemnation, from Syrian surprise attack, we also protected the Palestinians and then Syria against Israeli preemption.

"The closer the U.S.-Israeli strategic relationship grew," the colonel explained, "the more the smaller partner was roped to the larger. U.S. global interests predominated over Israeli regional goals. Of course, for a time it was symbiotic, politically. The Clinton administration used the Rabin and Barak governments for moves that otherwise would have sparked widespread pro-Israel opposition in this town, and the Israelis used Clinton as a talisman with their own public to make palatable otherwise unacceptable appeasements of the Arabs. Call it a suffocating embrace, for the little guy."

Levinson, a gruff, heavyset man who owned several independent service stations in Fort Lauderdale, was a savvy if rough-hewn politician. He was not afraid to ask questions, naive or otherwise, and his boisterous self-promotion notwithstanding, almost always understood the answers.

"So it's like major refiners and independent stations," Levinson said. "The guys with the product call the shots."

"Exactly."

"Why tell us?" Marcus asked. "If the White House obviously knows all this, the Israelis must know it."

"Because," Samuels nearly shouted, "the administration lies to the Israelis. It pretends the information is ambiguous, 'subject to further analysis.' Given its hesitancy and isolationism, it has to be able to give the Arabs the benefit of the doubt, and to withhold some of it from the Israelis. Go easy on your enemies, hard on your friends–that's why all those slogans about peace and multilateralism, about a new, less-violent world order remained just slogans.

"I argued about this with the White House chief of staff, and finally he said, 'Colonel, aren't you making too much of this? After all, we're talking about small, faraway countries for which we would care little–if not that a few of them have a lot of oil.'

"'Munich,' I said to him, and this guy–whose father was in diapers during World War II, said, 'What's Germany got to do with it?'

"And," Samuels continued, "We aren't sharing the most damning information with the Israelis. Haven't been for months."

"But the Israelis have a spy satellite of their own, and a pretty decent intelligence system, don't they?" Bernstein inquired, almost plaintively.

"They did launch a replacement surveillance device of their own, yes, Ofek-6. A nice, compact piece of work. But we think they've had some trouble with it. Maybe Arab sabotage. Maybe someone else..." he said. "As for Israeli intelligence, perhaps it's been compromised from within."

The colonel, Marcus decided, was a conspiracy theorist. Well-informed, but a conspiracy theorist nevertheless, seeing hidden hands where there were no arms. But when Samuels called a few hours later to beg for a one-on-one conversation as soon as possible, Marcus had agreed.

*　　*　　*

"So Pollard was right," Samuels was saying. The brilliant, naive jerk was right. You ever hear of a guy named Sid Solomon? A Jew, worked for D.I.A. during the Yom Kippur War. When he realized Defense Intelligence knew the war was coming, two or three days out, and that the agency was not about to inform the Israelis, it nearly broke his heart. Well, as penitence, Solomon quit not long after, moved to Israel, and raised a family in one of the settlements across the Green Line, one of those dismantled not long ago in Israel's assisted suicide.

"Anyway, he wrote an article about it, eighteen or nineteen years later, in the Jerusalem Post. Claimed there were secret units, secret rooms at the Pentagon, C.I.A. and so on, from which Jews with even the highest security clearances were barred. Units so black hardly anybody outside them even knew about, except for two cabinet secretaries and the president.

"After I read the article–I was a major then–I just picked up the telephone, dialed Israeli information, got his number, and talked to him. Talked to him a couple of times, hours on end. Damn expensive." Samuels trailed off, his head sagging into his hands.

"What was I saying? Oh yeah, Solomon. He couldn't convince me at first.

Sounded a little paranoid, a little too much the autodidact's tour d' horizon. After all, I was a Jewish officer in U.S. Air Force intelligence, with a security clearance of my own, and no one had ever stopped me from getting something on a need-to-know basis.

"But, based on what he claimed, I started nosing around. I couldn't confirm his allegations, but judging by the cul-de-sacs that should have been through streets, the silence and even hostility I stirred up from people that—until I started my little hunt—I thought were buddies, I got a pretty good idea of the size and shape of the 'off-limits-to-Jews' zone.

"Solomon was right. And a decade later Pollard bumped into the same black zone. The part that let Bush the elder run guns to the Iranians before Iran-contra, trying to free the dumb-ass hostages. That's why Pollard started dumping folders full of documents about Iraqi chemical weapons and Syrian missiles and Iranian nukes on the Israelis. You know, in 1991, when Saddam launched his Scud missiles at Tel Aviv, and every Israeli family had a 'sealed room' to hide in and gas masks to wear, it was mainly because Pollard had spilled the beans. And that's really why the poor scapegoat got the rug pulled out from under his plea bargain and got life in solitary instead of ten years. Not because Weinberger first thought the espionage damage really done by Aldrich Ames had been caused by Pollard, but because Pollard would have exposed Vice President Bush's tie to the Iranian-Lebanese terrorist connection, and exposed America's deception of Israel, contrary to the U.S.-Israeli memorandum on strategic cooperation."

"The names and dates are right, I'll give you that," Marcus said. "But the whole thing sounds pretty fanciful."

"Fanciful? Fanciful!" Samuels shook his head, discouraged at the ineptitude of his congressional student. "You ever hear about the 'level battlefield' doctrine? At the same time we signed the memorandum of understanding in '83, some other senior people at Defense and Central Intelligence—Weinberger, Inman and others—fell for this idea. While our public policy claimed that the Arabs would make peace only with a strong Israel—hence our hefty military aid—our private policy, this thing at the center of the 'off-limits-to-Jews' zone, held that only a strong Egypt, strong Saudi Arabia, Jordan, and so on, would neutralize Israel's domineering posture, and be likely to accept it back in the pre-'67 lines.

"Never mind the religious, cultural roots of the war, the necessity of police states like Syria, Iraq and Iran to have an external enemy to deflect popular discontent onto, never mind the Arab-Islamic cultural hostility to Western—to American, to Judeo-Christian—success. I mean, damn, if the World Trade Center and Pentagon attacks taught us anything." Samuel finished his fourth glass and nodded to the hovering waitress for a fifth.

"Oh yeah, the 'level-battlefield' doctrine. Well, the bean counters decided it was Israel's military qualitative edge that made the Middle East unstable. It was the defense-intelligence establishment's counterpart of the State Department Arabists' idea that the Arabs, not the Israelis, were the aggrieved party in the Middle East."

"Your point?" Marcus said, simultaneously fascinated and irritated.

"Uh-huh," Samuels slurred, lapsing into a drunk's maddening familiarity.

"This level battlefield nonsense: Idea was, if only the Arabs—who outnumber the Israelis about fifty to one—had more tanks and planes, just as good as the Jews, then there'd be peace. Each side would be strong... but not strong enough to beat the other. That's what they figured, anyway—forgetting that at some point quantity overwhelms quality, if those with the quality aren't totally on top, or lose their morale. The AWACS deal back in '81 was the start of it. Turns out it and the other multi-billion arms deals that followed weren't just to recycle petro-dollars and maintain jobs in U.S. defense firms. No... they also were 'to encourage the Arabs to support the peace process.' It was a double game, with a weaker Israel as one object. By '91, with the Egyptians rearming with U.S. money and material, and the Syrians included in the Gulf War alliance, thanks to a fungible Saudi payment of $2 billion—which they immediately spent on weapons—it was happening. Like always!" This last Samuels practically shouted.

"If you can't handle your liquor, not to mention your theories, I'm out of here!" Marcus swore at him in a whisper.

Samuels slowly put down his new drink and looked directly into Marcus' eyes. The congressman thought the colonel was about the cry. "Don't you see, they're letting us down again. Not just letting, but abetting. Abandoning." Samuels sobbed. Tears ran down his cheeks.

From a few booths off, the waitress observed them. Can't be two gays quarreling, she thought. Two old, successful homosexuals this indiscreet? Not even today, not in Washington. Can't be. She edged closer and strained to listen.

"Here," Samuels said, opening his briefcase and sliding an unmarked folder toward Marcus. "See that you read this. Read it an' unnerstand it. I'm sending a copy to Admiral Win Fogerty. And now, please leave me alone."

Damn, the waitress thought. The suit is leaving. I wonder what they were arguing about? And what was in that folder the colonel passed to the congressman?

Samuels wiped his face, stuffed the handkerchief back into his pocket, and stared at the other patrons, especially the women in their business-like suits. The Hillary look, he thought. He had them figured, all right. As they claimed equality with men, an unconscious femininity—counterbalance to feminism—called for higher heels, skirts with deeper slits, retro-tailoring from the 1940s and '50s accentuating bosom, hips or both. Accept us as peers, the female half of the white-collar world demanded of the male half. See me for what I am, signaled each individual female in her own jewelry, coiffure, and eye shadow—womanly.

God, Samuels thought, filtering the images through that of his ex-wife, that belle of the South seared into his brain like an icon. What hard, brittle, beautiful faces. What firm, compulsively exercised, diet-denied bodies. What a grim charade!

And the men: marathon runners, M.B.A. body-builders, Ph.D. tri-athletes— most overcompensating for the fact that they'd never tested themselves in battle against other men, tested their own courage against imminent death. Tough on themselves as they might be, it was all voluntary—leaving them spiritually soft, and they knew it. Probably not a combat draftee among them. So they hid from the timeless skirmish between men and women, letting the latter proclaim the war over and pretending it was so. On the off chance representatives of these inverted camps successfully mated, he knew the result. He had seen it many times in this town—one child, one-private schooled, impeccably turned out, over-wound child. Two if they were Catholic. Busy with external lives, property owners barren of hearth and home, they collected their mandatory, solitary offspring they way they purchased BMW automobiles and Club Med vacations.

He wanted to shout at the women: "Don't you understand why these guys make lousy husbands, lousy fathers, lousy lovers? Because you've won. You've vanquished them. What do you expect of the defeated?"

The joke, like so many others, was on him, Samuels realized, even through the haze of alcohol. He was a dinosaur to them, a bitter disappointment to himself. They had invested so much in their post-modern life-styles they didn't comprehend that what they had was a style, not a life. As for him, he had neither, just three grown children each living about as far from him as possible and in touch just enough to maintain appearances but not to penetrate his loneliness.

He stared at his copy of the papers he'd passed to Marcus. The words blurred, replaced by images of a small boy on a school playground. This boy was thin and awkward, a target of ridicule from his more athletic classmates. Sometimes they taunted him with cries of "sissy." At other times, they circled him, like a wolf pack around a stray sheep. Then faces he still remembered shouted "coward" and "Jew-boy!"

The youngster ran home after school, seeking solace, seeking an explanation. His mother had none, except to say that "maybe they learned it at home. They don't really mean it." In his child's pain, he felt they meant it, all right.

He turned to his father. "Don't bring me those stories," the old man shouted. "I don't want to hear them again. I went through it—now it's your turn. They'll grow out of it, and you'll grow tougher." And then his father turned away.

As soon as he could, the boy turned away too. He made his way not as a Jew but as one of the others. Or so he had imagined for many years.

"Here you are, sir!" the waitress said brightly, having calculated finally that Samuels was worth cultivating. She placed another drink on the table. "Hard duty?" she asked sympathetically.

Samuels eyed her. Not bad. In fact, damn good. But a decade late.

"Thanks," he mumbled, then pretended to look at his papers again, as if they were not committed to memory. He cupped the cold, squat little tumbler in his hands, slowly brought it to his lips. Honest, he thought, unlike my waitress. One of the last honest drinks left—the Manhattan and the martini both counted. Simple mixes of crisp hard liquor, almost astringent, powerful and genuine. To move alcohol from bottle to brain with economy and, yes, sophistication, nothing could beat them. He'd noticed years ago that most people—especially most younger people, no longer ordered such drinks. They no longer drank mixed drinks much at all. The specialty at Bullfeathers, in fact, was some concoction called Chesapeake Bay Iced Tea. Another small, sweet dishonesty.

At last Samuels rose to leave. He walked unsteadily across the hardwood floor, bumping into other patrons.

"Excuse me," a well-dressed, better-coiffed young man demanded as Samuels brushed by him. Samuels felt the weight of the briefcase in his hand and snarled at the man. "All right, sonny, you're excused!" The younger man backed up like a compact car suddenly thrown into reverse.

Samuels lurched two blocks up to Independence Avenue and hailed a taxi. The driver was Haitian. His black face and French name shown from the license on the right windshield visor. Cab drivers, store clerks, waiters, emergency room physicians, government economists–hardly anyone is born here anymore, Samuels thought. And no one acts like it matters. A common language without a common culture? No such military, he knew. And probably no such nation.

"Where to, mon?" the cabbie shouted over reggae-rap music throbbing monotonously, ominously from a tape player.

"Seventeenth and Pennsylvania," Samuels said, asking for the corner along-side the Old Executive Office Building. The OEOB, next door to the White House, served as headquarters for much of the presidential staff. The cab driver worked through the rush hour traffic past the Smithsonian Castle, around the Washington Monument, up Fourteenth Street to Pennsylvania. In the back seat the officer wadded several sticks of gum and put them into his mouth, chomping vigorously to freshen his breath. He also slipped his .45 caliber service automatic from the briefcase into the waistband of his pants, concealed by his dress uniform jacket. Samuels exited the cab and dropped a thick envelop addressed to his old colleague Admiral Chester W. Fogerty into a mailbox. Just in case Marcus forgot. He then walked up Pennsylvania Avenue, took a last look at the placards of the full-time disarmament supplicants squatting across the street in Lafayette Park, and turned into the staff gate for the OEOB.

Samuels swiped his National Security Council staff pass through the auto-matic reader at the guard house and the wrought-iron gates swung open. He walked through them and around a metal-detector, past the Chevrolet Suburban parked in the drive to obstruct any gate-crashing truck bomber, and up the steps.

The Old Executive Office Building, a massive block of turn-of-the century gray Gothic revival, was in many ways the archetypal American county court-house writ large. However, here toiled not only clerks and technicians required to answer the president's mail and screen his invitations, the professional liaisons to the professional ethnic organizations, the speechwriters and image mongers, but also the intimate, trusted advisors who helped set the nation's direction–to the extent that a heterogeneous country of 285 million people stretched continental-ly across 3,000 miles could have its direction set consciously by anonymities instead of subconsciously by beliefs.

The hallways, with their impractically high ceilings, burnished brass wall lamps and high-gloss black and white parquet floors really were corridors of power, on occasion. And along one of them Samuels had a friend–an acquain-tance, actually–the vice president of the United States. In this ponderous yet sym-metrical great gray heap (before the euphemistically-named Department of Defense moved to the Pentagon, this building had housed the War Department) the vice president maintained an office, balancing the one he used in the Capitol as president of the Senate.

A shadow-less figure who not long ago had seemed on his way to becoming a forgettable senator, the vice president appreciated Samuels. "You know,"

Charles Hobart had explained to his wife, "I found him unusual—opinionated, experienced in martial affairs, a little dangerous and hence quite unlike most of my political acquaintances. You excepted, of course," the vice president had laughed. "Anyway, when the colonel had called to say it was urgent that we meet, I made time."

Samuels misunderstood their relationship, and pictured himself as the vice president's unofficial national security consultant. And he expected Hobart to take his Middle East plan to the president himself.

The colonel darted past the vice president's personal secretary as she ushered him into the office. Samuels glared at her, and, slurring the words, said, "Okay, you can leave now. This is a private session."

The vice president said nothing, but nodded. The secretary closed the door behind her. Hobart could smell the whiskey fumes rising from Samuels, even though he'd obviously just chomped a pack of Juicy Fruit.

"Colonel, you're drunk," the vice president stated.

"Sorry, sir. But I wasn't when I called," Samuels replied.

"You've got five minutes. Don't waste them," Hobart declared. He was surprised at his own firmness. Hell, he might have won the New Hampshire primary with that tone of voice. Of course, he might have done a lot of things besides becoming the disappearing vice president to an egomaniacal chief executive. Like gotten elected as attorney general of Wisconsin again. Something more worthwhile.

Samuels had pulled a sheaf of papers from his briefcase and spread them on Hobart's desk and began mumbling. His disjointed presentation related somehow to the Arab-Israeli war. From what the vice president could gather, the colonel thought the use of nuclear weapons imminent, that such use could entangle the U.S., harm security interests in the oil producing countries, and that America had an obligation to help the Jews avoid destruction.

"So you see, Chuck, vital U.S. interests are at stake!" Samuels shouted. Then he belched.

Hobart asked, "But why haven't I heard of this before?" He was morbidly curious, in spite of Samuels' boorishness.

The colonel giggled. "I may be drunk but I'm not naive. You haven't heard because a certain fake-boobed former weatherwoman thought you weren't important enough to be told. Or that you took too much of Hersh Hestin's money when you ran against Johnston in the Iowa caucuses and New Hampshire primary, that you're too close to the Jews, or that you might get in the way of her own presidential ambitions. And because the few people on the president's staff who know about my analysis disagree—the stupid bastards!"

The vice president was torn. Samuels was clearly drunk, probably manic, on an "I'm right and the rest of the world is wrong" rant familiar to anyone long in politics. On the other hand, Hobart already suspected that his connection to Hersh Hestin and the pro-Israel lobby had poisoned his standing with Mrs. Johnston—the nation's better-than-natural, MENSA-rated First Lady and former Queen of Indianapolis' Weather.

"Tell you what," the vice president said. "You come back here tomorrow,

16   *Total Jihad*

sober, and give a proper briefing to me and my senior staff, and then I'll decide whether to go to the boss with this."

"I'll tell you what!" Samuels flashed. "I'll take it to the boss, now, with your assistance!" Then he stuck his .45 in Hobart's face.

The vice president was terrified, yet part of his mind continued functioning normally, or hyper-normally—as if he was in an unfolding car crash, registering every detail of the split-second disaster in mental slow motion. Even before the colonel began yanking him toward the door, he smashed his foot onto the silent alarm under his desk.

A large, rectangular hall runs around the outer rim of each of the first five floors of the OEOB. It is dissected by two shorter interior halls. One can cross to the Oval Office in a minute.

"C'mon Chuck, move!" Hobart threatened. "Don't make me drag you. I might stumble and accidentally squeeze the trigger."

The vice president stood—he was nearly as tall as Samuels—and began to walk. He expected a detail from the basement security office, in full riot-gear, to intercept them at any moment.

Of course, Samuels knew how White House security operated as well the vice president did. Expecting the same thing, he decided on an evasion.

First he hit an elevator call button, then said "we're going to walk downstairs to street level and stroll over to the Oval Office, two good friends going to see a third on urgent business. I'll just keep my pistol concealed. But you'll be a hostage to leverage a meeting with the president under a safe passage guarantee. After he hears me out, I promise I'll surrender."

Samuels was well into this reverie when he tripped at the top of the southeast stairwell. He involuntarily jerked the trigger. The .45 slug ricocheted off a metal banister, sounding to Hobart like an artillery piece echoing in the stairwell.

The colonel swore and grabbed the vice president's arm to hurry him down. But it was too late. Secret Service agents were pounding up the stairs. One shouted for Samuels to halt and drop his weapon.

Leadenly, now in the same slow-motion mental imagery as Hobart had experienced moments before, Samuels released the vice president. They were on the landing between the third and fourth floor in the southwest stairwell in the Old Executive Office Building. Then, his service automatic still in his right hand, the colonel pivoted in a crouch toward the security men. Later Hobart would swear had heard the colonel say something really weird: "No more Jew-boy."

In less time than it takes for a thought to register, he heard Samuels mutter, heard the gun shots from above, watched Samuels pitch forward as if hit by an electric jolt, and saw him dead on the parquetry. His heart and lungs were shredded by the machine pistol fire.

Copies of the papers the colonel had handed to Congressman Marcus and mailed to Admiral Fogerty tumbled from inside his shattered briefcase. They littered the tiles around Samuel's sprawled body. Blood from gaping exit wounds in his back made a small puddle beneath him, encroaching on his plan to save the Jews.

Marcus, still an occasional golfing buddy of the vice president, had collected these details against the administration's black out. So it was that Patrick Beadle got his anonymous tip.

"This Beadle, of the Middle East Spectator?"

"Yes," the journalist responded, an uncomfortable feeling in his stomach. The serious voice sounded like work coming, maybe hard work.

"You hear about the shooting at the White House yesterday?"

"At the Old Executive Office Building, you mean to say?" Beadle responded, trying to preserve his British public school veneer and to sound like he knew more than the sparse details released so far.

"Right. Listen. I work on the Hill. Samuels privately briefed some members on confidential matters relating to U.S. involvement in the latest Arab-Israeli war. Things aren't what they seem. Samuel knew too much about the sell-out of Israel. You've got White House sources. There's a Pulitzer here."

"Wait!" Beadle shouted into the receiver, British reserve evaporated. "What do you mean, 'knew too much?' And who are you?"

But his caller had hung up. Beadle's caller I.D. showed only "unpublished number."

Two hours later, two largely futile hours on the telephone to contacts at the White House, National Security Council, Pentagon, State Department and Congress, Beadle had nearly given up hope. What a labyrinth! He'd almost abandoned the effort of confirming the bizarre tip. The few sources who talked—all not for attribution, most off the record altogether—added supposition, rumor, theories about the plight of the Jews; as if he cared. He learned there were voices in the administration, a few, urging more forceful American action. But nothing more. Everyone in this town liked to talk, although many made it a practice not to say much. One couldn't be misquoted that way. So Beadle decided to do what worked best in such straits: socialize.

He glanced at his gold Rolex. It wasn't that the Middle East Spectator paid him so well—his car was used, his shoes resoled, his upper Connecticut Avenue apartment building in truth not as well maintained as the address suggested—but the Rolex had been a gift from Chairman Arafat himself. On such fortunate coincidences, he knew, his reputation rested. It was time, the Rolex confirmed, for the Secretary of State's annual reception for the foreign press.

Just before his thirtieth birthday, Patrick Beadle had won the British equivalent of a Pulitzer for chronicling the fall of the Shah of Iran. He'd been there mostly because the wire service he worked for at the time had cut costs by not filling the post of the recently-retired bureau chief, and left him to his own devices in the midst of revolution. Beadle made the most of his opportunity, and stayed on. His dispatches seemed both urgent and exotic as the once lively, if corrupt, Tehran became outwardly the morbid city of the mullahs. Supporters of the ousted Shah and skeptics of Khomeini's direct connection to Allah fell before the firing squad, byline by byline. The city's real life flowed surreptitiously, behind shuttered windows and contained in private courtyards, but of this he did not write until one of the komitehs, which were everywhere, finally upbraided him for the whiskey bottle tipped in the incomplete privacy of his hotel room. Beadle returned to England something of a hero.

There, a few years later, he befriended the somewhat uncertain new American ambassador. That ambassador now was secretary of state, and liked to reminisce with Beadle about his London days. The latter never dissuaded him.

Beadle left his tiny cubicle at the White House press room, strode through the basement of the Old Executive Office Building—police were still stopping anyone without authorization from reaching the upper floors—and crossed Seventeenth Street. He walked opposite the Corcoran Galley, its would-be artists on the steps, their clothes fashionable grunge, as distinct from the encrusted grunge of the homeless squatting on the lawn a few feet away. He stepped quickly past the superb old red brick Octagon House at Eighteenth and New York Avenue, where President James Madison and wife Dolly had lived after Beadle's ancestors torched the White House nearly two centuries earlier. He soon reached the State Department and went in through the Diplomatic Entrance on C Street.

Beadle passed through the metal detector, once more wondering how much low level radiation, repeated several times daily at the entrances to official Washington, would prove fatal for the first terrorism generation. He ran his magnetized press pass through the reader, and pushed open the turnstile. Beyond the armed guards an elevator stood open at the west end of the two-story lobby. In the foyer itself the flags of the one hundred and eighty-five or so nations recognized by the United States were on permanent and colorful display. Many of those countries, Beadle knew, were less important than half the states in America. But, to him, they were infinitely more interesting. Without Boston and New York, San Francisco and, well, Washington, Beadle doubted he could tolerate the country. It would be like what, France without Paris? A crude, often thuggish France—with lower class Spanish dialects replacing French. Oppressive, he thought.

A special-duty operator pressed the elevator button for the seventh floor.

"I hope you're getting overtime for this," the reporter said.

The young woman, with high, exotic African cheekbones and artificially long, menacing-looking fingernails, offered the merest smile. She said nothing.

It seemed to Beadle that nearly all the State Department police and receptionists, guides and public contact personnel—who sometimes doubled as special duty elevator operators—were black. Nearly all the high-ranking diplomats were white. He himself was comfortable with this, but took care not to let on. In fact, in his periodic "Letters from Washington" in the Spectator, he occasionally offered the lament that "a half-century after legal desegregation, twenty years after the recognition of the multicultural imperative, official Washington remains nearly as segregated, functionally, as official London. Maybe more so." Two birds with one stone. So satisfying.

At the reception itself, in the exquisitely remodeled Franklin Room, the waiters and bartenders were mostly Hispanic or of Middle Eastern origin, with a few Koreans and Vietnamese thrown in. The same was true, Beadle thought—not, of course, that it mattered, not really—at most office buildings, hotels and anywhere else one of the catered receptions around which official Washington revolved was in progress. Entering the long hall he automatically glanced out through the series of French doors on the southern side. They opened to a shrubbery-bordered balcony that looked across the Potomac River toward Alexandria and Reagan

National Airport. Just below, on the other side of Constitution Avenue, stood the marble magnificence of the Lincoln Memorial. Along the Mall to the east, the Washington Monument was bathed in late afternoon sunlight. Further off but still visible through the same doors gleamed the Jefferson Memorial. It was one of his favorite views in a town that, absent the perks of his job, he wouldn't really care for. Beadle had savored the scene many times previous, covering state dinners and receptions for all sorts of foreign dignitaries.

The scene inside afforded its own panorama. The room itself was about sixty feet long, with three chandeliers spaced evenly along the high ceiling. A gold-trimmed cornice joined the cream-colored ceiling to the walls and fluted, carnation-colored marble columns surrounded the entire room, standing out from the walls at eight-foot intervals. Between these hung generally somber oil paintings of previous secretaries of state. But the portrait of the nation's first diplomat showed a ruddy-faced Franklin with a small smile about his lips and a knowing twinkle in his eyes. Beadle had been in this room on more than one occasion during which that portrait of Old Ben, wise and mischievous, seemed more vibrant than the faces of most of the living. Beadle felt certain that Franklin could have charmed that elevator operator into activities he himself would never dare suggest.

The secretary of state, having cut short a golf vacation in the Caribbean to deal with the latest Arab-Israeli crisis, nevertheless showed a bit of tan and the satisfaction of a man whose last round had been a good one.

"Patrick," the secretary said, breaking from a growing knot of anonymous scribes cosseting him for attention. Once more he greeted Beadle like a rescuer. "Nice to see you," he said, real brightness in his often-mimicked monotone.

"How are you?" Beadle asked politely. To his surprise, the secretary of state told him.

"I just had my annual physical, and everything's fine. Even had a damned colonoscopy. Ever since Reagan they've made that mandatory out at Bethesda." Beadle had difficulty imagining the secretary of state in a worthless hospital gown, secured to an examining table and being thus probed; the man seemed to have been born in a dark business suit, dark wing-tip shoes to match. Beadle thought it a measure of the Americans' national lack of taste, or perhaps lack of sense of place, that even a cabinet officer found a colonoscopy fit for small talk at a public event. Next thing you know, they'd be comparing prostate exams.

"Well, there's your scoop, ladies and gentlemen of the press: 'Doctors Proclaim Secretary of State Fit in Case of Succession Crisis.'" The reporters, who had regrouped around Beadle and the secretary, stared. They did not know the secretary to joke. But Beadle did, so to save this inestimably valuable source yet again, he began to laugh uproariously. The secretary joined him and, after an uncertain second, so did the others.

Suddenly, the secretary stopped. "And remember," he admonished them in mock solemnity, "this entire reception is off-the-record. Why, it isn't even happening." Then he laughed some more.

To stress the point, the department's chief spokesman, an icy Foreign Service Officer still awaiting his first ambassadorial posting, stepped in: "And I, at least, am not jesting. No stories about the physical. No stories about the vacation."

Giving his tight-lipped, professional smile, he added," This is a social occasion. Period."

In Washington, as Beadle had learned early, social did not always mean enjoyable. But for him no occasion was purely social, and he took advantage of the spokesman's interruption to steer the secretary toward the dessert table, laden with tiny chocolate and cream delicacies. Somewhere, among the black, Hispanic, Korean and Vietnamese catering staff was a pastry chef with an unerring Viennese touch, he thought.

"You were at a White House meeting with the president and vice president yesterday. What the hell happened over there?" he asked in his most Etonian inflection.

The secretary of state brought his head close to Beadle's. Within five minutes–including time for both of them to chomp several of the miniature desserts– the reporter had confirmed the story of Samuels' killing. "But don't quote even a 'high administration official.' Nothing more than 'a usually well-informed source.' Got me?"

"Got you."

Sometimes, Beadle thought, stuffing two more napkin-wrapped pastries into his jacket pocket and slipping through the throng of reporters still eating, drinking and talking–mostly to each other–if one worked long enough, the job could seem easy. He glanced at his Rolex; he had five minutes to walk out via one of his favorite rooms in Washington, a gallery off the main hall. It was a miniature museum of America at birth.

In it he examined once more Jefferson's desk, a drafting-table device the Virginian had designed himself. Beadle looked at the original of the Treaty of Paris in its glass case, the signatures of Franklin, Adams and Hay virtually unfaded. On the wall was a Rembrandt Peale portrait of Washington, and in a cabinet stood full sets of serviceable yet well-wrought silverware by one Paul Revere.

How, Beadle wondered, would the children of electronic mail and digital pictures retain their own history? Virtually? Would that be history, really? With no past, no past of parchment, wood and metal, would they have a material future? Or would it all be plastic and electrons, instantly moldable, readily shattered, instantly accessible, revisable, deleteable? Whatever, he decided, in what's left of my lifetime, history still is always in the making. And he was about to give it another push.

As he stepped into the elevator for the ride back down, his face must have shown a more positive, confident expression. In any case, the operator seemed to reappraise him. She smiled, more of a crease about the lips, really, but a smile of sorts. He smiled back, and was suddenly aware of her scent. "Are you here full-time?" he asked.

"Here, no," she said, meaning the elevator. "At State, sort of. I do translation, French, for the Bureau of African Affairs, when I'm not in school. American University, in the graduate program for international relations."

The best kind, Beadle thought.

"Here's my card," he said. "Perhaps I can call you. As a source."

"Perhaps," she replied.

As the elevator stopped, he pulled the pastries out of his pocket and handed one to her. "They're extraordinary," he said. "Try it."

She closed the door and headed back up. Another cheap English journalist, she thought. No more than a bachelor's degree, for sure. Still, the pastry was excellent.

As for Beadle, he hailed a cab on C Street, the story already in his notebook, the woman on his mind, feeling younger than he had in months.

Marcus read The Middle East Spectator story closely. It identified Samuels correctly and revealed that he had appeared with Assistant Secretary of State M. Grace Pittson before the House International Relations subcommittee on the Middle East only hours before his death. In fact, one of the accompanying pictures from the hearing showed Marcus himself, in the background but visible. Jeez, either I'm starting to show my age or that's a particularly grainy print, the representative thought.

According to the Patrick Beadle-bylined story—God, how Marcus detested that arrogant, greasy-haired British antisemite—Samuels "seemed almost irrational" with committee members at the end of the meeting, and "nearly fought with Rep. Jonathan Marcus (D-Va.) on his way out." Little attention was paid, however, to the substance of the colonel's warnings. A reference to his personal contingency plans, misidentified as a Pentagon threat assessment, was buried deep in the story. "Usually well-informed sources," not otherwise identified, described Samuels as a "mid-level analyst with a history of personal problems."

The country buzzed with the story of "the White House shoot-out." For two days. It then was eclipsed by a federal court ruling citing free speech protection for homosexual acts in music videos. And one day after that came the jubilant confession by a prominent television talk-show host that he once had been married to an illegal alien who organized farm workers for a union subsequently revealed to have Mafia ties.

* * *

Alexandria, Virginia (April 24, 2007)—"Now, these pictures from the Middle East." Jeri Levi looked toward the image of the anchorman. "Shh!" she hissed at the children, playing on the floor behind her.

Another riot. Police clubbing demonstrators, clouds of tear gas, rocks being thrown. God, she was sick of it. Arab police, Jewish rioters.

Rabbi Jeri Levi was sick of it, but not used to it. She stared at the television, like a devotee before a priest, at the pictures beamed from six thousand miles away. The longer she watched, the more agitated she became.

On the screen, dust rose and mingled with tear gas, partially obscuring the end of the protest. An American reporter, fresh-faced but with a voice trained to portentousness, intoned "the end of another outburst organized by the Zionist underground. How long this will continue before peace between Arab and Jew returns to the Holy Land remains to be seen. But as Prime Minister Mahmoud

Terzi told me today, 'All we are saying is we will give peace a chance,' Moving words. Tom...."

Through the open sliding glass door to the deck a breeze drifted in, brushing the rabbi's cheeks. It irritated her. In a refurbished Federal-era townhouse near Old Town in Alexandria, a block west of the Potomac River, with her two children fighting over Legos on the floor behind her, Jeri Levi spat out a prayer: "Almighty God, I beseech you: send someone to stop this. Now!"

The report had been no more fatuous than a dozen others she had seen or read in recent days, but the sight of fleeing Jews hit hard. "Peace–why does it mean something for everyone but us?" she demanded of the uncomprehending screen. Levi, rabbi of Alexandria's Or Kodesh–Holy Light–Reform temple, one of the first and still one of the comparatively few women rabbis to head a large, urban American congregation, was talking back to the television. Again.

"What did you say, dear?" asked her husband. Hal Levi entered from the deck, from which he had been watching pleasure craft move through late afternoon sunlight to their berths at the Alexandria Yacht Club.

"Land-for-peace. Wasn't that what the United States promised Israel after the Persian Gulf War? What Rabin and Peres, Netanyahu and Barak made endless concessions for? Final resolution of the Arab-Israeli conflict–mutual recognition, compromise, internationally guaranteed security? Well, Israel gave up the land and this is the peace."

"Jeri, give it a rest. You're becoming obsessive. Okay, I admit it–things have been disappointing since Israel finally withdrew from the territories and the Palestinians established their republic. And this war–tragic, of course. But objectively, it does not affect us," Hal Levi said.

Objectively. As if that was not a subjective term, especially when he used it, she thought. Talk about abused words. Like when he said love and meant sex. Like peace, which in Tibet, Cambodia, Sri Lanka, Bosnia, Northern Ireland, Sudan, Angola, Kosovo, a dozen other places and above all Israel had been process, not peace; death, not life.

"The Palestinians didn't just set up their own country, or have you forgotten? With their en masse 'family reunifications' plus Israel's Arabs–a demographic fifth column–they've have made the country a 'bi-national secular democracy.' That was part of the covert deal for Egypt and the Saudis to join America's 'war against terrorism,' which turned out to be mostly the battle in Afghanistan–letting bigger terrorists, like Iran and Syria, off the hook, and pretending that China, the great proliferator, wasn't the worst threat of all. In the end just buying off a little of the hostility of the Arab street over Iraq at the Jews' expense. So, a free Jewish state no longer exists. Not de facto anyway. Israel now is more of a circumscribed international protectorate–and not very damn well protected.

"And how can you say it doesn't affect us? Those Israelis, or should I say hope-to-be former Israelis, many of them former Russians, Argentines, Ethiopians in lines snaking around the U.S. Embassy, begging for visas to America, an America closed to all but a trickle of Jews–that doesn't affect us? Antisemitic demonstrations at Georgetown–doesn't affect us? Followers of Farrakhan and

Sharpton in Congress—doesn't affect us? Denial—the strongest Jewish trait."

"No sermons, please," Hal interrupted. "I'm a husband first, congregant only second." He refilled his whiskey and soda and returned to the deck.

How had she come to marry this man, this stranger, this, accidental Jew who fathered her children, she thought. Ah, the delusion that one can make another person, unrelated by blood, over in one's own image. The delusion that one can understand a person of the opposite sex, especially one who does not want to understand himself. The delusion that American Jew and Jewish American can intermarry. That was how.

Jeri Levi sighed, picked up her tumbler of rose and soda, went out to join her husband and tried again. "Remember the lines of Lebanese Christians, waiting for visas so they could flee Beirut in the Eighties? Now it's the Jews turn—partly because of American self-deception, partly due to Israeli demoralization, and partly because American Jews refused to end our exile and go build our homeland."

Hal Levi gave his wife a searching look. "Exile? I've never been in exile. Homeland? This is my homeland—Alexandria, Virginia. The United States of America! And there've been more rabbis in my family than in yours—even counting you. So stop sniffing fire and brimstone, Jeri. Please."

Rabbi Levi turned and walked back inside, alone.

* * *

West Jerusalem (April 24, 2007)—"They're burning effigies of the president and the secretary of state in front of the American ambassador's residence again."

"Good! But better if they can get the originals."

Pnina Yehezkeli had been Meir Sarid's secretary for years, starting long before he became prime minister. She enjoyed his dry humor as much as anyone did. But it was getting harder, she thought.

"So?" Yehezkeli asked.

"The minister of police knows?"

"Yes, and he'll be here soon."

"Okay, let him handle it. If they set fire to the residence, I don't care—but make sure the ambassador is safe. We may need a hostage," the prime minister said. After recognizing the Arab Republic of Palestine, the United States had moved the residence of its ambassador in Israel to southwestern Jerusalem, at the same time turning the U.S. consulate in eastern Jerusalem into its embassy for Palestine. But most official chancery functions remained in the large beachfront complex in Tel Aviv. Washington thereby mollified the Jews while hoping to minimize offense to the Muslims.

In his office, the door closed behind him, Sarid did not feel much like joking. What he felt like was retaking the entire West Bank and Gaza Strip, booting out the Palestinian Arabs, firing a few missiles at Damascus, Baghdad, Washington, D.C., and the other enemy capitals, and transferring the ultra-Orthodox Jews out of west Jerusalem and out of his hair and into the holy cities of Nablus and

Hebron once the Palestinians were gone. Then converting the Israeli Arabs–to Hinduism or Buddhism if not Judaism. Good thing I'm a moderate, he thought. Now there's a punch line.

"Good morning." Uri Eshel, professor of Jewish history, former Israel Defense Forces chief of intelligence, now acting minister of police, opened the door and shambled in, as always with a greeting instead of a knock. On leave as professor at Hebrew University–the west campus, the east campus on Mount Scopus was now Sheik Yassin madrassa–he tossed a few sheets of paper, the morning police intelligence report, on the prime minister's desk.

"Summarize it, please. I haven't had my coffee yet, or anything to eat, so I don't feel like reading." Sarid, in addition to a bad right ear–a reserve officer's memento of Lebanon, 1982–suffered from low blood sugar. He had convinced himself years ago that he could not read on an empty stomach. And he loved to read. As a consequence, the prime minister, like most Israeli politicians, needed to lose twenty pounds. Maybe thirty.

"Okay. Two killed in yesterday's riots in Ariel. Twenty-three injured–twenty Jews, three Arab policemen. Three serious injuries, all Jews. The Jewish enclaves are quiet today," Eshel said, referring to the handful of settlements remaining in Samaria–in the former West Bank, now with the Gaza Strip and eastern Jerusalem, Arab Palestine.

"Prime Minister Terzi has been all sweet reasonableness in public, telling American reporters the Jewish settlers must be given more time to accustom themselves to their status as Jewish citizens of the Palestinian state."

"But privately?" Sarid asked.

"Privately, his police have let us know bluntly they are at the end of their restraint in dealing with rebellious Jews. They're practically guaranteeing a massacre next time," Eshel answered.

"They understand that could mean war, whether our government wants it or not?"

"They don't believe we have the military option any more. They've got big, powerful sponsors vying for influence–Syria and Egypt, and to a lesser extent, Iraq, the Saudis, even Jordan and Iran. We've got, who? The Americans? President Johnston's word, like his judgment, is a joke. As for the Europeans, they've never cared whether we lived or died, so long as they weren't inconvenienced by interrupted oil supplies or their growing numbers of Muslim citizens. The synagogue burnings and "death to the Jews" marches in France and Italy and Holland when Sharon went into the territories in April, 2002, confirmed that. Reconfirmed it, to be specific. And we're so divided internally, Jew against Jew, Jew versus Arab."

"Old Shamir was right about one thing," Sarid mused. "We need the Russians."

"Russians, Americans, British, Indians, Chinese for God's sake–we need an ally somewhere, in addition to the Turkish military," Eshel said. "But what's in it for any of them?"

"I'm not sure. What else in that summary?" the prime minister asked.

"We're close to an arrest in the car-bomb murder of the Arab mayor of

Nazareth. Evidence points to the Sicarii faction of the Zionist underground."

"What else?"

"We think we know who ordered the assassination of the minister of agriculture. And you're not going to like this."

"Who?" whispered the prime minister.

"His colleague, the minister of religion, Rabbi Moshe Ben-Chesed, the Sicarii leader."

"Civil war," Sarid said flatly. "We put that man on trial, even file charges, and it's the war between the Jews, ultra-Orthodox versus radical secular. And they'll force all the rest of us to take sides or get caught in the crossfire."

"It's civil war if we don't," Eshel said. "Remember what happened when we arrested the triggermen?"

The prime minister remembered.

"Damn it! Damn it to hell!" Eshel had lumbered into Sarid's office around noon a week earlier, cursing as he came. His broad face was furrowed and red, and he seemed to be glaring at something or someone beyond the building walls.

"What is it this time, Uri?" Sarid asked, the nervous edge back in his voice.

"Those idiots, those adolescent killers! They've done it again, and this time I don't know how we'll keep the lid on!"

"HaSicari'im?"

"Yes," Eshel snapped. Sicarii—literally, the daggers—the name given to the first-century Zealot assassins who fought their fellows Jews first, the Romans second, the name still there in Jesus' disciple and betrayer, Judas Iscariot—Yehuda the Dagger Man, assassin in a cell of revolutionaries. Now the name belonged to a tiny but well-supported group of ultra-observant Jewish fanatics. First heard from in 1988, the modern Sicarii had progressed, if that was the word, in the subsequent two decades, from daubing graffiti to beating political opponents to firebombing, and finally murder.

Eshel, a barrel-chested man with a surprisingly soft voice, dropped into one of the comfortable, well-worn armchairs in Sarid's office. The prime minister looked at this reserve brigadier general and acting police chief, and wondered again at the illusion he created, unconsciously, of a man taller and more graceful, even aristocratic-looking. Physically a thick, squat descendant of Slavic Jews, somehow Eshel's commanding presence caused contemporaries to see him on a grander scale, the way Herzl's peers looked at a man of just above average height and saw a giant.

Sarid tugged at his scarred right ear and silently reproached himself again: Why couldn't I have been more like he is? Aloud, reluctantly, he asked, "What have they done this time?"

"Murdered the minister of agriculture. Shot him in cold blood, in broad daylight, on Ben Yehuda pedestrian mall. In front of witnesses, as if they didn't care, as if their 'purity' would protect them."

Sarid slumped at his desk. "Arrests?" he asked flatly.

"Two thin, wan, yeshiva *bouchers* in their black frock coats, black hats and side curls. Neither of them is twenty. They told the arresting officers that 'no Jewish court will convict us for punishing an apostate who voted to surrender the estate of our fathers and also married a shiksa.'"

"Public reaction?" Sarid mumbled.

"Thousands–maybe tens of thousands–of people massing in a spontaneous rage in front of B'nai Shammai Yeshiva in response to calls broadcast on secular radio stations. And that's not all: streaming up to the backside of the yeshiva is a like number from the ultra-Orthodox neighborhoods around the corner. Only months after losing nearly half of Jerusalem, when Jewish unity has become a condition for Jewish survival, the center of the city is filling with Jews bent on spilling Jewish blood."

"Welcome to post-Zionist Israel," Sarid muttered. "The police are out in force?"

"And the army. We got permission from the Palestinian government in east Jerusalem and from the United Nations Jerusalem Supervisory Committee to use up to ten light armored vehicles to back up the police," Eshel said.

"Good!" exclaimed a suddenly animated Sarid. "Uri, if there is any violence, any at all, either between the haredim and the hellonim," the prime minister said, referring to the fervently Orthodox and the secularists, respectively, "or against the police, I want it smashed! Like we should have done years ago, before these groups got the idea they were bigger than the public at large and somehow above the state itself."

"You've got it," Eshel replied.

The first line on Sarid's telephone flashed. He picked it up and grimaced. It was Mahmoud Terzi.

"Yes, I know about the demonstration," Sarid said.

"Demonstration? It's a riot."

"We've got our police out in force," the Israeli prime minister responded. "Any violence will be contained in west Jerusalem, I assure you."

"See that it is," said the prime minister of the Arab Republic of Palestine. "You know, Meir, the U.N. Jerusalem Supervisory Committee agreed to let you police your own people on the condition you do it cleanly, thoroughly. If it gets out of hand, it won't be good for the Arabs, and it won't be good for the Jews.

"By the way, all the networks already are on the scene, especially the Americans. So if you need them, my forces are standing by only a few blocks away."

Hanging up the telephone, Sari said, "Uri, he's still looking for excuses to assert Arab authority over Jewish Jerusalem. Make sure he doesn't get it."

Eshel made sure. In the process more than three dozen Jews died–haredim, hellonim and police, at one point all firing at each other. But in western Jerusalem only. Mahmoud Terzi did not get to send his troops across the line. Not this time.

*   *   *

Washington, D.C. (April 25, 2007)–Congressman Jonathan Marcus looked up from his desk to see Felicia Sanchez standing before him, hands on her hips–broad, curved, voluptuous. God, he thought, what lovely female anatomy. He smiled to himself, thankful once again for having reached puberty before feminist totalitarianism had set in, of having been single before herpes, before AIDS, before the Packwood affair and its bastard offspring like the Clinton and Condit cases. His vision uncluttered by dogma, he could see Felicia Sanchez as she was, as a man sees a woman. Art appreciation, Marcus thought. No, he corrected himself, life affirmation.

Her dark and comely face reminded him of the Song of Songs, although he had never told her so. Today it wore Sanchez's patented "You never listen to me so you're going to be late, again, Congressman" look. Marcus had been reading Info Briefs from the Congressional Research Service, the branch of the Library of Congress that on short notice made senators and representatives sound informed. These on his desktop computer dealt with the situation in Palestine and Israel. Behind CRS's academic tone, they told an ugly story: one-party rule, brutality, occasional disappearances in Palestine; rage and underground plotting, political and religious polarization within Israel; chronic economic instability and social tension in both and Jordan as well.

Glad for the interruption, he asked with mock seriousness, "What is it this time, Ms. Sanchez? A committee inquisition to roast some assistant secretary of state caught between the department's old lies and its new ones, or maybe an interview with a secular cleric from The Washington Post?"

"You wish," Sanchez replied with amiable directness. "It's lunch all right, but with Myron Mandelbaum and the Honorable J. Willard Coffin III, former ambassador to Jordan, former assistant secretary of defense for security assistance, founder, president and principle supporter of the Foundation of Americans Concerned for Middle East Peace."

"SOBs like him helped cripple Israel! Now the vulture hovers, waiting for the kill. I agreed to this?"

"Of course. Myron asked you."

Myron Mandelbaum—Marcus' former law partner—and Coffin had gone to school together and stayed in touch ever since. Marcus was certain most of the effort on that score had been Mandelbaum's. And now Myron had trapped him into another of his countless ideological "hands-across-the-water" meetings, trying to reform the world over lunch.

"The old sentimentalist. He still thinks it's worthwhile for disagreeing gentlemen to break bread together, converse in polite tones, and find that damned 'common ground' of his. As if foreign policy, as if politics were an administrative law court writ large, not a global criminal proceeding to which all the plaintiffs and defendants come armed. As if Coffin and I were gentlemen. Well, what's the venue? Maybe the food will compensate."

"Afraid not," Sanchez said. "You're on your way to the private dining room at the National Lawyers' Club."

"That's the best he could do?"

"Be sympathetic. Ever since Myron's wife died, the Club's been his real home. And Coffin's a member too. They can just sign the chit."

"Good, because I'm not paying for this fiasco. I may be a Democrat, but I'm not a masochist," Marcus said, hurrying out.

As late as the Reagan years, the National Lawyers' Club, a few paces off Pennsylvania Avenue near the International Monetary Fund, had exuded a certain panache, an air of polished wood paneling and prestige. Senior partners from the city's top firms made a point to dine there, meeting colleagues who served as ranking counsels at the various federal agencies, as political strategists and White House advisors. Efficient old black waiters hovered in attendance and the food satisfied all but the most censorious palate.

But that generation of men, the one that had fought in World War II or Korea and had won the right to oversee Washington's transformation from provincial Southern city with a part-time legislature to ravenous spider at the center of a national web, that generation was gone. Its successor, with members likely as not to have avoided combat in Vietnam, to title themselves attorneys, not lawyers, and to favor Mercedes over Cadillacs, joggers, not golfers, this generation did not join the National Lawyers Club. It either bragged of twelve hour days and catered lunches in the office or took care to be seen at whatever expense account restaurant—The Palms, La Colline, or I Ricchi—was currently mandatory.

Yet the club hung on. Traditionalists—including a few who still retained the financial and professional clout to command attention—kept it going. Myron Mandelbaum was one of them. And despite Mandelbaum's dogged, reflexive hopefulness, Marcus was devoted to his old friend.

At the reception desk in front of the second-floor dining room sat a thin old woman, her face pale and wrinkled. A bouffant of platinum hair overwhelmed the features beneath. The woman pointed a bony finger, decorated with a huge diamond ring and ending in a brilliant red enameled false nail, into the dining room. "Mr. Coffin's table is that way," she intoned.

Only one of seven chairs remained open. In addition to Coffin and Mandelbaum were a youngish-looking woman in a prim business suit set off by a pair of incongruously large dangling gold earrings; a dark-complected man of late middle age; a tall, bony fellow with longish red hair in need of a shampoo, and a stocky woman with thick black hair in tight ringlets and an ample bosom, her initials etched into the gold frames of her glasses, the initials of her designer on her dress.

"Glad you could make it, Jonathan," Mandelbaum said, rising part way out of his seat. "You know my compatriot, Will Coffin. M. Grace Pittson, the new assistant secretary for Near Eastern Affairs, is here from State. Next to her, I'm sure you'll remember Achmad el-Rashid, former Egyptian ambassador to Israel and now at the Brookings Institution. Next to him is Patrick Beadle, Washington correspondent for the Middle East Spectator of London. And last but not least is my good friend Zelda Zoltin, the new executive director of the American Jewish Conference."

Marcus shook hands with the ambassador, immediately on his right, and nodded at the others.

"I like to think that this sort of ecumenical little group is a testimony to the friendships once can make in this town over the years, if one gets to know people as individuals, not positions," Mandelbaum continued. "I asked you all here because of something Will said to me recently. I wanted to see what you all thought of it and to let my old classmate have the benefit of your reactions."

Coffin, sitting straight and oddly still, hands folded like a preacher's, a half-smile frozen on his face, came to life:

"As some of you may know, I served a number of years as this country's ambassador to Jordan. I don't mean to sound melodramatic, but something happened there one day that changed the course of my life."

Already Marcus was only half listening. What a pompous ass, he thought. The hell you don't mean to be melodramatic—that's how you see yourself. Why in heaven's name didn't you take your self-inflation and your money and go back to Wall Street and leave the Jews alone?

"So at the end of the day I stopped with then-Crown Prince Hassan and the lovely Queen Noor—I knew her as a young woman, Lisa Halaby, here—at a refugee camp outside Amman. Suddenly, what seemed like an endless procession of little children, some in rags but all bright-eyed and eager to see their distinguished visitors, came running out of the shacks and alleys. They surrounded us, clamoring for a glimpse of the Prince and the Queen, begging for attention. As the Crown Prince recounted the hardships of their lives and the seeming hopelessness of their fate—these were, after all, third-generation refugees—I felt my bachelor's heart go out to them. I vowed then and there to champion their cause.

"A few years later, after I left the Foreign Service, I used some of the family funds to endow the Foundation of Americans Concerned for Middle East Peace. I was quite singled-minded about fulfilling my pledge on behalf of those homeless, oppressed little children. It made me the target of the more reactionary elements in the American Jewish community, but I persevered. And, in some small way, I think I contributed to resolving the larger Palestinian-Israeli quarrel.

"That brings me to the idea Myron mentioned. I believe that the Jews of Israel, certainly the fair-minded majority of them, desperately want to close the book on the bloodletting and hatred. But the remnant of Zionist nationalists, especially in the Jewish settlements, and the religious zealots in Israel proper won't let them.

"Now, the American Jewish community, which did so much to help establish and secure the Jewish presence in Palestine generations ago, which manfully supported the Israeli-PLO accords and a West Bank and Gaza Strip Palestine, must provide one more heroic service to their brethren and indeed, to the world: persuade the Jews of Israel to agree to a referendum among the Arabs of the Galilee and Negev on whether or not to join the Arab Republic of Palestine, and to the Palestinian Arabs' right-of-return to their original homes inside what became Israel.

"The sooner the Zionist thugs among them stop inciting resistance on this matter, the sooner final peace will come. In exchange, I'm sure the United States government will guarantee no violence from either side."

"The United States government guaranteed, just in my memory, the survival of South Vietnam, the territorial integrity of Bosnia, the rebuilding of Somalia, freedom for Lebanon, democracy for Kuwait, a multi-ethnic Kosovo, freedom for Taiwan and a lot of other overseas commitments we wouldn't keep. An equitable Arab-Israeli peace—'secure and recognized borders'—always has been in that category," Marcus barked. "I know it if the Israelis don't. As for your third-generation Arab refugees, they were unique in the world, refused resettlement by their Arab brothers and refusing it from the Jews so they could go on being a living reproach against Israel."

"Jonathan, Jonathan, please. You'll get your turn." It was Mandelbaum.

"So I'd like to hear your thoughts on how that might be done, without seeming meddlesome or anti-Jewish—which God knows I am not," Coffin finished.

Marcus fumed as, one-by-one, the others seriously discussed the subject. Beadle, who always had datelined his stories Tel Aviv even when filing from Jerusalem, averred that "many progressive, post-Zionist Jews in Palestine would welcome such a push from the American Jewish community. They are weary; their children are emigrating to Australia, Canada, the United States, wherever they can get in. They fear the ultra-religious that are strangling them culturally and the Israeli Arabs beginning to outnumber them by fertility rates. They need our help to make the reasonable Jewish voices we all knew prevail again."

Mandelbaum did not test Beadle's late-blooming rhetorical love for reasonable Jewish voices but turned to the stern-faced woman from the State Department. She demurred. M. Grace Pittson noted that she was present to listen, not advocate. "After all, domestic developments do have their foreign policy implications, don't they?" she said smoothly.

Marcus, speculating on strangling Coffin, Beadle, and Pittson in turn, studied the woman's wardrobe. The muted colors and conservative cut of the fabric said, I am a professional, you will respond accordingly. The earrings and heels rejoined, Don't forget—woman on duty.

Marcus was fooled by neither apparel nor rhetoric. Here was a first-class operative, tight-lipped and hard-assed, eager for American Jews to do the administration's dirty work and pressure the Israelis to abandon their last shred of self-determination, of dignity, in their shrunken Israel. It was just what Prime Minister Mahmoud Terzi had demanded, in that soft, lulling voice of his, during his triumphal American visit a few weeks before. At a mutually congratulatory fete hosted by the Conference of Presidents of Major American Jewish Organizations and the National Association of Arab Americans—to which Marcus let his wife, Madeline, drag him—Terzi had insisted, softly, on two items Israel and its American Jewish supporters had, until the second intifada of 2000 to 2002, convinced themselves were non-negotiable. These were "self-determination for the Arab Galilee and Negev," and the "right-of-return," the obscene Arab conscription of the Jews' biblical claim to Eretz Yisrael, the Land of Israel. Conference leaders objected, but softly, politely.

Marcus had watched as Terzi, on "Meet the Press," smoothly insinuated his demand for the five million Palestinian Arabs he claimed as refugees—the much-multiplied generations of the half-million who originally fled the War of Arab Rejection in 1948—to what they claimed were ancestral homes inside "Israel proper." He, as Arafat in 1999 had done, now defined this as the minuscule Jewish area allotted under the 1947 U.N. Partition Plan, the plan the Arabs had gone to war to overturn at the time.

His demand was a short-fused demographic time bomb; added to the 1.5 million Israeli Arabs and "reunified" Palestinian Arab families, their presence alone would vitiate the idea of a Jewish state, especially in its shrunken boundaries, already shorn of Judea and Samaria.

Nevertheless, Zelda Zoltin was ready to enlist. The American Jewish Conference–one of the few groups out of the more than four dozen in the Conference of Presidents with more living than deceased on its membership rolls–had a broad agenda. To the AJConference not only Israel but also separation of church and state, feminism, fighting antisemitism (that from the right if not the left), homosexual rights, environmentalism, government funding for the arts and, above all, unrestricted abortion on demand somehow were Jewish issues, urgent Jewish issues.

Conference leaders had realized by the 1991 Persian Gulf War that divisions among their members over Israel threatened group unity. Subconsciously, many Jewish American activists wanted the burden of their obligations to a Jewish state lifted. They just could not admit it. Like the Israelis on the front lines, they too were weary of the decades' old struggle. So the sooner the last vestiges of the Arab-Israeli conflict were relegated to history, the better off the AJConference would be. Hence its leaders' relief, even joy at the 1993 White House handshake between Arafat and then-Prime Minister Yitzhak Rabin. The temptation to bask in the afterglow at joint banquets with the National Association of Arab Americans and the Arab American Anti-Discrimination Committee–yesterday and tomorrow's vituperative critics of Israel–was more than they could resist.

"My organization is not endorsing any specific outcome," Zoltin said. "And we note that any solution must assure Jewish security. But we are most interested in facilitating any moves that lead to reconciliation among peoples, so we stand ready to help Ambassador Coffin reach out to our Jewish American brethren."

The presumptuousness, the self-centered provincialism, the lethal euphemisms of these professional Washingtonians, Marcus thought. But before he could respond, el-Rashid administered some reality therapy:

"When I served as ambassador, the Israelis–even with their big military–saw themselves as besieged. They were right. How much more so now? If I must work in Washington because of assassination threats at home from both right-wing Islamic fundamentalists and left-wing Arab nationalists, how can you think of asking the Jews in Palestine to welcome as neighbors, as returning long-absent landlords, people in whom hatred of Israel and Israelis was inculcated early and invoked often? Might as well ask the Jews to disarm."

"I was getting to that," Coffin said.

"Don't," el-Rashid commanded. "The Jewish state's already gravely compromised territorially. With the Palestinian Arab 'right-of-return,' it will be finished socially.

"Don't you understand Terzi's next non-negotiable demand–once he gets the return? Not just reference to the 1947 partition plan, but it's full imposition. And with that Israel will nearly vanish. Instead of being the size of your Massachusetts, it will be as big as two or three American counties–seven hundred square miles in three barely contiguous parcels. The Palestinians alone will be able to put it out of its misery, only they won't be alone. Many of the Arabs will join in the festival, the great ritual slaughter.

"And then those Jews who do survive will be reduced again in the Middle East to second-class citizens, inferiors, to dhimmi status, and elsewhere to stateless wanderers, powerless, living always at the sufferance of others."

Coffin and Beadle stared, mouths agape, at el-Rashid. Zoltin's face flushed. M. Grace Pittson wiped her mouth with her linen napkin, daintily. Mandelbaum, stumbling to find something hopeful to say, made little clucking noises.

Marcus, thoroughly pleased with el-Rashid, one of Egypt's oppressed Coptic Christian minority, broke in with practiced sincerity: "I thank the ambassador for puncturing our Anglo-Saxon ethnocentrism. Even after all the evidence to the contrary, we apparently need to be reminded now and then that we're not dealing with a labor-management dispute here. As Oliver Wendell Holmes Jr. said, regarding the necessity of the American Civil War, 'You can't reason someone out of something he hasn't been reasoned into.'" Marcus rose, looked at his watch, and added as apologetically as he could, "Sorry, but I'm late for a hearing. Just enjoy your desserts."

Where, thought Beadle, have I heard that voice before? Must have been at some hearing, or one of those disgusting pro-Israel PAC receptions.

* * *

Alexandria, Virginia (June 2, 2007) – Jeri Weinrib – by her teens a curious blend of Orthodox Jewish tradition and influences of the women's movement of the early '80's – spent her junior year in Jerusalem at Hebrew University. There, amidst new friends and ancient surroundings, she determined to become a rabbi. In doing so she surprised herself as much as her family and friends.

Knowing that an Orthodox pulpit would be impossible, a Conservative one rare, she enrolled at the Hebrew Union College in Cincinnati, the seminary for American Reform rabbis. A decade later, in her mid-thirties and married, Jeri Levi moved from assistant rabbi for a small congregation in suburban Detroit to the larger Or Kodesh as its spiritual leader. She came to feel at home in her role, except for the times Marvin Kammelman started in on her.

The congregation itself mixed long-time residents of metropolitan Washington – many of them federal and military retirees – with younger members in an odd, informal alliance that rewarded both the oldsters and the couples with children by keeping the temple not only open but growing, the Hebrew school expanding. Or Kodesh worked across a generational divide: there were comparatively few middle-aged congregants. The veteran members, suspicious at first of a woman rabbi, had taken to agreeing lately with the younger faction and a Washington Post reporter who had featured Or Kodesh for the Saturday Religion page and lauded its "charismatic" woman rabbi.

Jeri Levi did not dwell on her growing stature within the temple but continued to work hard. Household chores, previously more or less equally divided, fell increasingly to Hal alone. This included the management of their two children, Justin and Deborah. Justin was in the fourth grade, Deborah in second. Hal worked as a bonds analyst for the D.C. branch of a New York brokerage house.

Until now he had handled his wife's career rather well, he thought, especially for someone to whom religion represented just one more compartment in a life of diverse interests. Lately, however, he sensed the same change in his wife as had the congregation and the reporter. It was more than self-confidence; that she always had possessed. But now there was a force, a power flowing through his wife that had never been there before. It made him uneasy.

"I had a dream last night," Jeri Levi said one June morning, less than a week before disarmament of the remaining Israeli towns and villages in Palestine.

"And you bring it up after breakfast? It must have been a bad one," chirped Justin, whose precociousness was by turns astounding and annoying.

An old superstition among some Jews, in this case handed down from grandmother to mother to son, forbade the telling of nightmares before breakfast lest they come true. It was the only such taboo the rabbi consciously observed. That and skipping over sidewalk cracks. Her grandmother, of blessed memory–a short, stocky woman with twinkling eyes–had survived private and public tragedies, had somehow learned anger without bitterness, and rarely misjudged people or events. Jeri still envied the woman's certainties.

"I was standing in the sanctuary. Close to me were a few members of the congregation. Outside were more, plus strangers. They stood at the doorway but did not enter. Behind them I could see smoke and fire."

"What else?" asked Justin.

"Marvin Kammelman, shouting at me that services were over."

"That's all, mommy?" Deborah wanted to know.

"That's all."

"Children, your 'charismatic' mother has begun to foretell the future in her sleep. At least, that's what she thinks," Hal said.

Jeri Levi glared at her husband, but said, "C'mon, I'm a Reform rabbi. Visions are for the Chasidim. Besides, you know the saying: 'Since the destruction of the Second Temple, prophecy has been given only to fools and children...'"

"You said that, I didn't," Hal Levi replied.

Oh, to be rid of this man, Jeri thought.

In her study at Or Kodesh later that morning, the rabbi's thoughts wandered from the Men's Club request for a second night of bingo each month. She had rehearsed mentally the conversation she anticipated with Marvin Kammelman, congregation president:

Yes, the bingo games do help make up the difference between parents' fees and the cost of running the Hebrew school. Yes, nothing fills the parking lot to overflowing like bingo, except Rosh Hashanah and Yom Kippur. A second night of bingo might even allow us to expand the adult evening courses.

Rabbi Levi had organized a series of mini-classes in basic Hebrew, basic Jewish history, basic Jewish ritual. Always the basics, she thought. The edifice of Judaism can never be built here since it cannot really be lived here, not in neighborhoods that are not communities, in subdivisions in which sidewalks lead nowhere, among friends who live ten miles apart. Not when the synagogue is an out-building and the real Jewish community center is a gym and a pool, the central Jewish activity a federation fund-raiser. So all we do is go on relaying the foun-

34   *Total Jihad*

dation—and the foundation only—year after year.

That was what the bingo proceeds enabled her to do, tutor the untutored, take the first step in the Jewish way of life and then—the weight of the general non-Jewish environment, the solvent of mass culture and the non-Jewish calendar itself against her and against her students—retake that first step the next year, and the next. And it was different, if not worse now, after the collapse of the illusory peace. When what had been touted as Arab-Israeli normalization appeared instead to become the prelude to the end of Israel, when Israeli counter-terrorism provoked violent antisemitism throughout Europe and some open hostility at home, many American Jews simply began peeling off, or accelerating their departures.

Psychically, they could not stand as Jews without the knowledge, however vague, without the connection, however tenuous, to a Jewish state that needed them, to an Israel that stood behind them, whose strength implicitly fused the Holocaust-shattered collective Jewish consciousness. Israel's own post-Zionist—or as Hillel Halkin put it, anti-Zionist—intelligentsia didn't want them, busy as it was revising or erasing Jewish history, the better to reject Jewish nationalism and meddling by Diaspora philanthropists. Non-Orthodox Diaspora Jews—seeking spirituality as a substitute for God; committed to "outreach" to but not conversion of non-Jewish spouses—returned the favor. They dropped out the Jewish collective, out of the Jewish nation, in search of a strictly American Judaism, or rather, Judaisms. The twin centripetal forces complemented each other in denying the Jews' identity as a Chosen People with a Promised Land and God-given mission.

Instead, these new branches of Judaism, the "post-denominational" delusions, blended ethnic assimilation, cultural dilution and radical individual autonomy. The new Jewish majority replaced an ancient, global peoplehood with local "faith communities." Their new Judaism was an extra-territorial religion, shorn of its national character, like Christianity after the failure of the Crusades.

The most extreme were doing in months what formerly had taken decades—dropping their affiliations, their participation, ending their contributions, some even changing their names. The post-World War II slow motion self-liquidation of a large part of American Jewry was suddenly on fast-forward. More than a few, no longer content to creep or walk away from their Jewishness, from Judaism, now ran. Consciously, rapidly, they sought protective coloration now that Israel and the psychic protection it formerly conferred upon overseas Jews had been compromised, now that women wearing the Star of David were beaten in the streets of Europe, men wearing kipot stabbed in cafes of Latin America.

But others reacted differently. Responding to the second Crown Heights pogrom and similar riots elsewhere, inspired by examples of Jewish resistance in Israel—or out of guilt for somehow not having done enough before—they restored previously nominal ties.

"Half the nearly six million American Jews never have been involved in community life," Jeri Levi had remarked to Sylvia Weinberg, Or Kodesh's veteran secretary. "And of the other fifty percent, with membership in at least one Jewish organization or institution, only about half of them were active. So this great edifice of American Jewry never rested on more than about one and a-half million people."

"We'll be lean and mean," Sylvia Weinberg said.

"We'll have to," Rabbi Levi answered.

Resuming her anticipated conversation with Marvin Kammelman, she heard herself telling the congregational president that bingo once a week is enough for now. At least it should suffice until our evening prayer services regularly draw the required minyan, don't you agree?

Daily prayers were a fixture in Orthodox congregations, morning and evening, and at least once a day in most Conservative synagogues. Their inauguration at Or Kodesh came both as a result of the insistence of a handful of members and of Jeri's own encouragement. The congregational president had opposed the idea until he recognized that a hard core would go on demanding it. A minyan, the required minimum of ten adults for congregational prayers–traditionally males but for years not exclusively so at most Conservative and Reform congregations–that was a fair exchange for more bingo. She envisioned herself honeyed moderation in her disputation with the perpetually disgruntled Kammelman.

The intercom buzzed in Rabbi Levi's office.

"The Shapiros are here to see you," Sylvia Weinberg said. "Shall I send them in?"

Sylvia Weinberg, a New Yorker transplanted to northern Virginia years before, shouted into her telephone from an office away. What Meyer Weinberg's widow lacked in polish she more than made up for with concern, selflessness and– prized by Rabbi Levi and her two immediate predecessors–nearly total recall of congregational affairs.

"Yes," the rabbi sighed. "Show them in." Naomi Shapiro had cornered her after Friday night services the week before. Mrs. Shapiro implored the rabbi to help her with "a little low-key family counseling."

Whatever problems the Shapiros were experiencing they must be more than low-key for the family to put in a temple appearance. It was not an uncommon gesture. Often, before coming to the rabbi with a personal problem, members who were veritable strangers otherwise would show up in temple. It was as if they meant to say, Here I am–remember me–I'm part of the congregation. So help me.

Ted Shapiro designed and sold sound systems for nightclubs, restaurants, office buildings, malls and the homes of the wealthy. He made a good living, good enough to keep Naomi in the latest fashions, which she took care to exhibit on her rare visits to temple–and to take the family on several trips a year to the Caribbean, South America or Europe. Style was Naomi's ruling passion, travel the means to express it. Business up and down the Atlantic seaboard kept Ted Shapiro on the road. That left Naomi in charge of seventeen-year-old Aliza, who inherited her mother's obsession with clothes and foreign locales but whose striking face belonged to no one else, and Todd, a pudgy, purportedly brilliant fifteen-year-old malcontent.

After they all were seated in her office, Rabbi Levi asked how she could help.

"Well, it's not like we have any really serious problems," Naomi Shapiro began, "but some things could be a little better, you know?"

"Not exactly. Maybe you could give me some examples."

"This fall we, that is, Aliza and I, went to New York so she could try to break into fashion modeling there. After all, Manhattan is the only place that really counts and Aliza already has done all the department store ads and television commercials available here. Isn't that right, dear?"

Rabbi Levi pivoted in her seat to look directly at the daughter. Aliza Shapiro had long, thick blonde hair swept wildly up and back from her forehead and sculpted down onto her shoulders. Her face, highlighted by gem-like brown eyes, displayed the prominent cheekbones of the high-fashion model. She was tall and her figure hovered on the bony side of slender, also like the magazine mannequins.

"Oh, mother," Aliza exhaled. Speaking the two words seemed to consume all her strength.

"Anyway, we went to New York for a week and with Aliza's portfolio made the rounds of the agencies and photographers. It's an excellent one. It cost us six thousand dollars to put together. Here," Mrs. Shapiro said, extending some mounted glossy color photographs. "Take a look."

Rabbi Levi glanced quickly through the prints. One showed Aliza in a Spanish-style costume with an embroidered skirt, a sombrero never seen west of New Jersey tipped rakishly over half her face, a coy expression showing on the other half. One long, tapered leg extended up behind her, a frozen implication of motion and excitement.

A second shot pictured Aliza in stretch blue jeans and a sequined bandeau top, an expensive little blazer thrown over one shoulder. She appeared to be striding threateningly toward the lens; on her face was an expression much too hard for any high school girl—the "thug mug" as fashionably transported from slum to suburbia. In the third photograph she lay stretched across a make-believe beach, wrap-around sunglasses dangling in one hand, two strips of florid-colored nylon pretending to be a swimsuit stretched taut across her nipples and merging to give minimal cover for her pubic triangle.

"It's called a uni-thong," Naomi Shapiro explained, as if a euphemism could make the suit legitimate.

"Very professional looking," the rabbi muttered, stricken by the girl's exploitation.

"Right, professional. That's just the thing. For four years now we've been working hard to turn Aliza into a professional. That's what she wants. And she's given up the normal things a seventeen-year-old has, including a car, boyfriends, an active social life, pizza, for God's sake. It's hard on her I know, but becoming a top model is something only a few girls can do, and Aliza is one of them. It's nothing to play at.

"Well, in New York she suddenly acted like she wanted to throw it all away. She got difficult to work with, surly and unresponsive. Hell, people won't put up with that in Washington, where they think fashion means navy blue, let alone in New York, where people innovate." Her mouth caressed the last word, as if it were a sacred formula.

"Worst of all, she started clinging to every male who gave her an interested look. Every time I turned my back it seemed she was sneaking off with another sleazy..."

"Oh mother, you just didn't like Rudolfo, admit it! This whole thing is only because I had to have the abortion," Aliza challenged. "After all, it's not like that was the first abortion in this family!" Out of breath, the girl fell back into the sofa.

"Shut up!" Naomi Shapiro snapped. Then, evenly, to Rabbi Levi, "As I was saying, Ted was out of town while we were in New York. Todd, who swore to us he could take care of himself for a few days, simply stopped going to school. Finally, I got a call from a neighbor–do you know the Irvings?"

The rabbi knew them. Another family like the Shapiros, whose temple contact hinged on their children's irregular Hebrew school attendance and the parents' fleeting participation in Rosh Hashanah and Yom Kippur services.

"Anyway, Mrs. Irving called to tell me that Todd had been detained by the police!"

"Not 'detained,'" Todd sneered, suddenly aroused, "Fucking arrested!"

"Now Todd," Ted Shapiro said evenly, "what have I told you about such language?"

"One of the boys he was with was held for possession of LSD! Those bits of flavored absorbent paper with the Disney characters on them that the kids buy and sell and put on their tongues? Can you imagine?" Mrs. Shapiro went on. "Call me conservative but I think fifteen is a little too young for LSD! Well, when I got back and Ted returned, we laid down the law: No marijuana on school days, no more truancy, no more weeknight rock concerts, no LSD at all.

"That was two weeks ago. You know what the sullen little bastard's been doing since then? Nothing, that's what. He stopped going to soccer practice–he's first-string goalie–won't have a thing to do with the high school science club–of which he's vice president–and refused to go to the temple youth conclave. To top it off, he's giving us the silent treatment. Isn't that right, dear?"

At this direct invitation, Ted Shapiro spoke.

"Yes, that's right."

Jeri Levi waited for more, but there wasn't any.

"What I really don't understand, and this is why I, why we decided to come to you instead of going to the psychologist–Ted and I agreed before we were married that we would keep a Jewish home. I always light candles on Friday night, we always attend High Holiday services, we celebrate Passover and Chanukah at home–we even had Todd's bar mitzvah at the Wall in Jerusalem, for Chrissakes! So why is this happening to us? Why are our children growing up like goyim?"

In spite of the pain she felt for this family, Rabbi Levi wanted to laugh. Naomi Shapiro's sincerity, like her arrogance and ignorance, was breathtaking. But a second outburst by Todd riveted her to the difficulty at hand:

"She's such a bitch!" the boy hissed at Jeri Levi. "And now, for some reason, she's decided that being a bitch in my sister's life isn't enough. She wants to be one in mine too."

Ted Shapiro finally acted. He rose, ripped off his son's headphones–for a moment Rabbi Levi clearly heard the dull, deadly thump of the rap music the boy had been ostentatiously tapping his feet to during the entire session–pulled the CD player from his son's waistband, and crushed them under his heel.

The boy tried to punch his father but the older male easily deflected the blow.

He jerked his son up and bundled him toward the door. "I'm sorry," he said, his tone still amiable. "Naomi, you finish this. We'll wait in the car."

Softly, Rabbi Levi asked Mrs. Shapiro a question. "When you light candles on Friday nights, do you do anything else?"

"Like what?"

"Oh, maybe say the blessings over the wine and over the bread, or even the father's blessing for the children, or for his wife, sing shabbat songs, discuss the week's events together, anything like that?"

"I don't understand," said Naomi Shapiro, genuinely puzzled. "I don't think we know any Shabbat songs. But what's this got to do with the children's problems?"

Soon she and Aliza left as well.

*　*　*

Ramallah (June 6, 2007)–"No violence. Do you hear me? No violence!"

The half-dozen men listening nodded silently.

"Good," said Yacoub al-Masri. "If we do this right, the remaining Jews are on their way out of this part of Palestine soon, and the rest of them out of it completely soon after!"

Yacoub al-Masri, man of many guises. A one-time student at Georgetown University–scholarships from both the Palestine Liberation Organization and the Carnegie Endowment for International Peace–he returned to Nablus before a District of Columbia police matter could intervene. Sentenced in 1983 to life in prison for the kidnap-murder of a hitchhiking Israel soldier, he was exchanged two years later, along with 1,150 other terrorists, for three Israeli prisoners of war.

Al-Masri was not alone in believing that act, by then-Prime Minister Shimon Peres and Defense Minister Yitzhak Rabin, set the tinder for the intifada in 1987. Not so much a convert from Palestinian nationalism to Islamic fundamentalism while in prison as an alchemist of the two, he now edited east Jerusalem's Al-Quds newspaper. And Yacoub al-Masri–literally, Jacob the Egyptian–had figured it out.

How to breach the security measures in the Arab Republic of Palestine that guaranteed the remnant of Jewish settlers and oust the colonists from their settlements, yet leave their government in old Israel unable to respond. At least, unable to respond without committing political suicide. Of course, failure to respond would have the same result. He had them.

Al-Masri, also covert chairman of the executive committee of the PLO, steered the group away from a terror campaign across the boundaries of Arab Palestine into Israel proper. That he left to the suicide bombers of Hamas, the Islamic Resistance Movement, to the drive-by gunmen of Palestine Islamic Jihad, to the battle-trained Hezbollah–the pro-Iranian, Syrian-supplied Party of God so adept at infiltration, ambush, intimidation and propaganda–and to his own al-Aksa Martyrs Brigade. Instead, he had won approval for something much different, more dangerous to the Israelis.

"Do you really think Israel will be able to play by 'Chicago rules' with us in east Jerusalem the way it did when we were in west Beirut, or even in Ramallah before the U.S. enlarged its 'war on terrorism'?" Mahmoud Terzi had said, arguing for the attacks. As prime minister, he retained his seat on the PLO executive committee—expanded to include representation for Hamas and Islamic Jihad alongside old-line Marxist revolutionaries like the Popular Front for the Liberation of Palestine and the Democratic Front for the Liberation of Palestine.

Terzi had taken over as chairman after Arafat and the pope had died in a plane crash while mediating the most recent Persian Gulf crisis. He relinquished the chairmanship when he became prime minister of Arab Palestine, Arafat's West Bank, Gaza Strip and east Jerusalem domain.

"'Chicago rules', indeed," Terzi snorted. "'If Palestinians from their new state hurt one Israeli, the Israelis will have an address at last, and hurt one hundred Palestinians.' Did The New York Times really believe that when our heroes mortar and infiltrate Israeli neighborhoods south of Jerusalem from Bethlehem, a few hundred yards away, the vaunted Israeli Air Force will be able to bomb the birthplace of Jesus in reprisal? Impossible! The world won't stand for it. They couldn't do it when Hamas kidnapped Nachson Waxman in 1994, holding him all the time just a few miles north of downtown Jerusalem, they couldn't do it when they had 40 of our best fighters surrounded in Nativity Church in 2002, and they definitely cannot do it now. They couldn't, or wouldn't, rescue the soldier bleeding to death at Joseph's Tomb in Nablus, or the two we lynched in Ramallah, a dozen miles from the Knesset.

"Israel once was able to hit us with impunity. That day passed long ago, by the time Colin Powell was on the phone, pressuring Ariel Sharon not to respond to every shooting and suicide bomber. CNN looked at Sharon's mini-invasion and saw Stalingrad. But we know the truth—two blocks here, one block there—the Israelis were afraid to really fight. Not afraid of us, but of American reaction. Hell, the West's adored King Hussein martyred 5,000 Palestinians in three weeks in Black September, but it took the Israelis two years to kill 1,600. Israel never will be able to attack the recognized Palestinian capital of east Jerusalem, not with every network in the world filming as the planes violate our sovereignty. Not with the European Union countries ready to reimpose economic sanctions. Never! The armed struggle will now triumph!"

"But why take even that risk?" al-Masri had responded. "And might not the armed struggle return an Israeli military presence to our soil permanently? Didn't Arafat ultimately lose his gamble with Sharon and have to give the Jews half a loaf? No, to get the Jews out, completely, quickly, virtually bloodlessly, we'll use a Western method, a method in the face of which liberal Jews, secular Israelis will be helpless—nonviolent civil disobedience.

"Imagine: our people will stage round-the-clock sit-ins in front of the gates to the Jewish settlements. We will form human chains—men, women and children, around the remaining Israeli security outposts in the hill country and on the highway chokepoints from the Jordanian part of Palestine. Left-wing Jews will join us, like they did at Efrat and Beit El in 1995, at Har Homa in 1998, Ramallah and Bethlehem in 2002. Not another intifada of stones and bullets—no rocks, no Molotov cocktails, no knives and axes—nothing but dignified, quiet, civil rights; an intifada of demonstrations. Well-covered demonstrations, of course. The Israelis will be out in weeks–a few months at the most, I promise you.

"And if things go too slowly, then two or three armed actions, 'out of frustration,' will be enough to force revision of the accords and give us complete sovereignty over our soil–not even the unarmed Israeli patrols, no settlers at all. This, in turn, will accelerate gaining our full right-of-return to the 1948 lands, to Jaffa, Haifa and Beersheva, by showing both our commitment and our righteousness. How will the Jews resist the growing international pressure for a referendum by the Arabs of Israel as well as by the '48 and '67 refugees? Especially divided among themselves as they are, ridden with their Jewish guilt. And a year or two after that, our large police force now an army, we will lead, not follow, the other Arabs in the total liberation of Palestine. Isn't that our name, what al-Fatah meant from the beginning–the total liberation of Palestine? Tel Aviv will be gone, the village of Sheik Munis will return, this time as a great city. Netanya will be gone, Um Khalid will reappear. Then the al-nakba, the shame of 1948, will be erased!"

The executive committee agreed. So it was that al-Masri was able to order his top aides to begin the great Dignity and Equality Demonstration. Hundreds of PLO members and supporters, hundreds of Hamas and Islamic Jihad activists, hundreds of cadres from the Popular Front, the Democratic Front and the Palestinian Communist Party, instructed on how to lead non-violent protests, mobilized tens of thousands of followers. They were the most dangerous Arab army the Israelis yet had faced. And the demonstrations were echoed inside Israel itself, with demonstrations co-sponsored by the Israeli Arabs' Islamic Movement and the new Peace Now-Canaan.

Befuddled, the Israeli government at first tried to ignore the demonstrations. But after several days, some settlements began running low on food. People were not able to get in or out for work, school, shopping. Soldiers assigned to the territorial outposts were unable to patrol, to rotate home for leave or return from reserve duty to civilian life. They grew restless, dispirited. The public was tense, confused, demanding action, demanding leadership, yet insisting on the maintenance of peace.

"If they won't get out of the way, drive over them!" Shlomo Ben-Porat, representative of the tiny far-right Revival Party and minister-without-portfolio, insisted at a cabinet meeting.

"Excellent, Shlomo. On camera or off?" Eshel said sarcastically.

"Then arrest them non-violently. You can do it, Uri. After all, you're a university man," Ben-Porat shot back.

"You forget we're not the lawful authorities there anymore," Sarid cut in. "Not over the Arabs, not over the land. Only over the Jews. As a result of the Clinton-Barak-Abdullah-Bush final status agreement we accepted after 'the war on terrorism' that somehow omitted terrorism against Jews, we're in charge only of the few Jewish villages and towns and the handful of unarmed Israel Defense Forces outposts permitted to remain in Arab Palestine. We can't arrest the citizens of another country on their own soil. Not legally, not as a matter of practical politics. Who'd back us up?"

"We need legal backing, not military. I say we file a complaint with the U.N.

Treaty Supervisory Organization, as provided for in any dispute over the implementation of the settlement, and simultaneously take this to the World Court. That'll force the supervisory organization, loaded with friends of the Palestinians, either to act or get out of the way," said Israel Miller, a long-time leader of the Likud Party.

Miller was deputy prime minister under Sarid, the Labor Party chairman, in a national unity government. The government had been formed to implement the division of Jerusalem, reallocation of water resources and air space rights, minor border modifications and Arab family reunification as part of the final status obligations. Its members were hardly partners, often not friends.

"Make it an issue of sanctity of treaties, the rule of international law," he stressed. "After all, we signed the damn thing—under duress from the Americans and the Europeans, but we did sign it. And so did the Palestinian Arabs."

"The World Court? Israel, that deck is stacked," replied Sarid. Although a Labor man and, as a son of leading Labor parents, a prince of the party, a party pulled ever leftward by its Meretz bloc and Israeli Arab allies, Sarid had been sympathetic to Another Way, one more of the 15 parties in the 120-seat Knesset. Proportional representation, a 1.5-percent vote threshold to enter parliament, and election by party lists rather than constituent districts long had been the curse of Israeli politics, that and the failure, from 1948 on, to adopt a written constitution. Together they made rule by unstable coalitions inevitable, law uncertain and fundamental principles ephemeral. Their effect was to render Israeli democracy more apparent than real, especially in crises. The Knesset, instead of being a forum for inter-party debate on crucial issues, was more like a confederation of clans always at war with itself over tribal matters, essentially the allocation of tax-supported plunder and of family status. Individual voters, represented by no one in particular, usually found themselves outside looking in.

Another Way had bolted from Labor after the 1993 Oslo Accords, ironically to uphold Rabin's 1992 Labor platform of no retreat on the Golan Heights or Jordan Valley, both gained in the 1967 Six-Day War. Sarid, in one of the incessant balancing acts to which Israeli prime ministers are condemned, tried to offset Meretz as a coalition partner with Another Way as counter-balance.

Meir Sarid was relatively young, fluent in Arabic and English as well as Hebrew, and personally untouched by the police-elections scandal that unseated the previous Labor leadership. Mid-level party hacks, with the tacit approval of their superiors, had organized covert groups of followers—funded by donations from wealthy Jews in France, England and America—to disrupt opposition meetings and rallies. Their ultimate exposure forced a housecleaning within Labor, and brought the uncharismatic, but unsullied, Sarid to office.

"Ein briera. Because there is no other choice," said Miller.

The rest of the discussion was perfunctory. The cabinet voted to complain to the U.N. Treaty Supervisory Organization—comprised of Canada, Saudi Arabia and Japan—the body established to uphold the settlement agreed to by Israel and the Palestinians, Lebanese, and Syrians. The cabinet also determined to proceed to the World Court.

Al-Masri was more than ready. He had anticipated that the Israelis might respond without force. So, without reconvening the PLO executive committee but after telling a handful of members steadfastly loyal to him, he published the following editorial in the July 4, 2007 issue of Al-Quds:

"Nearly thirty years ago, after Israel's treaty with Egypt, this newspaper wrote that 'Israel provides a good reason for every Arab, whether leader or ordinary citizen, to act violently against any Israeli he may meet anywhere. Any tie between Arab and Jew is forbidden, as is any peace agreement. Every Arab leader, king, president, officer or ordinary citizen must work for the destruction, liquidation and extermination of Israel.

"'This must be the legacy of every father to his sons and grandsons, and this goal must be passed from generation to generation. No Arab may rest or sleep until revenge has been taken.'

"But this paper said after Oslo that it was time to leave the old path, time to convince the Jews we are not against them, only against the racist crimes of Zionism and the Zionists. We tried to do so by accepting the peace process and Arab Republic of Palestine. The rise of the Israeli peace movement and the post-Zionist intellectuals—honestly self-critical at last showed there were moral, truthful Jews we could work with for a peace of the brave.

"Nevertheless, a Palestine of only the West Bank and Gaza Strip, of only part of Jerusalem, is a half-measure. In it we are not completely sovereign, Arab Palestinian unity not completely restored. The Israeli army still watches over us from strategic sites of Arab Palestine, the Israeli Air Force controls the skies above us.

"Yet we ourselves are forbidden an army. We do not threaten Israel. We demand not an army of our own but, for the sake of self-determination, equal rights, and above all, peace:

"• Immediate liquidation of the Israeli observer presence on our soil;

"• Restoration of the right-of-return for all Palestinians whose family homes are not in Nablus, Jerusalem or Hebron but Haifa, Jaffa and Ashkelon, not in the West Bank but the Galilee, not in the Gaza Strip but the plain of Sharon or the Negev, in accordance with U.N. General Assembly Resolution 194;

"• In exchange, we will consider agreeing to the 1947 U.N. General Assembly Partition Plan, Resolution 181, which, after all, is Israel's basic international legitimacy.

"To push these just demands, the core of the Middle East problem, to the top of the world agenda, Al-Quds calls for a mass 'Green March,' a peaceful demonstration for dignity and equality, by all citizens of the Arab Republic of Palestine who are able to walk. Two days hence we will start from Jenin and march, in celebration and dignity, singing and carrying our holy Koran and our Bible, to the illegal fence separating us from our brothers and sisters in Arab Galilee. We will, without weapons, push down the fence and embrace our brothers in Palestine!"

Al-Masri headlined his editorial: "The Way to Peace."

Palestinian Arabs responded to the proposal with rapturous enthusiasm. All but the most dour members of the P.L.O. executive committee were swept up by the support for al-Masri's "Green March."

"This is not mugabalah," Sarid said, sliding a copy of the Al-Quds editorial across a table in the Knesset dining room to Israel Miller. "This is al-Masri's bottom line after negotiations at the U.N. and the World Court–Dismantle the Israeli observer position and remaining settlements in Palestine, implement the 'right-of-return' and he'll talk about another–no doubt temporary–peace with the microscopic, truncated Jewish statelet of the '47 Partition Plan, the Israel his grandfathers tried to strangle.

"From our hallucinations of 'the New Middle East' back to their 60 years belated endorsement of the partition plan. The Arab-Islamic mentality–seeing themselves simultaneously as permanently aggrieved and permanently superior, therefore entitled–expected always to be indulged in 'no-fault' aggression. The Americans and Europeans encouraged them in this, pretending they were the victims and pressuring us, not the aggressors, to make the concessions. As they have, one way or another, since the Arab riots of the '20s and '30s, since the Arabs' refusal to make peace in '48 or '56, in '67 or '73 or 2000. We had to understand their frustration, we had to induce them to negotiate, as if peace was a value only to us."

Arabic, a language of poetry more than prose, tends to extremes of vocabulary and construction. Speakers often employ exaggeration, even violent hyperbole–mugabalah–in order to make a point tacitly understood as more limited. Generations of Western scholars lived by parsing the underlying reality and generations of Middle Eastern minorities suffered by denying the dreams embodied in it.

"'Just for local consumption,' 'just openers for the final status revisions,' that's what the State Department–and some of our own intellectuals–will tell us, even now, after all evidence to the contrary," Sarid said. "As if the twentieth century was not full of anti-holy men with their tracts full of horrific vows, from Lenin's pamphlets to Hitler's Mein Kampf, from Mao's Little Red Book to Khomeini's cassettes and Pol Pot's Paris musings. There always have been warnings, and always denials by 'progressives'."

Said Miller, "The Hebrew prophets faced the same problem. Watching the Judean political factions quarrel violently among themselves in this city 2,600 years ago over whether to align with Egypt against Babylon or vice versa, Jeremiah said of the glib leaders of his day: 'They heal the wounds of the sons and daughters of Israel lightly, crying "Peace, peace," when there is no peace.'"

* * *

Washington, D.C. (July 10, 2007)–"The chief of staff just blew me off! Like I was nothing. Like AIPAG didn't count anymore. Can you believe it?"

Lo, how the mighty are fallen, Congressman Marcus thought to himself. It could not have happened to a more deserving jackass than Hersh Hestin. Too bad the situation was so serious. Otherwise, Marcus could really enjoy this.

"Sit down, Hersh, and tell me what happened," Marcus said, ushering the breathless Hestin into his private office. Standing in the half-open door, he turned back to Felicia Sanchez. "Felicia," he said softly, "would you have an intern fetch us some coffee? I think Mr. Hestin will want one of his pick-me-ups."

The president of the American Israel Political Affairs Group would fortify the coffee with the golden-brown Kentucky bourbon from the engraved silver flask in Marcus' desk. Two Jews two generations removed from Poland, sitting in the shadow of the U.S. Capitol, sipping sour mash. The flask had been a peace offering from Hestin himself, after he had tried and failed to steer Jewish campaign contributions away from Marcus a few races back. Then, according to the AIPAG leader, the congressman "had gotten too big for his damn britches!"

Marcus rarely touched the bourbon—except perhaps when he and Sanchez worked late. Given the congressman's hectic schedule and his wife Madeleine's mountainous suspicions, that happened rarely.

The latest Israeli-Arab settlement—imposed as one inducement for European cooperation and Arab acquiescence in America's post-Afghanistan war on terrorism—had meant, to the White House at least, the diminution of Israel as a point of foreign attention. This led quickly to a decrease in interest in the pro-Israel vote. That vote turned out to be comprised of many pro-Israel evangelical Christians, who did not generally elect Democrats anyway. The overall Jewish vote—at least the non-Orthodox component—turned out to be something else, a small but moneyed slice of the Democrats' constituency of post-liberal left minorities. In any case, as the Jewish community continued to age, assimilate, to succeed at birth control and out marriage, the Jewish electorate, however segmented, kept shrinking.

Hersh Hestin—unknown to most Americans, including to most American Jews—had been one of the country's most influential political players. Secretaries of state and Israeli prime ministers used to take his telephone calls, senators canceled appointments to make room for his unannounced drop-ins and mere representatives begged to take him to lunch. Hestin headed AIPAG, the registered pro-Israel lobby.

But he and the other AIPAG leaders, like many politically active Jews, long ago had confused influence with power. When Israel—Jews with land of their own and guns to defend it—lost power, the Hersh Hestins of the world lost influence. These American Jewish "leaders" either had never learned, or conveniently forgotten, that a king has power, his vizier only influence and that conditionally. Medieval court Jews lived with their bags packed. Hestin and AIPAG, having mistaken access for authority, flattery for loyalty, relearned the old lesson with brutal clarity.

Now, having been unceremoniously ejected from the White House by the president's chief of staff after pulling one of his legendary unannounced visits, Hestin wandered the halls of the Cannon House Office Building like a beggar. He felt condemned to irrelevance in the waiting rooms of members who now had neither the need nor the time to see him. So he was glad to be able to sit in the private office of Jonathan Marcus and relate the outrage done him.

Marcus was that rare Jewish congressman who in the old days had told Hestin where to stuff an AIPAG dictum, in this particular case an order to vote for a modified Saudi Arabian arms sale, and still hung on to pro-Israel campaign money reflexively raised and arbitrarily donated by AIPAG board members in their legally separate but electorally parallel functions as political action committee leaders.

Only a few years before, before implementation of the final status accords, Hestin had been brimming with schemes. Schemes to increase aid to Israel and to the Arabs, encourage Iranian "moderation" by dropping the pistachio sanctions—which his Lincoln Bedroom buddy Bill Clinton had done, and to fund a mirage-like Turkish-Syrian-Israeli water project if only Syria would make peace. Schemes to punish members of Congress who did not wish to grease a grand Arab-Israeli settlement with taxpayer dollars or who just annoyed him personally, and to place friends of AIPAG's in senior White House, State Department and Pentagon posts. But now the Johnston Administration sat on its hands while the Israelis struggled to enforce that grand settlement and the treaty that had brought into being the Arab Republic of Palestine, divided Arab east Jerusalem from Jewish west Jerusalem and returned Israel to its pre-'67 lines as a snake-like territory nearly 300 miles long but just nine miles wide near its most populous point. A peace AIPAG, co-opted and comfortable, had lobbied for.

American Jews, assimilated as individuals, were marginalized as a group. No one needed to care what they thought, or feared, or wanted, now that a treaty covered the Arab-Israeli conflict, now that Jews were a but a remnant domestic group, now that antisemitism, like philosemitism, was just another spice in the country's multicultural, non-judgmental stew. Hestin, a child of the '60s, had been dazed by events neither he nor his generously paid senior staff admitted were happening.

To admit they were happening would have meant acknowledging failure, or at least to learn from it. That AIPAG's lay leaders, like the FBI senior staff after September 11, 2001 hated to do; after all, it meant having been wrong. Early in Reagan's second term they had decided, almost unconsciously, to let themselves be co-opted by whomever occupied the White House, by whichever party was in power in Israel, in exchange for access, frequent and first-name.

They mistook their own slogans about "the unshakable U.S.-Israel strategic partnership" for reality, as if Israel couldn't become another Taiwan, Lebanon, or Bosnia—small and smaller places of real or imagined national interest that, in or just after crises, fell off American radar. They had convinced themselves that who they knew inside the Beltway counted more than who the anti-Israel crowd, the news media, progressive clerics and revisionist academics reached outside it—even though that often included their own children. The odd exhilaration Hestin experienced the night of September 13, 1993, celebrating that day's Rabin-Arafat handshake at a party co-sponsored by AIPAG and the until-then detested National Association of Arab Americans, was as a taste of forbidden fruit. Intoxicated, he and his colleagues sobered up only when that taste soured with the second intifada. Now, deprived of the pretext for his obsessive political meddling, Hersh Hestin—who once confessed to his formerly Baptist wife that he suspected God was preparing him to be a prophet if not the Messiah—was perplexed.

But hardly broken. Hestin still possessed his fortune, generated by the tool manufacturing business his grandfather had started and that Hestin now ran, more or less on automatic pilot. The grandfather, a Russian-Jewish immigrant and tinkerer, had held a patent on the socket wrench, that all-American device. The father had expanded the firm by successfully developing the cordless power drill. Hestin himself took care to hire competent managers and stay out of their way. He did not see it like that of course. He believed it was his higher calling to oversee, and, as necessary, correct American politics.

As president of AIPAG, Hestin had had two invaluable assets: The first was a mailing list of 55,000 passionate pro-Israel activists, with its sub-list of several hundred proven donors, men and women who could and frequently did write five-figure checks at a moment's notice. The second was political clout of overblown proportions, based partly on a handful of dragon-slaying stories by journalists looking for sensation and partly on tips from the lobby—the tips themselves based on leaks from the administration or Israeli embassy—about government policy changes. These assets allowed him to get away with bragging, in public, about his tennis victories over two consecutive secretaries of state.

But after the Arab-Israeli settlement, all Hestin had was the mailing list. That and a lot of vengeful Washington chickens coming home to roost. Marcus could not care less if the chickens pecked Hestin's pampered carcass clean—he wanted the mailing list. He did not know why, but he knew he had to get it, even if half those on it were demoralized now by Israel's reverses. So he provided an old adversary with a little solace.

Marcus watched Hestin pour the whisky into his coffee, sunlight glinting through the Venetian blinds and off the HH monogram engraved into the silver flask. He took in the HH monograms on Hestin's gold cuff links and their clones woven into his custom-made Italian silk tie. The man, a walking logotype for himself, was dressed for the good old days so suddenly gone.

"That bastard kicked me out of the White House! Can you believe it?" Hestin repeated.

"I can. When the Assistant Secretary of State for the Near East or the Assistant Secretary of Defense for Security Assistance come up to testify these days, they don't bother to hide their contempt for Israel's friends on the committee. Especially the Jewish members. A couple of years ago they were gray, gutless bureaucrats, the kind of Washington careerist who could hurt you only if your back was turned. And now they think they can walk over us. And if that's the case with them, the politicals in the West Wing must be feeling omnipotent," Marcus said.

"God, you're verbose. Just say they're finally acting like they've got balls!" Hestin rejoined.

"No, like they think we don't."

"I want to get even!" the AIPAG president fairly screamed.

"I want to save the Jews," Marcus said quietly. "And you," he said to Hestin, fixing him with an uncompromising stare and speaking like a father to an unruly son, "are going to help me."

* * *

The Hague (July 15, 2007)–The U.N. Treaty Supervisory Organization rejected Israel's demand that the pact ending the Arab-Israeli conflict and creating Arab

Palestine be retained as negotiated, with the five-year period of "confidence-building measures" before either side could make new demands. "Changed conditions demand changed thinking," the supervisors declared. "Palestinian grievances are real and must be redressed. Fresh negotiations should begin at once."

At The Hague, a majority of justices—some from oil-poor third world nations, some from major Western trading partners of the Arab states—suggested the Israelis cease being "so stiff-necked." They also did what the U.N. Security Council, fearing a U.S. veto, had not done—proposed their own comprehensive solution. It called for "splitting the difference":

Israel should get out of the territories completely, no settlements or even unarmed military observers retained on the strategic highpoints, no rights to over fly Palestinian Arab airspace, no patrols along the Jordan River. Complete sovereignty, including the right to an army and to military alliances with any other Arab state, for the Arab Republic of Palestine. In return, Arab Palestinians would relinquish any claims to land inside Israel's 1948-1949 boundaries. However, U.N.-appointed arbitrators would decide on a referendum for the Arabs of the Galilee and Negev and a large increase in the number of Palestinians covered by "family reunification" to Israel proper.

Pier Vandenhagen, the World Court's presiding Danish judge, issued a solitary dissent. Vandenhagen invoked the memory of Danish resistance to the Nazis, of the dangerous, selfless acts of many of his countrymen who had fought the Nazis and shielded the Jews two generations before. He pointed to his country's support for Israel during the 1973 Yom Kippur War—alone among Western Europe's democracies and for which it joined the United States on the Arab oil embargo. "If any people deserve at least to have its case heard, it is the Jews of Israel. If any other people have had their very right to exist called into question repeatedly, by a majority of U.N. member countries, this Court is unaware of it; when Serbia expelled the ethnic Albanians from Kosovo, it at least did not try to tell the world they were not a people. And if any other people have waged such an heroic, exhausting struggle to reestablish their nationhood as have the Jews, this court would look sympathetically on their claims.

"For us not to hear them but to put them at risk by means of a scheme dangerous to their security places this Court on the side of those who threaten the Jews and their state. Historically, on the side of the Czars, the Nazis, the Soviets, the side of Arab dictators and Muslim bigots. By now that is something no person who calls him or herself civilized should do.

"That the big powers, especially the United States, helped impose a settlement and then connived to disregard it is clear. They have acted like Britain after it issued the Balfour Declaration regarding the Jewish national home in Palestine, then cut off immigration—taking back by deed what it had promised in words. For us to refuse Israel's case is to confirm the axiom that international law is invoked successfully by the strong, who do not need it, and appealed to in vain by the weak, who do.

"I cannot be a party to such actions. Therefore, I resign from this court."

In a one-page statement issued separately by his office, Vandenhagen noted his grandfather's participation in the World War II Danish underground. "He would understand my decision to go to Israel now and share the present danger. It is a matter of principle."

The judge's decision was a one-day news story. So was his murder on a crowded street in The Hague forty-eight hours later. A taxi driver described the gunmen as "dark, Middle Eastern-looking." He said he lost sight of them as they escaped toward France in a late-model Mercedes with diplomatic license plates. No one else remembered seeing anything at all.

*   *   *

Alexandria, Virginia (July 23, 2007)–"Israel was right to reject the World Court's plan. The United States was wrong to join the U.N. trade embargo," Rabbi Levi said, delivering the sermon near the end of the Braverman bar mitzvah.

"Warmonger!" a man shouted from the back of the temple. "It's the Israelis who never give peace a chance. The Israelis! And they're stirring up trouble for us American Jews."

Rabbi Levi did not recognize him. Probably one of Paul Braverman's relatives, she thought. Or one of the growing number of "messianic Jews" from the "Jews-for-Jesus" congregation in the church up the street, who brazenly attended, and at times disrupted, services at Or Kodesh. Like the bar mitzvah boy's father, the "Jews-for-Jesus" were unwilling either to shut up as Jews or put up as Christians and refused to acknowledge their dual shame.

Ushers surrounded the man and walked him out.

Poor Joshua Braverman, Jeri Levi thought. Poor Joshua. As if the two years of struggle on his part to learn his short Hebrew Torah portion and the cantillation that went with it, and the conflict between his Jewish father and non-Jewish mother–she wanted the bar mitzvah, he did not–had not been enough. Now the ceremony itself threatened to degenerate into a brawl. Rabbi Levi put her hands on his shoulders. "It will be all right," she said softly. "Yehiyeh b'seder. It will be all right."

She resumed her sermon. "Awake, all those who slumber," she said softly.

Something insistent in her quiet tones caught the congregation's attention. Silent faces stared intently at her. "Jews–it is the eleventh hour, and still we walk, as if entranced, toward the precipice!"

Now her voice was louder–controlled, but penetrating. Not an eye moved from Rabbi Levi's countenance. "Once more danger approaches–this time not from one source but from a host, an evil host. Yet we Jews look on as if detached, as if this were not our battle, as if it was happening to someone else, as if glimpsed on a video.

"When they rioted in Crown Heights we said, 'How awful, what happened to those Chasidim.' When they bombed the Jewish community center in Buenos Aires we lamented, 'How terrible, what happened to those Argentines.' When they blew up the children in the Tel Aviv disco we said, 'Now the world will understand at last the evil ranged against the Israelis'–yet the world said, 'We understand the Palestinians rage.' And when they destroyed the World Trade

Center, when they struck the Pentagon, the world said, 'Let us stamp out this evil,' this evil but not that evil that strikes the Jews.

"'That evil the Jews bring on themselves, and must appease... so its twin will not strike the rest of us.'

"After the Holocaust we said, 'Never again!' And imaged that the world spoke in unison. But 'never again' nearly repeated itself in 1948, in 1967, in 1973. If we were not alone we were nearly so.

"Nevertheless, after the miracle of '67, after Sadat's peace trip in '77, we convinced ourselves that our equality was established, that peace—one day—was inevitable. But as the Chosen People with a divine mission, we went back to sleep. We slept not because history's oldest hatred had dissipated, let alone because we had fulfilled our mission of bringing Torah into the world, but because we were in denial. So we awoke one spring five years ago to burning synagogues in France, tens of thousands of marchers in Holland—where Anne Frank metaphorically metamorphosed into a suicide bomber—in Italy, shouting 'Jews into the sea.'

"My children!" Jeri Levi shouted in what was not a shout but in fact the piercing call of a spoken shofar blast, a surreal vocal note of holy clarity that none who heard it would ever forget: "Awake, and act! Otherwise it is the last moment for the Jews as a people, for the Jewish people. Now!" Another vocal shofar blast, not hanging in the air so much as filling it, then rising, quavering and, as Rabbi Levi's long exhalation ended, shattering into hundreds of crystalline aural shards, figuratively piercing each breast.

She collapsed on the bimah. For a moment the synagogue was silent but for the perceptible whoosh of the air conditioning. The chronic Saturday morning kibbitzers were hushed. Then congregants were helping her up, and color began returning to her face. She sat for a few minutes in her chair, facing a stunned congregation, a bewildered Joshua Braverman standing uncertainly beside her.

She stood, placed her hands on the boy's shoulders, and in her normal voice resumed. "To those who hate the Jewish state, the Jewish people, the idea of Judaism, to them the very name of this congregation, Or Kodesh—holy light—is a provocation. Joshua Braverman, in such a time we receive you into the congregation of Israel. You will be counted as an adult in the minyan, the minimum of ten required for communal prayer. You will be called to recite the blessings before and after Torah readings, like any other adult. But maybe we should expect more."

Aware they had heard, had witnessed a sermon unlike any before it at Or Kodesh, congregants were puzzled to hear the rabbi announce there might be something more for a bar mitzvah boy.

Rabbi Levi continued. "For too long we argued over 'who is a Jew' when the real question is what is a Jew for? After the Exile, the end of the ghetto, after the disappearance of the shtetl and failure of both assimilation and reborn religious obscurantism, after the Holocaust, we have had only one answer. To build Israel—the people and the nation. But not just one more little country, one more needless nationalism. No, as the Chosen People, on the Promised Land, heeding and exemplifying the Word of God. Ki me'Zion, taytseh Torah, u'davar Adoni m'Yerushalyim. 'From Zion shall go forth Torah, the word of God from Jerusalem.'

"Otherwise, we are like the wicked son who, at Passover, asks of the Exodus,

'What is this that God has done for you?' for you and not for me, for you but not for us. Otherwise, Judaism, until a few generations ago a way of life, becomes either a 'drive-through' life style or archaic cultism."

"Nonsense! Sheer nonsense!" It was Marvin Kammelman, president of the congregation. He stood, snorted, and stamped out.

Rabbi Levi stopped abruptly, startled. When she concluded, it was in a light, lyrical voice, almost as a song: "And now, the ancient priestly benediction," she said, placing her hands lightly over Joshua Braverman's forehead. "May the Lord bless you and keep you, and make his countenance to shine upon you."

The sanctuary began to stir again. Congregants and Braverman guests gaped, then struggled to extract an explanation from each other for what they had just heard. Kammelman, who had sat through the sermon in fuming fascination before his outburst, skipped the kiddish luncheon; he would not miss much, he thought, with Paul Braverman paying. Besides, this time that accursed woman rabbi had gone too far! All that zealotry about Chosen People and antisemitism and Israel. Upsetting. Damned upsetting! The temple existed for people's comfort and enjoyment, not their distress, Kammelman said to himself. Maybe now he could mobilize a majority of the board and rid himself at last of Mrs. Rabbi Jeri Levi!

Kammelman had not even been on the board, let alone president, when Or Kodesh hired Jeri Levi. He had just relocated to northern Virginia to be near his married daughter, a moved she regarded without enthusiasm. In his early sixties, he arrived to semi-retirement, he said.

A successful Long Island insurance agent, Kammelman was a driving, driven man. Bullish in appearance and manner, his large, tired-looking pale blue eyes offset by an imperious voice, he averaged a secretary a year. He arrived at the office an hour earlier than anyone else, remained an hour later, often skipped lunch but snacked incessantly, and stayed awake at night wondering what he had left undone. His in-basket was empty every night, his out-basket full.

Bouts of high blood pressure left him with periodic nose bleeds. When he felt the intended beneficiaries of his chronic monologues were not listening, he was not above changing the bloody tissue paper in his nostrils for dramatic effect. Obsessed with punctuality and neatness, especially in others, he invited people to "discuss matters" and then invariably lectured them. In New York he inclined to dark suits and stripped ties. In suburban Washington, in semi-retirement, he wore dark sport coats, gray slacks, and kept the stripped ties.

He also retained the ability to manipulate, intimidate, cajole and, when unavoidable, charm people into doing just what he wanted them to do. Even those who quickly decided they could not or would not deal with his abrasiveness recognized his dogged intelligence. Insurance had made him prosperous. In Alexandria he had announced that "home and business security systems are the insurance of our day," and waxed wealthy. He joined Or Kodesh to keep his wife quiet–a constant motivation for Kammelman. Then, aggravated at how the temple operated–"a bunch of GS-13's on the board, $75,000-a-year bureaucrats trying to tell me how to run things"–he determined to straighten it out.

Although he dominated the board, Kammelman never felt he prevailed in the contest of wills with the woman rabbi and what he called her clique. In reality, a majority of the congregants supported Jeri Levi, many avidly. That exasperated Kammelman, and from the moment he joined the board, he began working assiduously to undermine her. In Levi, Kammelman recognized one of those rare individuals who not only anticipated but also preempted him. He gave up long, direct meetings with her, which he usually left deflected if not deflated. Confounded by her ability to absorb his attacks, then bounce them back at him with a midrashic reference or old rabbinic story, he turned instead to short, insistent telephone calls. Long determined to get rid of her, Kammelman saw in her newly-erratic behavior his opportunity.

"A rabbi," he once had fairly shouted at Sylvia Weinberg, apropos of nothing, "should know how to follow orders, say the right prayer at the right time–and shut up!"

The most disagreeable part about being Or Kodesh president for Kammelman was the necessity of sitting on the bimah each Saturday morning, enduring the services as if they were important, and in essence functioning in the sanctuary, on public view, as part of the rabbi's entourage. "I feel like a Democratic Speaker of the House, having to nod and smile in the background while a Republican president gives the State of the Union, knowing it's all mush!" he once bellowed over the phone at his son in Chicago.

His son, Marvin P. Kammelman, Jr., rarely visited but sent greeting cards to his parents several times a year. He also styled himself M. Peter Kammelman, collapsing Marvin and dropping Junior.

For Kammelman, Senior, the meaning of Judaism lay not in its laws, not in the ethics the laws inspired, and not in what Jeri Levi called history–to him fables–but in its social and ethnic ties. He tried, without seeming to be anti-religious, to discourage Rabbi Levi's institution of a daily minyan. It reminded him of Orthodoxy. The Orthodox, with their rituals and self-righteousness, their fedoras and fastidiously covered women, made him uncomfortable. He thought them fanatics, and worse, old-fashioned.

"Nothing worthwhile happened before the twentieth century!" he snapped at Sylvia Weinberg on his way out of a meeting with the rabbi. Jeri Levi had quoted Scripture again to discourage his plan to double Sunday school fees. "That is, nothing with the exception of Thomas Alfred Edison."

"Alva. Thomas Alva Edison," Sylvia Weinberg corrected.

"Nothing, damn it!" replied Kammelman, slamming the door behind him.

Of late Kammelman had begun delegating the responsibility of adorning Rabbi Levi's bimah to the congregational vice presidents.

Also out the door ahead of hungry celebrants pushing from the sanctuary into the social hall was Hal Levi. He too was upset by his wife's sermon and did not trust himself to speak to her at the reception. It was two miles to their riverside townhouse, but he set off, leaving the kids playing with Sylvia on the temple playground and abandoning his car in the parking lot. He hoped the walk would help him cool down. Hal Levi feared for his marriage. Hell–he had married a rabbinical student, not a self-anointed prophet!

When Jeri Levi returned home after the Braverman reception she saw Hal on the deck, staring towards the Potomac.

"I'm home," she shouted, choosing for the moment not to make an issue of his early departure. He nodded but kept his back to her.

She went inside and, suddenly quite exhausted, climbed the stairs to the master bedroom. Sprawled across the bed, she fell asleep almost immediately. And Jeri Levi dreamed. It was a dream of herself, delivering a sermon she had never written, in a voice not her own, a dream of cold shoulders instead of greetings, and of Marvin Kammelman and her husband ascending skyward in storm clouds. She awoke convinced of the enormity of her transgression. Convinced, but curiously detached, unafraid.

Hal Levi had been watching his wife from the doorway. Seeing her fully awake, he moved into the bedroom, closing the door behind him. "That sermon this morning; where the hell do you get off with that nonsense? First the dreams, now this, this affront to the entire congregation! I'm not sure I can take much more of this holier-than-thou crap!"

She answered through clenched teeth. "A–It wasn't nonsense. B–You can't take anymore? You're not the one going through this, being overcome by some strange energy, doing and saying things I know are right but doing them almost not of my own volition, having these dreams, then feeling wrung out. Maybe you were right, maybe they're not just dreams. Whatever, I never asked for them and I sure can't ignore them. And C–as for holier-than-thou, I believe what I say. Monday I'm going to enroll the kids in day school for next year. You're right; we should practice what we preach."

"Do that–give the kids up to Orthodoxy, and I'll fight you for them!"

"Hal…."

For the second time that day he fled her presence. But two days later Jeri Levi kept her word and enrolled Justin and Deborah in Gesher, the Northern Virginia Hebrew Day School. Even though as a congregational rabbi she qualified for a one-third subsidy, their combined tuition still cost her more than $12,000. Hal Levi called a lawyer and took a room at the Old Town Holiday Inn.

*   *   *

Jenin (July 13, 2007)–"Allah akbar!" Yacoub al-Masri shouted into the microphone.

"God is great!" two hundred thousand voices roared in response.

Al-Masri could not have been more satisfied. Standing on a small platform on the back of a flatbed truck, trying to make himself heard through a public address system cobbled together for the march, he faced a great crowd, excited and excitable, of Palestinian Arabs. Behind him, just beyond the chain-link and barbed wire fence, a smaller but still sizable mass of Israeli Arabs, perhaps another one hundred thousand. Between them, on their side of the boundary, a thin line of Israeli border police–mostly tough Druze and Bedouin led by Jewish officers– and a handful of Israeli regular army troops struggled to maintain the demarcation line between Arab Palestine and Israel.

More than twenty-five years of tireless, tedious organization, dangerous covert work and armed struggle finally bore fruit: al-Masri had managed all this less than two years after the "final status" agreement between Israel and the Palestinians had been signed. Less than two years after the accords between Israel and Syria, Israel and Lebanon had taken effect—with tens of billions of dollars in U.S., Western European and Japanese aid, modern baksheesh, as lubricant.

"Salaam!" al-Masri shouted. "Salaam and shalom and peace! For Moslems, Christians, Jews, Palestinians and Israelis. Peace for us all! The peace of the brave! The peace of victory!"

"Victory!" tens of thousands of throats screamed back at him.

"Freedom!" al-Masri shouted. "Freedom and unity!"

"Unity!" the masses cried out. "Allah akbar!"

Cameras rolled. Al-Masri smiled, and spoke of the great time soon coming when they all would be victorious, united. Well-traveled, well-paid American correspondents, using the scene as backdrop rather than focal point, were already intoning their "stand-ups" and voice-overs, talking over al-Masri, showing the peace and freedom march, silencing the call to victory. The bright superficiality of television, the monomania of the myopic lens, relayed instantaneous images yet immediately insulated the audience from their meaning.

Explaining rather than reporting, the broadcast correspondents missed it when al-Masri glanced at his watch and made his way back through the frenzied mass. The cameras, focused on the reporters rather than the crowd, never caught the initial outburst, only its aftermath, and that only in part.

"Tear gas!" a Border Police sergeant shouted. A canister had come arcing up from somewhere in the front of the crowd on the Palestinian side. Then a barrage of them. While the police and soldiers struggled to put on their gas masks, Israeli Arabs on the other side began pelting them with rocks and firing ball bearings from sling shots. Quickly the troops were shooting tear gas grenades of their own in all directions.

The rally disintegrated into riot. Arabs at the rear of the crowds pressed forward to see what was happening. Those in the middle, where the responding Israeli tear gas grenades fell, tried to flee to the rear. And those at the front of the melee—some out of anger, some under orders—rushed their side of the fence and began tearing it down, with bare hands, poles from their placards, even wire-cutters. Israeli Arabs rushed to help them.

"Rubber bullets!" commanded the Israeli Defense Forces major in charge. Standing orders called for rubber bullets to be fired from more than seventy-five yards and aimed only at the waist down. The major knew that was impossible—the mob was too close, too many. Only seconds later, after seeing the first of his own men go down, some to gunshots from somewhere in the surging crowds, he bellowed "Live ammunition, at will!" His men, already squeezed against the fence, a mob only a few paces in front of them, another at their backs, were firing point blank, rifles on automatic. Bodies fell about them, but the bloodied, frenzied mass came on, engulfing them, ripping their weapons from their hands. The major was shot dead while radioing for the reinforcements he had been denied earlier, out of fear that heavier security might appear repressive.

Before departing a small hill nearly a kilometer away, al-Masri witnessed the collapse of the border fence. "Good. Very good!" he exulted. "We have had our tea party. Soon we shall have our war of independence. Independence from the Jewish presence, that is."

*   *   *

West Jerusalem (August 1, 2007)–Prime Minister Sarid pressed the telephone receiver tightly against his good ear. He could not afford to miss a word the president of the United States was saying, not now, and the connection was bad. A Syrian missile–a Chinese copy of a Russian SS-23, modified according to German plans– had blasted a telecommunications relay station north of Jerusalem just that morning. It knocked out trunk lines around the country and demolished satellite dishes. So instead of the crisp immediacy he usually heard in trans-Atlantic calls, Sarid listened as the president's boyish voice echoed through a well of static.

"Meir," Barry Johnston said familiarly, although the two had never met, "you'll be glad to know that the Syrians have told us, through the Egyptians, that they've agreed to a ceasefire. Seven a.m. our time. What's that for you?"

"Two p.m., Mr. President," Sarid replied. "That's a little more than an hour from now. I'm relieved, and I thank you on behalf of the people of Israel." The prime minister paused, then rushed on. "But this is only a ceasefire and the Syrians could strike again any minute. So could the Iraqis. Their ground forces are mobilized on the Jordanian border. Jordanian troops have entered Arab Palestine, in violation of the agreement..."

"At the invitation of the Palestinians," Johnston interrupted.

"And Saudi Arabia is reinforcing Jordan, including with top-of-the-line U.S.-built aircraft, in violation of U.S.-Saudi agreements. Mr. President, I must ask you again: what about our re-supply? My country will not, cannot agree to implementation of the World Court verdict regarding the Galilee and Negev–any more than you would permit Hispanic Americans in Texas and California to vote on reattaching those states to Mexico–so the Arabs may well attack again."

"Some in my party might not think that amiss," Johnston laughed, his mind wandering.

"Missiles and bombers from Iraq and Syria have cost us hundreds of tanks and dozens of planes, large amounts of ammunition and petroleum stocks already. Our casualties, from chemical and biological warheads as well as conventional, are nearly fifty thousand–more than in all our previous wars combined. Mostly civilian."

"I know. Things have been tough. But the Pentagon tells me you boys gave a good accounting of yourselves. They say the damage in Baghdad and Damascus is extensive. I don't think the Arabs are going to be in any hurry to launch a second strike. Anyway, we're going to be talking about you people at the National Security Council meeting this afternoon. Have Ambassador, ah..."

"Tarbitsky. Yehuda Tarbitsky."

"Yes, my friend Ambassador Tarbitsky. Having him standing by. And Meir, this is really a bad connection. I can barely hear you. Have someone check your lines."

Sarid heard the phone click dead. Bad connection, hell! The president had stiffed him again. Johnston did not want to talk about replacing Israel's losses—those that could be replaced. With a ceasefire pending, the prime minister now worried more about American reliability than Arab intentions.

Had it only been thirty-six hours? In less than two days this had become the most destructive of all Arab-Israeli wars. Like the 1948 War of Independence this one too saw devastation hit civilians more than the military. And like the 1973 Yom Kippur War—which Israel nearly lost in the first two days—many had feared this explosion but few had forecast it. Of course, in retrospect, the descent was plain, Sarid thought, fingering Eshel's dog-eared memo.

He stared out the window of his office in the Kirya, the government compound on Kaplan Street just opposite the Knesset building, and tugged absently at his scarred right ear.

In January, 1983 he and an aide were escorting an American television crew down a supposedly secure Beirut side street. Suddenly, a grenade came hurtling out of a passageway between two buildings. Down, down he shouted then and a thousand times since in nightmares and daydreams. The news crew, fresh from El Salvador, hit the ground instinctively. So did Sarid, pulling himself into a ball, his legs up over his abdomen, his hands clasped behind his head and bringing it down toward his chest. But the aide, a bookish American immigrant fresh out of Hebrew University, froze. The blast tore off half his head.

The prime minister came back to himself and focused on the scene outside his window. Positioned on a low hill covered with evergreens, the early modern masonry block of the Knesset dominated a large area of western Jerusalem. Nearby was the Israeli Supreme Court building, its Jerusalem stone finish, like that of the Knesset, gleaming golden in the sun. The Knesset dated to the late 1950's, the Court building to the mid-'90s.

The Knesset opened as an assertion, still fanciful to most, of Jewish sovereignty. The High Court building was inaugurated between the justices' startling loss of nerve in the John Demjanjuk case, when they decided not to retry the Ukrainian-American and their demoralizing rejection of Jewish nationalism in the Katzir case. In the former the justices denied the evidence that if Demjanjuk was not "Ivan the Terrible" of Treblinka, then quite likely he had been Ivan the guard at Sobibor. In the latter they found real estate restrictions for Jewish neighborhoods in the Jewish state somehow anti-democratic. Within a few years, Sarid thought, Israel's chief jurists had gone from weariness with Holocaust memories to implicit rejection of the moral necessity of a Jewish country.

The court building itself, an audacious architectural blend of ancient and modern, was meant to be a manifestation in stone of the biblical imperative, "justice, justice thou shall pursue." Yet in that case, wondered Sarid, why did we free, over the years, so many thousand Arab terrorists and suspects for a few dozen Israelis? Why did we never try and execute their men and occasionally women, for murdering our children? Why did we agree to live with fear while they walked among us in security? He thought of Yitzhak Rabin caving into European and American pressure in 1993 and letting 400 Hamas and Islamic Jihad leaders just exiled to Lebanon return. This blunder, one of countless Israel miscalculations of future Arab behavior in response to present Israeli concessions, contributed much to the kidnappings, stabbings, axings, shootings and suicide bombings that punctuated the Oslo "peace process." Impelled in part by the court, it was one of many decisions, Sarid thought, that helped grind a fragmented Israeli society into even smaller bits.

So for the missile that demolished most of one wing of the court, Sarid felt only ambivalence. For the one that struck across the small valley west of the Knesset and court, just missing the Israeli Museum and the Dead Sea Scrolls' Shrine of the Book, he could not avoid ironic empathy. The warhead—technology supplied by expatriate Russian scientists, funded by U.S.-purchased oil, and completed in labs purchased whole from France—had pulverized the Billy Rose modern sculpture garden. At least the Arabs had done one thing right, Sarid mused. If it had been the Arabs. He could not rule out the Sicarii, those Jewish religious-nationalists warring against modern secular culture as well as their fellow Jews. They already had taken advantage of wartime chaos to assassinate one cabinet member, one Knesset member, and set fire to two movie theaters, and that was only in Jerusalem. Someone, perhaps in response, had blown up a classroom in a well-known yeshiva, killing eighteen young boys. It was wartime, and camouflaged by the fog of war enemies domestic as well as foreign satisfied the sometimes suppressed but never satisfied human appetite for human blood.

Between parliament and the museum a lone army jeep picked its way along the normally busy Ruppin Boulevard, dodging the bomb craters. Damn those Americans! What were they waiting for?

"Pnina," the prime minister said into the intercom, "please find Professor Eshel and ask him to see me immediately."

Eshel now was acting director of Shin Bet as well as minister of police. He had taken the second appointment early yesterday, after delayed-fuse penetrator bombs hit the Shin Bet's headquarters. The reinforced subterranean offices—which probably would have survived low-tech warheads—proved no match for the lethal sophistication of the Arabs' Western weapons. The agency's director, his deputy, and several senior aides—among many others—died in the blast.

Shin Bet, or the General Security Services, Israel's equivalent of the F.B.I., as the Mossad was to the America C.I.A., continued operating in the West Bank and Gaza Strip after they became the Arab Republic of Palestine. Agency operatives worked, too, on the Golan Heights, now once more Syria's southernmost province. But just barely.

Israel's abandonment of its Southern Lebanon Army allies in the spring of 2000—part of then-Prime Minister Ehud Barak's desperate diplomacy to reach a deal with the dying Hafez al-Assad, made being an Arab partner of Israeli security a dubious undertaking. Palestinian double agents—increasingly common as Israel made plain its determination to leave virtually all of Judea and Samaria, no matter what—had rooted out the "collaborators." Most of them.

Sarid glanced again at the memo Eshel had written a few long weeks ago. Under "Indicators of War," he read:

• Erosion of deterrence—lack of strategic depth following withdrawal from the territories; an Israel "strong enough to take risks for peace" now found itself with increased risks and no peace; strained relations with an America determined to keep its jerry-built anti-terrorism campaign going; proliferation of high-technology and mass destruction weapons to the Arab/Islamic states and Israel's "post-Zionist" demoralization—too many Jews, like kidnap victims dependent on their captors a la the Stockholm syndrome, saw the Jewish state through Arab propaganda as basically flawed, even illegitimate and therefore not worth fighting for;

• Intensified Islamic fundamentalism in Arab Palestine, Jordan, Egypt and among Israeli Arabs—the radicalization of Palestinian leadership, religiously and nationalistic;

• The "Palestinianization" of Jordan—the Hashemite dynasty and its backers, always a demographic minority, have been submerged not only by Palestinian population growth, but also by Palestinian "assimiliation" into the Jordanian establishment, including the military. There would be no more Black Septembers like the three-week war in 1970 that resulted in the P.L.O.'s expulsion to Lebanon. In any case, King Abdullah, with his Palestinian wife, Queen Rania, does not appear to be the warrior his father had been;

• Return of the oil weapon to Arab hands due to decreased U.S., U.K., and Russian production, increased demand world-wide. The near-record gas prices that set American drivers groaning in the summer of 2000 and spring of 2001 were but a precursor of what had followed;

• The wars among the Israelis—our enemies see the bitter, increasingly bloody clashes between ultra-Orthodox and secular Israeli Jews, between political left and right, between Israeli Jews and the fast-growing Israeli Arab minority, nearly 25 percent of the total;

• The weakening relationship between Israeli Jews and the American Diaspora, having less in common with each passing generation, differences sharpened by "who-is-a-Jew" arguments and post-modern withering of ancient tribal ties and ethnic sense of peoplehood.

Under "Indicators for Peace" Eshel had written:

• Arab memories of previous Israeli military success, an unbroken chain from 1948 through 1956, 1967, 1973 (despite Israel's initial setbacks) and in Lebanon in 1982. (Qualified by recurrent examples of Israel's military ineptitude since, including "Operation Accountability" and "Operation Grapes of Wrath" in Lebanon against Hezbollah in the '90s, failure to quickly suppress either of the first two intifadas and by Arab generational turn-over that has resulted in a new class of leaders without personal experience of decisive Israeli power);

• The tacit understanding of our sophisticated nuclear and chemical warfare capabilities. No enemy regime which starts an all-out war can count on finishing it. (Qualified by Arab realization we can defeat but not destroy them, not being big enough or wealthy enough to occupy and punish them indefinitely. So for them all-out war might not be necessary, just a series of attacks, none of which cross the nuclear threshold but which require additional Israeli concessions to halt. They can always loose to fight again. We cannot.)

That was it; six omens of war, two indicators of peace. And those two were qualified. So when missiles struck throughout Israel, when the Palestinian paramilitary police opened fire in the streets of Jerusalem, Eshel had not been surprised. Neither had Sarid. Staggered, but not surprised.

*   *   *

Damascus (August 1, 2007)–In the modern bunker-like Mohajirine presidential palace dug into a low hill overlooking the capital from its western fringe, a meeting in some respects like that in Jerusalem between Sarid and Eshel had just adjourned. Syria's new strongman, for the moment alone in his situation room, considered his position. Ibrahim Abu Bakr did so the way a chess master analyzes the board, looking many moves ahead, visualizing alternatives, anticipating his opponents. He did so quickly, with a degree of complex cunning superior to the formal interpretations of many better-schooled than he.

Abu Bakr knew how the Israelis had gotten themselves so isolated. The end of the oil glut–the depletion of British and Norwegian North Sea reserves, the decline in American domestic production, the post-Soviet decline of Russia's antiquated petroleum industry, combined with rising demand from Japan, China, South Korea, Taiwan, from Germany and the growing economies of eastern Europe. These intersecting trends pushed Middle Eastern oil producers back on stage, and Israel off. That and the new post-Christian culture of so many postnational European Union countries, countries in which both Pope John Paul II and the Rev. Billy Graham had lamented that the lamp of Christ was flickering. With it, ironically, went the spirit of national particularisms, of French, German, Italian identities self-confident enough to resist the non-violent Muslim invasion by immigration of Christendom. So American and European commitments to Israel in the wake of the Israeli-PLO accord and Israel's treaties with Jordan and Syria were met tardily, grudgingly and incompletely.

As Japanese products competed with American, as the Euro began to joust with the dollar, political as well as economic diktats started to issue from Brussels, not to mention Tokyo and Berlin, Paris and London. Hence the Europeans' betrayal and the Americans' belatedness over Bosnia, Rwanda, the Sudan and a dozen other international inconveniences. Hence the anti-terrorism campaign aimed at Osama bin Laden and Afghanistan's Taliban regime but not at Iran or Syria, at the Al-Qaeda networks and Hezbollah but not at Arafat and his Tanzim or Al-Aksa Martyrs Brigade.

In America, massive military cuts throughout the first Bush and Clinton years, and an insufficient rearmament during the second Bush administration assured there could be no repeat of the powerful U.S. Persian Gulf deployment of 1990-'91. Iraq, having successfully outlasted sanctions, had resumed its nuclear, chemical and biological weapons programs. Saddam Hussein's successors, dissembling as democrats, saw them to fruition. Iran, never really interrupted, accelerated them. From Libya and Syria to China and North Korea—with complicity from industry in Russia, Germany, France and even the United States—profiteering and proliferation reigned, diplomatic rhetoric notwithstanding.

And there was something else, Abu Bakr recognized. The cursed Holocaust generation had died off at last! With it went the remnants of Christian guilt. The West, ever more amorphous, less Anglo-Saxon culturally, less masculine psychologically, less connected to its classical heritage—including its barely acknowledged Jewish ethics—felt no more need to hear the Jews and their eternal whining. It felt both more open to and intimidated by its own rapidly growing Muslim populations. Hence its insistence that in fighting bin Laden it fought only Islamic radicalism rather than Islamic triumphalism. That meant less hesitation in sacrificing the Israelis, especially if it could be called making peace instead. And the Israelis, sapped by decades of futilely fighting others, now sought personal vindication fighting among themselves. These things he and his intelligence chief had just reviewed. The results:

"For the first time since 1948, our pilots penetrated Israeli air space and struck major targets. The missiles, with both conventional and chemical warheads, exceeded expectations. The Israeli cities of Kiryat Shemona, Safat and Karmiel will have to be rebuilt—if the Zionists can afford it and if we let them. Counting other major northern targets in Haifa, Afula, Nahariya, Tiberias and Akko, we estimate up to fifty thousand Jews dead, twice as many wounded. That's more than double the casualties for them as in all their previous wars."

"Conservative estimates, no exaggerations?" Abu Bakr had asked.

"No exaggerations," his intelligence chief said. "Probably underestimates."

"How ironic. They thought by holding onto Arab Galilee and the Arab Negev they could save their little country. They didn't understand that insisting on their 'rights' would mean losing what they would not enforce. And monetarily?"

"It will take billions—tens of billions—for them to rebuild the north, probably one-third of their gross national product."

"Excellent," said Abu Bakr. "Billions they don't have and won't get from anyone else—and would need to spend first on their military, anyway. This is really it then, the beginning of the end of the accursed Jews and their little tumor of a state! The beginning of a new Arab golden age, led by Syria, by us!"

*　　*　　*

West Jerusalem (August 2, 2007)—Sarid and Eshel sat hunched over the telephone, awaiting the call from Washington. "It is different this time, isn't it?" Sarid said. "In this war they never planned to invade, only to cripple us while keeping their militaries intact. They gambled that by not actually sending troops across the border, international pressure would keep us from launching an all-out counterattack."

"That was no gamble. It already had been proved in 2002, when not even outrages like the Passover massacre or the Megiddo bus bombing were 'bad enough' to permit us to hit the Arabs so damn hard they wouldn't do it again," Eshel responded.

"Besides, in this case they knew their people had no choice but to absorb more punishment than ours. And there's no doubt we punished them. But our air and missile strikes mostly hit their military and industrial installations—many of those sites hardened years ago in anticipation of this kind of warfare. Underground facilities and dense air defense. So we struck back, hurt but did not incapacitate them, and lost our best planes... and best pilots.

"I'm afraid this is the start of a new War of Attrition, like that with Egypt along the Suez Canal in '69 and '70. Like that waged by Arafat after September, 2000. It's meant to deplete us, soften us for a main assault still to come. That helps explain the chemical weapons: not only death, but also demoralization. The psychological impact of Jews dying in their own land from poison gas and germ warfare was not particularly subtle. The millions we spent on protective gear, filtration units for the shelters, distribution of antidotes for troops and civilians alike to chemical and biological agents—on an even larger scale than we did after Saddam's Scud missile attacks in '91—was never enough. Not against this new generation of agents...."

Sarid interrupted him. "There's never been enough—not enough money, not enough material, not enough land, not enough water, not enough diplomatic support, and—even with the Russian immigrants—never enough Jews. It always boiled down to that. Never enough Jews returning to the Jewish state, or staying put in it. So we wait on the Americans and that forty-seven-year-old former television star and president, Barry Johnston."

"Not completely," Eshel said.

"What do you mean?" the prime minister asked.

"Don't you remember? We've had the American Embassy bugged again—this time with external pulse sensors, the things Elcint started developing for the Americans during the Reagan administration to use on the Russians at the strategic arms talks. Only this technology is two generations further along."

"I approved?"

"Sort of. I knew you would, so I went ahead, right after I submitted that memo on factors for war."

"You ought to be indicted—and given a medal. Washington doesn't have a clue?"

"Not yet, not as far as I know," Eshel said.

"Good," said Sarid. "What have you got?"

"Well, Ambassador Jennings has relayed the facts pretty faithfully—his new Egyptian wife notwithstanding. But what he gets back from the White House shows how the Americans vacillate where Israel's concerned. The Japanese and Germans—dependent on Middle Eastern oil—hold U.S. debts worth hundreds of billions. And they're making very undiplomatic noises about calling in loans, reducing trade, canceling remaining base rights and so on if Washington does anything that might upset their Arab suppliers. The U.S.-headquartered multinational corporations echo them. So do Kowalsky and Elijah Khalid's followers in Congress," Eshel explained.

Again the telephone rang. Sarid nodded to Eshel who picked it up and said, "Mezrad shel rosh hamemshala"—the prime minister's office. Sarid meanwhile stretched in his high-backed chair, seeking a posture that would provide relief from the nervous exhaustion accumulated over the past three days. He tugged at his ear until Eshel frowned at him.

"Uri, that you? Let me speak to Meir," said the voice at the other end.

"It's Yehuda," Eshel said, handing the receiver to the prime minister. Yehuda Tarbitsky, one of the country's last living links to the pioneering pre-state genera-tion, was Israel's acting ambassador to the United States. He was reprising the job he had retired from nearly a decade earlier. Tarbistky reluctantly returned after his successor disappeared. That envoy had left his modern, low-slung white resi-dence on a cul-de-sac in fashionable upper northwest Washington one evening around dusk for a quick stroll. Two bodyguards accompanied him. None of them ever were seen again.

Some residents had glimpsed a big, black Mercedes with diplomatic plates in the area about the same time, but that was routine; other ambassadors lived near-by, including the always hospitable Sheik Abullafiah Sabah of Kuwait, whom Israeli envoys liked to visit informally for tea and talk—in that golden age between the Persian Gulf War and the second intifada. The case was unusual, even for a city full of unsolved homicides: no bodies ever found, no arrests ever made.

"Do you have word about resupply?" Sarid asked hurriedly.

"No, no," Tarbitsky said, his familiar hoarse voice sounding faint. "Only a tip from a source on the National Security Council: the Egyptians have relayed an Arab settlement proposal to the White House, and the president likes it. Of course, he always likes any settlement that makes him look like a successful bro-ker, the details be damned. Reminds me of Peres, or Clinton. Anyway, knowing what the Arabs wanted before the war, this sounds like more trouble."

"Johnston told me he was going to call you the minute he had word on our request. He said they have an N.S.C. meeting set for late this afternoon."

"He lied, Meir. How many times do I have to tell you, American presidents sometimes lie—to us, anyway, and Johnston lies all the time to everybody. The N.S.C. meeting's been underway for more than an hour, and I don't think resup-ply's on the agenda. I'm going to try the Hill to see if we can make any headway on that front," Tarbitsky said.

"Too bad we don't have the majorities in Congress we did in the old days," the prime minister responded. "They never should have let you retire in the first place."

"Thanks, Meir, but we both know it wasn't me. It was the Americans them-selves, unable to sustain their militarily build-up after September 11, 2001 in the face of domestic needs, imagining they could split the difference between Arab and Jew diplomatically, listening to the incessant voices in the news media, the professoriate, the clergy, portraying us as oppressors, the Palestinians as a civil rights movement."

"Yeah, and the American Jews themselves, so many afraid to speak out for Israel the minute we stopped conceding, the minute we stopped being popular. And deluded—like so many Israelis, to be honest—into agreeing that if only we met the Arabs halfway, two-thirds of the way, three-fourths of the way, ninety percent of the way, all would be well. Oh, hell. That chapter's closed. Call me as soon as

Total Jihad

you've got something."

Tarbitsky hung up the secure phone in his second floor office at the Israeli Embassy, off Van Ness Road above the University of the District of Columbia. The wall coverings around the windows, peeling in David Ivry's tour as ambassador and only patched, not replaced, now were undeniably shabby. He shrugged; decor was not a priority. Tarbitsky ordered a car to take him down Connecticut Avenue to the Old Executive Office Building. It was there, next door to the White House, that the N.S.C. staff worked, and where he expected to get details of the Arab proposal to the United States.

On the way he used his secure cell phone—at least it was supposed to be secure—to call Congressman Jonathan Marcus.

"Yonatan," Tarbitsky said. "They are getting ready to screw us again, maybe worse than before."

"I've heard rumors," Marcus replied.

"They're not rumors. Can you at least get the usual suspects to demand hearings. If we can't derail this thing, maybe we can dilute it."

"Certainly," Marcus replied. "It's about time this administration started playing to U.S. interests in your part of the world, not just Egyptian and Saudi Arabian. Maybe the day after tomorrow, as soon as the administration releases the details."

"Tomorrow morning. An emergency session." Tarbitsky was pleading.

"I'll try."

Jonathan Marcus was a veteran member of the House International Operations Committee's subcommittee on the Middle East. Before the 1993 Israeli-PLO Declaration of Principles, before the Rabin-Arafat handshake pulled the rug out from under Israel's best friends in Congress, the subcommittee had served as cockpit for legislative-executive branch battles over U.S. Middle East policy. Arms sales, peace initiatives, foreign aid packages, anti-terrorism campaigns—all were monitored, sometimes fought over, occasionally blocked and frequently modified in the subcommittee. But after 1993 the Israeli Embassy in Washington spent nearly as much time lobbying to prevent U.S. oversight of the PLO as it did working for its own interests. In that incongruous role, the embassy, AIPAG and pro-Israel congressmen helped sidetrack strict scrutiny of what even then-Israeli Chief of Staff Ehud Barak had warned were holes in the Swiss cheese of the Oslo Accords.

In the old days, any Jewish representative not on International Operations—then called Foreign Affairs—was suspect; any member, Jewish or not, who intended to raise serious money from the pro-Israel PAC's clambered for a seat on the Europe and Middle East subcommittee. Even now, it and a parallel panel of the Senate Foreign Relations Committee functioned as a sort of regulator on the State Department, a last bastion for Israel's friends in Washington.

"If Barry Johnston's going to sell out the Israelis, at least we'll make him do it in public," Marcus swore to himself.

Congressman Marcus slumped in the big black leather chair in his private office and stared out the window. From his suite in the ornate, early twentieth-century Cannon House Office Building, he looked across Independence Avenue to

the Capitol itself. He had won four elections before accumulating enough seniority to afford such a view. He used to find the vista—featuring the high, heavy but
graceful Capitol Rotunda, topped by the Goddess Liberty—inspiring. But lately he
had come to see it through a film of grime, and wondered why the windows were
not washed as often as they used to be.

Yet to walk into the granite and marble building every morning, to come
through the eight-foot tall heavy wooden door—his name etched in a polished
brass plate bolted to it—greet his staff and take his place at the desk of a U.S. representative still felt like the privilege and obligation it was. Sometimes, flanked by
the flags of the United States and of Virginia, his office walls covered with pictures
of himself and countless celebrities, astronauts, presidents, kings and dictators, he
shook his head. How the hell did I get here, he would wonder.

For the grandson of the penniless—and, truth be told, somewhat shiftless—
Anatoli Markevitch, for the son of Washington restauranteur Benny Marcus, the
name on the door and the seat with its Capitol view was an American allegory.
The stops along the way at Yale—where he had been surprised to find the school
motto in Hebrew—at the University of Virginia Law School, and as a senior congressional staffer appeared in retrospect both obligatory and preordained. A short
walk through the tunnel from Cannon to the House carried him to debates with
sharp, ambitious men and women from all over America, occasionally on matters
of importance. For that the endless round of banquets, fund-raisers, Rotary Club
speeches, interviews and visits to schools, shopping malls and old-age homes all
seemed worthwhile. And the deference—paid by staff, lobbyists, constituents and
even colleagues—was heady, addictive.

So what happened to the self-satisfied, periodically autocratic Congressman
Jonathan Marcus of earlier terms? Physically, he was much the same: solidly built,
a bit taller than average, thick hair combed back, no glasses on a face that looked
at least five years younger than it was. Some gray in the black hair, a few extra
pounds around the middle were the only outward concessions to advancing age.

But psychically, something gnawed at him. Had almost from the beginning.

In August, 1981, mid-way through his first term as chief of staff to then-Rep.
Millard Broyhill (D-Va.), the Senate approved the sale of $8.5 billion worth of
sophisticated armaments to Saudi Arabia, including five Airborne Warning and
Control Systems planes. The fifty-two to forty-eight vote came over the objections
not only of Israel but also of its many supporters on the Hill. Marcus himself had
helped work to defeat the proposal by a three-to-one margin in the House, but
Senate approval was enough to let the deal proceed.

After the vote in the upper chamber, a colleague of Broyhill's, Rep. Nick Joe
Hollings, a man of impeccable progressive credentials and one who often joined
him in rebutting the Israel-baiting of Representative Ignatius Kowlasky, met him
on the House floor. The other man grinned.

"Well, the Jewish lobby finally lost a big one," he gloated. "I was glad to see
it. You know Israel's going to get compensation… and in the meantime, maybe
the vote'll teach those people a little humility. 'Reagan or Begin' indeed!"

Broyhill looked surprised, but said nothing. Marcus, however, replied: "Israel will go broke financing that kind of arms race compensation." Hollings was still chortling when, after a pause, Marcus turned back on him. "Those people? We people have been force-fed humility and worse for two thousand years. We're finished with it!"

The smile vanished from the lawmaker's face. He challenged Marcus. "It's just like Zbigniew Brzenzski said—you American Jews better decide which country is yours!"

"Can you love your wife and your kids simultaneously? Well, I love the United States, and I love Israel," Marcus growled.

"That's enough," Broyhill said softly. His admonition when they were alone in the office was considerably firmer. Marcus dismissed the Hollings' episode at the time as isolated, unimportant. But similar occurrences in succeeding years he could not discount. They began to form a pattern: The reaction, especially in the Pentagon and State Department, to the Pollard spy case in 1985; the tolerance, even enthusiasm, among many blacks, for the Jew-baiting of racists like Louis Farrakhan; the phenomenon of the Skinhead gangs and Aryan Nation/Christian Identity killers; the popularity of the kaffiyeh—to Marcus a cloth swastika—on college campuses and city streets as a fashion statement. A statement which, under its multicultural camouflage, said "people who make news by killing Jews are fashionable" and the popularity of hate-filled sites on the Internet and short wave radio.

For Marcus personally there had been the especially disconcerting matter four years ago of Mohandas Gandhi Elementary School. He had attended the Arlington County School Board meeting personally to hear the proposal to rename Golda Meir Elementary in honor of the Indian independence leader. A local group calling itself Clergy and Laity Concerned quoted Gandhi's teachings on brotherhood and non-violence, and noted the demographic changes in the neighborhood, which had drawn many east Asians and left few Jews. When the congressman, who had not intended to speak, noted that Gandhi's non-violence was more applicable to fighting a flagging British imperialism than rising German Nazism—"He told the Jews of Europe to offer their necks to Hitler and sway him with pacifism"—he had been booed.

"We in the peace community are disappointed in you," one of the activists replied.

"And I'm appalled at you. You're not in any 'peace community,' you've just shanghied the words for a little psycho-drama."

The board approved the change. The local weekly upbraided Marcus for "stooping to petulance and pettiness." His staffers warned him that such "personal indulgence" could loose votes. "Screw 'em," he had replied. "Once in a while a man has to tell the truth, if only to remain a man."

"Please see to it that it's no more than once in a while, then," an aide replied. "To paraphrase T.S. Eliot, voters cannot bear too much truth."

Alongside hostility to Israel had grown an argumentativeness, a combativeness toward the more outspoken Jewish members of Congress. It was odd—there were twice as many Jews in the House and Senate now as when he'd first arrived, elected to fill the vacancy after Broyhill's unexpected death. Many of the Jewish members represented constituencies with few Jews. And so long as they kept a fairly low profile as Jews, and demonstrated unswerving loyalty to Democratic Party orthodoxy—nearly all of them were Democrats—they could succeed. But let them appear to stray, even a little, like Senator Joe Lieberman on affirmative action, morality and missile defense, and they would be rebuked by the party, by the professional voices of its all-important black constituency, by academia and the news media. Under Congress' club-like veneer, beneath its bogus collegiality, grew a callousness not so much toward individual Jews but certainly to Jewish concerns, to Jews as a group. And as the Jewish population itself aged, assimilated and shrank in numbers the comparatively few open antisemites grew bolder, and then more numerous. Hence passage of Kowalsky-introduced legislation to kill the tax exemption for United Jewish Appeal. Marcus could no longer deny his unease.

* * *

Alexandria, Virginia (August 2, 2007)–Madeline Marcus was fat. Again. She told herself so repeatedly, so it must be true. And when Madeline Marcus could not make her husband miserable she worked on herself.

How could any man love a fat, middle-aged woman; a fat, middle-aged woman with bad skin? She had found her silent litany both convincing and boring, so she resumed smoking, and resumed drinking.

Madeline Marcus, as Irit Gold a one-time runner up for Miss Israel–before her family emigrated to Virginia and her father became a senior U.S. government researcher–blamed her marital celibacy, her global unhappiness, on Felicia Sanchez, that Mexican whore her husband kept on his payroll. But it did not work, not for any length of time. Madeline Marcus was honest enough to know exactly what she was doing. But not motivated enough, or perhaps too afraid of change, to stop doing it.

Predictably, her skin erupted. Again. For at least three generations the women on her mother's side–Ashkenazi Jews all–were predisposed to a number of physical ailments, including diabetes, breast cancer and, worst of all as far as Madeline was concerned, acute psoriasis. This was exacerbated by nervousness and a familial inability to sweat properly. Instead of sweating, they tended to overheat and turn beet red. "So Israel was out of question, don't you see?" her mother used to tell total strangers.

Madeline suspected that the skin condition was related to the fertility problems. A woman on her mother's side who had regular periods and conceived without fertility drugs was an oddity. And not just in her family, she realized, but among her friends as well. God, the Ashkenazim in America must be as inbred as the Hatfields and McCoys, she thought.

Maybe that was why so many dermatologists and fertility specialists were Jews, she ruminated. Or Koreans; they must be the Jews of Asia. Whatever the reason, her skin had flared anew into angry splotches, red and scaly, from her hairline down along the jaw and onto her arms, thighs and breasts. Especially on her breasts.

A friend at the country club referred her to a new dermatologist. "Weird, but a wonder-worker," the woman had said. So Madeline Marcus now huddled unhappily and–to her mind–undignified in an examining gown which revealed more than it concealed but did so in a sickly, unerotic way, in a strange doctor's waiting room.

Staring at a new eruption under her big, heavy breasts, she wondered again, is man-woman attraction-revulsion the inescapable backdrop to everything? And why do men almost always have the advantage–except right after climax, when they are spent and weak but have gotten what they wanted anyway? Would a man, any man, sacrifice himself for me, right now? What would anyone pay me for on my own? I made a house for him, raised two children, and they all take it, or me, for granted, act like they think they could have done better without me. To hell with them all.

She was unconsciously scratching the blotches, had some raw and bleeding, when P. Sidney Nathanson, M.D., entered.

"Hello."

A tall, hard man who looked to be roughly her age, Nathanson had close-cropped white hair. Pale blue eyes peered out from behind thin lenses set in gold frames. He spoke tonelessly.

"So, Mrs. Rappaport sent you to see me," he said, trying to put her at ease. "That means I have at least one satisfied patient."

Madeline Marcus thought he sounded insincere, despite his little smile. Still, it was hard to evaluate a stranger, especially a man, when he was completely clothed and she was nearly naked, she decided.

"Now, what seems to be the problem?"

If you can't see it, Mrs. Marcus rejoined silently, nothing I tell you is going to help. Then she recounted once more the long history of her skin disorders, displayed the current eruptions, and told Nathanson of the string of dermatologists she had seen, never getting more than temporary relief.

"I'm afraid that some people, yourself included, have a familial weakness for psoriasis and related conditions. Stress, maybe diet, maybe climate–but especially stress–contribute. No doubt you've heard that before."

"Yes," Madeline said, almost hostile.

"And it was probably right," Nathanson continued, unperturbed. "But what you may not have heard is that there are new drugs that often can clear up cases like yours–or cause a marked improvement–and usually in a few days or a week at most."

She felt a surge of hope, the first optimism she had felt about anything in a long time. "Really? I had no idea "

"Of course," said the doctor matter-of-factly, "They can have side effects, especially if used in quantity for extended periods. In fact, there are indications that some can linger in the bloodstream, accumulate and cause brain damage; perhaps even strokes. But rarely. Very rarely."

Of course, thought Madeline Marcus. Isn't there always a trade-off?

"I'll try it," she heard herself say.

"You might be a candidate, but first, let me take a closer look at you," Nathanson said. As he peered at her rash, scraped some of the scales, felt her skin, he talked on. He commented on the Star of David she wore around her neck.

"Very nice. Looks like eighteen carat," he said.

"It is," she replied, making sure he understood that the six-pointed star, and she herself, were the real things.

"You know, we Jews have to be cautious, even here, especially now. It's better to wear that magen David under your clothes, rather than outside. We bring too many of our problems onto ourselves. That's what my wife says, and I believe her."

"I never thought much about it," Mrs. Marcus said, hoping he would change the subject.

"Have you ever wondered why there is so much hatred for the Jews, why there always has been, why it lurks just beneath the surface in otherwise pleasant people? I'm a physician, trained in science. I look at symptoms and search for causes. We can't pretend that with society it's any different. There is cause and effect. Antisemitism is the effect. The cause is we Jews ourselves. Of course the effect is disproportionate, but maybe we are too successful, superior—you know Jews have won more than twenty percent of all the Nobel Prizes awarded to Americans, yet we're barely two percent of the population? So we're resented. The same thing happened in Germany between World War I and World War II—the Jews, finally emancipated from the ghetto, seemed to be on the verge of dominating cultural and mercantile life. So they hated us—not because they 'knew' we were inferior but because they suspected we might be superior. As a physician, I consider it only natural. Don't you think so?"

"No, not really," Mrs. Marcus said, now alarmed at the way Nathanson rambled. She already suspected that he was not Jewish, that Nathanson was not his name and that maybe he wasn't even a doctor at all, but some dangerous fraud. And she was getting a little angry as well.

"My husband knows a lot more about this," she said, hoping to frighten Nathanson into dropping the subject by invoking a higher authority. "Maybe you've heard of him—Congressman Jonathan Marcus? I'm sure he'd like to talk to you sometime about this. He says that non-Jews use Jews for scapegoats no matter what we do: If the Jews are rich, we cheated them; if the Jews are poor, it means we're dirty and not fit to live among them. Either way, the result's the same, he says, because in the end the problem isn't really Jews but Judaism—it won't go away, meaning Christians and Muslims, who think their religions came to complete or supercede ours can't be sure they're right. So they don't like it, or us."

By now Nathanson had stopped examining her. He was consumed by the conversation he had begun. She sat on the table, uncovered from the waist up, inflamed blotches across her chest, and he talked on, oblivious.

"I'm not sure. You know Hitler's grandmother or something was Jewish. He changed his name from Shickelgruber. Sounds like shekel grubber, don't you think? And Marx, and Christ too. All Jews, all trouble-makers. That's what my wife says. That's why we have to be so careful."

"Pardon my asking," Madeline Marcus said, wanting to flee, or at least dress, yet now morbidly fascinated by this peculiarity in front of her, "but is your wife Jewish?"

"As Jewish as I am," Nathanson said. "Converted, of course, but went through the mikveh and everything. Let me tell you, she knows a lot more about Judaism than I do, that's for sure, the reasons for the holidays and all that."

Mercifully, the discussion and the visit came to an end. She had the prescription for a new cream filled, despite the potential side effects. She was supposed to apply the cream, Cosmenex, sparingly to the rash and scaly patches, then surround it with petroleum jelly so it would not damage normal skin. Madeline hated the feel of petroleum jelly, but used it at first. The ointment worked wonders on her psoriasis; the scales rapidly shrank, the rash retreated and paled. But where the balm touched unprotected, unaffected skin when Madeline forgot the Vaseline barrier, it left a lingering rust-like stain.

*   *   *

Washington, D.C. (August 5, 2007)–The revised final status agreements were supposed to end the 125 Years' War between Arab and Jew over the Promised Land; they were overtaken by the Green March Riots. The riots became the pretext for the Thirty-Six Hour War. Now fears of Israeli nuclear retaliation overtook the war itself and the hearings Marcus had instigated. Instead of focusing on a new armistice between Israel and Syria and the Israelis and Palestinians in particular and between what was left of the Jewish state and the Arab world in general, the hearings concentrated on how to restrain the Jews and clamp a lid on the post-war turmoil coursing throughout the Jewish, Palestinian and Jordanian segments of what many hoped would be Confederated Palestine.

Barton Goldberg, the venerable chairman of the House International Operations Committee, did not look too bad for a man lying in a hospital bed, the plastic tubes of a respirator pinching his nose. A certain tightness along his neck and jaw, a hint of hollows under the eyes were the only visible signs of what the doctors termed a "mild heart attack."

"I'm okay, Jonathan" Goldberg said. "Really, I am. They told me I'll be out in a few days. Just too much stress, the war and everything. Hell, I had worse pains when Rabin shook hands with Arafat." He managed a weak laugh.

"Lots of us did," Marcus said, trying to joke. "We just denied it. Anyway, don't worry. We'll take care of the committee until you get back."

It's the law of discontinuous change, Marcus ruminated as he drove east on Pennsylvania Avenue from George Washington University Hospital toward the Hill. You extrapolate from the present for years, expecting tomorrow to be like today, until one day the unseen stresses, the accumulated marginal changes and suppressed minor problems coalesce along old fault lines into a new reality. Then, BOOM!–without warning only to those living normally, the ground shakes. And as one nears the moment of crisis between old and new, history accelerates, leaving yesterday's wisdom and yesterday's leaders behind–although often dangerously still in office. It happened to the Soviet Union and Yugoslavia in the 1980s, to Israel and Indonesia in the '90s and, Marcus feared, it was happening to America now.

"It is clear, is it not, that Jewish police and para-military units—no matter how well-intentioned—no longer can keep order among the Palestinians of Israel. I mean, the Arabs of Israel?" asked Representative Ignatius Kowalsky, presiding in Goldberg's absence.

"It is, Mr. Chairman," said Assistant Secretary of State for Near East and South Asian Affairs, M. Grace Pittson. As an afterthought, she added, "Unfortunately."

"How serious is the ripple effect in Arab Palestine and Jordan?" the chairman asked, giving the secretary her next cue.

"Very serious," the diplomat replied. "Our best information are that Jordan and Arab Palestine—which as you know have been discussing a merger, although the kingdom seems reluctant—and Israel itself are all being destabilized by the continuing turmoil. We are, this morning, issuing an advisory against travel by American nationals to any of the three countries, extending our embargo on weapons shipments to the area, and consulting with other members of the Perm Five in New York."

Marcus found the choreographed charade nauseating. No doubt staffers for the chairman and assistant secretary had outlined if not specifically rehearsed this ersatz testimony. And the assistant secretary's chronic Britishisms—"our best information are" and her diplo-jargon "Perm Five" for the five permanent members of the United Nations Security Council—galled the congressman. Worse, the entire exchange was an artifice to conceal what was really going on at the top of the Johnston administration, consideration of yet one more partition of eretz Yisrael.

When his turn came, Marcus struggled to cut through the cant:

"Is the administration really considering a new U.N. Mandate for Palestine?" he asked, the question based on a tip from Tarbitsky.

Pittson looked flustered, but only for a moment. Blandly, professionally, she answered, "No, not exactly..."

"Then what, exactly?" Marcus demanded.

"Well, we are only in the early stages of consultation with our friends and allies in New York about a U.S. protectorate for Israel proper."

"And what do the Israelis think of this?" Marcus asked.

The assistant secretary paused again for a moment while one of her aides, a senior State Department lawyer, whispered into her ear. "We have not discussed it with them yet. Nor, to be fair, with the Palestinians or Jordanians. That would be premature, since the details have not been agreed to at the U.N. And, of course, we're still waiting for them to officially rescind their nuclear ultimatum. After that," she said, attempting to make unctuousness pass as reasonableness, "of course, we would have to come to Congress, if a commitment is to be made to keep certain American forces, under U.N. authority, in the Jewish autonomous region, in Israel, to safeguard it from attack, protect the Palestinian Arabs who live there, and control the Jewish zealots."

"Then the Israelis themselves, since you haven't spoken to them yet, are not in the category of 'friends and allies'?" Marcus wanted to know.

"Our special relationship with Israel continues unchanged, unshakeable," the assistant secretary replied. Marcus imagined he saw the tiniest smirk at the corner of her perfectly composed lips.

"Not to mention invisible," the congressman inserted, mostly for the record.

"If it was premature to inform Israel about the discussions at the U.N.," he went on, "considering Israel's fate remains at stake—why was it not premature to slap an embargo on arms shipments to the Israelis after the war with Syria since, after all, Israel's fate remains at stake?"

"You seem to be overlooking the destabilizing effect of the Israeli nuclear threat," Pittson almost snapped, then added more evenly that "we embargoed arms to Arab Palestine and to Jordan as well, congressman, as you know."

"We weren't supplying Arab Palestine with any major weapons and Jordan gets little, whereas the United States has been virtually Israel's sole source of important weapons systems—other than its own domestic arms industry—for decades, Madame Secretary, as you well know. And the fighting was not between Israel and Jordan or Palestine, but between Israel and Syria. Syria gets its guns from Russia, China, Iran, France, Brazil, Germany and us—to compare apples to apples. Of course, that's something this administration's never been too good at."

Marcus' allies on the panel, particularly Representatives Lany Levinson from Florida and Mel Bernstein from California also tried to pin down the administration witnesses. But with Kowalsky in the chair, the administration's supporters on the committee combined with pro-Arab, anti-Israel members to shield the assistant secretary and her counterpart from Defense, to conduct them back to calmer waters whenever the Jews and their friends made things too choppy. After nearly three hours, the hearing ended inconclusively.

As it did, Marcus' cell phone sounded. He snapped it open, said "Marcus here," and listened. "Damn! Are you sure?"

"I'm sure," came the voice of his foreign policy staffer.

Marcus snapped the phone closed. "Gentlemen," he said to Levinson and Bernstein, "we already may be too late. The King of Jordan's been assassinated. And not only the king, but apparently the crown prince and most of the government."

*　*　*

Amman (August 5, 2007)–Much of Al-Nadwa Palace, on the crown of a dun-colored low hill at the outskirts of Amman, lay in rubble. Huge chunks of masonry and steel beams mingled with bits of precious metal decoration and splinters of mahogany paneling. Silvered shards of mural-like mirrors and pieces of crystal chandeliers sparkled amidst the debris. Buried beneath were the remains of the American educated King of Jordan, his Palestinian queen, his uncle the crown prince and much of the rest of the governmental and military leadership of what had been, until moments before, the Hashemite Kingdom of Jordan. Somewhere too, in what had been the kitchen, lay the earthly remains of Sami Shakurti. He had done his work perfectly, even if he had not known exactly what that work had been.

Shakurti was one of the first recruits to al-Masri's Palestine Islamic Army twenty-plus years before. The Palestine Islamic Army began in the early 1980s with less than a dozen teenaged nationalists. They found the local Fatah cell of Yasser Arafat's Palestine Liberation Organization insufficiently devout, even though Arafat–like the Islamic Resistance Movement, better known as Hamas–like al-Masri himself, had roots in local offshoots of the old Muslim Brotherhood of Egypt. Shakurti had aided al-Masri in the elimination of the army's first traitor, Ali Haikmat, and the execution of their first Zionist war criminal, a hitch-hiking soldier. He had fled with al-Masri to the caves of Tubas, and eventually escaped into Jordan with him.

Others had ridiculed Shakurti for his stammer and his congenitally twisted spine. Some did even worse; they ignored him. But al-Masri had accepted Shakurti as he was. The simple act won him Shakurti's unquestioning loyalty.

Al-Masri invoked that blind allegiance when he sent Sami to the Jordanian capital a year ago with instructions on gaining employment at the palace. Shakurti, in his childlike excitement, imagined he was meant to be a spy. Al-Masri did, in fact, find much of use in Shakurti's reports from the royal household.

For example, the King–black belt in judo, airplane pilot, Harley-Davidson motorcycle enthusiast like his father–was a nutritionalist. An early intestinal problem converted him to a fresh fruit and vegetable fanatic. And as he grew into the arduous task of ruling a tense, fragile kingdom at the head of a minority dynasty, pressured on all sides by more powerful, self-interested neighbors including Iraq, Saudi Arabia, Syria, the Palestinians and Israel, he became obsessed with how long he slept, how much he exercised, precisely what he ate. He demanded quantities of steamed fresh vegetables, and chopped–sometimes pureed–fresh fruit at every meal.

Al-Masri's people arranged for Sami to carry into the palace kitchen each day cartons brimming with produce. And one day, concealed beneath the oranges and grapes, bananas and avocadoes, carrots and beans, tomatoes and cucumbers, he carried in enough Cold War surplus Czech-made, Libyan-supplied Semtex plastic explosive to level the entire kitchen and dining wing of the palace. But all Sami Shakurti knew–and had reported–was that night a banquet was to be held, a banquet at which not only the king and crown prince, but also the prime minister and military chief of staff were to attend, with their aides and their wives.

Also that night, a mere seventy miles away, al-Masri was to address a rally in his native Nablus.

Before speaking he had prowled his spacious, sparsely furnished hillside home. He looked out across the narrow valley which squeezed Nablus into a dense, monochromatic concentration of stone and masonry. The al-Masri clan (the name literally meant the Egyptians, denoting family history), venerable and influential in the West Bank's largest city, occupied several large, neighboring houses clinging to the slopes. An uncle, a Palestinian nationalist, had been mayor under the Israelis, and assassinated by Abu Nidal. Whether on contract for Arafat, or against his wishes but at the behest of the Popular Front for the Liberation of

Palestine-General Command, a Syrian proxy, was never quite clear. A cousin had been Jordanian Foreign Minister and later a member of parliament before being forced out by Islamic militants. Yacoub al-Masri had studied his prominent relatives and determined to capitalize on their advantages while avoiding their vulnerabilities.

Nablus, two dozen miles north of Ramallah (where the prophet Samuel had sat in judgment of the Israelites), was an eastern Naples, Roman successor to biblical Shechem. In Shechem, Abraham made his first home in Canaan. In Shechem, his grandson Jacob dug a well, a well from which water still trickled nearly four thousand years later.

Yacoub al-Masri was certain of his lineage as a descendant not of Abraham but of Ibrahim. Descended not from Isaac but Ishamel, not as a Hebrew but as a son of the great Arab nation. Ishmael, not Isaac, was the son Ibrahim bound for a sacrifice at the behest of Allah. The nation descended from Ishmael—the Arabs, not the Jews—was destined to rule. Mohammed himself had proved that. Yacoub al-Masri would merely reassert it.

The world of Islam once stretched united from the Atlantic Ocean to the Indus River, from southern Europe to central Africa, and leapt all the way to Indonesia. One thing, one powerful dream, one unrelieved compulsion, drove Yacoub al-Masri: to lead the Palestinian Arabs in reuniting that world. Israel, like Carthage of old, must be destroyed before his new Rome could reestablish its empire. So he had struggled for more than twenty years, first to whittle away support for the Jewish state, then to whittle away the Jewish state itself.

"Not much longer," he said, staring at a radar installation sweeping the skies from its perch atop Mount Ebal, at an early warning station belonging to the Israelis. Up there, after the Six-Day War, Israeli archeologist Adam Zertal had uncovered an altar dating to the time of Joshua, an altar built without mortar—like the one Moses, on God's instructions, had enjoined Joshua to build as recounted in Exodus. Al-Masri knew the story; Mousa had told his lieutenant to build the altar to Allah to help pave the way for Islam. And the Jews—like Esau trading his birthright for Yacoub's stew—had given the shrine, and others like it, to the Arabs in the "final settlement."

"Not much longer!"

So intent was Yacoub al-Masri that he did not notice as his wife, Fatima Tlass al-Masri, entered the room and moved to his side.

"But be careful," she said, putting her hand on his arm. Surprised, al-Masri jerked back, as if from attack. Seeing her, his apocalyptic mood broken, he smiled and kissed his wife's forehead.

"Umm Jihad," he said, lovingly pronouncing her "mother of struggle," "I will take care, but I will not hesitate. Like your romantic hero, Napoleon, I will analyze coldly and act passionately." They embraced, and she kissed him full on the lips. Later, as he held her head in his lap, stroking her long black hair, he said, "What can you tell me of your travels? I already know that Jordan is ripe. And Saudi Arabia?"

"As soon as the king in Amman falls, the king in Riyadh will find himself 'protected' by his brother, the defense minister, who is with us. And if the defense minister, a pompous fool as the Americans have learned to their dismay, gets cold feet, the chief of staff, his cousin, will seize control. You know the chief of staff is both Palestinian by marriage and a member of the Brothers. In Syria, Abu Bakr already is snorting, pawing the earth, ready to finish the Jews. Unlike his predecessors, he has rallied the Brothers to his side rather than tried to obliterate them. So the Syrians will be more unified than they have in years. The Iraqis won't be able to restrain themselves. That means that when we move, the shaky regime in Egypt must either join us or fall."

"Many criticized me then, but not so many now. They see I did well to make you my chief," al-Masri replied.

"I know," Fatima said lightly.

"Take nothing for granted!" he exploded.

"Yacoub, Yacoub, you must relax. Control yourself and all else will go well."

He sighed. "I'm sorry. You know how I feel. But the stakes are so high."

That evening, at the rally, he spoke like one in ecstatic fervor:

"My brothers, the moment approaches! Soon we will redeem ourselves and our stolen land. No foreign doctrines, whether of the West or East, will corrupt the purity of our action. We obey only Allah, trust only the Koran.

"The arrogant Jew, as it is written, we will kill him wherever he hides. We will slay him with our rifles, and if not with our rifles, then with our knives. If not with knives, then with our hands. And if not by our hands, then with our teeth! And the corrupt among us, those not pure in Islam—they shall be overturned!"

The roar of the crowd, tens of thousands of aroused voices, drowned all else. Al-Masri smiled tightly, and waited for quiet. When it came, he shouted, "By belief, action, strength, martyrdom, we will regain our usurped rights, our manhood, our Arab leadership. The stain of al-Nakba, the disaster of 1948, the humiliations of 1967 and 1982 will be removed with the new istisal, the elimination! Allah truly smiles on us, that we live in such a time. Be ready!"

Again the tribal thunder of the crowd rolled over his last syllables. He did not mind the interruption. The emotional pitch of the masses energized him. He knew they would follow him to glory. Even the knowledge that among the churning sea of bodies moved the spies and informers of Israel, of Mahmoud Terzi's corrupt Palestinian regime, of Jordan, Syria, and, no doubt, Russia and the United States did not trouble him.

He glanced at Fawzi Khadoumi, his chief bodyguard, standing near the edge of the platform. Khadoumi, one hand over an earpiece, looked at his wristwatch. His tall, strong body stiffened, then his sharp, scarred face opened into a frightful grin. Catching al-Masri's eye, he nodded vigorously, pointing to the earpiece.

"Arabs, listen!" al-Masri shouted into the microphones. "I have word. Our time has come! The corrupt king, he who has walked the streets of Tel Aviv, who drank tea with the murderer Sharon at the Black House of shame in Washington, he who did the bidding of the British and American infidels, this outsider is dead. Jordan is ours; the East Bank and the West Bank are united!"

A deafening roar of approval split the black Samarian sky. It echoed the explosion that had shattered the night in Amman and it foreshadowed explosions to come.

In his palatial office in eastern Jerusalem, Ra'is Mahmoud Terzi, president of the Arab Republic of Palestine, listening to the speech over an amplified cell phone, wondered how that damned al-Masri invariably knew what was happening before he did. Nevertheless, the ra'is prepared his armed motorcade for the one-hour drive to Amman. There he would formally declare the merger of Jordan and Palestine into the United Arab Republic of Palestine.

And the Israelis—and Americans—be damned, he smiled to himself. I don't care what the treaties say. This land is all part of the Arab nation, the Arab nation of Palestine. If they don't like it, they can go drink the sea at Gaza!

In Riyadh, the diabetic king granted full operational power to the minister of defense, who immediately closed the borders to civilian traffic, and cut official communications with the outside.

In Damascus, President Abu Bakr ordered his commander to prepare to attack—the Palestinians if they would not heed him, the Israelis if Arab unity prevailed.

In Baghdad, the order went out to the Iraqi Army in Jordan to help the Palestinians gain control of the late king's military if necessary, and prepare to strike west with alacrity.

In Cairo, the embattled government watched the huge pro-Palestinian, anti-Israeli street demonstrations, heard the rumblings from sympathetic army officers, and wavered.

In western Jerusalem, Prime Minister Meir Sarid, whose country had remained on full alert after the Thirty-Six Hour War, called the White House to demand an immediate end to the arms embargo and the commencement of resupply to his depleted forces.

And in Washington, President Johnston reluctantly cut short his late afternoon swim. He climbed out of the White House pool, toweled off his naked body, toweled off his second wife's second breasts—surgically augmented, like his own neck and chin not long before the last campaign—and said, "Resupply, my ass! God, what the hell's wrong with those Jews? We've given 'em what, $90 billion, $100 billion in loans and grants— mostly grants—the past fifty years, and now they want more? They're going to scare those Arabs into another war if we don't stop them."

The First Lady, a former television weather forecaster and staffer for Johnston when he was a senator from Missouri, squeezed the president. "To hell with the Middle East. It's going there anyway. Let's take a long weekend at Camp David—without the kids. That way, whatever goes wrong, we can blame on the secretary of state." She let him go, slowly, dragging her nails lightly across the presidential scrotum.

"War is hell," the chief executive panted.

*　　*　　*

Kibbutz Nof Benjamin (August 6, 2007)—"Jerusalem is impossible now."

"Because of the Sicarii?" Jeremy Marcus asked.

"No," said Aharon Tabor. "They've been isolated pretty much in Mea

Shearim and a few other ultra-Orthodox neighborhoods. Because of the terrorists infiltrating from east Jerusalem."

"Terrorists?" the boy questioned. "What about the Palestinian policemen?"

"The terrorists are the Palestinian policemen, and women. One of the loopholes of the 'final settlement'," Tabor explained.

"And it's the reverse in Tel Aviv," he continued. "Left-wing extremists–Jewish radicals–intimidate and, on occasion, murder, those they suspect of being sympathetic to or involved with the religious nationalists."

Jeremy Marcus had remained in Israel when, as the ceasefire in the Thirty-Six Hour War took hold, the rest of his high school tour group fled back to the United States. He listened intently to the conversation in the Tabor family quarters at Kibbutz Nof Benjamin. Aharon–son of Ambassador Yehdua Tarbitsky, one of the kibbutz's founders a half century earlier–his friend Ehud Kenaan, their wives and children filled the apartment.

Nof Benjamin, like most remaining kibbutzim, had been determinedly areligious. But in recent years members had recognized that in times of plenty, times of ostensible peace, let alone in days of constraint and trouble, the kibbutz experience alone was not enough. It no longer sufficed to keep its children from emigrating, from marrying non-Jewish Europeans who came to the collective farm as volunteers, or from adopting at least the outward elements of Palestinian pop culture. Not without strong attachments to Jewish tradition as counterbalance. So changes had been made. For example, on Fridays, after the biggest meal of the week in the communal dining hall and the only one featuring table cloths, wine and challah, many families returned to their rooms for oneg shabbat. Wives said the old blessings over the candles, husbands blessed the wine and the children. Then coffee, tea, and an abundance of the inevitable cakes and cookies were served. The name of God, the Jewish God, was again invoked, after a lapse of half a century, in the ancient formulas.

Now, while the younger children played on the small patio off the living room and the wives interjected their opinions as they straightened up the kitchen, the men and older children–some home on weekend leave from the army–talked about what everyone called ha matzav, the situation.

"Headquarters believes the international observers are looking the other way as arms and men infiltrate across the Jordan into Judea and Samaria–excuse me, into Arab Palestine–and Jerusalem itself," Tabor said.

"Surprised? That's what international observers always do," Kenaan said evenly. "UNIFIL did it when the PLO, and later the Hezbollah, brought contraband into south Lebanon. And, to tell the truth, they did it when we armed the South Lebanese Army."

"The point is," Tabor said, "that we don't have a handle on what's happening in eastern Jerusalem, let alone the rest of the territories. The spy satellite is not working–someone knocked it out, we're not sure who–and the Americans still won't give us real-time intelligence on what's going on in Syria, Jordan, Iraq or Saudi Arabia."

"Just like 1973 and 1991," Kenaan observed. "But didn't we leave a lot of surveillance gear, and some agents, in the West Bank and Gaza when we pulled out?"

"Yes," Tabor replied. "But don't speak to me about 'the West Bank.' That was a Jordanian coinage, like 'Palestine' was a Roman forgery, a Latin corruption of Philistine–non-Arabs finished off by the Babylonians six centuries before Christ, a name revived by Rome to blot out the real name. It's Yehuda, damn it–the land of the Jews, and Shomron, another name for Israel. If the British could use those names during the Mandate, then Jews ought to have been able to use them since."

"Alright, alright," Kenaan interjected, perturbed. "What about the agents?"

"Well," said Tabor, a reserve Army major, "a few of the Arabs work for us. Not nearly as many as before we started negotiating with Arafat and he started murdering 'collaborators', or before Barak so cleverly abandoned the South Lebanese Army. Talk about hanging your friends out to dry! But there are still some, settling intra-Arab scores, or because they're afraid of Palestinian thuggery–like all those Arab east Jerusalemites a few years ago who, when given the choice of Palestinian or Israeli citizenship, would have taken Israeli, if we and the Americans had let them–or because they're mercenaries. If Jewish criminals could sell stolen guns and stolen cars to Arab terrorists, then Arabs of the territories could work for us. And," he said, referring to Israelis originally from Arab lands, "there are still a few Sephardim with the looks and the language to pass unremarked on the other side of the green line."

"What do they tell us?" Kenaan's curiosity, like that of most sabras, was palpable.

"That scores, hundreds of Arabs–mostly men of military age–arrive each day, and don't leave at night. And this has been going on for a month. We know construction has been booming in what they call Arab Palestine ever since we evacuated, with new settlements–airbrushed 'refugee' camps, really–everywhere for the Palestinians flocking back under their so-called right-of-return. Money from Saudi Arabia, Kuwait, the United Arab Emirates, Japan, Libya, it doesn't matter, it just pours in. Even so, construction alone can't account for the numbers of men flooding across the river."

A television news bulletin interrupted their conversation. It reported an explosion at Al-Nadwa Palace. It also told of three major terrorist attacks within Israel at approximately the same time. In each case men in vans, apparently bullet-proof, pulled up to crowded public places–a movie theater in Haifa (a city which, because of its mixed Arab-Jewish population in pre-state Israel, never enforced shabbat blue laws as severely as the rest of the country), a late-closing restaurant in Tel Aviv, and a Jerusalem synagogue–flung open the back doors, fired rocket-propelled grenades, and sped away. Altogether, more than one hundred Jews were dead, close to three hundred injured.

Immediately after that, the announcer began reading an alert message:

"Attention all reservists. Attention all regular army troops on leave. This is tzav shmoneh. Repeat: this is tzav shomneh. Emergency mobilization. Return to your units now. All reservists, all regular army soldiers on leave–return to your units now.

"Special orders: Mistral, deploy to point Aleph. Mistral, deploy to point Aleph. Spilling Wrath, consolidate point Bet. Spilling Wrath, consolidate point Bet. Vengeful Redeemer, secure sector Gimel. Vengeful Redeemer, secure sector

Gimel. Infinite Justice, take sector Heh. Infinite Justice."

"What...?" Jeremy Marcus started to ask. Even as he rose to his feet, he watched Tabor bolt across to a bedroom. There, the door still open, Tabor flung off his white shabbat shirt and kicked away blue jeans, pulled on camouflage fatigues, strapped a holstered 9-mm. automatic pistol around his waist and hoisted a bulging duffel bag over one shoulder.

"Come with me," Kenaan said to Jeremy. "I'll drop you at the kibbutz switchboard. You can get a special line—no doubt our little national circuits are overloaded right now—and call your father, tell him what's happening, have him tell you everything he knows, then come to the parking lot next to the dining hall in five minutes to report to us. Concentrate when you listen to him."

"The shit's hit the fan, right?"

"There are not enough fans for what's happening now. And don't say shit. You're home now. Say chara, with a barely hard 'ch'. It's Arabic, but we stole it from them because..." Kenaan smiled.

"Because they don't know shit!" Tabor shouted, finishing an old gibe and, having already kissed his wife and children, burst out the front door.

Part II

> *"They have healed also the hurt of My people lightly,*
> *Saying: 'Peace, peace' when there is no peace."*
> –Jeremiah, 6:14.

Mediterranean Sea, near Cyprus (August 7, 2007)–As commander of the U.S. Sixth Fleet in the Mediterranean Sea, Admiral Chester Wingate Fogerty followed not only satellite coverage of the bombing of Al-Nadwa Palace on Cable News Network and the British Broadcasting Corporation, but he also scrutinized the cable traffic and other secure communications now flooding into his flagship, the nuclear-powered aircraft carrier U.S.S. John F. Kennedy. As a born-again Christian, he also kept his Bible ready for background analysis. Deep background. Jeremiah had warned shortly before the fall of the First Temple of Solomon to the Babylonians under Nebuchadnezzar in 586 B.C.E. that Jewish leaders who followed the conventional wisdom of their day and put their faith in help from a foreign power–in that case the "weak reed" of Egypt–would be proven false. Unfortunately, all the people would suffer for it. And now, only a few years after Israel's then-prime minister, Ariel Sharon, had admonished the United States not to sacrifice Israel's struggle against Palestinian terrorism to its own Arab-Islamic coalition against bin Laden's terrorism, Fogerty wondered. Would Washington impose a Munich-like settlement on Israel, as Sharon had feared? Would America prove to be a weak reed?

He knew President Johnston–a man who pretended to believe that all disputes were the results of misunderstanding, that there was no conflict that could not be resolved through meditation. Such a man believed, or said he did, that the worst peace was better than the best war, that reconciliation mattered more than justice. To such a man there ultimately was nothing worth fighting over, at least nothing that he would admit to in public. One did not wish to appeared rigid, after all, or judgmental of other people, other cultures. Especially not to focus groups of suburban women voters. So he talked endlessly of conflict resolution and never, God forbid, of victory.

Yes, Johnston would sell the Israelis out–hell, had been selling them out from the start. Well, Admiral Chester Fogerty thought to himself, there might be a little something I can do about that, the good Lord willing.

Having watched the progressive dismantling of Israel from the 1993 Oslo Accords to the "final status settlement" a little more than a decade later, and the concomitant intensification and melding of Islamic fundamentalism and Arab nationalism, he had anticipated this day. Nevertheless, he still was not ready, not emotionally. He felt that the explosion in Amman would precipitate a personal time of testing. It would be worse than those he experienced as a new ensign in Vietnam thirty-five years ago, or as a commander in the Persian Gulf War. It would be like the year after his son died, hit by a drunken driver, the year before "Win" Fogerty found Jesus. It would try his soul.

So Fogerty stood on the bridge, gazing into darkness rent by brilliant orange flashes from the exhausts of the old F-14 Tomcats, the F-18 Hornets, the new F-22's he wasn't, according to NATO qualms, supposed to have. As his interceptors and bombers were launched screaming from the deck to fly their expanded patrols, he smelled the heady mixture of salt sea air and aviation fuel. He remembered the warning of Isaiah, that prophet of peace and justice, echoed by both Jeremiah and Ezekiel, voices of retribution and redemption: "They heal the wounds of the sons and daughters of Israel lightly, crying 'peace, peace' when there is no peace."

They had foreseen wars; he smelled one coming. As another Jew, the apostate Lev Bronstein—known to the world as Leon Trotsky—once observed: "You may not be interested in war, but war is interested in you." Trotsky, father of the Red Army, murdered in Mexican exile by Stalin, and whose grandson ended up living on a religious kibbutz in Israel.

Fogerty contacted fleet headquarters again, asking for updated orders. There were none. Repeatedly he pressed his superiors, repeatedly he volunteered his own suggestions. Their replies were slow, evasive. HQ hinted that Fogerty's concern, his persistence, were annoying, perhaps eccentric. Angered, Fogerty was not surprised.

He remembered his first visit to Haifa years earlier. After finishing an official inspection of the port and Israeli naval base, the admiral accompanied Captain Simcha Horowitz on a tour of the city. He especially wanted to see Elijah's Cave on Mount Carmel, which overlooked the harbor. A tourist trap, of course, but Win Fogerty, pausing to meditate, tried to put himself in mind of the man—pursued by the corrupt Jewish establishment of his day, defiant of his enemies and righteous before his often unappreciative people—who once found refuge there.

The two officers and their aides strolled through the then still respectable Hadar business district part-way up the mountain, watching the early evening shoppers crowding the streets. Later, on the crest of the Carmel ridge, they stopped for drinks and the ubiquitous sweet cakes at the Little Haifa Cafe. Virtually invisible in the shadow of the twin spires of Panorama Towers, a modern high-rise defiling the Carmel, the cafe occupied an old two-story building at the end of HaSavyonim Street. Partially covered by thick green hibiscus vines with their vivid purple trumpet-like blossoms, the building marked the northern end of Carmel Center, charming intersection of small shops and sidewalk cafes that served the fashionable residential neighborhood astride the main spur of the range.

HaSavyonim Street itself ended on a bluff more than three hundred feet above the bay. The sidewalk, supported by concrete columns, arced out into a little observation platform.

"See those lights in the middle distance?" Horowitz asked.

"Yes," replied Fogerty, "and I think these old aviator's eyes can make out another cluster twinkling faintly beyond them."

"Good for you. Of course, we're lucky it's clear tonight. The first lights are those of Akko, about ten miles across the bay to the north. Beyond them another six miles or so are the lights of Nahariya, a resort town. And, about four or five miles north of Nahariya—somewhere in that blackness—is Rosh Hanikra and the Lebanese border. We could hail a taxi and be at the gates of hell in half an hour."

Fogerty had known the claustrophobic nature of Arab-Israeli geography before; now he understood it. But the northern border that night might just as well have been a world away. The city of Haifa, its high- and mid-rise apartment blocks, banks, shops, synagogues, mosques, churches and single family villas, clinging to the slope of Carmel and graced by the gardens and gold dome of the Baha'i Temple, spread out and glistened before him. Beyond was the great curving bay itself.

"Looks a little like San Francisco, doesn't it?" Horowitz said, gesturing at the city below.

Remembering his shore duty there years before, Fogerty nodded. "Like a little, civil San Francisco."

At the cafe, after conversations about ships and men, training and the special problems of patrolling the vital, crowded and potentially vulnerable coast, Horowitz began discussing ha matzav, "the situation." "I'm a fairly observant Jew," he said. "Not Orthodox by local standards—some American Orthodox don't qualify, and our local holy men keep moving the goal back—but I take my religion more seriously than many. Not just the rituals, but the meaning. And every year, in the cycle of Torah readings, I come back to two stories.

"The first is from Exodus. As Moses and the Israelites escape from Egypt and head for the Promised Land, they encounter the tribe of Amalek. The Amalekites say, 'Let us fall upon them and slay them all.'

"In rabbinic tradition—of which we possess a suffocating surplus—this story is taken as symbolic, showing that anti-Israeli passion is ancient and unreasoning. The Amalekites could just as easily have said, 'Let us stop them and levy tribute,' or even, "Let us kill the men, keep the women for ourselves, and sell the children as slaves.' But no: 'Let us kill them all.'

"The sages said that in every generation the Jews will have to face a new Amalek, Fortunately, so the story goes, the Israelites won their first battle for survival. But the lesson was plain: we will have enemies not because of what we do but because of who we are, the people of the Book.

"The other story is a prophesy from Isaiah, which promises that when the nation of Israel is found righteous, when it has redeemed itself and is reestablished on its own soil, then will every man be able to sit in peace in the shade of his fig tree, enjoying the fruits of his vineyard. 'And none shall make him afraid.'

"I believe in both stories, as metaphor and promise. Our 'state of siege,' as you mentioned, while unique, does not necessarily seem unnatural. I, and my people, are suspended between Amalek and the vineyard, between destruction and redemption. I suppose your Pilgrims felt much the same way about their 'new Jerusalem' in Massachusetts Bay Colony."

"No question about that," Fogerty replied, lifting his glass of Yarden white, an excellent wine from the lost vineyards and winery of the Golan Heights. "The question arises concerning what their successors in Massachusetts and the rest of the country think about such things, if they think about them at all. Most Americans now use the phrase 'God-given' to connote gifts, not rewards."

From second in command on a patrol boat in the last brown water units of South Vietnam, to the bridge of his own destroyer playing cat-and-mouse with Soviet submarines in the early '80s, to a deputy commander's role in the Gulf War, Chester Wingate Fogerty had been a good sailor. But he had done nothing to commend his memory to future seamen, to future generations of freedom-loving Americans, to believing Christians. And, the Lord willing, he meant to be remembered.

The Russian presence in the Mediterranean had shriveled after the fall of the Soviet Union. But the size and capability of Arab navies escalated. American vessels frequently encountered ships from Syria and Libya, from Egypt and Algeria. No aircraft carriers or heavy cruisers, but plenty of European and U.S.-built destroyers, missile boats, submarines and even landing craft on maneuvers. Darting among them were the technologically advanced missiles ships and fast patrol boats of the Israeli Navy. And, no doubt, somewhere close to the coasts of major Arab countries were Israel's three Dolphin submarines, German-built diesels carrying advanced cruise missiles. What the cruise missiles carried was classified, extremely so.

Fogerty retained his regard for the Israelis, despite their current debilities. This stemmed only partly from his religious convictions. Part of it was sheer professional respect. What their little fleet accomplished in both 1967 and 1973 wrote the book on modern small ship coastal defense and blockade. Their advancements in electronic navigation and weaponry, including remotely piloted surveillance vehicles–sophisticated drones–ship-to-ship missiles and anti-missile systems adapted by the United States largely at his insistence, leapfrogged some aspects of America's own military technology. And repaid their cost many times over, first in the Persian Gulf, later in Afghanistan. And he valued Israel's lesser-known support of U.S. forces in moments of crisis. In 1978 and again in 1987 when U.S. Mediterranean strength was drawn down to permit assembly of a second Indian Ocean-Persian Gulf battle group, the Israelis tacitly expanded their own patrols. When Qaddafi challenged the Sixth Fleet with his "line of death" in the Gulf of Sidra in 1981 and again in 1986, the Israeli Navy extended its operation north and west to help cover for American ships concentrated off Tripoli.

Fogerty also remembered with pleasure days when Haifa had been a regular port of call, the days before President Johnston and Secretary of Defense Obey. The days before the restrictions of the agreements creating the Arab Republic of Palestine. In the old days, the facilities of Haifa port were excellent, and the local population–unlike that in many NATO ports–was hospitable. Captain Horowitz, always a gracious host, became a friend.

Fogerty continued to exchange an occasional letter with the Israeli after the treaties with the Palestinian Arabs and the Syrians. He took care to make them personal and non-controversial as befit private communications from the Sixth Fleet Commander to an officer of a friendly but non-allied country. He put his messages between the lines, sometimes using Biblical allusions. The Israeli's responses made clear his concern over the growing Arab forces off his country's coast.

"I suspect that the children of Amalek are gathering once more," he had written in his last letter. "I pray we will have the same success as the first time."

Dated August 6, it arrived ten days later. But what quickly became known as "The War of Arab Unity"—even though it included the non-Arab Iranians—overtook Fogerty's reply, and the lives of millions.

*   *   *

Kibbutz Nof Benjamin (August 6, 2007)–"Without the King, without the Crown Prince, all hell will break out in Jordan," Aharon Tabor shouted to Ehud Kenaan as they ran with their duffel bags toward the kibbutz parking lot.

"Don't think so," said Kenaan. "Jordan, even before the treaty, was something of a mirage. There had never been a political crisis in Jordan–like in 1948, 1958, or 1970–without either British troops on Jordanian soil or U.S. or Israeli troops mobilized on the border to prop up the dynasty. There'd never been a succession, except the last one, without British officers in charge of the Army. As a country, as an economy, Jordan was always artificial, with a Palestinian Arab majority, with cash flow dependent on subsidies from Saudi Arabia, contraband trade with Iraq, or foreign aid from the United States or Britain. What's happening now is just icing on the cake."

"For Prime Minister Terzi, not for us," Tabor replied.

Jeremy Marcus got through to his father on one of the kibbutz's special lines, normally used by Nof Benjamin's high-tech plastic fittings plant for export business. "The Israelis are on full mobilization. Major Tabor told me to tell you they'll need immediate, large-scale resupply!"

"We know. Tell him we'll do everything we can in Congress to pressure the administration, and have him tell his superiors. But I can't promise. Things are different now. Make sure he understands that," Congressman Marcus said. Jeremy thought his father's voice sounded hollow, disembodied. "And Jeremy, be careful. Stay indoors, in solid buildings...."

"Jeremy, you get the next flight home! Do you hear me? The next flight.... I never should have let you go on that 'study mission.' It was your father's insane idea!" Madeline Marcus had picked up an extension. "I lived there–I know how God-awful dangerous it can be!"

"Mom, there are no civilian flights now. Ben-Gurion's closed to all but essential traffic."

"No excuses," Madeline Marcus shrieked. "And forget about that girl, what's her name? You're a congressman's son. You better be able to get a flight." She was crying.

"Sivan. Her name is Sivan," Jeremy said softly. "Mom, don't worry. I'll be back as soon as I can." He could not bring himself to say home. He was not sure anymore just where he belonged. Jeremy put the phone down lightly.

The kibbutz parking lot looked like a family reunion in reverse. Everyone was hugging, kissing, shaking hands, saying tearful goodbyes while trying, with little success, to smile. Children, husbands and wives, grandparents, neighbors jumbled together.

But quickly the ninety reservists—about one-third of the adult male population—in uniform for mobilization, rifles in one hand, bags full of gear in the other, shirts untucked, boots unlaced, formed as a unit. Three of the kibbutz's bus-like vans, normally used to transport workers to the fields and groves, were commandeered for military use. Aharon Tabor, as commanding officer, climbed into the front seat of the first van, opposite the driver. Before he did Shoshana kissed her husband and held him tight.

She had salvaged this man, then not yet twenty, from the wreckage of an earlier war. Once more she tried to memorize every crease, every line in his face, the glint in his eye, the smell of his skin. She noticed a dot of fresh blood on his neck, just below the ear, where the graft was the roughest. She dabbed it away and said nothing. Nothing but "I love you. Be brave, be careful. Hurry home. I love you."

The door closed, shutting out the life he had lived until five minutes ago. Tabor gave the driver instructions and they headed out the kilometer-long drive to the old coastal highway, Route 4, south a few minutes toward Hadera and then northeast on Route 65. They drove toward the Eron pass—a gateway for pharaohs, for Solomon and Allenby—near Megiddo toward Afula. There they were to rendezvous with their full unit, and Tabor had no doubt, be quickly dispatched to whatever objective the general staff decided would come under the fiercest attack soonest.

Tabor's unit never reached Afula. Thirty minutes into the trip, just outside Umm al-Fahm, the three buses were ambushed. A rocket-propelled grenade hit the second vehicle, which burst instantly into a flaming orange ball. Screams from inside the van stopped as suddenly as they had started, and a thick plume of black smoke raced skyward.

This is not supposed to happen! Something like this happened here only once before—the suicide bombing in 2002 near Megiddo, and that was a civilian bus, even if 13 of the 17 dead were soldiers returning from leave. But an attack on a military convoy in Israel itself? Not since 1948. Something had gone wrong, very wrong, and Aharon Tabor was furious.

Umm al-Fahm, one of Israel's largest Arab towns, climbed a slope above and just south of Route 65. Touched by the Islamic fervor of the Sons of the Village movement as early as the mid-1970s, Umm al-Fahm elected an Islamic fundamentalist municipal government in the late 1980s, and sent an Islamic Tendency member to the Knesset in 1996. Closely watched by the Jewish authorities, the municipality preached non-violent separatism—publicly, at least. In fact, the buses of Egged, Israel's large national transport cooperative, were stoned outside Umm al-Fahm as early as 1980. Energized first by the rise of Ayatollah Khomeini in Iran, later by Hamas and the Palestinian Islamic Jihad, Umm al-Fahm considered itself part of Arab Palestine regardless of where diplomats drew lines on maps.

Tabor caught sight of muzzle flashes in the hills above the road. "Yoni," he shouted to his second in command, Captain Yonatan Shamir, "Acharai!"

After me!

Until late that afternoon Shamir had been at work managing a resort hotel on the beach in Netanya, forty minutes south of the kibbutz. In the small new marina lay a little Sunfish sailboat. Yoni and Adva Shamir were passionate about their sailing, and the boat symbolized their recent arrival as the bourgeois their European-born socialist parents always had warned them about. "That's what comes of a country with tourism as a major industry and hotel management as a trade for a kibbutznik," Shamir's father had fumed. Regardless, with the baby, and both their jobs, they had little enough time for sailing. But on Friday afternoons the boat and the world—as caught between the setting Mediterranean sun and the beachfront skyline—was their personal treasure.

With a wave of his left arm, a late model Uzi submachine gun already blazing from his right, Tabor led his men out of the remaining vans, off the road and into a shallow ditch. He thought he glimpsed Ehud Kenaan leaving the third van with his communications men. Tabor knew Kenaan would be reporting by satellite phone and portable relay to Afula. His troops took cover and then slowly spread out. A second RPG found its target and the lead van, now empty, exploded. But a flash from the launcher showed Tabor where the attackers were concentrated.

"Yoni, to the left and up! Ehud," he shouted to Kenaan, who also held captain's rank, "stay here. Keep them pinned down, and contact headquarters. The rest of you with me, to the right and up!" Having thus divided the remnant of his force, about 60 men, into thirds, Tabor began a pincer movement toward his attackers.

Gunfire crackled up and down the hillside. Kenaan and his men set up two mortars and began hitting the area from where the heaviest firing came.

"More fire from the flanks! More fire," Tabor shouted up the line.

Weapons set to automatic, Shamir and Tabor's squads poured in round after round. Heavy return fire answered them. Movement was difficult.

"Damn!" Shamir muttered to the man beside him. "They must have the same night vision gear we do." Thanks to Israeli equipping of Arafat's forces—part of the intermittent, post-Oslo cooperation between Israeli and Palestinian police—they did indeed.

The Jews worked uphill with difficulty. The Arabs, pinned by the mortars, could not move at all. Sounds of battle, intense only moments before, grew sporadic.

Then, in a new burst of gunfire, the Arabs tried to withdraw uphill. The Jews cut them down. After an eternity of less than ten minutes, it was all over. Tabor's men converged on the Arabs' position.

"Yoni, Yoni!" Tabor shouted. He stumbled. At his feet lay Yonatan Shamir. The captain's stomach was torn open. Blood soaked his uniform and the ground beneath. Aharon grabbed his friend's hand and felt it already growing cold.

"Medic!" Tabor screamed.

Yoni stared at Aharon. His eyes were wide with fear. A gurgling sound came from Shamir's throat as he tried to speak. A medic now knelt at his side. The man, another friend from Nof Benjamin, glanced at Tabor and shook his head. Yoni Shamir was dead.

Shamir, the thirty men in the second bus, and three other soldiers shot during the battle were gone. Ten more lay wounded.

"Nearly fifty percent casualties, more than a third dead," Kenaan reported for Tabor to regimental headquarters. In ten minutes, in a little ambush at the side of a two-lane highway inside what had been Israel proper, the unit from Nof Benjamin suffered losses worse than any it had experienced in the 1973 Yom Kippur War, in the 1982 war against the P.L.O. in Lebanon, far worse than anything incurred while policing the intifadas after 1987 and 2000.

"We count eleven enemy dead," Kenaan reported. "No prisoners."

"Don't want any prisoners," Tabor spat.

Something had gone very wrong indeed, and not only on Route 65 outside Umm al-Fahm. Ambushes and raids just inside the pre-1967 green line along the hundreds of miles of serpentine border with Arab Palestine. Ship-launched missiles and submarine-borne commandos landing at a dozen places along the 90 miles of coast from Haifa to Ashkelon. Accurate Scud-D's and even more advanced tactical ballistic missiles carrying both block-buster conventional warheads and poison gas, striking highway junctions and arsenals, airfields and communications centers. Thousands of Jewish dead, tens of thousands wounded. An Israel unable to fully mobilize its citizen army or get all of its air force aloft, an Israel in pain, confusion and fear.

For Yacoub al-Masri, Mahmoud Terzi, Ibrahim Abu Bakr, for al-Ikwan al-Muslimi—the Moslem Brothers and its generational offshoots, Hamas, Islamic Jihad and the rest—for tens of millions from Tangiers to Tehran, the War of Arab Unity was well started. Except for the dumbfounding counterattack by ships and planes of the U.S. Sixth Fleet on Syrian and Libyan ships off the Israeli coast, things were on course and ahead of schedule. And even that American intervention proved brief.

* * *

Rota, Spain (August 14, 2007)—News media sensationalism, like The Middle East Spectator's story on the death of Col. Abner Samuels, did not interest Admiral Chester W. Fogerty. Far from Washington he continued to study both the accounts of the Samuels' case and the contents of the envelope the colonel had mailed in his last hours on earth. Fogerty was uniquely placed to piece the puzzle together. Under military administrative detention at the huge U.S./NATO naval base at Rota, Spain, he expected to be court-martialed for having committed, however briefly, U.S. Sixth Fleet planes and ships on behalf of the Israelis in the War of Arab Unity.

Nevertheless, up to now, no one had said a word to him about court-martial. As an admiral, he continued to be treated with respect, albeit frosty. His accommodations in the base guest house were anything but penal. He had unrestricted use of a telephone. He was certain it was tapped, but called his wife in Alexandria,

Virginia daily. And, incredibly, no one had searched him or his papers yet. Having done his best to memorize Samuels' plan, he tore it into tiny pieces and flushed them down the toilet.

Chester Wingate Fogerty was deputy chief of naval operations when the state of Israel agreed on the White House lawn in September, 1993 to progressive dismemberment. It seemed such an obvious calamity at the time that he suspected the Israelis were following some intricate master plan in which the Oslo Accords were themselves but a feint, apparently to lull Syria into nuclear disarmament. However, by the time Rabin was assassinated two years later, he understood there was no master plan, hardly a plan at all. What had happened, he explained to doubting colleagues, was that the Israelis—who had survived forty-five years in the Middle East on the basis of worst case planning—were now, out of a war-weariness they called "a new paradigm", staking all on best case planning. And doing so when their enemies gave them barely an undergarment with which to support Miss Rosy Scenario.

Fogerty's insight allowed him to determine in what ways Samuel's plan made sense, and in what ways it erred. The admiral wasted little time on the personality failures that must have led to Samuels' bizarre last day. He focused instead on the alarm the late officer had tried to sound, a Forrestal from familiar country. He found Samuels' fears—at least on the strategic as opposed to the personal level—neither bizarre nor paranoid.

He watched Israel appeasing, retreating, as if it had been the defeated aggressor, as if its patron, the United States, rather than the Arabs' ally, the Soviet Union, had collapsed. The failure, he believed, had been spiritual, not objective or material. The Israelis, or at least the ruling elite—post-Zionist, Jewishly secular, even anti-religious were, after three generations of war and rumors of war, desperately seeking normality. They convinced themselves first that they, like their Western European reflections only an hour or two away by plane, were entitled to it, and second, that like their American diaspora cousins, they no longer needed to defend by force their right to be Jewish. So, in the midst of an Arab-Islamic Middle East trying mightily to reject them as an organism rejects an alien protein, the otherwise successful Jews found themselves worn down by a relentless 60-year campaign of hot and cold warfare.

Fogerty understood the transfiguration of pan-Arab nationalism—from the defeat of Nasserism by Israel in 1967 and the would-be Nasserism of Saddam Hussein by the United States and Great Britain in 1991—into revolutionary pan-Islam. That was the meaning of the fall of the Shah of Iran in 1979, the 1981 assassination of Anwar Sadat and the 1989 defeat of the Soviet Union in Afghanistan. He observed the consolidation first of the Palestine Arab Republic and then of Jordan into the United Arab Islamic Republic of Palestine, in tenuous confederation with Syria. He recognized the renewed reliance of the growing economies of Western Europe and Japan on Middle Eastern oil. And he noted the inroads made in the West, even in the United States, by a radical Islam running under the flag of multicultural equality, of a mindless regard for unassimilable "diversity," banners that provided useful camouflage even after September 11, 2001.

Early in his career Win Fogerty had managed a base drug treatment program in San Diego. The base commander had first refused to admit there was a problem. Then he attempted to define the problem away as merely a matter of "generational change" and personal experimentation. As parts of the base itself became no-go areas at night and intra-service crime soared, he minimized a law enforcement response. Not until an officer's wife was murdered for the thirty-four dollars and bank credit card she carried in her purse by two enlisted men serving under her husband did the commander begin to allot more money for security and for treatment.

It was a pattern Fogerty would witness again and again by those in leadership positions, and not just in the Navy. It seemed especially common to those without belief in absolutes of right and wrong. Open-mindedness—or rather, a willingness to discard uncritically old verities in the name of progress—seemed to go hand-in-glove with a moral hesitancy, a lack of command rigor.

About this time Fogerty experienced a religious re-conversion. God had not saved his older son from death caused by injuries sustained in an automobile crash, a crash not his fault. But faith in God had saved his wife. And her faith—not a simple acceptance of the unexplainable as "God's will" but rather a realization of the impossibility of human justification for the divine coupled with a profound certainty in the necessity of God—pointed Fogerty back to his own belief.

In his drug treatment program on base, Fogerty began to talk not just of healthy and unhealthy, of legal and illegal, but also of right and wrong, moral and immoral. Seeking to reach those in the program, especially the recidivists, he began not to talk at all, but to preach against "the idea of salvation through good intentions, of feeling good instead of doing good, of pretending that man is not born only a little lower than the angels and only a little higher than the animals, and therefore denying that every day is a battle for each of us between doing right and doing wrong, between good and evil.

"Those whose definitions of right and wrong come only from inside, only from what they themselves believe true, good, appropriate, momentarily gratifying, are worshipping an idol—themselves. Since the self is transitory, they have nothing lasting to fall back on, and all their values amount to so much fleeting opinion. Ultimately, they can allow themselves to do anything, to feel nothing for anyone else. If I am describing you, I am describing a person who will have even more difficulty in breaking an addiction, in staying clean than someone who does believe in a higher power.

"No, not all who pray to God are good. But only those who believe God might be listening have a real expectation that their prayers will be answered. If you want easy validation, it's all around. But it can never redeem you. For that you'll need forgiveness, for God's help to change."

Before Fogerty took over, recidivism in the base drug treatment program was more than fifty percent. Under him it dropped to roughly one-third. However, its planned three-year life was cut to two, mostly to make moot a suit against it by the American Civil Liberties Union on grounds it violated church-state separation.

Regardless of its end, the effort won Fogerty a devoted following among enlisted men and their families as well as among some officers. It also earned him a reputation among some superiors as "Chet the Bible-Thumper." But perhaps most of all, it reinforced his confidence in his own decision-making, in his own risk-taking and innovation. Plenty of people inside and out of the Navy were not surprised when they heard that the Sixth Fleet had intervened, if briefly, on the Israelis' behalf.

As for Fogerty, he'd already told the commander at Rota he was looking forward to a court-martial. "Why?" his fellow admiral had asked, uncomprehending. "Because," said Fogerty, "it'll be a bully pulpit!"

U.S. Navy Adjutant-General Delbert Bump III thought the same thing. However, in his case it was utterly without relish. "To hell with Fogerty! To hell with that sanctimonious Bible-thumper!" he thundered to his senior staff again. "The man deserves a court-martial. Damn it, we'd be within the law to hang him for treason...."

"Sir, I must remind you, the United States was not and is not at war with Israel. It does have a commitment—not as direct as its mutual defense pact with South Korea, or even as clear as the relationship with Taiwan, to be sure—but a commitment nonetheless to Israel as a major non-NATO ally and partner in strategic cooperation. And its relationships with the Arabs states involved in the War of Arab Unity was premised in part on those states not going to war against Israel. So the charges against Admiral Fogerty, no matter how serious, cannot include treason...."

"I know that, Captain Revson. I know that!" Delbert Bump III glared. "I also know that one more nit-picking, legalistic remark like that, and you're off this case."

The A-G hated it when Revson reminded him, with sarcasm lurking just behind his case law technicalities, of the difficulties of the Fogerty matter. He knew that naval command, the Joint Chiefs of Staff and the White House itself all wanted to avoid the publicity a court-martial of Fogerty would shine on America's failed Middle East policy, on its ever more precarious, ever more inflationary dependence on oil controlled by countries whose leaders, at least some of them, expected Christians everywhere to begin converting to Islam now that the Jews had been defeated. The First Lady herself, still basking in news media coverage of her latest visit to the Islamic center on Massachusetts Avenue, had made plain the White House's insistence not to be further embarrassed on this score when she awakened him from a sound sleep the night before.

* * *

Jerusalem (August 7, 2007)—"Look at this!" Prime Minister Meir Sarid demanded, pushing a print-out from Le Monde, the big French daily, onto the center of the cabinet table. A page one editorial blamed the Jews for the latest Middle East war, since "they should have let the Arabs of the Jewish part of Palestine, the Arabs of the occupied Galilee and Negev, vote on whether or not they wanted to join their brothers in the Arab Republic of Palestine. They should have permitted the hundreds of thousands of Palestinian refugees wishing to return to their rightful homes inside Israel—to Jaffa, Ramle, and Haifa—to do so. By denying the elementary human rights of these long-suffering victims," Le Monde pontificated, "the stiff-necked Jews brought destruction on their own heads and danger to us all."

"So the French are dependent on Arab oil. So they have millions of Arab and Muslims migrants as permanent residents and new citizens. So they're arrogant bastards. What else is new? We saw the French establishment turn a blind eye to Muslim attacks on Jews back in 2002. Who gives a damn about the French?!" said Deputy Prime Minister Israel Miller. "Tell us what the Americans are doing."

Miller, a self-described "relic" of Israel's infancy, a lanky New York City boy too young for Korea but just old enough to have fought under Dayan in the Sinai in 1956, was a little stooped now, a little heavier a half-century later, but still vigorous. He liked the younger, technocratic Sarid, but was finding it ever more necessary to keep the latter's attention focused as the unremitting pressure intensified.

"You mean the Americans who let Vietnam fall, Lebanon collapse, the Shah be overthrown, Somalia disintegrate, who let the Bosnians bleed and held the U.N. back for the Rwandan slaughter? Those Americans, always with their peace processes, not with peace?" Sarid retorted. "The Americans, who'd move heaven and earth to kill Osma bin Laden but not understand their real enemy is the ideology that prevents a single democracy from taking root in the Arab-Islamic Middle East? We called the White House the moment the attacks began, and we've been calling ever since. The American ambassador, Jennings, says not even he has been able to get through."

"There are some kind of demonstrations, or riots in Washington, apparently not far from Capitol Hill. Sharpton was on 'Larry King Live' demanding that 'no African American go to war for no Israelites.' Johnston's distracted—as usual."

"Distracted or swimming," Miller said. "Is Egypt quiet?"

"No," retorted Uri Eshel. "Our diplomats and the Egyptian media both report big pro-war demonstrations in all the major cities. In parliament, members of the Brotherhood are insisting that Egypt join the jihad. Mossad sources say there's unrest in the military." Already holding the police minister's portfolio and substituting as head of General Security Services—the domestic undercover arm formerly known as Shin Bet—or internal security, Eshel now stood in for the chief of foreign intelligence as well. The latter was part of a handful of cabinet ministers and Knesset members missing in action.

"Forget the Americans for now," the prime minister snapped. "Let's deal with what we can control."

"Influence maybe, not control. Not anymore," said Defense Minister Shaul Simon Tov. Like so many Israeli politicians, Simon Tov was a former general. Unlike so many others of that ilk, he had not jettisoned martial knowledge to accommodate political ambition. Simon Tov had won the defense minister's post through a combination of strategic foresight and popular support based on a straight-forward charm. As a result, he had many enemies in both leading parties.

He now stood before a series of maps that blanketed one long wall of the cabinet room. With his pointer, he gestured toward the top of the left-hand map, the one of northern Israel.

"Okay. As you know, the Syrians finally transcended the law of the French generals and stopped fighting the last war. This time they're acting like we used

Total Jihad

to, fighting the next war. As for us, without strategic depth, without allies, we've been doing what we could. That is, staging an orderly retreat.

"When we pulled troops out of the enlarged concentrations around Lake Kinneret and Jerusalem—necessary because we'd given up the strategic depth of the Golan Heights and Jordan Rift Valley—to counterattack the Arab beachheads on the coast, Syrian forces stationed on the Golan executed flanking maneuvers. They left the international observers untouched on the Heights, and poured through the Beka'a Valley in Lebanon and then down into the Hula panhandle." Here Simon Tov's pointer tapped the chart, "and across the Yarmuk River, cutting through northwestern Jordan. In a classical pincer, they're circling Lake Kinneret toward Tiberias from north and south." Another rap of the pointer tip against the map. "The fact that we agreed to partial demilitarization below the Golan, in exchange for Damascus doing likewise above, has not helped us any. Now the Syrians have smashed through Metulla and the ruins of Kiryat Shemona left from the Thirty-Six Hours War in the north, and face only what resistance we could muster locally at Safat. So now, should we try to defend Tiberias, or regroup to defend the approaches to Haifa?

"My assumption is that they'll detail a sufficient force to occupy the ruble of Safat, but send the bulk of the northern column west across Route 85—our new and improved Route 85—toward what was Karmiel and on to Akko on the coast. I don't think they'll invest much on Tiberias, because if they're successful to the west, Tiberias will be encircled anyway. So their southern column probably will try to move quickly along old Route 77 toward Kiryat Bialik and the outskirts of Haifa. If they can manage that, they'll lay siege to the city. At least, that's what I'd do if I were them. Especially since we're only talking about an advance of 30 miles or so. If they can manage it in the next two days, they'd be in perfect position even if the diplomats arrange a ceasefire."

"Damn it, Shaul," the prime minister swore. "how can you be so matter-of-fact about everything? This is life-and-death, for God's sake!"

Simon Tov, taciturn to the point of bluntness, stiffened. "It's my job. If I am not matter-of-fact about military decision, if I allow myself to act on the emotions I feel, you can be sure the result would be more death—more Israeli deaths—than if I, and the rest of us, maintain our self-control. As for God's sake, I've been in the Israel Defense Forces, fighting for this country for thirty years. He can work His wonders alone, no doubt."

"Sorry," said Sarid. He looked it too, and worse. "Please continue."

"All right. Now each of these Syrian armies, and that's what they are, armies in their own right, has approximately 80,000 men, with full complements of armor, mobile field artillery, helicopters for airborne infantry and fighter-bombers for close air support. Combined they equal the size of our standing army. And, as you know, fighting on our own soil this way, defensively and reactively, rather than offensively, preemptively and on Arab ground—whether the Golan, south Lebanon, Judea and Samaria, Gaza or the Sinai—has crippled our ability to control our own territory and air space and therefore to be able to mobilize fully. So while we've got units in place near the Karmiel junction to block the Syrians, at least for a time, Route 77 is relatively open to them.

"As a result, the chief of staff and I have decided to concentrate on establishing the strongest Haifa-Akko defense perimeter we can, as quickly as we can."

Simon Tov let that sink in. There was uncharacteristic silence in the cabinet room as it did. For the first time since the tiny, beleaguered Israeli army abandoned the Negev early in the 1948 War of Independence to focus on saving western Jerusalem, the vaunted IDF was, in essence, trading a large portion of Israel to invaders.

"But bad as it is, the north is not our primary problem. Things are worse—or soon will be—within two dozen miles of this room." Here the pointer came down hard on Ramallah, Jericho and Hebron, just north, east and south of Jerusalem.

After the rapid growth of new Jewish neighborhoods northward from the city center in the 1980s, Arab Ramallah actually had become a suburb of Jewish Jerusalem, ten miles from the Western Wall. Jericho, the ancient oasis 20 miles east and 3,000 feet down—far below sea level in the Jordan Valley—had become part of the first phase of the autonomous Palestinian Authority in 1994. Hebron, site of King David's original capital more than 3,000 years earlier and burial place of Abraham and Sarah, Isaac and Rebekkah, Jacob and Leah almost a millenium before that; scene of Arab massacres of Jews in the 1920s and '30s, flashpoint of murderous Muslim-Jewish hostility in the '80s, the place of Baruch Goldstein's killing of 29 Muslims at prayer in 1994, remained a center of Islamic fervor. It had bedeviled British, Jordanian, Israeli and even Palestinian authorities in turn. The Arab municipality—140,000 people—was united in two things only: suspicion of whomever held power, and hatred of the Jew.

The Jews—at least those religiously minded or nationally conscious—considered Hebron one of their four holy cities, along with Tiberias, Safat and Jerusalem itself. And a troubling city, ever since the Israelite spies returned to Moses carrying its luscious grapes and bearing fearful tales of giants among its people, their fear undermining God's promise and condemning a generation to wander and die in the wilderness.

"In Hebron and outside Ramallah, protected in the small valleys to the north, the Palestinian police, or army, is reinforcing itself—with Iraqi, Jordanian and Saudi Arabian help," Simon Tov reported. "Or perhaps I should just say the Palestinian-Jordanian Army. And resupply comes not only by truck, but by transport helicopters and, of course, drawing on all the materiel smuggled in since the start of autonomy. Likewise in Jericho. In fact, the combined infantry and armor battle just east of Ma'ale Adumim, in its second day, includes Palestinians, Iraqis and Jordanians with Saudi equipment. That's what you hear when you go out of this bunker and up to the street."

Ma'ale Adumim, the largest of the post-1967 "settlements," in truth a beautiful modern suburb of red-tile roofed masonry duplexes, irrigated greenery and Scandanvian-style playgrounds, resembled an affluent neighborhood of Phoenix or San Diego. It remained a Jewish town according to the final settlement between Israel and the PLO, in exchange for land inside the '67 green line along the lower Jordan Valley. Clearly visible from the old Mount Scopus campus of Hebrew University and linked to western Jerusalem via a bypass around the Arab neighborhoods on the city's eastern side, Ma'ale Adumim had become a suburb-turned-bastion.

"Jerusalem, of course, we will defend at all costs," Simon Tov said. "And that's what it looks like we'll pay, because we won't be defending only Jerusalem, but also the corridor down to Tel Aviv."

"Like '48 in reverse," said Israel Miller.

"Not exactly," Simon Tov replied. "In some respects, we're much better positioned to defend the capital, but worse to protect metropolitan Tel Aviv and Haifa."

"What about Beersheva and the Negev? What about the Arava and Eilat?" asked another cabinet member.

"What about Egypt?" Miller virtually shouted.

The tension, already thick, seemed about to suffocate them. The prime minister felt the meeting spinning out of control. Partly to concentrate everyone's minds, partly to get answers, Sarid slapped the table with the palm of his hand, then asked, softly but firmly, "what about nuclear weapons?"

Before Simon Tov could answer, one of three red phones on the large, polished mahogany table began flashing. Cabinet Secretary Ruben Elchanan, a political acrobat who had held the job under successive Labor and Likud prime ministers and then returned with Sarid, answered it. He listened briefly, his face grave, then handed the receiver to Simon Tov.

The defense minister pressed the phone to his ear, his neck and jaw muscles tight. He asked few questions, instead grinding his teeth as he heard the voice at the other end.

"Okay," Simon Tov whispered, partly into the receiver, partly to the others in the cabinet room, as he put down the telephone. "There is new information from all fronts, mostly bad.

"A sizable naval task force, apparently Iranian and including at least one submarine and one missile ship bought from Russia, has swept through the few patrol boats we left in the Gulf and is shelling Eilat while Saudi planes are bombing the city."

"And in Eilat we have..." Prime Minister Sarid started to ask.

"A tiny garrison, just the kind you'd keep in a resort border town in peacetime," Simon Tov finished. "All we could spare. And it's got 120 miles of exposed desert highway behind it as a supply line."

Iranian cutthroats are attacking a barely defended Jewish city of 40,000, and the defense minister continues his briefing routine, Sarid thought. Damn Simon Tov and damn his self-control, the prime minister thought to himself, full of envy.

"... The news from Cairo is also desperate. The military command–feeling pressure from middle-level officers and the enlisted men, many of them supporters if not members of the Islamic Group or Egyptian Jihad–presented the civilian government with an ultimatum: join the holy war or resign. The government, its ministers fearing for their lives, and smelling victory, ordered national mobilization."

Prime Minister Sarid, long a defender of the 1979 treaty with Egypt, despite the Egyptian's endless violations of key provisions regarding normalization, tourism, cultural exchanges and even military cooperation, felt his heart sink. In a few hours, he realized, his country had gone from cold peace to the brink of hot war with the Arab giant: Egypt with its 80 million people, one-third of the Arab world; Egypt, with its American-reformed, American-armed military; Egypt, with its limitless supply of troops.

In fact, a column larger than either of the Syrian armies now ravaging eastern Galilee sped through the tunnels—illegal under the '79 treaty but long winked at by Israel, under U.S. pressure—beneath the Suez Canal. It crossed the flat low dunes and asphalt roads of northern Sinai. It moved in American-built armored personnel carriers and trucks, led by American-designed and licensed tanks built in Egyptian factories, followed by American-made artillery and covered overhead by U.S.-manufactured warplanes. This force, beyond the dreams of a pharaoh or a Nasser, was the legacy of Anwar Sadat's reorientation from Moscow to Washington and the colossal "sweetener" from Camp David. The new armies of the Nile were possible due to the baksheesh of realpolitik— the $2-billion plus in annual U.S. military and economic aid that lubricated Egypt's peace with Israel ever since 1979. They rumbled eastward, reversing the course of battle that had prevailed in the Sinai in 1948, 1956, 1967 and, ultimately, 1973. The Egyptians were doing what so many Israeli politicians and American Jewish notables had assured themselves never would be done.

"The Egyptians have brushed aside American and other personnel from the multi-national peace-keeping force and appear headed toward Beersheva," the defense minister said, tapping his pointer at a succession of spots, progressively closer to Israel, on the wall map of the Sinai. Beersheva, the place where Abraham and Abimelech had sworn peace in the oath of the wells nearly 4,000 years earlier, was now a city of 300,000 Jews—many of them old immigrants from Arab countries, or newer immigrants from the former Soviet Union and Ethiopia.

"As we saw in Bosnia, Cambodia, Rwanda, Azerbaijan, Sierra Leone and elsewhere, peace-keepers can become war-monitors whenever the balance of power shifts," Miller interrupted. "And no one rescues the weak, certainly not in time."

"Whatever," Simon Tov continued, annoyed at yet another of what he considered Miller's pointless historicisms. "Beersheva is our fourth-largest city. It is home to a major air base. And it blocks the southern end of the expressway north toward Tel Aviv as well as the highway through Hebron to Jerusalem. We will try to defend it."

"Try?!" shouted Miller. "We must!"

"Yes, Israel, we must," Simon Tov snapped. "We must do many things. But with what, and for how long? We've eliminated the Arab beachhead between Herzylia and Netanya—at heavy cost in men and material—but still must block the Syrians outside Haifa and defend Jerusalem as well. Judging by the standards of '67, '73, and '82, by the third day of a major war we would be on or returning to the offensive. But now, due to the deadly distraction of the coastal salient, the Syrian and Iraqi conventional and chemical missile strikes on depots, highway junctions and other mobilization points, and the necessity of impromptu response on multiple fronts on our own territory, we are not even fully mobilized…"

Total Jihad

"And won't ever become so, will we, Shaul?" Sarid asked. It was more a statement than a question.

"Not in the strategic sense, no," Simon Tov answered flatly. "Even if we could be assured of getting every man and woman to their posts–which without undisputed control of the air and ground west of the Jordan River we cannot–we're starting to reach our red lines on consumption of ammunition and fuel, not to mention equipment. Just as the Yom Kippur War used supplies at a greater rate than in '67, and the Six-Day War consumed materiel faster than World War II battles, two or three times faster, so this 'War of Arab Unity' is proving even more voracious. And the Americans still refuse to begin any resupply. And counting the Thirty-Six Hour War as well, we've suffered nearly 25,000 military deaths, equal to all of our previous wars combined."

"Civilian deaths?" Sarid asked, almost listlessly.

"Don't know. But early estimates suggest at least as many as the military," Simon Tov answered.

"That's nearly one percent of the total Jewish population. Proportionally, as many losses as in '48!" Miller erupted. "I can't believe it!"

"If we ever get out of this basement bunker and get a chance to look around, you'll believe it, Israel," Simon Tov told him.

"Then we must use nuclear weapons now," the prime minister stated. "That, or consider terms of surrender." Now it was his turn to sound as maddeningly matter-of-fact as the defense minister had earlier.

For the second time in the history of modern Israel, a government discussed using nuclear weapons or surrendering. The first consideration, during the early hours of the 1973 Yom Kippur War, lapsed only as the battle turned. Now another Israeli cabinet debated the politics and practicalities of incinerating its Arab neighbors. During the argument, an errant shell from a long-range Iraqi self-propelled artillery piece firing in the battle of Ma'ale Adumim exploded in the aboveground portion of the Knesseet building, rattling the ministers' jaws and the teeth in them.

In Ramallah, the Jordanian-Palestinian, Iraqi and Saudi forces–using Israeli designed and American-manufactured satellite controlled range-finders–had locked onto key targets throughout the city.

*　*　*

Amman (August 8, 2007) – "The noose is tightening," Radio Amman declared. "Only unconditional surrender will save the Jewish civilian population. As for the military, nothing will permit the genocidal Zionist storm-troopers to escape the people's justice, or war crimes trials for their offenses against the Arab nation!"

Judith Miller, Israel Miller's wife and, like him, an American teenager who had responded to the Holocaust and Israel's independence by emigrating to help build the Jewish state a half-century earlier, flipped off her radio. More mugabalah, she thought. On the other hand, real bombs accompanied this bombast. From the Miller's pleasant French Hill apartment, with balconies east and west suffused by dawn and dusk respectively, on former "no-man's-land" on the northern side of Jerusalem near the site of the 1967 Ammunition Hill battle that helped reunify the city, she could hear explosions. Out there, in the middle distance, Arab artillery was finding its targets in the center of Jerusalem. She saw an explosion rock an apartment building a few blocks away. Long after the blast died off, she stood trembling. Suddenly, her own residence seemed claustrophobic.

Maybe I'll go down to the makolet and see if there's any more bottled water, she said to herself. Although Judy Miller, like her neighbors and Israelis every-where, had been hoarding what she could the past seventy-two hours, she decid-ed to chance one more trip. Besides, sitting still indoors was making her nervous. For security reasons, she couldn't call her husband on his cell phone. So, taking her cane, she picked her way down the stairs and eased out the door, hugging the wall of her building. She had reached the corner market, its windows shuttered but door still opened, as a shell fell short of the ministry of police to the southwest. It blasted through the roof and blew the store's contents out into the street, Judy Miller with them.

* * *

Beersheva (August 8, 2007)—"Hurry, hurry," shouted Assaf Adebele, gesturing to the large family crammed into the small Peugeot. The father, a red-faced Slav of about fifty, grunted as he worked the steering wheel and gear shift, trying to maneuver the car out of an alley next to a buff-colored, mid-rise apartment build-ing of the type still common in Beersheva and in older neighborhoods through-out the country. Adebele was one of the last military policemen in the southern part of the city, prying stragglers out of their homes. We always wait too long, he thought, of his parents in Ethiopia and of Jews throughout history. Prisoners of hope, of despair, or simple human inertia, we overstay.

Furniture and clothes, lashed to the roof of the Peugeot, tilted crazily to the right. Inside, the wife, a stocky match for her husband, screamed at him, at the three or four children in back—Adebele was not sure of the number, partially obscured as they were by more family possessions—and the world itself. Screamed and cried. The children cried. The man cursed. The Peugeot got stuck on a high curb.

"Jose, Jose!" Adebele shouted at another MP down the block. "I need your help!" Thus it happened that in the middle of the War of Arab Unity, Assaf Adebele, a Jew from Gondar Province in Ethiopia, and Jose Rosenblum, a Jew from Buenos Aires, Argentina, pushed the overloaded little vehicle back onto the pavement and helped the family of Lev and Ludmilya Borowitz from Novosobirsk, Russia, flee Beersheva in the largest single migration of Jewish refugees since the Third Reich.

"Amazing!" exclaimed Major General Abdul Hamid, commander of the Egyptian Third Army. "Simply amazing!" His lead elements had stopped on a sandy ridge barely five miles southwest of Beersheva, digging in and waiting for the bulk of the Egyptian army behind them to catch up. In a helicopter above,

General Hamid–binoculars pressed to his eyes–focused on a point at the northern edge of the city. He watched a thick dark line protrude out and north, away from Beersheva.

"How many would you say, Osama–a hundred thousand?" Hamid asked his executive officer.

"Nearly twice that many, for sure," Col. Osama al-Kadr replied, putting down his own binoculars. "At least half the city's population."

"Allah be praised! I'd like to get a closer look," Hamid said excitedly.

Just what al-Kadr feared. His chief, a career military man who achieved his general's stars more due to loyalty to President Hosni Mubarak and the secular nationalists who'd led the military and government throughout the 1980s and '90s than to his soldiering, had a disturbing habit of forgetting the real enemy, whether Israelis or Islamists, and obsessing on the transitory. Much of al-Kadr's work consisted of shepherding him back to the mission, as tactfully as possible.

"Between us and them are Israeli forces, and they still have some aircraft and mobile surface-to-air missiles," the colonel said.

"You're right, of course," the general replied. "Take her down," he ordered the pilot. He had seen enough, regardless. Behind a thin cordon of Israeli troops, what must soon become virtually the entire population of Beersheva and surrounding villages and towns was fleeing, most of it north on the Route 40 expressway toward the southern end of Israel's coastal plain and, ultimately, greater Tel Aviv sixty miles away.

Let them go, the general thought. Within twenty-four hours he would have the city nearly enclosed inside an arc of armor, artillery and infantry extending from the southeast to the northwest. Since escape eastward through the northern Negev toward the Dead Sea meant flight into a wilderness and running northeast toward Palestine and Hebron, which blocked the way to encircled Jerusalem, was hardly better than staying put, the Jews had no choice but to scurry toward Tel Aviv.

Hamid did not care. His full force was not in place yet, so he could not stop the refugees, and he certainly did not want to be bogged down with that many civilian prisoners, not when he could become the liberator of Beersheva, which the Zionists stole from Egypt nearly 60 years before, and conquer the important airbase next door.

"If our planes can be based at Beersheva, instead of west of Suez, it will more than double their effective time over targets for the siege of Jerusalem and the coming encirclement of Tel Aviv," Col. al-Kadr insisted again.

"Much as I do not like to admit it," Gen. Hamid replied, "you are right." Al-Kadr was often right about such things, the general thought. Perhaps too often. If I was not certain of the man's loyalty, I'd have him shot, the general mused. The chopper landed gently, reassuringly.

As they stepped out of the helicopter, Hamid studied his map. That always made al-Kadr nervous. The squinting expression the general wore under tension was gone. The colonel waited, ready to agree, demur or mumble.

"We should detail some units south along Route 222 to clean out Retamim, Revivim and take Sde Boker. And as the rest of the force catches up to us here, we should reinforce the detail, push east and take Yerocham and the air base there. Reclaim the Negev—and block any advance north by the damned Iranians. Right?" Gen. Hamid felt expansive.

The general's political instincts, in this case preempting a possible Iranian move northward out of Eilat, were on target. As far as Col. al-Kadr was concerned, Iran's attack on Israel's Red Sea port was unwelcome at best, classical Persian meddling in Arab affairs at worst. In any case, he doubted that the Israelis left anything more than token forces in the isolated villages and kibbutzim of the Negev Desert.

"Right. And may I say, sir, capturing Sde Boker quickly, with all the symbolism involved, can do the Third Army and its leader nothing but good," al-Kadr said. "After all, Ben-Gurion is buried in Sde Boker."

"Perhaps we can dig up his bones and grind them to dust," General Hamid laughed. "But then, there's no need now."

*   *   *

Jezreel Valley (August 9, 2007)—"Everyone in place?" Major Aharon Tabor shouted to his unit.

"Ready," the men of Nof Benjamin and other members of the reserve detachment responded from a dozen spots, concealed amid rocks, bushes and hastily dug foxholes.

"Good," Tabor answered them. "Okay. Look, no long speeches. We know why we're here: The Syrians are moving west, toward Akko and Haifa. Every hour we hold them up is one more hour for the bulk of the army to prepare to defend the western Galil. "This is an elite unit. When we joined, we joined as volunteers. There's no higher calling—not rabbi, professor, doctor or prime minister. Without us, no Israeli could be any of those things.

"We lost our comrades, too many, outside Umm al-Fahm. Some of us might not make it through today. But this is not going to be Umm al-Fahm. This time we're going to surprise the Arabs. We've got the high ground, we've got the equipment, we've got the training—and we're fighting for our families, our homes, our country, ourselves. We'll be outnumbered. But this is a bottleneck. They've go to come to us in small groups, and in small groups, we'll beat them. This is going to be Thermopylae, Thermopylae without traitors to betray our position. Just don't waste ammunition."

Because, Tabor thought, there's no more where that came from.

He looked to the northeast, across the intersection of routes 77 and 65, at this point both narrow strips of two-lane asphalt. Just beyond the junction, Route 77 dropped into the declivity of the Lake Kinneret basin. Route 65 meandered down from the north.

A few miles to the south was Mt. Tabor, its solitary dome overlooking what had been, even for a few years after the Rabin-Arafat handshake, tranquil rolling farm country of Jewish towns and kibbutzim and Israeli Arab villages. Tabor, where Deborah and Barak defeated Sisera and his Assyrians in a clash of sword and shield more than 3,000 years before.

A few miles to the northeast he could see the little plateau of Hattim, riding like an empty barge high on the horizon. The Horns of Hattim, where the light cavalry of the Moslems under Saladin, the great Kurdish leader, slaughtered a parched and exhausted armor-encumbered Crusader army on a broiling July 4, 1187. In doing so, they ended the Latin Kingdom of Jerusalem.

Not this time, Tabor vowed, not this time. We're not alien Crusaders—we're the Indians, and we've taken back our Manhattan. No more reservations—we're going to keep it now.

How long he stared out at history he did not know. Five minutes, an hour?

"Smoke and dust to the east. Here they come!" shouted the sentry high up the hill. "Wait. Something's happening... they're stopping!"

Tabor scrambled up the final thirty feet of the hill to look for himself. Why would the Syrians stop just now? It made no sense. No sense, unless they suspected his ambush.

"Small Israeli unit on hill 17," Khalil abu-Jahsin said into his microphone. Jahsin, eighteen years old, was sitting in his bedroom, in his parents' house on the northern edge of Tur'an village. Through his powerful Israeli Army binoculars, provided by his immediate superior in the Fatah Hawks, he had been watching Aharon Tabor's unit ever since he caught sight of it just after dawn, scurrying about the hill less than two kilometers away. He used his low power radio to contact local headquarters. The radio, originally supplied by the American CIA to the Palestinian Authority police, had like the binoculars found its way from the police through the Tanzim—the Fatah militia in the West Bank and Gaza Strip—to his Fatah Hawks cell of Israeli Arabs. Headquarters, in turn, was in touch with Syrian intelligence.

"I want artillery to hit that hill, hit it hard! Then let the helicopter gunships saturate it," Lieutenant General Rifaat Habib ordered. "After that, commando units attack from the north and east. And don't take long. Every minute we sit here means better-prepared Israeli defenses at Haifa!"

General Habib, a childhood schoolmate of Syrian leader Ibrahim abu-Bakr, and a graduate of the French military academy, was more excited than he been on his wedding night almost thirty years before. But less apprehensive. After all, this—leading a Syrian army through Israel—was new, something no other Arab general had done before, at least not since al-nakbah, the humiliation of 1948. And he, Lt. Gen. Rifaat Habib, would be the Arab to avenge that still-burning disaster. In fact, he was doing so already, having devastated the Israeli defenders at Tiberias.

Of course, in the back of his mind he half-suspected that if he failed he would not long survive the war, and if he succeeded abu-Bakr might mark him as a rival to be eliminated. No matter. If he succeeded, he just might be able to eliminate abu-Bakr. Meanwhile, the network of Israeli Arabs—since the first intifada many had insisted on being called Palestinians, although to Habib the whole lot of them, Palestinians and Israeli Arabs combined were merely southern Syrians—continued to prove invaluable.

"Incoming! Take cover!" Tabor shouted. Round after round from the Syrians' 120-millimeter mortars exploded on his position. The air, rent by the barrage, crashed together with deafening concussions. The earth heaved and soil and rock rained down on his men. Occasionally a shell struck a newly-dug foxhole or trench directly, casting a man's shredded body skyward in bloody bits at one with the dirt and stone.

Tabor, nearly buried by debris, heard the helicopters before he saw them. It was almost too late. Hugging the other side of the hill, the Brazilian copies of U.S. Cobras popped over the crest, their nose cannons, rocket pods and large-caliber machine guns blasting at nearly every inch of dirt and rock. Only steel-reinforced concrete bunkers would have protected, partially, against such a heavy, close-quarters, aerial assault.

Moving automatically, his body on adrenal overdrive, his eyes momentarily all-seeing, his mind curiously clear and orderly despite the infernal ringing of his ears, Tabor shouted one order to launch the Stinger short-range ground-to-air rockets, another for everyone else to stay covered. He saw one of the six or seven attacking choppers explode into an angry orange-and-black ball of roiling fire and smoke. Fragments from the downed helicopter apparently struck a second, and it limped back toward Syrian lines. But two other helicopters, hovering like angry wasps just a few feet over the unit's hastily-dug defenses, spit death at the men below, ripping the bodies of those Jews who had had the effrontery to stand and fight.

Tabor felt an explosion of fire in his leg as he collapsed into a rock-lined swale near the top of the mount. From the end of the barrage to the moment he lost consciousness was perhaps ten seconds. So he did not hear the lead units of the Syrian army resuming rolling westward. He did not hear them blasted to bits by the virtually undetectable plastic mines his men had planted at the junction of Routes 65 and 77 just before dawn that morning.

"Clear the wreckage! Clear the wreckage!" shouted a furious Lt. Gen. Habib. "We're taking too long. I must see Haifa before nightfall!" His shouts, thought an aide, sounded like cries.

*   *   *

Eilat (August 10, 2007)–Hosein Sarifani was laughing. His was a huge, soul-stirring belly laugh. In another context, it would have been amusing, contagious, the kind of laugh that could set onlookers to smiling and chuckling themselves even without knowing the cause of Sarifani's mirth.

In this context, however, it was a joyless eruption, a human self-contradiction. Sergeant Hosein Sarifani was counting the Jews arrayed before him. What a motley lot; children, young women, old women and old men, and a handful of males of military age but decidedly unmilitary bearing. Huddled around a white flag of surrender, the reality of this dejected rabble looked nothing like the fierce and blasphemous Zionist hordes, the impudent Israelis of Iranian propaganda. And Sergeant Sarifani appreciated irony as much as the next man. Maybe more, when it played to his ego.

"We're not going to eat you," he shouted in Farsi. From their expressions, he could tell that a few of the prisoners–obviously unbelievers who'd run away after the sainted Ayatollah Ruhollah Khomeini had proclaimed the Iranian Revolution–understood. "On no, we don't eat Jews," he said reassuringly. "We butcher them, but we don't eat them!" And Sarifani laughed again, uproariously, at his own joke.

Striding quickly to a cluster of Jews, the big sergeant spied a young woman, perhaps twenty years old, with strawberry blond hair and blue-green eyes. As he approach her, she stared at, and, he thought, through him with a mixture of fear and anger. "A Russian," he shouted. "I love Russians!" With that, he grabbed the collar of her blouse and ripped it downward.

"Chose the women you want–if there are any," he told the troops. "Castrate the men and shoot the children!" Suddenly, Sarifani screamed. He had relaxed his choke-hold to the point that Avital Resnikov had been able to bend forward and sink her teeth into his beefy forearm. The sergeant involuntarily jerked back. As he did so, Resnikov began to run. Instantly, Jews were running in every direction, Iranian soldiers chasing them, shouting and shooting. Incredibly, a few Jews who had been able to conceal guns, were shooting back. Sarifani pulled his bayonet knife.

"Don't kill the girl. She's mine! When I'm done with her, she'll beg me to slit her throat–which I will!"

Sarifani crumpled to the ground, a crimson stain spreading on his back.

They'll think the Jews did it, or call it friendly fire, Corporal Ali Musavi thought with satisfaction. By Allah, what a bully Sarifani always had been. A crazy, oafish bully. He deserved it. And I deserve this fair-haired Russian princess myself.

Two days earlier Eilat had been a small resort city at the southern tip of the Negev Desert, a little jewel squeezed between the shimmering blue water of the Gulf of Eilat–an extension of the Red Sea–and the rust colored hills of the Sinai whose reflections at dawn and dusk gave the water its name. Now it was smoking rubble. And across the rubble Iranians searched for Jews to kill. The order had been to take no prisoners, and with the exception of the two surviving senior Israeli officers, none were. More than thirty thousand dead, ten thousand missing. It was the biggest pogrom in sixty-odd years.

* * *

Ramallah (August 10, 2007)–It was evening, and it was morning. The fourth day. Yacoub al-Masri stood above the Arab city of Ramallah, on the long hill of Tel-En Nasbeh, the ancient Mizpah of the Hebrews, not far from where the prophet Samuel had sat in judgment of Israel. Not far from where an Arab mob lynched two Israeli reservists only a few years earlier, ripping out their intestines in a celebratory frenzy carried on newspaper front pages around the world. Two deaths–such a tragedy, al-Masri thought. Tens of thousands of such deaths, in this fourth day of the War of Arab Unity–a mere statistic.

"Now if you look straight ahead," Mahmoud Terzi told him, "you can see the northern front, with Iraqi and Palestinian troops facing Pisgat Ze'ev and the other settlements the Jews built between Al-Quds and Ramallah." Al-Quds, the Arabic name for Jerusalem, was one more example of the Christian and Islamic compulsion to appropriate Jewish themes. It was an acronym born of the Arabic phonetization of the Hebrew name for the Temple itself–haBeit el haMikdash– the most holy house. And Ramallah, once largely Christian, now overwhelmingly Muslim, was–like Bethlehem, Nazareth and eastern Jerusalem, an example of the Arab-Islamic tendency to abrade Arab-Christian as well as ancient Jewish communities both through population growth and suppression of religious minorities. "First the Saturday people, then the Sunday people," had long been the cry. But given Zionist persistence, it had worked in reverse order for several centuries, with Christian Arabs emigrating steadily from Palestine, Syria and Lebanon or intermarrying and converting. And the three children of the covenant continued their existential war over inheritance, so far to the same bloody end.

"To the east, you can glimpse the Jordanian and Palestinian lines," Terzi continued. "We've won a great victory, taking Ma'ale Adumim this morning. Of course, the Iraqis helped."

Al-Masri could see little to the east, the normal mid-morning haze of dust thickened by the lingering smoke of battle. But, staring through a pair of powerful binoculars, he did detect an omen: between eastern Jerusalem and Ma'ale Adumim, across the dun-colored hills, with their ancient terraces and occasional olive trees, nothing moved. This was not a morning like any other, this was a dawn of dreadful anticipation.

"We are just a little over four miles from central Jerusalem to the east," Terzi said. "Of course, the Saudi and Palestinian forces are in Bethlehem just to the south. The Jews pulled out of Adumim before dawn this morning, rather orderly, I must say. They'd already evacuated what was left of the Etzion bloc earlier. So their defensive perimeter in the south now runs through Gilo, less than two miles from downtown, as the crow flies."

"For the Jews, only vultures will fly today," al-Masri said.

Terzi hated this man, hated the way he talked, walked, stood. Hated and feared the way he knew. "What do you mean?" he could not help asking.

"When the Jews stage no more orderly retreats, but flee in a rout, the vultures will feast."

Riddles. The man speaks to me in riddles, Terzi thought. It's some kind of tactic. But I will trump the arrogant bastard. The president of Arab Palestine glanced at his watch. It was just before eight a.m.

"Look to the southeast, quickly!"

Al-Masri looked toward where Terzi pointed. Black dots just above the horizon, coming from the direction of the Dead Sea, quickly resolved themselves into formations of jet planes, of sleek Saudi and Egyptian fighter-bombers tearing through the air. Suddenly, as if in a post-modern silent movie, plumes of black smoke were rising all over western Jerusalem and anti-aircraft rockets burst like deadly flowers of orange and black in the sparkling blue sky. "Maybe today we will take Jerusalem," Terzi enthused.

"Maybe," al-Masri replied flatly. "And if not today, certainly tomorrow." Mahmoud Terzi, al-Masri thought, his most temporary excellency the president of Arab Palestine, looks ridiculous, his beetle-like body clad in a steel helmet and flak vest, bifocals and stubble beard. Like the doomed salon socialist Allende, waving his pistol and retreating into the Chilean presidential palace just before Pinochet's generals arrived. Like Dukakis in his tank before the Americans picked the elder Bush.

Al-Masri, Terzi thought, looked inscrutable, his face a perfect void. Like his heart, the president understood in a flash of insight, empty but for hatred. Damn it, how does he know what he knows, and what is it he's thinking of now?

Al-Masri knew, had planned long ago, that as soon as the bombing of Jerusalem started, his fighters from al-Ikwan, the Muslim Brothers, and from the more devout members of the Palestine Liberation Army—the merged alumni of Hamas, the Islamic Resistance Movement, and the more religious members of Arafat's Tanzim and of the Palestinian police—would launch a guerrilla blitz of the city, from within, from east to west. A few blocks, that was all, and they would be in the Jews' living rooms. It was a gamble, but al-Masri figured short odds. In any case, it was a necessary gamble. When Terzi's Palestinians and their Iraqi, Jordanian and Saudi allies entered Jerusalem, it must not be to receive the Jews' surrender. It must be to find his men already in charge, himself ready to proclaim the Islamic Republic of Palestine, incorporating and succeeding all that had gone before. And with himself as sharif if not caliph or imam. Satisfied, he began climbing down from the observation post in the minaret of Bir Zeit's Ibrahimi mosque. Terzi, still perplexed, followed.

*   *   *

Jerusalem (August 10, 2007)—"Listen, listen, damn it!" Defense Minister Simon Tov screamed. Already hoarse, trying to make himself heard above the bombing, he feared losing his voice completely. And every damn cabinet member was talking at once. Half of them wouldn't have made county commissioner in the United States—but such fatal mediocrity was a by-product of Israel's fractious, proportional parliamentary politics with two dozen parties on the ballot, one dozen in the Knesset.

Maybe the overnight move across Sederot Ruppin from the basement of the blackened shell of the Knesset to the sub-basement of the Israel Museum had been a mistake. Feeling better protected, surrounded by the tangible reminders of nearly 4,000 years of Jewish history on this very land, the ministers had found their voices again. Like players in a bridge game gone amuck, each one seemed compelled to trump the other, rhetorically, in what threatened to become an endless debate about authorizing the use of nuclear weapons. They already had approved assembling the warheads and delivery systems.

"Shut up, already!" Simon Tov bellowed painfully. Finally, his colleagues fell silent. The defense minister glanced at the prime minister, who reclined in his chair, his eyes closed, right hand pulling on his right ear. Before any of the others started again, Simon Tov spoke:

"The Arabs have advanced about a mile west from Ma'ale Adumim since late this morning. We mined both the old Jerusalem-Jericho road and the new bypass; they expected it, and are using mine-sweeping tanks, but can't make quick progress. We might have been able to pin them down completely, but as I tried to outline a few minutes ago—until bedlam broke out—Arab commando units have infiltrated much of western Jerusalem. Commando units," Simon Tov snorted. "These are the Palestinian police we created and armed out of the old P.L.O., that the Americans trained, and we expected to run joint security patrols with! These 'partners' of ours even have some of our artillery batteries under close small arms fire. So instead of trying to cut the noose around the city, we've had to divert forces to counter-terror search-and-destroy missions. It's been block-by-block, door-by-door in some areas, including Rehavia, where some of you live. It's time-consuming, with many casualties.

"And since the Arabs hold the advantage in the air—not that we aren't making them pay—we can't really get over to offense."

"Their initial targeting of our airbases and depots paid off, all those years they spent developing missiles and warheads—with the help of everyone from the Argentines to the North Koreans, the French and Russians, the Pakistanis and Chinese. It paid off, didn't it?" Prime Minister Meir Sarid said softly, as if musing, eyes still closed, chair tilted back, rubbing his ear with a rhythmic motion.

"Yes," Simon Tov sighed. "We've got some planes up, as I said, and are contesting over most targets, but their early rounds of bomber and especially missile attacks hurt, taking out planes but, even worse, crippling a lot of runways. And, as you know, we've held back ten remaining F-15-I's and twice that many F-16's to escort them if we go nuclear. And, gentlemen and ladies, we've only got a few more minutes to decide."

"Because of the other fronts?" It was Israel Miller.

"Right. The Saudis and Palestinian forces, reinforced by Pakistani mercenaries, moved out of Bethlehem this morning toward Gilo. Their tanks rolled right over Ramat Rachel...."

"Destroying Rachel's Tomb? Like Joseph's Tomb in 2000?" Miller thundered. "Maybe now even the haredim will fight for their country, at long last!"

"Or fight what's left of us godless Zionists for bringing this destruction on their heads," Simon Tov replied. "Thousands of them were out dancing last night, celebrating their imminent deliverance from heretics such as us. A few were shot by snipers—some from Arab-controlled areas, some from Jewish neighborhoods."

Miller gasped. But the defense minister continued. "Meanwhile, the Palestinians and Jordanians, with Iraqis, have reached the northern edge of Pisga'at Zeev...."

"And the highway to Tel Aviv?" the prime minister asked.

"Still open, but under artillery and aerial bombardment."

"Casualties?" the prime minister inquired.

"We started the war with nearly 150,000 troops, regular army and reserve, in the greater Jerusalem theater," Simon Tov said. "As of this morning, about 120,000 were still effective. They're fighting combined Arab-Islamic forces of twice that number. And doing a good job, considering our unusual lack of air

Total Jihad

superiority. But doing a good job on defense, on managing a slow retreat to interior defensive lines.

"In the north, the Syrian advance on Haifa seems to have stalled, although I have no idea how long we can hold our present blocking positions at Achihud and Hasolelim. Some elite units in forward ambush along Routes 85 and 77 did slow the Syrians. Now signal intelligence indicates some sort of argument between the field command and headquarters in Damascus. Regardless, we've got about 100,000 troops well-deployed and fortified, in and around Haifa, facing the Syrian pincer, which has something less than 200,000 soldiers combined.

"Haifa itself has not suffered as much damage as Jerusalem. The Arrow antiballistic missiles protecting the port have had a better success rate, for some reason, than those here, and one airbase in western Galilee has been repaired to nearly full functioning...."

"Beersheva and Tel Aviv?" the prime minister asked, his inflection between a question and a command.

"Beersheva is fully occupied by the Egyptians, with detachments already firing on Dimona and Arad and approaching Sde Boker. Meantime, the Egyptian army continues to pour into Beersheva. It captured the airfield at Hatzerim and transports arrive virtually non-stop. Without question the Egyptians are staging for a push north toward Tel Aviv."

"How long?" Sarid wanted to know.

"At the rate they're assembling, three days. Maybe two. They've got around 200,000 troops in and around Beersheva right now, division-sized detachments in the northern Negev, and are moving fighters and bombers to Hatzerim as well. We've left a blocking force outside Kiryat Gat and another near Kfar Silver on the coastal expressway outside Ashkelon–altogether about 50,000 men."

"Tel Aviv?"

"Harassing small arms and light artillery fire from the Samarian foothills in the direction of Petach Tikva and other outlying suburbs, the Palestinian police back at their old terrorist tactics–attacking civilian vehicles along the roads, firing their 'illegal' mortars into residential neighborhoods. But we've got several thousand troops, border police and civil guard on aggressive reaction, so that's pretty much under control, at least right now. And about 60,000 army and reserve for the defense of the city itself. The potential for a Sarajevo rerun exists, of course, but only if the Egyptians close in from the south and a regular force, Iraqi or Syrian, manages to occupy the western ridges of Samaria."

"Chances for improvement?" This time is was Miller.

"Dim," Simon Tov acknowledged. "Good as our forces are, we're outnumbered and, unlike past wars, unable to use speed and mobility to concentrate temporarily superior numbers at strategic points. Our high casualty rates–close to twenty percent of the active military–are unlike anything we've ever suffered before. And, on full mobilization with the enemy on our own soil, we can't replace them. Finally, as you know, we're low on materiel–fuel, ammunition, replacement weapons, artillery, armor and planes. Nothing, not one planeload, has arrived from the United States since the war started. And we already were down from round one, the Thirty-Six Hour War."

"I know," sighed Sarid. "It's still 'under review.' President Johnston told me so himself an hour ago. Again."

"And my evaluation was just of the military," Simon Tov added. "In the civilian sector, in greater Jerusalem, among the Beersheva refugees pouring into Tel Aviv, things are worse. Especially psychologically.

"But frankly, we don't have time even to worry about morale. The bottom line is that we're almost out of gas, literally. Modern warfare is omnivorous. Like the well-armed South Vietnamese in 1975, our main problem is not on the battlefield, difficult as those circumstances are. Our main problem is not bleeding to death, but dying of thirst and hunger, you might say. Thirst for gasoline, hunger for ammunition.

"Supplies from Egypt–from the Sinai oilfields we developed–stopped even before the Egyptians entered the war. The Europeans closed down our spot market purchases–as they did with 'all belligerents,' as if this hurt the Arabs–and never mind we were paying triple the pre-war rate. In Washington, America's Camp David I promise to be our 'worst case' petroleum supplier is 'under study.' Apparently Johnston thinks our circumstances not quite worst case."

"In that event," said Miller, "we must stop talking and act. Israel must issue an ultimatum: the Arabs must accept an immediate ceasefire, followed within 48 hours by a supervised withdrawal to the lines that existed five days ago–that is, before they invaded–or we turn their capitals to radioactive waste."

"And if they return the threat?" It was Simon Tov.

"If they return the threat, we've still got a draw at worst, with no more retreating," said the prime minister.

Knesset members not part of the cabinet had been gathering in the sub-basement all morning, those still alive and able to get to the museum. The vote to authorize the use of nuclear weapons went sixty-five in favor, twelve opposed, with ten abstentions. The other thirty-three members of the 120-seat parliament chosen in the 2005 snap election were absent: missing in action, wounded, captured, dead or–in the case of most of the fourteen Arab members, defected.

Shulamit Dayan, leader of the left-wing People's Progressive Party–whose ideologues now called themselves Canaanites, not Jews–voted no, saying "Israel cannot be a light unto the nations if we destroy the nations. Besides, it is nationalism that is to blame. Had the Zionism been less racist toward the Arabs in the beginning…"

Rabbi Baruch Schnorrenstein clamped his hands around Dayan's neck. Thick fingers began to squeeze. Shouting, other Knesset members pulled them apart, Dayan purple-faced, Schnorrenstein bleeding from Dayan's long, deep scratches.

The rabbi's number two in the Degel HaTorah (Torah Flag) Party, finally explained that he was voting yes for the same reason Dayan had voted no: "We Jews cannot be a light unto the nations if we let them destroy us."

Eli Avichai agreed with both of them, saying "the world needs Jewish light, this is plain. And only sincere repentance averts the severe decree. But since we cannot repent for our enemies' sins, we must repent for our own. It is in God's hands." He abstained.

"We have two more decisions to take," Sarid shouted over the pandemonium. "As we can see, it gets progressively more difficult to assemble the Knesset. Until such time as the war ends, or we regain control of most of our territory, I urge that we delegate authority to a small war cabinet–headed by myself and ministers Simon Tov and Miller–and suspended the full Knesset indefinitely, subject to recall by the war cabinet. The rest of you will then assume full-time leadership roles in your localities."

This passed by voice vote, over strong objections by Dayan's Progressives to a "right-wing Zionist dictatorship."

"Okay, one more thing. Defense Minister...."

"Given the course of battle, we've had no choice but to revise the plans made in the first days of the Yom Kippur War," Simon Tov explained. "We've got to establish a new paramilitary underground, just in case. Worst case scenario– excluding unconditional surrender, which I do–is that some imposed settlement, Arab victory on the battlefields or combination of the two deprives us of any overt Jewish armed force. And disarmament could set the stage for more bloodshed, this time all ours. Like the Druze and Christians in Lebanon, the Muslims in Bosnia and Kosovo, we will need our own militia–not to fight a civil war but to defend ourselves against the conquerors... and, maybe, if the time ripens, to lead us back to independence!" The stoic Simon Tov flashed with uncharacteristic emotion.

"A throw-back to the Haganah?" Miller asked.

"Exactly. Only this time we'll start much further along, using sophisticated arms of the IDF, which we must cache throughout the territory we still control in the event of a ceasefire or imposed settlement," Simon Tov explained. "This new underground, based on cells operating from every kibbutzim, moshavim, every Jewish town and urban neighborhood, will incorporate the smallest IDF units– those that survive and those we can recreate–in civilian dress. And some cells, some units, will be so deep underground, according to our new plans, that I cannot mention them even here."

"I so move," said Miller. This time the vote was unopposed, the PPP members having decided, after a brief huddle, to abstain. With creation of Magen Israel, Shield of Israel, and the small war cabinet authorized, the last Knesset of the reborn state of Israel, its business completed–so far as possible–adjourned sine die. Most of its members, like the delegates to the World Zionist Congress in 1939, would never see each other again. Those not on the war cabinet made their farewells, slowly climbed the stairs from the sub-basement to the basement and then exited a secret tunnel. Emerging near the Israeli Supreme Court building into smoke and dust-filled air, the sounds of war in their ears, they saw the Shrine of the Book–its Dead Sea Scrolls removed for safe-keeping–miraculously intact across Ruppin Boulevard. Then they started picking their routes home as best they could to begin organizing Magen Israel...

...Rabbi Bar Kochba Blum–that was the name he was best known by–did not have far to go. A Knesset member from the non-Zionist Degel HaTorah Party, Blum managed to find an Egged bus still running, another Daliesque touch in a city where war already had merged the spiritual and surreal. As the sole passenger, he rode the two miles east back to his ultra-Orthodox neighborhood of Mea

Shearim, the driver weaving nonchalantly around craters left by Arab artillery and burnt-out vehicles. Judging by the sound, at one point near Rehavia, they passed within a few blocks of house-to-house fighting. Near the end of the line a shell exploded just behind the bus, tossing the rubble of a building destroyed by an earlier blast like vegetables in a salad bowl.

Probably a 105 howitzer, Blum thought. He was surprised that the Jordanians still would be using their old American guns. On second thought, they'd probably given them to the Palestinians.

"What about the negotiations? Isn't there supposed to be a cease-fire?" Blum said, making conversation with the driver.

"Negotiations!" the driver snorted. The man wore his old civil guards' helmet and flak jacket, an automatic pistol holstered on his hip—but slowed at each customary stop as if he expected commuters, shoppers, and students to board as usual. "Negotiations are how we got into this!" the driver said, gesturing at the burned out buildings lining the route. "They called it a peace process because it was a process, not peace. Anyway, talk doesn't matter, not now. I just heard a radio bulletin before I picked you up. Apparently we've given the Arabs an ultimatum: stop fighting or we nuke you."

"I heard something about that this morning from a friend who has a friend high in the military," Blum offered.

"Ceasefire. There's another phony word. What it really means is, like the U.S. deal during the second intifada, ceaseless fire. We cease and they fire," the driver said.

"And one way or another, so will we," Blum replied. "God willing." Then he asked the driver, "why are you still out here?"

"Got to do something. Poison gas killed my wife; my son disappeared somewhere in the fighting at the Netanya-Tulkarm salient. My daughter emigrated to Australia years ago. If I stop driving, I'll kill myself before the Arabs do. And what are you doing out during a barrage instead of hiding in a shelter somewhere."

"You ask questions like a rabbi," Blum offered.

"If so, we could all be rabbis by now," the man replied grimly.

"Well, I am a rabbi. And like you, I'm looking for something to keep me going."

"That's a funny thing for a rabbi from Mea Shearim to say," the driver mused.

"I used to be a funny rabbi," Blum said.

"Well, maybe you'll find what you're looking for," the driver offered.

"Baruch HaShem," Blum said. "I have faith. And you be careful."

"Baruch HaShem," the driver responded. Blessed be the Name of God.

Blum stepped past shattered glass in front of Rabinovitch and Son, Jewelry and Religious Articles. Before the war the Rabinovitch family, like many others in this old quarter of narrow streets and aggressively pious Ashkenazim, had prospered. They sold not only to their neighbors but also to the thousands of diaspora Jews who entered their shops each year in search of something to take back for themselves or their families—holy souvenirs, gifts, totems from eretz Yisrael.

And the Rabinovitches, staunchly anti-Zionist and anti-state like most of their neighbors, contributed to Rabbi Bar Kocha Blum's small but well-regarded yeshiva. There men and boys studied Torah and Talmud from dawn until well after dark. They also studied subjects never suspected by the Rabinovitch clan and the yeshiva's other haredi supporters.

Outside the school a banner proclaimed: "Zionism and Judaism—Diametrically Opposed." It was replaced with a fresh one as needed. In the spiritual ghetto of Mea Shearim the struggle between eighteenth century Lithuanian Jewish Orthodoxy and nineteenth century Russian Jewish nationalism, between those who prayed for the Messiah and those who meant to pave his way, persisted oblivious to the twenty-first century imperative to synthesize the two or perish.

Despite appearances, Blum was no ordinary rosh yeshiva. After the first Palestinian Arab uprising began in late 1987, and some fringe Jewish religious groups resumed their support for Yasser Arafat as one of G-d's chosen instruments to scourge the blasphemous Zionists, military intelligence increased surveillance of both east Jerusalem Arabs and the Old City's Jews. Not long after, HaDavar HaKotel (The Word of the Wall) Yeshiva opened. Reb Blum, who indeed had trained at a yeshiva once, became its second director about the same time Ehud Barak became prime minister. Now, he led his students in both prayer and patrol.

Off Mea Sharim the rabbi moved through even narrower alleyways. The main streets of his neighborhood barely tolerated a motor scooter cart and a pedestrian passing abreast. He remembered this same stretch less than two weeks ago:

On the little walk in front of his yeshiva—the space actually was just a flattened portion of the curb—a large, handsome Arab woman sat in her customary spot. She wore a black, Bedouin-style dress, richly embroidered with threads of red and gold. She sold the big, spherical purple and green grapes of the Hebron hills, the kinds of grapes that must have been familiar to Abraham and Isaac, the kind the spies brought back to Moses. The woman was familiar to Reb Blum and he to her.

"A cluster of each, Nuri," the rabbi said, bending over the big, battered wooden tray between her knees.

"Bavakasha," she would reply in Hebrew, holding up the glistening grapes, trophies of fertility from a deceiving land.

"Shukran," he answered in Arabic, an exchange of please and thank you between well-acquainted individuals whose peoples teetered at the brink of war. He was not what he seemed; what was Nuri?

"Rabbi," she had said to him once, "are we all to die here, Arabs and Jews?"

"As we live, we must die, of course. But do you mean, Nuri, in war?" He had been surprised at her directness and her intensity.

"Yes. In war for this land."

"Only God knows. I pray it will not happen."

"But it has happened before," she said flatly.

"Yes, but we believe nothing is inevitable, if men only turn to righteousness."

"Rabbi," she said, looking directly into his eyes and holding his glance, which he suspected was a deliberate cultural transgression, "it is going to happen. We both know it. Why don't you and your students go back to America?"

"Back to America? I was born here."

"But you are a Jew, not an Israeli?" She seemed bewildered.

"Nuri, I am both."

She studied him, perplexed.

"Should I ask why you don't go to America? No doubt we both have relatives there."

"No doubt. Maybe we should both go," she said, her gaze again averted.

Had there been a hint of a smile on her lips then, he wondered once more.

Just beyond her he had stopped to inspect the new door and frame Arab workers were installing at the yeshiva's main entrance. The original had been damaged, again, by secular Israelis, helonim who protested in front of the school after Blum announced that he would prefer seeing his neighborhood under Arab rule than that of "this pagan Jewish government we are cursed with, this government not of Jews but of Hebrew-speaking Canaanites." This, during the controversy over the Education Ministry's new high school history texts that had replaced pictures of Ben-Gurion with those of the Beatles, that related Israel's 1948 War of Independence from the Arab perspective, had gotten Blum 30 second of television news exposure. Contributions to the yeshiva rose markedly in the days following.

"Salaam, rabbi," said one of the workmen. "We will be done soon, as you can see. This door will be much stronger than the one before. The Zionists will not bother you again." He spit out the word.

"It is good work, Ghassan," Blum had replied....

But artillery did not discriminate between good Jew and evil Zionist, or even between Jew and Arab along the intertwined battle lines of Jerusalem. On the sidewalk now a few children scavenged amidst debris. A solitary adult hurried past Blum, anxious to complete some crucial mundane errand and return to his lair before the next bombardment. As in the new neighborhood of Ramot, astride the "no-man's-land" of 1949-1967, as in fashionable French Hill, Rehavia and working class Givat Shaul, the explosives and chemical munitions had wrecked their havoc in Mea Shearim. But for Reb Blum and his followers only the terrain had changed, not their assignment.

* * *

Washington, D.C. (August 11, 2007)–"Desperate Jewish Rattle Nukes!" headlined the New York Post. "Arabs Fear Israeli Missiles," announced the Boston Globe. "Israel Threatens Nuclear Holocaust," bannered the New York Times. "World Peace at Risk," advised the Washington Post.

As it often did in times of foreign crises, the American capital erupted into a frenzy of mostly purposeless sound and motion, from congressional hearings and White House statements to televised news conferences and think tank symposia. In the executive mansion, however, in the Lincoln bedroom, President Barry Johnston glided in and out, in and out, prolongedly in and out of his wife's smooth, shapely if somewhat artificial body. He glanced at the newspapers he had placed, fanlike, above her head on the pillows. Overseas drama excited the president—so long as it remained overseas. Toying with the first member at such times, denying, denying, denying and then only at last yielding to executive pleading, excited the First Lady, leaving her doubly lubricated. They both agreed they had never had such good sex until coming to the White House—not even under the lights, after hours, in the television studio in Indianapolis.

"God, how I love foreign affairs," the president moaned.

The First Lady smiled, said nothing, and knocked her cigar ash on the carpet.

"The truth is, congressman," Assistant Secretary of State S. Grace Pittson was saying, "oil-related multinational corporate interests and international diplomacy have always explained only half of America's persistent Middle East involvement. The other half, understood if less frequently expressed, was the fear that a nuclear Sarajevo was more likely in the Middle East, and of course along the Indo-Pakistani border, than elsewhere in our multi-polar post-Cold War world."

"You mean," asked Rep. Jonathan Marcus, "that the moral commitment to a democratic, Western-oriented Jewish state was just window dressing?"

"Not at all. Just that as a calculation of international involvement, that was a bilateral issue for us, whereas the question of nuclear confrontation was and is multilateral," Pittson returned. Marcus imagined he could hear her thinking: Ball's in your court, congressman. Again, with backspin.

So the Jews had counted on three halves to U.S.-Israel relations—strategic, diplomatic, and moral—without checking their proportions too closely, Marcus understood.

"We regard the threat to use nuclear weapons, regardless of provocation, as so fraught with international danger as to be impermissible," the assistant secretary continued.

"The threat has been made before, achieving positive results without actual use, hasn't it?" Marcus pushed.

"Not really. If you're referring to 1973, the Israelis had sustained more than 1,800 dead—but were telling their own people and us that the total was just six hundred. Golda Meir's government wanted to avoid being pressured internally or externally, so it lied about how bad things were while ordering its small arsenal of nuclear weapon components assembled into deliverable bombs. The Soviets responded by sending a ship carrying atomic warheads into Alexandria harbor. President Nixon then ordered U.S. forces worldwide onto full alert. At that moment Israel regained the offensive and U.S.-Soviet diplomacy starting working on a ceasefire...."

"So the nuclear bluff went unproclaimed and uncalled?" Marcus finished.

"Ostensibly. And most of the world remained blissfully unaware of how close a thing it was. But we learned a lesson: Close is too close, even as bluff. This time we cannot be sure the Israelis are bluffing," she said. "And I cannot overemphasize how seriously this administration regards such a threat."

"Are you saying," Marcus demanded, "that Israel is the cause of the trouble? What about the threat to the Jews of Palestine?" he asked. "The Arabs' demand for unconditional surrender, with 'war crimes' charges for all senior members of the Israeli military and government, can hardly be considered conciliatory, can it?"

"Congressman, as you know well, we are pursuing every possibility to reach a ceasefire and resume the peace process. But one can hardly expect the parties to do so under threat of annihilation...."

"Peace process," Marcus scoffed, "has as much to do with peace as processed cheese has to do with cuisine. What you're saying is the Jews, under siege by invaders, are supposed to accept a surrender and hope it becomes a truce. But if they threaten to take the aggressors down with them, like Samson in the Philistine temple, we decide—on behalf of the Arabs—that cannot be allowed," Marcus said.

"I didn't say that, congressman," Pittson replied.

"You didn't mean to say it, perhaps, but that's exactly what I heard."

Felicia Sanchez suddenly was at Marcus' side, whispering into his ear.

"Let me see it," he said.

She placed a neatly folded print-out of an Iranian newspaper article on the polished mahogany table in front of him. Beneath it was an English translation from the Farsi. "Government Will Reply to Nuclear Attack Against Arab Allies," proclaimed the headline. Warning "the Zionist usurpers" against "any suicidal actions," the story quoted senior officials in Tehran as promising nuclear retaliation for any Israeli attack, and not necessarily at just Israeli targets. It also quoted European Community representatives as saying that the War of Arab Unity "has claimed many lives, Arab and Jew alike, but in addition has set the stage for realization of the just rights of all people in the area, as part of a unitary greater Palestine."

Marcus understood that the Europeans, their own capitals within range of Iranian, Iraqi, Syrian and Libyan missiles, were acting as a stalking horse for the Arab-Islamic parties. "Warfare," intoned the statement of European nations molded by repeated warfare, "solves nothing. It is no longer necessary in any case." Of course not, now that the Jews—by international agreement—were to be defeated, the congressman thought.

"Are you aware of an Iranian ultimatum?" he asked Pittson.

"I was getting to that," she said.

"This hearing is pretty irrelevant, isn't it?" Marcus replied. "The deal's been cut, over the heads not just of this Congress, but the Israelis, irrespective of American commitments." Standing, he added, "I don't have time for this dog-and-pony show." He stalked out through the paneled door behind the raised dais, banging into a row of filing cabinets on the other side in the staff room as he went. Never before in public life had Congressman Jonathan Marcus simultaneously felt so furious and so frustrated.

*   *   *

Ramallah (August 11, 2007)—Also furious, also frustrated, was Yacoub al-Masri. The Americans, the Russians, even the Chinese, had ordered Mahmoud Terzi—ordered him!—and his Syrian, Iraqi, Jordanian, Saudi and Egyptian allies—to stop fighting. The American and Russian presidents agreed on one thing, and that one thing they made clear: They would tolerate no nuclear war in the Middle East, especially not now that the parties had plenty of medium range ballistic missiles and even a few legitimate ICBMs. If the Arab armies did not halt, if the Israelis did not surrender and both parties did not stop troubling the rest of the world, the big nuclear powers would rattle their own doomsday weapons in the direction of the Middle East. Off the record, of course. All this before his men had taken western Jerusalem, before he could depose Mahmoud Terzi and proclaim the Islamic Arab Republic of Greater Palestine.

"The war is over, my friend," the Russian ambassador had informed Terzi. "If you persist, we can bomb your sacred al-Quds for you. If you want to liberate the dust of what was holy al-Aksa mosque, keep fighting. We'll blame it on the Israelis and only the two of us will know the difference. And please don't feign surprise. What do you think the American ambassador is telling Prime Minister Sarid right now? 'Accept the ceasefire, prepare to turn over your heavy weapons and your offensive aircraft to the United Nations peacekeepers, or U.S. planes will strike Tel Aviv, and America will say 'the Arabs did it.'"

Terzi, close to tears, demanded to know why. "Haven't we been loyal to you—at no small cost to our movement and our people—from the '60s to now? From the first hijackings—always Western planes, never yours—to fighting American hegemony after Camp David, in Beirut against the Christians and as your eyes and ears in Damascus and Riyadh, as your seconds in El Salvador, Nicaragua, even for Ceausescu in Romania at the end. Why do you betray us?"

"Don't be naive," Ambassador Alexiev responded. "You are one of our players, but not the only one. Never forget that. We are big, our interests global. Like the Israelis to the Americans, you are a piece of our puzzle—we are not a part of yours. And we most definitely are not ready for World War III. Not now, not here. And not over Islamic issues, not when we've repacified Muslim Chechnya and are having to do the same in Uzbekistan."

"I will never make a pact with such a Satan," al-Masri announced when Terzi relayed his conversation with the Russians. "I will avenge this day and complete our victory! It is the will of God!"

"Meanwhile," al-Masri went on, controlling his bitterness, "the world will learn of Mahmoud Terzi the peace-maker, and of Yacoub al-Masri the holy man. For the time being, the open war suspended, we must resume the psychological war to continue weakening the Jews and strengthening ourselves. This should have been the final battle, but the end will come soon, I swear!"

Al-Masri stated this without sarcasm or self-deprecation, speaking as if to himself—or to an audience of thousands of believers, but not as one man in conversation with another. Terzi realized that he himself might just as well have been a piece of furniture. Once more he recognized how much he loathed and feared this mahdi, this messiah-dervish, this dangerously indispensable man.

I must have the mukbarahat, the secret police, double surveillance on al-Masri, Terzi said to himself. My self-sainted revolutionary needs a short leash.

I must have the Brothers in the mukbarahat increase Mahmoud's dosage, al-Masri said to himself. My president, beetle-like though he is, with the tell-tale trembling lips, looks altogether too alert for a man getting so little sleep.

"You have another reason for agreeing to the ceasefire," Fatima Tlas al-Masri said to her husband later that night. In his residence, a newly-built palace in neo-

Ottoman style on the northern edge of Jerusalem, well-kept but sparsely furnished, not far from the cease-fire lines, they had talked long and deeply, al-Masri using his wife as sounding board, critic and intimate advisor. She was the only person he tolerated playing this triple role.

He lay with his head in her lap as she stroked his thick black hair. On the sofa in front of them stood a low tray of finely wrought brass, bearing small china cups of thick, strong sweet coffee and baklavah, wrapping honey, nuts and raisins within its layers of delicate pastry. Large, perfect green and purple grapes sat next to the baklavah. Pistachios filled a bowl of filigreed silver. Fatima, once more watching her weight, occasionally nibbled at the grapes but ignored the baklavah. Her husband, his appetite fueled by an ambition both boundless and focused—and feeling its object tantalizingly near, but just beyond a seemingly insurmountable barrier—consumed the coffee and pastry in voracious bursts.

"And what is that reason?" al-Masri asked, testing her.

"Arab unity," his wife responded. "Our solidarity, unprecedented compared to past wars with the Jews, is hardly perfect. And the Persians," she said, referring to the Iranians, "are a wild card. They use Islam to try to dominate the Arabs and to be the predominate regional power in dealing with the Americans and Russians. We need to neutralize them."

"You're right. The Persians are congenitally istikba, arrogant bastards. On their own they destroyed Eilat—I had plans for that port—and threaten the Europeans with missiles. Not that the Europeans shouldn't be threatened, but to our purposes, not Tehran's! What else?"

"Islamic fervor grips the masses in Palestine, in Jordan, Syria and Saudi Arabia, and influences them in Iraq and Egypt as well. But you know better than I, for it is you who taught me, that centuries of rivalry don't vanish overnight, not even with victory over the Jews."

"Again, right. Iraqi and Syrian units whose paths crossed on the way to Jerusalem and the Jordan Valley traded shots, just as in previous wars. The Saudi royal family, weak and corrupt as it is, is rumbling about holy Jerusalem being its only goal, that the war aims of those eight thousand endowed princes and princesses don't include Tel Aviv and Haifa. It wouldn't surprise me if they fear the Iranians will march east from Eilat toward Mecca, not north to Tel Aviv. More?"

"Cairo, Damascus, Baghdad—the three classical centers of Arab culture—do we really think they will tolerate us upstart Palestinians leading the Arab world from Jerusalem and Amman? Even now Ibrahim abu-Bakr thinks he led the war against Israel, not us, and that Syria is number one, the 'beating heart of Arabism,' as the elder Assad used to claim. And the Egyptians in Beersheva—as far as we're concerned, they're the Arab version of the Persians, or worse, the French."

"All you say is true. But we have people in place everywhere except Iran. If the Russians and Americans have forced us to detour, it will be short and return us to the main route further ahead than we are now. So for the moment we consolidate our victory, unify our forces—beginning with the Palestinian, Jordanian, and Syrian sectors, then neutralize the powers, especially the Americans. That won't be hard, since that is what they really want, especially the Johnston administration—to be open-minded, even-handed, neutral. Neutered.

"Meanwhile, the Jews in their little beachhead, no longer even a Palestinian statelet, become our subjects. Subjugate them we will! The Jews will relapse to their proper Islamic status of dhimmi, lesser people, protected monotheists, but—like the Christians—protected at our pleasure and properly taxed because they refused the Prophet and the Final Revelation."

"Our biggest problem," said Fatima, a natural pragmatist for whom her husband's theological insistence approached obsession, "will be getting the Syrian, Iraqi and Egyptian armies off our soil." Stroking her husband's forehead, feeling again his feverish heat, she added quietly, "the Egyptians talk like Beersheva and the Negev belongs to them."

"They'll all go, all right," al-Masri said. "Under Western prodding and U.N. cover, the Syrians and Iraqis will go—but it'll cost us diplomatically. They have no claim, at least not one anyone else accepts; Syria got the Golan back before and no one else thinks Palestine is really south Syria. At least not anymore. It's the Egyptians who'll be trouble. They've got a point from the '40s about Beersheva. But after the U.N. issues its 'balanced' withdrawal recommendations, and after I proclaim the restored caliphate, none of the Arabs will have a choice."

Despite the heat from her husband's body, when Fatima al-Masri heard the word caliphate, she felt a chill shoot down her spine. A chill of apprehension, not anticipation.

*　　*　　*

Kibbutz Nof Benjamin (August 19, 2007)—Shoshana Tabor stroked her husband's head, her fingers lingering at the edges of the skin graft, the stigmata from that war more than twenty years ago. Thank God it was dry, she thought. But her eyes were not on re-knit wounds of an old battle. They stared down at his legs, both encased in white gauze and plaster, one held in position by a brace with a chain hoisted over a pulley.

The second week had been much better than the first, she thought. He rarely screamed at all anymore, not when he was awake. Still, he ought to be in a hospital, she worried, not Kibbutz Nof Benjamin's little clinic.

"There's no point in talking about it anymore," Aharon Tabor insisted. "Sure, a hospital would be better—but in a hospital I would be a sitting duck for the new Arab authorities. There's going to be a round-up of former IDF officers, a purge. Count on it."

"How can you be sure?" she replied. "Here you can't get the care you need. God, you of all people know how long and hard rehabilitation from combat wounds can be, especially if you get started wrong. These make-shift casts and jerry-rigged traction... I'm certain the veterinarian did his best, but you're no bull, only as stubborn as one."

"C'mon," he tried to tease her. "You've called me a bull once or twice, if I remember right."

"Bullheaded, I think it was." Then she leaned over and kissed her virtually immobile husband. Aharon Tabor did manage to slip his right arm around his wife's neck, and keep her face on his.

It was less than two weeks since he lay in a coma, partially buried by artillery-tossed rubble, on the hill above the junction of routes 77 and 65. After the Syrian Army resumed its advance, a small group of Arabs from Tu'ran had gone to scavenge on the battlefield. A party of Jews from nearby Bet Rimon–with whom they had, in the days of Israeli sovereignty, exchanged wedding visits–intercepted them. The bodies of the Tu'ran residents were buried in a common grave on the hillside, among them Khalil abu-Jasin, 17, former spotter for the Fatah Hawks.

Aharon Tabor, whose right arm, twitching among the stones, caught the eye of a searcher, had been dug out and carried along back roads, away from the advancing Syrians, to Kibbutz Nof Benjamin that same night, lying on a mattress in the rear of an old Chrysler station wagon, once part of the motor pool at the U.S. ambassador's residence in Herzliya. Tabor had been the only member of his unit not killed or captured. Although the ceasefire included provisions for a prisoner exchange, Israelis who'd returned from Syria in previous wars often did so maimed in body, mind or both–if they returned at all.

"In the exchanges so far, no Jew over the rank of sergeant has been returned. It's the opposite of when we used to make those insane trades–one thousand terrorists for three soldiers, that sort of stuff–before the first intifada. Now we give up a dozen captured Arabs for fifty or sixty Jewish P.O.W.'s, but none of the latter are commissioned officers. Funny, how every single missing officer 'died in battle.'"

"What's really happening?" Shoshana asked, although she knew.

"The order's gone out to liquidate the leadership, and potential leadership. It's why Lenin had not just the Romanovs shot but all those 'class enemies' as well. It's why Ho Chi Minh had 10,000 Vietnamese village headmen and traditional story-tellers massacred over the years. Why revolutionaries and illegitimate conquerors always eliminate those who might challenge them. And if our new overlords ever get the chance, they'll do even worse in our big coastal ghetto. Why not?"

She had no reply.

He understood her silence as agreement. "So that's why I'm here, and why, if any outsider starts snooping around, even if it's a Jew, you must hide me."

"Where?"

"Remember the little children's reading room in the kibbutz library?"

"How could I forget?"

It was there they first kissed, as fourteen-year-olds chaperoning younger children one night an age ago.

"I've already ordered two men I know to be loyal to build a false front over it, with a cot and the other necessary supplies inside. It'll be ready in a day, two at most."

"You are suspicious of other Jews? Really?"

"Someone betrayed our position to the Syrians. Even if it was done by Israeli Arabs, we know the hard left of the peace movement, the Shenkin street types, the ones who, when they went on vacation, told people they were from 'Palestine,'

Total Jihad

not Israel, who called themselves 'Canaanites,' who insisted that Zionism was racism, were everywhere before the war. Maybe not that numerous, but enough. So they must be everywhere now."

"Dissent is one thing, Aharon. Treason is another."

"Of course. But given how fragmented our society was even before this war, even before Oslo, for that matter, given how 'peace' became a totem to so many, so many delusionaires, no one is automatically above suspicion."

Shoshana Tabor looked her husband full in the face once more. She knew him better than anyone else, maybe as well has he knew himself. Yet he still surprised her. Not that he wouldn't be anticipating, issuing orders, even in his current condition. No, but his complete, oddly unegotistical confidence that those orders would be carried out, carried out by men who recognized him as their natural leader and wanted to serve him, was both uncanny and well-placed. She did not know where it came from, how he understood or maintained it, but it was one of the qualities she loved him for. Over the years, she had met more than a few men whose respect for Aharon was as unshakeable as her love. And women, too, she mused.

Ehud Kenaan knocked, then entered Tabor's apartment. "The pain any better?"

"Yeah," Aharon responded. "Each day's an improvement—unless I try to move my legs."

"Any idea how long that'll take?"

"The vet says not long for the left leg, a couple of weeks and the cast can come off. As for the right leg, he's not sure; says the femur was shattered, basically, right above the knee."

"So you'll limp a little. It'll certify your war hero image. People already are beginning to talk."

"Well, tell 'em to stop. None of us, me, you or any of the other IDF survivors need one bit of notoriety. Not now, not under this new regime. We need to be anonymous—invisible, if possible—until we figure out what to do next. What we can do next."

"That's been done," said Kenaan, who had participated with the rest of the Nof Benjamin unit in the defense of Haifa when Tabor's elite squad had gone to set the ill-fated ambush.

"What do you mean?"

"I met last night with Knesset member Uzi Peled, or member of the former Knesset, to be exact, and a couple others from our reserve divisional headquarters. The IDF may have been disbanded, according to the terms of the ceasefire, but not before the war cabinet authorized formation of a Jewish underground. We've already got a structure, a national structure, in place. That wheel doesn't need to be reinvented. What we need to do is grease the damn thing and put a tire on it...."

The two men—friends, fathers and warriors—talked on until Tabor, feeling his medication, began to doze. This time his dreams were pleasant: of kibbutz fields white with the snow of cotton, the green fronds of banana trees unable to hide their forty kilogram bunches, tractor trailers hauling loads of plastic pipe from the kibbutz factory, of children laughing on the playground, adults lingering over coffee in the dining hall, of Shoshana, always Shoshana. And of arms caches, of ambushes successful this time, of American ships shelling Arab armies. Of an uncountable sea of Jews dancing in the streets of Jerusalem.

Shoshana Tabor watched her husband move in his sleep. She felt his forehead. It was warm and damp. Hair slick with sweat curled up from the graft on the nape of his neck. Two little droplets of blood glistened at the hair line. But his lips smiled. Delirious, she thought.

* * *

Alexandria, Virginia (August 19, 2007)—"Come home now. Peace of mind awaits you, salvation for your souls!" The Rev. Gary Goldenberg, Jewish apostate, ordained Southern Baptist minister, leader of the multimillion dollar Messianic Jews of Jesus, Inc., looked into the lens and implored his television audience. "Accept Yeshua as your savior and know the bliss of redemption! Recognize Yeshua as King of the Jews, as your personal savior—and shed the bitterness, the gall, the despair of the War of Arab Unity! Join Jews of Jesus today, become part of the new Israel, the true Israel, the suffering servant washed in the blood of the lamb, God's chosen on this earth and in heaven! You know today's headlines, you've seen God's final rejection of the false Jews who, stiff-necked, remained in the synagogue of Satan. Come home now. True peace, human brotherhood and divine love await you. Call 1 800 I Yeshua. That's 1 800 493-7482. Operators are standing by."

Goldenberg was wearing a dark business suit, an embroidered tallit of white, blue, purple and gold and a matching kipa. He stood on a mock bimah, with a Torah scroll unrolled before him, a small but gleaming golden crucifix off to one side. A telephone bank staffed by a team of operators worked on the other side. As the credits rolled, music of Ha Tikvah, "The Hope," Israel's national anthem, rose over the ringing phones.

"I'd like to slit his throat," Jeri Levi said, clicking off the little portable television in her study. In what had been her study.

She was now a rabbi without a pulpit. Her erratic behavior, in the eyes of Marvin Kammelman and other Or Kodesh officers, had led to a showdown. They accused her of "disturbing and accusatory sermons," actions "out of character" for a Reform rabbi—enrolling her children in a traditional day school among them—and, regardless of their own varied marital statuses, castigated her for separating from Hal.

She responded by indicting the board members—and by extension, more than a few of her congregants—for lax ritual observance, insincerity, and ignorance in the faith. That sealed her fate. But her threatened lawsuit did get their attention. To avoid it, the board's attorneys agreed to honor the remaining year on Rabbi Levi's contract. She got four hours to clean out her study, under the watch of security guards hired by the board. Disappointment mingled with relief as she packed the items from her desk and cleared her bookshelves.

"You know, Sylvia, it's funny," Jeri remarked, as Sylvia Weinberg stood watching, her eyes wet. "There's so little here that's really mine. Books and papers, papers and books, a few boxes. That's it. the material evidence of my existence as Or Kodesh's rabbi."

Sylvia embraced her. "I don't usually say this, but this time, rabbi, you're wrong. There was plenty in this building, in this congregation, that was yours–the spirit of this place. Before you, it was a synagogue. You made it a congregation. After all, in life it's never really the place, or the possessions. It's the people. And plenty of people here–not many of them machers on the board, I know–but plenty of people would follow you into a new congregation...."

"Thanks, Sylvia, but I'm not going to split Or Kodesh to satisfy my own ego."

"I know this sounds corny, but I mean it: Don't worry, something will turn up, something good. It always does." With that, the two women parted.

Rabbi Jeri Levi was unpacking those few boxes at home the next morning, rearranging the books on the shelves over a small desk in the alcove off the family room, when the telephone rang.

"Rabbi Levi?"

"Yes?"

"This is Jerry O'Malley. I'm program director at WBLS, the non-denominational religious radio station. I was wondering if you'd like to do a weekly show for us, for a small fee, of course."

Ah, she thought sardonically, WBLS–plucky little "Bless Radio." An earnest, strange blend of religious and commercial broadcasting with Protestant, Catholic and even a little Jewish programming "for all good people of good faith." She opened her mouth to tell Mr. O'Malley thanks but no thanks when she felt a surge of excitement.

"Yes," she heard herself saying, "let's talk about this in person."

They met for lunch two days later at Moshe Hunan's, the only kosher restaurant in all of the northern Virginia suburbs. Forty-five thousand Jews, one kosher restaurant. There it was in a nutshell, or fortune cookie message: We don't care enough.

"Anyway," O'Malley was explaining, "it's easy for WBLS to get Protestant programming. Why, some clergy start their 'electronic ministries' before the paint dries on the Sunday school bus. Local productions and national syndicates from each of the major denominations supply more than we can use. There's certainly enough Catholic material, though not as varied, from the Washington diocese. And it comes in English, Spanish, Vietnamese, even Korean. But Jewish stuff, well, we've been scrambling, I hate to say."

"What do you have in mind for me?" Jeri Levi asked.

"I think something basic to start, say fifteen minutes commenting on each week's Torah portion, then current events from a Jewish perspective in the second half. Old Testament themes are big with most of our listeners, in any case..."

"Hebrew Bible, not Old Testament, at least for me."

"Of course. Sorry. In any case, minus commercials, station breaks, time and temperature, all that, you'll have about twenty minutes of air time. At first it would be taped at your convenience. If you catch on, we could add half an hour for listener calls. But that would mean you'd have to do it live, at the same time each week.

"As for payment, we'll see how things go. If you sell enough ads to cover the cost, we'll cut you in for a share of the gross. How's it sound?"

O'Malley gave her a little grin. Rabbi Levi liked the grin, a mixture of personal sincerity, self-promoting self-satisfaction and, yes, religious excitement. "If I sell the ads?"

O'Malley nodded, still smiling.

Rabbi Levi smiled back, just as mischievous. "It sounds okay. No, it sounds great," she said. "But let me suggest a special debut…"

O'Malley's heart warmed. He was sure the impulse to phone this woman had been a godsend. The fact that she was hot right now, with news of her departure from Or Kodesh in the local headlines, didn't hurt. "Like what?" he interrupted.

"Some of my backers from Or Kodesh–the saving remnant, you might say– have rented the small theater at Northern Virginia Community College's Arlington campus for me Sunday evening, sent out flyers and put up posters, e-mailed a notice to various lists. I'm to speak on 'The Jewish Crisis.' Maybe you'd like to tape my talk for rebroadcast."

"Tape it, hell," O'Malley said. "Oops. Forgive me. I mean heck, if it's as good as the sermon that got you fired, we'll air it live!"

The Washington Area Board of Rabbis memo, urging members of the respective congregations to shun Rabbi Levi's new "unauthorized" activities, of course had the opposite effect. People actually began to talk about her coming broadcast with anticipation. This made Rabbi Heskel Greenberg, a relentless moderate and unforgiving consensus-builder, uneasy. He sensed a renegade, and renegades by definition rocked the boat. Rocking the boat was bad, especially for Jews so often already in stormy seas. Rabbi Greenberg, master of behind-the-scenes-leadership, cultivated a quietude in which he soundlessly crushed boat rockers.

As the Sunday night speech approached, Jeri Levi felt an increasing exhilaration. Having been stripped of Congregation Or Kodesh, she was going to try to gather a new one of her own. To what end, she wasn't certain.

Northern Virginia Community College's Arlington campus was a neat quadrangle of relatively new beige brick buildings, a landmark in a changing neighborhood of weary commercial streets where a once-Jewish population had given way to Indochinese, and the latter had begun to yield to Hispanics and blacks. An extension of the Metro Orange Line had reinvigorated business, real estate prices, social turn-over and crime, itself met by newly-vigilant police.

People dissatisfied with the pious but pointless messages heard in their own synagogues, messages divorced from their own yearnings and dumb in the face of Israel's peril, crowded the little theater. Maybe this Levi woman could satisfy their hunger, ease their spiritual isolation. If not, perhaps she could at least satisfy their curiosity. The two hundred seats filled fast; late arrivals stood along the sides of the hall and packed into the back. In the lobby several dozen folding chairs were hastily set up for the overflow and loudspeakers connected to one of two microphones on the podium. The second ran directly to WBLS' remote unit.

"Man, it's warm in here," Jerry O'Malley muttered to himself. He was handling the control board at a table just off stage. The crowd settled in only as Jeri Levi walked to the podium, which was flanked by the American flag and the now-unofficial banner of the former state of Israel.

"You in charge here?" A big man in a dark suit flashed official identification at O'Malley. Another man, almost as large, accompanied him.

"Yes, why?" O'Malley asked.

"Fire marshal's office. We've got a complaint about this gathering. Let me see your permit."

Rabbi Levi had been right, O'Malley thought. Rabbi Heskel Greenberg was pulling strings. But forewarned is forearmed. That Sylvia Weinberg was a gem. He pointed the men to the front row of the auditorium. "See those two fellows with the briefcases? They're lawyers for the station. I'm sure you'll find everything's in order, sir. And let me know if you want to stay for the sermon; I'll find you some seats backstage."

The fire marshal glared and moved off to confer with the lawyers. These Jews, O'Malley thought to himself. They sure keep each other on their toes, to be polite about it.

Jeri Levi began with a prayer, first in Hebrew, then English, for the welfare of the assembly, the United States, and the Jews of Palestine. Then, slowly, somberly, deeply, she said, "Brothers and sisters, we are in danger. Great danger. And this looming threat is our own fault. At bottom it comes not from the Arabs, not from our abandonment—once more—by the 'good people' of Europe and North America. No, it stems from our own refusal to end the exile, from our willful dispersion and fragmentation. It keeps us weak, wherever we are. And it is an old story:

"Nearly three thousand years ago the united kingdom of the Jews split after the death of Solomon. Within two hundred years, the ten tribes of the north were destroyed by Assyria.

"Judah, the southern kingdom, carried on. Eventually, abandoned by its erstwhile Egyptian ally, internally divided, it fell to Babylonia. When the Persians conquered Babylon and let the Jews return from exile, many of them stayed put, undermining those who did return.

"Centuries later the Maccabees reestablished the Jewish state, defeating first the upper class of Hellenized Jews and then the Greco-Syrians. But their offspring became corrupt. Again Jew intrigued against Jew. Sadducees maneuvered against Pharisees, Roman party versus the anti-Roman party, Zealots against the establishment. Rome, at first referee, became dictator.

"And so on, until, when Zionism arose more than a century ago, the secularists fought the religious, the Socialist battled the Orthodox. The amcha—the people, the grassroots—scattered. Many escaped to the New World, many more throughout Europe, a remnant to Palestine. And because we were scattered, because Palestine was not yet rebuilt, the Holocaust was even worse than it might otherwise have been. Even in the Warsaw Ghetto, there were Jewish fighting factions that barely spoke to each other.

"Because we ten tribes of the West remained in exile, Israel emerged small and stunted, its Zionism twisted inward and, like its Judaism, distorted by the experience and intellectuals of eastern Europe. The little Jewish state grew over-burdened, forced to fight repeated wars and, wearied, to accept a false peace.

"Of course our enemies rejected Israel, called it illegitimate. Why not, when most of us free Jews rejected it?

"Why does this matter so? Because, it turns out that small plot called Israel, with Jerusalem at its heart, is the spiritual center of the world, the portal between heaven and earth. And this world cannot be redeemed until the Jews—fulfilling our divine obligation to be a light unto the nations—show the way from our own nation, redeeming ourselves by redeeming eretz Yisrael as the world's holy land!

"In the words of our great sage, Hillel, 'If I am not for myself, who will be for me? But if I am only for myself, what am I? And if not now, when?'

"Brothers and sisters," Rabbi Levi cried from the depths of her soul, "if not us, who? If not now, when?"

The crowd, young and old, affluent and working class, affiliated and unaffil-iated, secular and observant, mostly but not entirely Jewish, buzzed with a strange excitement.

"Now!" it shouted in answer, surprising itself, astonishing each person, Jew and gentile, who shouted, "Now!"

When Rabbi Levi finished, nearly all the spectators broke into waves of applause, a vigorous, emotional endorsement. The rabbi's children, Jason and Deborah, moved up the aisles, collecting donations. Whether from heat, excite-ment or both, several people fainted. Jeri Levi herself seemed to collapse over the microphones. Jerry O'Malley could not have been happier. He'd seen tent revivals and coliseum crusades; the rabbi looked like a hit. This little bit of Jewish rabble-rousing would be rebroadcast two or three times, each airing to higher rat-ings, he was sure.

Part III

"As in the days when you left Egypt, I will show you wonders."

—Micah, 7:15.

Alexandria, Virginia (August 29, 2007)–That there would be no court-martial did not surprise Win Fogerty. The speed with which the Navy disposed of him did. Less than two weeks later he was back home in Alexandria, Virginia, as if flung ashore by a breaker rising suddenly from a calm sea. Fogerty sat in the perennially bright breakfast nook of his small, well-appointed home on Vassar Road, the robin's-egg blue ceramic floor tiles sparkling with reflected sun from the jealousy windows on three sides. He sipped fresh-brewed coffee and read the morning's Washington Post, smiling in spite of himself at the paper's misguided analysis of the meaning of Col. Abner Samuels' death.

Fogerty had received "administrative sanction," an obscure regulation under which the judge advocate general ordered his reduction in rank to captain, a fifty percent cut in his pension, termination of all base privileges and immediate "retirement"–with the requirement Fogerty not discuss publicly the matters leading to his separation from the service. Violation could lead to reopening his case, court-martial, imprisonment, complete elimination of his pension, and so on. So he was now 62, a civilian, unemployed, and in de jure disgrace. De facto, he was a hero to many. Compared to the Jews, he mused as he read Washington's rejection of Jerusalem's nuclear ultimatum, he was doing fine.

Still, Fogerty thought, Samuels had it at least half-right: given the proper materiel–which, with proper planning, could be obtained–the Jews would rise once more. Provided they wanted to, provided they had the will. In that mood the ex-admiral's eyes ran across a brief item noting that "Rabbi Jeri Levi, host of WBLS Radio's weekly 'Jewish Renewal' program, will give a second public sermon, 'Israel, the Jews and America: Triple Crisis,' Sunday evening at 7:30 p.m. in the rehearsal theater of Northern Virginia Community College, Alexandria campus...." He made a note to attend.

In her DuPont Circle apartment–a narrow basement conversion shared with two other young women–Lorraine Lansky also read the Post that morning. She had decided not to study for her international relations course at Johns Hopkins

School for Advanced International Studies nearby on Massachusetts Avenue until after her shift as a part-time waitress at Bullfeathers. Glancing across the photo of Samuels her eyes suddenly stopped. You fool, she reproached herself. You served this drunk just before he got himself shot at the White House. Lansky stared at the picture, her model's face contorted by the concentration of her mind's raw ambition. You won't be the next Hillary Clinton if you can't put it together faster than this, she muttered.

Because there in the background, she saw another face, of the man Samuels had been talking with, arguing with in Bullfeathers that afternoon. She read the cutline: Col. Abner Samuels, testifying before the House International Operations Committee shortly before his death. In the background, Acting Chairman Rep. Ignatius Kowalsky (D-Ill.) and Rep. Jonathan Marcus (D-Va.).

Bingo! Lorraine Lansky thought. I've found my ticket; I'm going to work for the International Operations Committee, for Rep. Jonathan Marcus. She leaped up and began to brush her long, thick blonde hair–a reflex action in moments of deep satisfaction.

The response to Rabbi Levi's second sermon without a congregation was even more spectacular than the first. In fact, it was a riot.

An hour before the scheduled start, throngs of people jammed the building that housed the rehearsal theater and spilled onto the sidewalk beyond. Parking space in a nearby campus lot and on adjacent side streets vanished. People began to leave their vehicles on sidewalks in front of closed shops. License plates from the District of Columbia and Maryland, as well as Virginia, and even a few from Pennsylvania, Delaware, New Jersey and New York were evident. Loudspeakers were installed hastily in front of the building. Police arrived to clear the street of pedestrians and parked cars. Nearly one thousand people were on hand.

Some had come because of the earlier coverage. Some responded to Jeri Levi's own publicity campaign. Others had heard by Internet word-of-mouth. Many outraged Jews attended as a protest over the Johnston administration's announcement that it had frozen Israeli economic assets in the United States "pending Israel's agreement to the final ceasefire and reparations plan." And others, perhaps surprised at themselves, came hoping to hear what they prayed might be the voice of God, a word to re-ignite the fire of faith from spiritual ash.

"It is true," Jeri Levi began, "that in many places and times Jews were forbidden to arm themselves, or keep arms they had acquired previously. Unarmed, concentrated in Jewish villages or outright ghettos, outnumbered, and psychologically crippled by our insistence on the sanctity of life and therefore reluctant to acknowledge the periodic necessity to take it–to kill or be killed–Jews made tempting targets.

"When we seemed too strong–as at York in 1190–first we were barred from possessing weapons; then the massacres began. When we seemed weak from the start–as in Kishinev in 1903, the pogrom could be planned, the hand-wringing afterward piteous.

"But when, like after Kishinev, we stopped trusting in others and only in God–I mean trusting in God without assisting Him, without working as His partner in repairing this world–and we armed and organized in self-defense, something happened. The next attack cost those who would shed Jewish blood some of their own. And enthusiasm for Jewish slaughter declined.

"It was a lesson the Jews who built Israel had learned from the anti-Nazi partisans, a lesson the still uncertain American Jews of the '30s and '40s understood–but rarely acknowledged–in the swagger of the Jewish gangsters, the Murder, Incorporated partners of the Mafia. It was a lesson those who lost Israel forgot. The world's post-'67 sympathy for the Arabs, at Israel's expense, the insistence that Israeli retaliation for Arab terrorism was itself aggression should be understood in part as the age-old rejection of the Jew's right to self-defense.

"The Israelis' increasing doubts about using force was itself a reemergence of the galut's skewed emphasis on the sanctity of human life–sacred, absolutely, but not one's enemy over oneself. This tension led to the denial by many that they had enemies.

"So Israel, especially its opinion-molding elites, became more like pre-war European Diaspora than its antidote. So the old conditionality of diaspora Jewish life–murder had been a leading cause of death for a millennium–returned. Meanwhile, if in Europe before 1939, in the Soviet Union before 1967, we were the Jews of silence, then in America, since 1967, we haven't stopped talking–and the din of a million monologues, a thousand tiny particularisms praised as pluralism, drowned perception.

"Now is the moment for unity, the last moment. It's time for an end to Reconstruction, Reform, Conservative, Orthodoxy. We no longer need–in fact, we suffer from–an intra-communal democracy that, like the last Israeli Knessets, is functional anarchy. No more the American Jewish Committee, the American Jewish Congress, the American Israel Political Action Group, Agudath Israel, the American Zionist Federation, the Zionist Organization of American, B'nai B'rith, Hadassah, the National Council of Jewish Women, Jewish Women International, Na'amat Women, Mizrachi Women, the National Conference on Soviet Jewry, the Union of Councils for Soviet Jewry, the Student Struggle for Soviet Jewry, the American Association for Ethiopian Jewry, the North American Association for Ethiopian Jewry, Jewish War Veterans, the Union of American Hebrew Congregations, the United Synagogue of Conservative Judaism, the Union of Orthodox Jewish Congregations, the United Jewish Communities, Israel Bonds, the Jewish National Fund, the New Israel Fund, Americans for Peace Now, Americans for a Safe Israel and all their scores of splintered offspring.

"Enough! Now is the time for Judaism and the Jews! Now, as at Sinai, is the time to do, and to listen. As one people. The Jewish people. Am Yisrael Chai! The Jewish people lives!"

Jeri Levi cried out with a hoarse masculine power that startled herself and all who heard her. Then, in a quieter, softer voice, almost her own, she concluded: "The Baal Shem Tov, Master of the Good Name and founder of Chasidism, said three hundred years ago that 'forgetfulness leads to exile, while remembrance is the secret of redemption.' Barely a generation ago, when he was freed from the prison that was Soviet Russia, Yosef Begun said, 'we must not forget those still waiting to be free.... Not to forget, that is the main thing.'

"Not to forget, that without the Jewish land, the Jewish people can live only stunted, unfulfilled. That without fulfillment–without repairing the world, starting by healing ourselves on our own land–we cannot be redeemed. And without the example of Jewish redemption the world will lose the light of salvation, the light it desperately needs.

"'And let Jerusalem be rebuilt speedily in our day, and Zion thy habitation... Thy children will become a nation great and might, their seed like stars in the illimitable heavens.'"

Applause and shouts from many, jeers from others, silence from more than a few greeted Rabbi Levi's pronouncement.

"The woman is mad... raving mad," said a middle-aged man to his companion.

"Maybe," smiled Wingate Fogerty, who had been standing nearby at the back of the hall. "However, she's absolutely right."

Police tried to disperse the crowd, futilely. Scores of people surged toward the front of the theater, threatening to trample those in the first rows.

Jonathan Marcus too was in attendance. He was present, he told himself, out of simple curiosity and his need to be out of his wife Madeline's presence. In her self-justifying anger at him she insisted that she could not fathom "what all the shouting over Israel is about. Jews have always lived in the Diaspora. What difference does it make now?"

Marcus found himself pushing to get to Rabbi Levi. On the street across from the campus theater, a claque of Indochinese youths, attracted by the crowd, heard the finish of the speech over loudspeakers. "Go home, Jews!" one shouted. "Get out of our neighborhood! Go back to where you belong, back to Bethesda!"

A knot of neo-Nazi skinheads on the opposite side of the street took up the chant: "Jews out! Jews out! To the showers!" They began throwing rocks, at the people outside Rabbi Levi's speech and at the Indochinese.

A brick smashed a plate glass window in the auditorium lobby. Some who had been listening to the speech outside charged the skinheads, overrunning the few police standing between them. The skinheads ran, but one tripped and went sprawling. Before he could regain his footing a dozen Jews set upon him with feet and fists.

Warning shots were fired. By the time police restored order the youth lay in an ambulance and a quartet of Jews sat handcuffed in the backs of patrol cars. Sirens screeched as the vehicles pulled away. Diagonally across the corner from the auditorium in which Rabbi Levi had spoke, Franks', a neighborhood carry-out, was ablaze.

Marcus was stunned. The future had arrived even faster than he expected, and right before his eyes. And what a speech! Twenty years and more in the House and he had never energized an audience like that, and neither had any of the other members, except perhaps Rep. Alim Abdul Kareem (D-N.J.).

Marcus pushed into the small backstage area. Jeri Levi slumped on a metal folding chair, one arm over Jason. Near her stood a middle-aged, clean shaven man, holding Deborah's hand. He wore a dark suit, open-collared white shirt, and non-descript black tie shoes. He issued commands that no one heeded.

"Get the rabbi a glass of water," he told someone. "Open the window," he told someone else. "Let's get some fresh air in here. Her color doesn't look too good."

No one paid attention. People milled about the rabbi, trying to converse with her, complimenting her on the speech. Levi, exhausted, mumbled her thanks. The children seemed frightened.

"You heard the man—the rabbi needs something to drink. Right now! And she needs fresh air," Marcus bellowed. That got their attention. "I'm Representative Jonathan Marcus, and if you want to help the rabbi, please clear out now." His authoritative manner, a combination of innate personality plus years of deferential treatment as a member of Congress, got results. He sent one woman for water, and instructed two men to open the back windows, which they did. Most of the others departed.

"Thank you, congressman" said the man in the dark suit. "I'm Jerry O'Malley, of WBLS Radio."

"My pleasure," Marcus replied.

"I'm a little surprised to see you here," O'Malley continued. "But then, I'm a little surprised at seeing about half the people who showed up."

"You work with Rabbi Levi?" Marcus asked.

O'Malley hesitated, then said, "I thought so, at first. But judging from the response, my station and I might just be along for the ride."

"What do you mean?"

"I've been in religious broadcasting for thirty years—starting with Jerry Falwell and the Moral Majority in Lynchburg—but I've never seen anyone generate such enthusiasm, and hostility, so quickly. Why, not long ago she was virtually unknown outside her own synagogue. Now she doesn't even have a pulpit but she's drawing people from five states, on a Sunday night, and causing a riot for good measure. If Jews didn't have a revival circuit before, they do now."

A revival circuit! Marcus felt a thrill of recognition. This Rabbi Levi could be the key, or one of them. To what, he wasn't quite sure, not yet. "Besides you and the kids passing the hat, is there any organization behind her?"

"None," said O'Malley. "Why?"

"Because, Brother O'Malley," Marcus said, putting an arm on the other's shoulder, "you've discovered the Jewish Billy Graham, and not a moment too soon. You had a small crowd last week, a small riot tonight. Rabbi Levi has struck a chord; to play a symphony, she'll need an organization. If you don't mind, I'm going to give you the names of two people to call first thing tomorrow. They'll help you help Rabbi Levi put together a team, a good one, in a hurry. It'll be good for her, good for the Jews, good for WBLS."

"You're on," O'Malley replied enthusiastically, taking the congressman's card, on the back of which Marcus had written the names and telephone numbers of his long-time campaign fund raiser and manager.

*　*　*

Jericho (September 11, 2007)—Mahmoud Terzi smiled once more into a multitude of adoring lenses. Digital, video, even a few older motor-driven thirty-five mil-limeter cameras–a swarm of photographic locusts consumed the moment so thoroughly their images would never be able to explain what it really had meant. The cameramen and women, from dozens of countries, veterans of a score of wars and revolutions, of natural and man-made disasters, captured everything in front of them and missed everything outside that narrow field of vision, every-thing beside or behind. The camera never lies, but it has such a hard time telling the truth, the whole truth. And so the pictures, still and action, beamed the pre-meditated tableaux around the world, illustrating once more the oxymoron called breaking news.

With a nod and a flourish Terzi cut the four intertwined ribbons–black, red, green and white, the colors T. E. Lawrence, the British Lawrence of Arabia, had chosen so long ago for the imperially designed flags of the Arabs' colonially designed nations and now the colors for, among others, Syria, Iraq, Jordan and Palestine. As the severed strands fluttered down, Terzi said, "I now proclaim this the Muammar Ghadafy Bridge and open it to the traffic of the united east and west banks of the Jordan, to the people of the Palestine Arab Islamic Republic!"

Applause rolled over him, from residents of nearby Jericho, from members of the diplomatic corps, even from some of the reporters themselves, a few of the oldest ones whom he had known ever since the retreat from Beirut in 1982. With the support of Yacoub al-Masri, the "spiritual leader" or imam of Palestine, his own omnipresent mukhabarat or secret police, and money from the European Union and the Americans, consolidating his grip over what had been Jordan, the West Bank, Gaza Strip, eastern and central Jerusalem, eastern Galilee and much of the Negev continued smoothly. Confederated with the new Islamic Republic of Syria under the slogan of "two countries, one people," Terzi was a leader to be reckoned with around the world. So the news media proclaimed. Yet they did not report, did not know, that he felt not a bit secure. How could he, not really know-ing if General Rifaat Habib in Damascus plotted against him, if al-Masri with his Khomeini cowboys in every school and mosque was his titular holy man or if he himself was al-Masri's political figurehead? He could not be sure even of his own secret police; C.I.A. trained, they seemed hesitant, excessively gentle. How he missed the Soviets, and especially the Jewish trainers in the East German secret police. Now there was a properly ruthless, utterly doctrinaire little bunch of Marxists! Ah, the world had changed, and not always to the liking of the leader the Palestinians called "the Old Man."

"We rename this the Ghadafy Bridge to honor our great Brother Leader, hero and comrade of all the Arabs. We blot out the name Allenby, and with it some of the last legacies of imperialism. At the same time, as Imam al-Masri has told you, we are renaming the Abdullah Bridge in honor of that great source of inspiration to all Muslims, Ayatollah Khomeini.

"We pledge, as president and imam, that the Palestine Arab Islamic Republic, confederated with the Islamic Republic of Syria and Lebanon, will be a strong, democratic and peace-loving member of the Arab and Muslim worlds, of the Arab League, the Conference of Islamic Nations and of the United Nations. We vow to remain in the vanguard of the struggle against the enemies of Arabism and

Islam! Our jihad for peace will be unrelenting. It is a revolution until victory!"

"He'd be hell at a shopping center opening, wouldn't he?" said U.S. Rep. Ignatius Kowalsky, head of the congressional delegation at the ceremony, wiping sweat from his reddening forehead with a handkerchief. "No doubt," replied G. Grace Pittson, newly-promoted from assistant secretary of state for Near Eastern and South Asian Affairs to deputy undersecretary of state, the department's third highest post. "Shopping center openings are one reason I entered the foreign service, not politics."

It was still hot, very hot, later that night when al-Masri, who had stayed behind in sleepy little Jericho when Terzi returned to Jerusalem, stepped into the private office of the head of Palestinian security in the Jordan Valley. A few blocks to the north lay Tel Jericho, the site first excavated by Dame Katherine Kenyon late in the nineteenth century, then in 1931 by John Garstang who determined that, yes, the city had burned and its walls collapsed around 1400 B.C.E. Travelers from around the world disembarked daily from their air conditioned buses, climbed the ancient mound and stared into the archaeologists' old slit trenches. From those gashes in the earth had come evidence of more than twenty separate civilizations, stretching back eight thousand years. Human beings had begun to settle at the oasis of Jericho not long after the end of the last ice age, leaving cave homes and nomadic hunting for houses and agriculture, for the protection and surplus grain the new way of life provided, for the writing and civilization it made possible. In honor of that true revolution in human history, a steady stream of tourists had come from around the world, looked, photographed, and tossed their cigarette butts, empty film canisters and soda cans into the trenches.

Twenty civilization, eight thousand years, leading inexorably to the glory that would be the new caliphate, the reunited, renewed Arab Islamic Middle East, thought Yacoub al-Masri.

"Well, what does the Old Man know?" he asked Jibril Dahlan, regional mukhabarat chief.

"No more than we want him to," said Dahlan. "He believes that the real Muslim Brotherhood leadership is in custody and that he calls the shots. He's insecure, yes, but who wouldn't be in his shoes? Still, he thinks he's watching you, not the other way around."

"And Gen. Habib?"

"He cannot be fooled. Neither can his inner circle, including security, be easily compromised."

"Every man can be fooled!" al-Masri thundered. "Every man who badly wants something he suspects he might never get, can be fooled–briefly but thoroughly–when it appears that object is suddenly, temporarily, in reach. In such moments, even wise men gamble, make themselves vulnerable, and fall."

Stunned at this outburst, Dahlan asked, "Every man?"

"Almost," amended al-Masri, thinking of himself. "What of the war criminals, Simon Tov and Sarid?"

"Consulting their U.N.-provided lawyers."

"Fine–so long as the result is as we discussed."

"It will be."

Al-Masri thought for a moment, then went on: "After their trials, only two more people will stand in our way—Terzi and Habib. Terzi, we know, will succumb to natural causes, a result of his many medical problems. Problems, ironically, made worse by his medication." Al-Masri laughed. "Habib we will buy or eliminate. It must be done. Then we will absorb the rest of Zionist-occupied Palestine and restore the caliphate.

Much had changed for Yacoub al-Masri over the years, as he went from teenaged guerrilla to American college student to holy revolutionary and Palestinian leader. His physical strength and appeal, his phenomenal memory and capacity if not for intellectual growth then for sheer learning and, above all, his monomanical focus brought him ever-greater influence and power. But one thing had not changed; the bloodshed that followed him like a tail to a comet.

Yacoub al-Masri was satisfied—not pleased, but satisfied—with Jibril Dahlan's report. Never patient, a visionary interested in the present only in so far as it led to the future he meant to mold, al-Masri had been compelled by the imposed end of the War of Arab Unity to bide his time. He did so now, resting in the cool, date palm-shaded villa his family had owned in Jericho for generations. Nearby were similar winter homes of the Jabari, al-Husseini, Nusseibah and Nashashibi clans, the families that had led the Arabs of Palestine for centuries now—under the Turks, the British, the Jordanians and even the Israelis. Now, he told himself again, they all would be under him, under the al-Masris.

Sometimes cooperating, more often competing, earlier aligned with the pretentious Hashemites in Jordan, lately more affiliated with the thuggish nationalists of the Palestine Liberation Organization, but always maintaining an air of nobility other Palestinians could not bring off, the clans influenced events even when they did not determine them. As it had in the beginning, with the British-appointed mufti, Haj Amin al-Husseini, so it was now in the end: the clans' tradition of leadership, combined with Islamic fervor and Arab nationalism, was embodied in one person—Yacoub al-Masri himself.

"It'll work, you'll see," a much-younger al-Masri had insisted. His companions that day in 1981 were not so sure.

"Look, others have done it before and not been caught. How better to strike a blow for the revolution, for our people? You want to fight the Israelis, right? I'm telling you rocks and firebombs alone will never drive them out. But this is how we can be heroes...."

His four friends shifted uneasily. They stood on a narrow side street off Faisal Boulevard, the main thoroughfare through the jumble of Nablus' central business district. A few blocks away the small green and gold dome of the Masri mosque gleamed in bright sunlight.

"You make it sound possible, easy even," said Ali Heikmat. "But your words are, Yacoub, still words. It's one thing for us to talk about 'liquidating' a Zionist soldier. It's another for us to do it. Most who try are arrested. We all know there are collaborators everywhere. And even if we succeed, the Israelis are likely to trace us and, even if we get away, bulldoze our families' houses."

"No one is forcing you, Ali," al-Masri said evenly. "The revolution is democratic. Each fighter must decide for himself. If you are afraid, okay. The rest of us

Total Jihad

will just have to struggle harder to make up for you. And, you know, some have succeeded already..."

Ali Heikmat looked downcast, but said nothing more.

"Has Fatah authorized this?" asked another of the young men.

"Of course," said al-Masri. "They sought me out after my return from America. Besides, aren't we all Fatah?"

Al-Fatah, the Movement for the Total Liberation of Palestine, was the largest of the Palestine Liberation Organization's eight often feuding factions. Fatah, the PLO mainstream–founded in the 1950s by Yasir Arafat (Abu Amar) himself along with Farouk Khaddoumi (Abu Luft), the Arab-assassinated Abu Iyad (Salah Khalaf) and the Israeli-assassinated Abu Jihad (Khalil al-Wasir)–later would belong to Mahmoud Terzi. Its cells dotted the West Bank and Gaza Strip, its Tanzim militia and al-Aksa Martyrs Brigade led the intifada in 2000-2002 and its shabib youngsters threw the rocks and took the Israeli bullets for both intifadas. But its on-again, off-again talks and security cooperation with the Israelis undermined it with the Palestinian "street," opening the way for the Palestinian opposition–Hamas (the Islamic Resistance Movement) and Islamic Jihad for Palestine, those who cheered bin-Laden when Arafat, for temporary cover when America was bombing other terrorists, bade them be quiet.

But al-Masri lied that day; no one had contacted him about organizing a commando and he did not plan to inform anyone else. Even before accepting a PLO scholarship for college in America, al-Masri had begun to doubt Arafat's organization, to wonder if Fatah ever could accomplish its stated goals. For more than a quarter century it had led the Palestinian Arabs from one defeat to another, claiming each new setback as another step on the victory march. As it accumulated international support and its leaders jetted from one capital to another, the Israelis gobbled up more Palestinian land, the people suffered new and endless humiliations. Meanwhile, the Zionists grew stronger, forced peace onto Egypt, brought in more accursed immigrants, built up their cities and farms, expanded their settlements. The PLO boasted of returning to Jaffa when it did not even control Faisal Boulevard in Nablus. Its leaders were famous, their pictures on the front pages of newspapers around the world. Famous, he began to think, not like revolutionaries, not like holy men, but like movie stars or Mafia chiefs.

He had an alternative, one he had been considering even before his semester at Georgetown University. If the old enthusiasm for the PLO, which by his youth flowed to further left factions like the Democratic Front for the Liberation of Palestine or to religious fundamentalists like the old Muslim Brothers or newer incarnations such as Hamas, could be fused under a new generation of leaders, the ground really could be made to shake–first under the feet of the ineffectual Palestinian establishment, second under that of the Israelis....

They finished their drinks, Kinley lemon and Queen's orange–soda brands that long had survived the British Mandate–and smashed the bottles against a nearby building. With the exception of Ali Heikmat, they agreed to join al-Masri. And when Ali's eyes would not meet his own, Yacoub knew that his childhood friend would have to make way for the revolution.

A few days later al-Masri rode an early morning bus west out of Nablus and across the old green line to the Israeli town of Kfar Saba. The trip took about forty-five minutes, with stops. He looked like any other Arab making the routine journey to the labor exchange in hope of being hired by an Israeli contractor for the day or the week. But once in Kfar Saba he split from the others.

Instead of going to the exchange he stopped at a hardware store and bought a large push broom. A few blocks on he began to push his way down a quiet residential sidewalk until he found what he was looking for—a car with yellow-and-black Israeli license plates and keys in the ignition. Seeing no one, al-Masri tossed the broom into the back seat and jumped behind the steering wheel. The car, a yellow Subaru 1300, was perfect. A make and model then popular all over Israel, it was not conspicuous. Bigger than another popular model, the Fiat 127, it made execution of his plan possible.

He drove unhindered through Qalqilya, the big Arab town just a half-kilometer east of Kfar Saba over the green line in the West Bank and continued past Karnei Shomron, a cursed affluent little settlement of Jewish commuters atop a small promontory—the Horns of Samaria—and back into Nablus. It took him barely twenty minutes. He hid the car in an abandoned garage close enough to his parents' house that he could keep an eye on it. Then he waited.

The next day's Hebrew papers carried a few paragraphs on the disappearance. Included was police speculation that an Arab-Jewish auto theft ring known to be operating in the Tel Aviv area had expanded northward. For years Arab and Jewish gangsters had cooperated in smuggling drugs and arms, and with Israeli tariffs doubling the price of automobiles, in the profitable trade of car heists and resale. Fine, thought al-Masri. Let them think so.

The following Saturday night four of them—Ali Heikmat pleaded illness—drove out of Nablus on the northwest road toward Tulkarem, another old Jordanian border town above Qalqilya and about ten miles inland from Netanya and the coast. There they expected to find Israeli soldiers at bus stops along the main highways, looking for rides to get back to their camps after spending shabbat at home.

They were not disappointed. Just west of Tulkarem a lone trooper stood in front of a dimly lit stop that served Moshav Nitzanei Oz, a long walk down the lane from the highway. His rifle was propped against the concrete block shelter and his duffle bag stood next to him in the stand. He had his arm out, index finger pointing toward Netanya.

Al-Masri slowed to a stop and in his best street Hebrew—he had been brushing up all week—said, "Need a lift? Hop in."

The soldier, a boy of about nineteen, hard and rangy-looking but beardless, hesitated. Something was not right. There were four people in the car already—they really did not have room for a fifth. And they were all men, about his own age. He could not be sure in the dimness, but they could as easily be Arabs as Sephardi Jews.

Sensing the soldier's anxiety, al-Masri said in an off-hand way, "Do you want a ride or not? We're in a hurry."

The soldier already had noticed the Israeli plates on the car, not the blue-and-black of the West Bank or silver-and-black of the Gaza Strip. And he was the one in a real hurry; he needed to report back at base before midnight. What the hell, he said to himself, griping his rifle and hoisting his duffel bag, "yehiyeh b'seder," it'll be okay. Yehiyeh b'seder, expressing the Hebrew equivalent of the British reassurance that "we'll muddle through regardless" was a cocky—or resigned—Israeli motto in those days, a national mantra. Yitzhak Rabin himself would complain, too late, that it was an anesthetic that smoothed the way from one short-sighted decision to the next.

The soldier climbed in, taking a seat behind the front passenger, and al-Masri accelerated back onto the road, still headed west, further into the ten mile wide spine of Israel north of Tel Aviv.

In an instant the two Arabs in back moved hard against him, pinning the soldier against the inside of the right rear door. He struggled to open it, but as he did the passenger in front climbed halfway around the seat and lunged at him with a butcher knife, striking a glancing blow across the shoulder.

They were piled together and the soldier could not bring his rifle up from the floor. He felt pain burning through his shoulder even before the one with the knife lunged again. And in the back of his mind he realized too that the driver was turning the car around, away from the Jewish coast and pointing east toward the Arab hills.

"Again! Again!" al-Masri shouted from the driver's seat. And the knife struck a second time, more painful than the first. But this time the point of the blade hit the collar bone and skittered along the rib cage. The blow did not halt the struggle.

"Hold him! Hold him, you idiots!" al-Mari urged, his foot on the accelerator, his hands fighting the wheel around a curve. The pair in back seemed to double their efforts, pinning the soldier for a moment to the back of the seat. He saw the blade flash again, filling his consciousness, as if the entire universe had now, for him, been reduced to this. He jerked to the right.

"Aaugh!" cried one of his captors. The momentum of the knife-wielder in front carried the blade into his compatriot's upper arm. The latter screamed and, for a moment, the soldier was free. He pulled the door latch and rolled out of the speeding vehicle, the wounded assailant under him.

"Damn it!" al-Masri shouted. "Now we've got to stop. This wasn't in the plan!"

The Subaru screeched to a halt, half off the two-lane blacktop road. Behind them to the west were fields and, just visible, a few lights from the soldier's home village, Nitzanei Oz. Ahead of them, only a few hundred meters, was Tulkarem. A car or bus might pass, or even a jeep from the Israeli border police.

"Find them, find them!" al-Masri urged, in a hoarse, excited voice. Almost immediately they stumbled onto Hindawi. His body lay in a heap at the edge of the road, just above a small ditch.

"He's neck is broken," al-Masri said, suddenly composed. "C'mon. We've got to find the Jew!"

"But he might still be alive," started one of the others.

"Hindawi? He's dead... like we'll be if we don't find the Jew." Then al-Masri had a second thought. "No, put Hindawi's body in the trunk, and jack up the car like we're changing a flat. If anyone comes, tell them we don't need help. I'll find the Jew myself. Now hurry!"

Al-Masri grabbed a large flashlight from under the dash and hastily began to track the splotches of crimson that that led away from the road and into a field of cotton. For a ghastly moment he thought the soldier might get away, that this beginning of his revolution also would mark its end. Then, hearing a noise, an animal-sounding thrashing, he took heart. His quarry could not be far.

The soldier, seeing, feeling his life spurt from the slashed artery in his shoulder, his heart beating faster and faster, fainter and fainter, felt dread, and urgency. God, let me kill them, he prayed.

Al-Masri found him, slumped in a semi-seated position, one hand draped across the barrel of his rifle, the other fallen under the ammunition magazine he had been trying to load. The right side of the trooper's uniform was olive drab. The top, left part of his fatigue shirt was a dark, wet umber. Yes, Yacoub al-Masri thought, Jews are much harder to kill in Palestine than in America. But it can be done in either place.

On a rocky hilltop just west of Nablus they poured gasoline over the car and, with the bodies of the Israeli and Hindawi inside, set it ablaze. Quickly they made their way down a timeworn shepherd's path to the city, pausing only once to look behind them at the pyre glowing against the black sky of Samaria.

"The city will not be safe for us now."

"No, Abdul Salam, it won't. That's why were going to my cousin's in Tubas, tonight. Go home, get a change of clothes, some money and something to eat, and meet me in the garage in twenty minutes. Say nothing!"

Even with its 120,000-plus residents and warrens of alleys twisting off the central market into the old casbah, Nablus could not hid him now, al-Masri realized. He knew most of the secret places and, after so many years of occupation, so did the Israelis. So did their informers. With an Israeli soldier dead there would be no perfunctory investigation, not like the American consulate's after that incident in Washington. And once word got out—and it almost always did, as rumor if not fact—his family's competitors, the other clans, might be willing, at least indirectly, to make sure the Israelis knew whom to look for.

As for Ali Heikmat, al-Masri knew that he himself must cut out that tongue.

Tubas was a small Arab town about ten miles northeast of Nablus. Near it a series of steep, rocky ridges hid a number of small caves. Yacoub al-Masri knew the area from childhood hikes.

"We will hide in the caves, emerging only to continue the revolution," he told his companions as they set out. "From this night on we are no more just young men of Nablus. We are the New Palestine Islamic Army." As a sign of his undisputed leadership, al-Masri slung the slain soldier's M-16 over his shoulder, stuffed the extra ammunition magazines into the back pockets of his jeans and set out at the head of his three-man army.

Few people lived in the immediate area of their hideout. Those who did guessed that the newcomers were outlaws, on the run either from a clan quarrel or the detested Israelis. Two or three aided the strangers, providing food and information, asking no questions in return. Al-Masri learned that the Shin Bet had been to his parents' house. And he heard that Ali Heikmat had been held by investigators for several days, then released, haggard and bruised. He sent word through an eager young courier—one of several recruits to his growing band—for Heikmat to meet him.

"So Ali has been beaten," al-Masri told his companions. "No doubt he asked for it, to 'prove' the Israelis tortured him, that he was no informer. I would like to inspect those pretty injuries myself."

Ali Heikmat understood al-Masri's invitation. So the next morning he boarded a bus for the coast. He had with him all his savings, plus those of his family. He planned to go to Ben-Gurion Airport, and leave the country. He would fly to America, where he had relatives, and escape this madness. Jewish soldiers did it after they finished their army service, he knew. Why shouldn't he?

But at the first rural stop west of the city a group of young men boarded the bus. Ali Heikmat paled when he saw them. Neither Yacoub al-Masri nor his other companions from Faisal Boulevard were among them. Nonetheless, the exchange of glances told Ali who had sent them.

His body was dumped on the outskirts of Nablus a few days after, his tongue cut out. Less than twenty-four hours later Israeli soldiers returned to al-Masri's home, this time with a bulldozer. "Your son," the captain in charge told his father, reading from a paper, "is suspected of organizing the murder of Corporal Shai Waxman, 20, of the Israel Defense Forces, and of Ali Heikmat, 19, of Nablus. The evidence against him has been seen and accepted by the civil administration court for Nablus. So by order of the military governor of Samaria, pursuant to the relevant Israeli and British emergency regulations in effect since 1967 and 1936, respectively, we must now demolish your son's room. You have five minutes to remove any of your own possessions—not his—that might be damaged in the operation."

Yacoub al-Masri's father began to protest. "You have no right. This is our home, our land. My son is a good boy, quiet and respectful. You are spreading lies about him. He has not been arrested or tried and you want to punish my whole family! This is unjust!"

The captain, a professor of social work at Tel Aviv University performing his annual reserve duty, could not agree more. He'd heard it all before, a half-dozen times. And he was weary of the whole thing—at age 47, a little overweight and out of shape, still having to lead other reservists chasing teenaged stone-throwers down alleys, into traps where Molotov cocktails waited to explode in their faces; of parrying the taunts of academic colleagues as a "fascist occupier"; of anticipating that his own son would have to endure similar duty. All because of the Arabs' unreasoning refusal to behave like good Jews and grant him the peace he craved.

But he had his orders—and perhaps more to the point, his wife's parents still lived at Nitzanei Oz, and knew the Waxman family well. In a country as small as Israel, a country full of Jews, everyone knew everyone, or at least someone else who did. "I have just cited you the authority under which we act," the professor sighed. "And we are both old enough to know you are lucky we don't seal, or bulldoze, your entire house. And sir, if it happens that you do hear from your son, tell him never to return to Israel or the territories. If he does, we will find him and deal with him. I'm sure you understand."

Mohammed al-Masri understood. Deal with him—it was the Israeli's way of saying an eye for an eye. There would be no due process, not for Yacoub, just summary execution by undercover agents, perhaps some swarthy looking Jews from Arab lands, dressed as young Palestinians, maybe even as women, who would one day suddenly surround Yacoub on the street, open fire, then jump in a waiting car and speed off to the safety of Tel Aviv, a half hour away. Rough justice, as his son dealt them.

Mohammed al-Masri's wife was wailing now, a high keening sound. A daughter pounded her fists on the chest of an Israeli soldier. "Okay," said the captain flatly, gesturing to the bulldozer operator. "Let's go." The legal niceties having been observed, the bulldozer's engine growled and its blade angled up slightly. The machine clanked forward toward the house.

As the captain watched, the masonry room with its plaster and glass crashed down upon itself, the bulldozer's tracks crushing its contents. The officer wondered again: Should we level the whole damn city, just get the hell out, or both? Or maybe expel the Arabs and hold the place for our American cousins. Our distant cousins who keep their distance.

Thank God his annual four-week active duty stint was coming to a close. It was driving him crazy. As usual. He could not wait to go home—30 miles and a culture away—and take an endless hot shower. He wanted to wash away the grime of Nablus, at least that which was on his skin, if not the enervating ambivalence embedded in his soul.

News of the destruction reached Yacoub the next day. His band, now grown to ten, urged him to flee across the border into Jordan. And al-Masri knew that the ridges and caves where they had been hiding could never conceal them from determined searchers. He expected those searchers soon.

Yet he hated to leave the occupied homeland without putting the M-16 to use. In the late 1970s, it was easy enough for the PLO, Family Jihad members and others to get handguns and an occasional grenade, often by breaking into Israeli households, sometimes by buying them from Jewish criminals. But automatic weapons still were difficult for individual Palestinians to obtain within Israel or the territories. Here was an M-16 with two banana clips—more than one hundred rounds—a prize with which to strike a truly demoralizing blow against the Zionists. But how?

With no plan, but a deadly determination, al-Masri and his top lieutenants set off along a ridge track paralleling the road east toward the Jordan River Valley. The narrow valley, part of the great African-Syrian rift, ran south from Lebanon and Syria. It passed through northern Israel, along the eastern edge of the West Bank, to Jericho, the Dead Sea and through the Arava Valley to the Gulf of Eilat and the Red Sea, the lowest depression on the face of the earth thanks to the historic earthquake fault line beneath it.

The quartet moved a few kilometers a night between the green Jewish agricultural settlements planted in the arid rift after the '67 War. They made their way to within sight of the border. A chain link fence, a barrier of parallel lines of barbed wire and a smoothly swept sand patrol road marked the Israeli side.

Troops in jeeps checked it frequently. Electronic sensors also warned whenever intruders tried to penetrate. And Jordanian soldiers on the other side, under orders from Amman, restricted infiltration to Israel out of fear of disproportionate retaliation.

"Look," al-Masri told him companions. "We'll make it. Both the Israelis and Jordanians guard the fence by looking the wrong way, as far as we're concerned. The Israelis are looking east, to Jordan. And the Jordanians too watch the east, trying to catch any mujahedin coming from their side. We'll surprise them both from the west. And in the process, I think we'll have a chance to use this." He patted the M-16.

The quartet waited through the night. Just before dawn a chance came. Al-Masri was ready. As a three-man jeep patrol passed on the security road below him, he opened fire. The driver fell dead and the other occupants scattered, both wounded. Before reinforcements arrived, Yacoub al-Masri had managed to cross into Jordan, his companions with him. The legend of the New Palestine Islamic Army, and of its leader, began to grow....

...A half-dozen years earlier, not long after the 1973 October War, he had been marked for leadership. A PLO operative in Nablus, an uncle, recommended he enlist in the Fatah Cubs. This would be "the generation that will fly the Palestinian flag over the walls and minarets of Jerusalem," as Arafat, icon and pedophile—oft-recorded in the act by Romanian secret police on diplomatic visits to Ceausescu—flattered them. Fourteen-year-old Yacoub took to the organization quickly, naturally assuming leadership among his peers in Nablus. After he finished high school, a year early, came the scholarship to Georgetown. Like a thousand other young Palestinians—some as medical students-cum-guerrillas in Romania; some, a bit older, as terrorist leaders-in-training in East German secret police schools; others leading cross-border raids south from Lebanese camps into the "Zionist entity"; many in Kuwait and the other Persian Gulf oil emirates, working as engineers and accountants, organizing the revolution and its finances, quietly subverting the ruling al-Sabah family in favor of Iraq's Saddam Hussein—al-Masri was groomed for command a generation hence.

But unlike most, he progressed on parallel tracks. As Yacoub the Palestinian nationalist grew, Yacoub the Muslim believer matured. A loyal, even privileged PLO cadre, he began to seek out and study at the feet of fiery holy men. And on his own, he blended both streams. So it happened that in the fall of 1979, after a stellar freshman year at An-Najah University in Nablus, he entered Georgetown, a bright, intense, alienated sophomore.

"You are to study, organize and agitate—but above all, study," his former Fatah Cubs leader instructed him, the leader who had initiated him into sex and given him his nom de guerre, Abu Buraq. "You will be contacted by GUPS, the General Union of Palestinian Students. They will help you get acclimated. Money will be no problem, but behave wisely. Do not attract undue attention to yourself. Act, but listen more than you speak."

His uncle was right. GUPS, the PLO's overseas university student front, got in touch with him his first day in Washington, D.C. It took a week before he made contact with the Organization of American Muslim Students. He had seen the group's poster in the student union. While the GUPS emblem, like that of the PLO, showed all Palestine–Jordan, Israel, the West Bank and Gaza Strip as one–the OAMS logo featured a united Arab-Islamic nation, from Morocco through Iraq.

Yacoub was to stay at Georgetown a least one year, and perhaps three or more, to complete his undergraduate degree and, if his organizational work warranted, begin post-graduate studies. He lasted only a semester. He could not cope with America, with its bustling bigness, superficial informality, blatantly sexual public culture. To him it was alien, disgusting, threatening. Not one moment in the four months he spent at Georgetown did he feel at peace.

One December night after his last final examination for the term, he reluctantly agreed to join a group of celebrating classmates. He accompanied them, two other young men and three women, to a crowded restaurant on M Street, one popular with students, area young people and tourists alike. Actually more of a tavern–it featured drinks and dancing as much as food–Mr. Harry's was loud, smoky and close. Al-Masri sipped a soft drink as the others ordered round after round of beer and wine. "It is against my religion," he explained, when questioned.

Rock music pounded at his ears, its monotonous beat irritating him. A pall of cigarette smoke hung in the air, giving him a headache. He could not understand how his acquaintances enjoyed themselves so, and he resented them for it.

After an hour one couple left and another moved to the dance floor, permanently, it seemed. As if by prearrangement he found himself alone with the third girl, something he neither expected nor desired.

"Hi," she said when they were alone, leaning across the table to place her face close to his. "I'm Judy, Judy Melman. I'm from New York. I don't think we've ever really talked."

"I am Yacoub al-Masri," he said, drawing back as far as he could. "I am from Nablus in occupied Palestine."

Judy Melman ignored his physical retreat. She stretched further across the table, her sweater now tight against her chest. "Occupied Palestine? Far out! So you're an Arab?"

Stunned by the girl's enthusiasm and her naivete and befuddled by her femininity, her closeness, her smell, al-Masri barely managed a simple "yes."

"That's great!" she bubbled. "I've never met an Arab before, not to talk to, anyway. We had one as a guest speaker in poli. sci. last year–Hassan al-something–from the PLO's Washington office..."

"Hassan Abdul al-Rahman," al-Masri said.

"Right. Boy, was he boring. On and on about British imperialism, American imperialism, Zionist imperialism. I only remember that much because when I was a kid, my father bought a Chrysler Imperial once. It was a big car. Very comfortable. I love big, comfortable cars, don't you? I mean, leather seats are absolutely the best..."

He was unfamiliar with Chrysler imperialism, but not surprised that Americans would name a car after it. But before he could respond, she asked, "What kind of car do you have?"

"I have no car," he answered, confused and curious over the direction her conversation took. Nevertheless, he took the opening. "As for imperialism, the British…"

"Class is over," the girl said, looking directly into his eyes, her own laughing. She took his hand. "Let's dance."

"I do not dance," al-Masri answered. He made as if to withdraw his hand, but she gently tightened her grip. It was true. He had never danced before, not with a woman anyway. At weddings, with male cousins, in boisterous circle dances, but never with a woman, especially a strange woman. It was the kind of thing that could cause a fitna, a conflict among believers, set off by the natural seductiveness of women. The only woman he had ever embraced was his mother, and then only as a boy.

But still Judy Melman held his hand, and it was not unpleasant. He wondered, as he often did at Georgetown—so much so he was having trouble sleeping lately. He had begun to fear for his soul. And now this girl, a woman, really, so close, so fragrant, so warm. He felt strange—faint but not ill. Not ill at all.

"That's okay. We can do other things than dance, can't we?" the girl asked, scooping up their jackets and leading him toward the door. "We'll go for a ride in my car," she said, as if issuing an order.

Outside all sorts of people jammed the sidewalk. The bars, restaurants and stores beckoned. Multicolored lights flashed from a dozen windows. Cars inched along M Street, two lanes in each direction and bumper-to-bumper. People shouted at each other, sometimes good-naturedly, sometimes not. Someone tossed a half-empty beer can, sending a trail of spray arcing over the automobiles. The smell of hashish, what the Americans called marijuana, hung in vapor trails at certain spots along the walk. The little gilt dome of the Riggs National Bank at M and Wisconsin seemed to preside over the roistering. Al-Masri felt claustrophobic. He wanted to run away, back to his room, back to Nablus.

"Here's my car," the girl said, stopping at a white Porsche two-seater. She opened the door for him and al-Masri got in, anxious to escape the crowd. The young woman drove past the university and sped quickly out along Canal Road.

"Where are we going?" he asked, concerned. Although he was not frightened—certainly not by a woman—the strangeness of the situation and her sense of command confused him.

"Just a little way. I have a favorite spot near here. I think you'll like it too," she said, and squeezed his thigh. Then, driving with one hand, she began to rub his leg, rub the inside of his thigh, firmly, rhythmically.

An odd, warm sensation surged down from al-Masri's chest. Before he could gather his wits—and half his mind shouted silently to the girl, go on, go on—she veered off the road into a little picnic area along the Potomac River and the old Chesapeake and Ohio Canal. She stopped the car at the far end of the dimly-lit parking lot, slipping the small vehicle in behind some bushes.

"What…?" he started. Judy Melman stopped him. Somehow she had eased out from behind the wheel of the sports car and across the transmission hump until she practically straddled him. She kissed him and at the same time pulled his arms around her. Her kisses were not hard—Yacoub had imagined that a woman's kiss in passion would be hard, a heavy pressure on his lips. But Judy Melman's kisses were neither hard nor soft, but a delicious tender touch, warm and moist. More, her kiss was firm, intoxicating. Now the strangeness ceased to threaten; instead it invited him, compelled him to go on as her willing partner. He kissed her back, euphoria swirling through his mind.

She slid his hands onto her breasts and he eagerly squeezed and rubbed and squeezed again. How did he know to do this wondrous, wondrously right thing, he asked himself? Nothing in his inexperienced imagination prepared him for what the girl did next. With her lips still on his, her face nuzzling his cheeks, her hands deftly unzipped his blue jeans.

"God, I just love it in a car. I don't know why…" She breathed in a husky exhalation. With that she slid down and enveloped his now free, erect member with her mouth.

A great rush of sheer physical pleasure overcame al-Masri. Almost instantly hard spasms jolted him. And on some subterranean level, in some distant, sluggish voice, he heard himself thinking: I have been defeated. I was not strong enough. This demon-woman overcame me.

"Well, that was quick," the girl said. She smiled but al-Masri thought he heard a trace of reproach in her voice. "Now it's your turn," she added. Gently, expertly, she massaged his testicles even as his penis—formidable just moments before—softened.

"What are you waiting for?" she callenged.

"I…" he stammered.

Judy Melman began to laugh. "Don't tell me this is against your religion too, like booze. You may be circumcised but you definitely aren't Jewish!"

Jewish! Now he felt something more than defeat. He felt humiliation. All the novel sensations of forbidden pleasure vanished, replaced by the more familiar, deeper ones of rage. Judy Melman had time to stop laughing but not to start screaming before al-Masri's strong hands found her neck. She was a strong, solid girl, but no match for him, especially not when he was possessed by the fury he now felt.

He shoved the body back between the bucket seats. Breathing heavily, he moved behind the steering wheel and started the car. At first he drove aimlessly, erratically along the river. Shadows from the tall, overhanging trees, the bright, pinkish light from the high-intensity vapor lamps above the road and the glimmering reflections from the silt-laden river gave the route a dim, surreal aspect. But al-Masri mastered his panic and doubt.

Yes, he had done the right thing. The woman was really a devil, a Jewish devil, sent to test him. He had acted correctly. There could be no doubt.

Al-Masri found himself at a large interchange, and recognized his location. A plan forming in his mind, he turned up the ramp and onto I-495, the Capital Beltway. He drove north along the Maryland suburbs and then followed the I-270 spur northwest into the countryside. He had been this way on a ski outing with the same students he had joined in the tavern. Skiing also disturbed him. All the women in stretch pants, as if in public in their underwear, their hips audaciously outlined. And, of course, he hated the wet, cold slopes. Yet the exhilaration of swooping down even the gentle beginners' hill thrilled him. So liberating, so frivolous. He could not reconcile these threatening opposites, and rejected a second skiing invitation.

A few dozen miles beyond the Beltway in Maryland, between Gaithersburg and Damascus, he pulled the car to the side of the road, opened the boot and jacked up the Porsche as if to change a flat. Then, when no headlights or taillights showed along the expressway from either direction, he carried the body across a low fence and into a wooded area. He dropped the corpse into a deep, tree and shrub-lined ravine. Quickly he removed all clothing and jewelry. Nothing would be left to help with identification.

Finding a large rock, he smashed it into Judy Melman's face. He brought the stone down repeatedly, until the face, barely an hour before so expressive of a free, coarse sensuality, was unrecognizable. Then he used leaves, dirt, fallen branches and rocks to hide his work.

The drive back was uneventful. He parked the car on a side street blocks from campus and wiped his handkerchief across the steering wheel, gearshift, and door handles. He carried the girl's clothes in a gym bag he had found in the trunk and, holding it with the handkerchief, tossed the bag into a dumpster near the cafeteria, a dumpster he knew was emptied early every morning. Then he walked the rest of the way back to his dormitory.

The next morning he rode the Metro to National Airport and took his previously scheduled flight to New York, to connect with an El Al Israel Airlines plane to Tel Aviv and home for winter break. He would not return.

"I detest America," he told his PLO backers. "Besides, I am an activist, an organizer, not a propagandist. I will be much more valuable to you here, among our people."

To his father, and only to his father, he added, "There was some trouble with a Jew. I could not stay."

Yacoub al-Masri threw himself into his studies and his work for Fatah at An-Najah University. He finished his second year as he had his first—with excellent grades and growing influence among the young Palestinian nationalists. Only one incident marred his second semester:

A young man came up to Nablus one day from the American consulate in eastern Jerusalem, the facility many Israelis in those days derided as "the U.S. Embassy in Palestine" for its concentration on Arab affairs.

"Sorry to bother you, Mr. al-Masri," the junior diplomat said, "but I'm here on business. The consulate has instructed me to gather some information on a rather unpleasant matter. I would appreciate your assistance."

"Certainly," al-Masri replied. He sensed from the man's diffident manner that he did not relish his task and wished to complete the visit as soon as was seemly.

"Washington police cabled us, through the State Department, for some information regarding the disappearance of a Georgetown University student a few months back. From what other students have told police, you may have been the last person known to have seen her."

"Who is this person?" al-Masri asked evenly.

"A classmate of yours named Judy Melman. Apparently you and some other students went out with her after your final exams first term."

"Yes, we did. But I did not know her very well. It was a spur-of-the-moment thing, as you say, all of us wanting to relax after the tests."

"What exactly did you do?"

"Well, it's been a little while now, but as I remember, one couple left early...."

"That would be Kozu and Sandra?"

"Yes, and the others–Manute and Becky–were dancing. Judy said she wanted to get some fresh air and I did not like the smoke and noise anyway, so we went out onto the sidewalk. She saw some other students, friends of hers, and started talking with them. They said something about going to a party; I was tired and said goodnight and went back to my room at the dorm."

"Do you remember who the other students were?"

"Just some boys she seemed to know. I hardly knew the people I was with– we were just in class together, that's all."

"Did anyone see you go back to your dorm?"

"I suppose so. But I roomed alone, and the dorm already was partly empty from people who'd finished exams earlier and gone home, or on vacation."

"You had a scholarship for your first year, I believe. Why didn't you go back for the second term?"

"I did have a scholarship. But my English–reading and writing, not speaking–was not good enough yet for college work. I was only getting C's and B's, and I wanted to get all A's, or mostly A's. You see, I want to go to graduate school, maybe medical school, and I must have better grades than I was getting at Georgetown. I felt the language problem was interfering with my studies. And besides, I was very homesick, as you can imagine."

The junior foreign service officer, deputy information and cultural attache, always more comfortable outside America than in it, could not imagine, but said, "Of course, of course. Well, thank you very much. These matters can be so... discomfiting. Well, good-bye!"

"But wait," al-Masri said. "You implied that Miss Melman disappeared."

"Yes. She was supposed to join her parents at their winter home in Boca Raton, Florida, but never arrived. The D.C. police found her car near campus, but not Miss Melman. Most disturbing."

"Yes. Unfortunately, your country can be very dangerous, I was told."

"We do have our problems," the diplomat conceded. "Well, thank you for your help."

When he left al-Masri's father had said, "Graduate school?"

"Why not?" the son replied. "Perhaps in Islamic studies."

That was the last they spoke of Judy Melman. And when the older man stepped from the room, Yacoub al-Masri permitted himself a small, previously suppressed smile. So it really was that easy to kill an American. The country was so big, the people had so little in common, they did not take these matters personally. They grieved often but showed little outrage. No wonder a man could go for years killing dozens of young women in Los Angeles, and another do the same to young boys in Chicago and be caught only because of their own carelessness. No outrage, no thirst for revenge, not justice, not morality.

∗   ∗   ∗

Aleandria, Virginia (September 25, 2007)–"Hello, is this the Grill Room?"

"Yes, señor."

"Is Madeline Marcus there? This is her husband."

"One second, sir, and I'll check."

Congressman Jonathan Marcus looked at the clock again; it was nearly five. If Madeline was going to accompany him to the fund-raiser at the Key Bridge Marriott that evening she was cutting it close. And if she had spent the afternoon at the country club, taking the sun for her psoriasis and sipping a succession of frozen daiquiris she would be too woozy to be presentable. Just thinking about it made him angry, and he knew that was just what she intended.

"I do not see her, señor."

"That's okay, I think I hear her now," Marcus replied.

He listened to the whir of the mechanical garage door opener as Madeline pulled in. A moment later she walked into the family room. Not walked, really, not the resigned shuffle that marked her drunken depressions, but nearly marched. She stepped with an erect, crisp, almost confident gait he had not seen in years.

Her face was flushed; at first he attributed that to an afternoon at poolside.

"Are you going to be ready in time? The reception's at 6:30 –drinks and hors d'oeuvres, then introductions and speeches at seven. I know how much you dislike these things, but this is for the Northern Virginia Home Builders Association. A command performance…"

"Don't worry, Johnny," Madeline sang out. "I won't embarrass you. And we'll be there on time; 6:30 it is–and out by 7:45 for some real food."

Johnny? She hadn't called him that in years, and when she had, things had been different between them.

"Are you okay?" he asked. Madeline was often depressive, or behaved like one–but manic depressive? This was new.

"I'm better than okay, I'm fine," she declared. "Now I'm going to take a shower, and don't want to be disturbed. I do have a bit of a headache, so could you leave the aspirin on the counter in the bathroom?"

"Certainly," he said, going to fetch the aspirin bottle from the kitchen pantry.

She had left the bathroom door partly open, as was her habit. As Marcus dressed he watched the steam drift out toward the bedroom. Madeline always ran her shower water hot and hard, another reason she claimed she could not live in Israel: the pressure and the temperature of hot showers in her homeland, the water heated by roof-top solar collectors, were both too low.

He knew she liked the hot jets of water beating on her skin, on the red scales of the psoriasis and on the pores that never seemed to open enough to cool her. For the same reason she liked the bedrooms windows "cracked a bit for fresh air" in the dead of winter, when he wanted the house hermetically sealed and toasty warm. But today, he thought, she was in there way too long for the psoriasis. Way too long. As if she was not just washing her skin, but washing her soul, he mused. Could my wife be having an affair, he suddenly wondered. If so, with whom? And should he be jealous, or relieved?

"Jonathan, we've got to talk." It was Morty Halpern, speaking in a roaring whisper, tugging at his arm and leading him away from a knot of developers. "Excuse me a moment, gentlemen," Marcus said, nodding at Halpern in mock exasperation. "I'll be right back." Then, when the two of them were alone, the congressman spoke to his veteran fund-raiser with genuine exasperation.

"Morty, what's going on? We really need to work those guys. You, of all people, know that."

"What's going on is my question. Who the hell is this Rabbi Levi woman, and that jerk, O'Malley, from the Christian radio station? Jonathan, you're going to have a tight race next time, a tight one. We can't afford to waste time or money with these religious loonies."

In his second race, in 1988, when they had budgeted almost a quarter of a million dollars, Morty Halpern went out and, by pleading, badgering and charming a good part of the Washington Jewish community, collected nearly $500,000. As the price of television politics escalated in subsequent years Halpern never faltered. When he felt he had begun to tap the limits of the local Jewish and liberal monied establishment, he went national. He brought in stars from show business—political groupies of the first rank—to do a turn at fund-raisers. He invented the technique, quickly favored by Democratic senators including Kennedy and Metzenbaum, of turning openings at trendy art galleries into campaign solicitations. He auctioned the work of noted artists and siphoned part of the proceeds into campaign cofferes.

Halpern did not sell anything, at least nothing tangible. No quid pro quo, no violation of federal election laws or congressional ethics, as defined by the members of Congress themselves. Nothing like that. Instead, he offered the intimation—certainly not a promise—of access to, not influence over, Marcus. Of course, by supporting the congressman, by opposing whatever threat to enlightened government and their own tax breaks the benighted Republicans might throw up, they were, Morty Halpern told them, fighting the good fight. Halpern sold donors on the idea that it was their duty, it was the highest form of political activity and civic virtue to give and give big to Jonathan Marcus. The honor would be theirs—especially if they gave more than their business or social rivals. By the time Morty Halpern finished with a prospect, the question was not "Why should I give?" but rather, "How much do you need?"

So Halpern felt fairly certain he could raise money for this Levi woman. The question was, why should he? How would it help Jonathan?

"Jonathan, every buck I get for this yenta rabbi is a dollar out of your till next year. What's the hook?"

Halpern, who ran a medium-sized advertising agency when not raising money for Marcus, never asked about ideology or philosophy, or even congressional log-rolling. At least, not directly. Instead, when dealing with motivation, in marketing or politics, he always looked for "the hook."

"The hook, Morty, is that she can do things in her way that I can't in mine.

144   *Total Jihad*

Things that need to be done now. You read the papers, see the television. Events are going against us. And I don't just mean Israel," Marcus interrupted himself.

He knew that Halpern, like his congressional chief of staff and campaign manager Mona Margolis, belonged to the majority of American Jews. The unaffiliated, reflexive majority. Members of no congregation, no Jewish social organization, never visitors to Israel. These were the people for whom Jewishness was an abiding but peripheral sentiment, Judaism an insubstantial curiosity. This flaw running through their own identity enabled them to look down on the non-Jewish world surrounding them (Halpern, asked to describe a Jewish home, sometimes joked, "the one with books in the living room") while schizophrenically embracing it. It left them unable to articulate a reasoned argument against intermarriage to their children, and freed the latter from any vestigial bonds of Jewish peoplehood. Hence the transformation of American Jews from deep-rooted ethnic group to a multi-faceted do-it-yourself religion. This left them, they believed, every bit as American culturally as Southern Baptists, pork rinds and stock cars aside.

In short, Halpern's attitudes were much like Marcus' own had been until, as a junior member of the International Operations Committee—then known as Foreign Affairs—he finally had toured the Middle East. In Israel for only the second time, and the first in many years, Marcus felt a powerful sense of belonging, of familiarity even though he spoke no Hebrew and knew next to nothing of that half of the culture which was Sephardi—Jews of Middle Eastern background. It was not so much coming home as it was arriving, finding one's place after a lifetime in someone else's frame of reference. No more "Marcus, that's a Jewish name, isn't it?" He returned many more times, twice at his own expense, and once stayed four weeks instead of the intended two. He thought Madeline might enjoy the extra time with her family. She had never let him forget how much she had hated the food, the rudeness of people in the streets, the hot, dry climate. "At least in New York you can go shopping," she said, comparing Jerusalem to another city she could not abide.

"It's going sour," Marcus continued, speaking to Halpern. "Politicians used to pitch for the Jewish vote, especially in presidential elections. Even if they disregarded us once in office, they didn't on the campaign trail. But you know what's been happening the past dozen years or more. The blacks, the Hispanics, Asians, even the Arab Americans—they've all gotten better organized, finally got their people registered and now are turning them out. It's changed the debate, how the issues are framed, even what words we can use in talking about the issues. Hell, I can't even use the phrase 'Arab terrorist' without someone calling me 'Islamophobic,' whatever that's supposed to mean!

"Look, Morty: when Jews were three percent of the population and voted like seven or eight in big states like New York, New Jersey, Pennsylvania, Florida, Illinois, California, and provided at least thirty percent of the Democratic Party's funds, we counted. Now we're two percent, vote like three, and campaign finance reform even has limited our financial clout…"

"Ostensibly," Halpern laughed.

"Yeah," said Marcus, "but people have picked up on the general trend. That's one reason you've had bipartisan coalitions of liberals and conservatives in

Congress the past few years, supported by minority members they don't otherwise speak to, all voting against any additional help to Israel, voting against tax breaks for Jewish charities at home."

"I may not like it, Jonathan," Halpern acknowledged, "but truthfully, most of this has to do with Israel. It doesn't affect me directly, and, be honest, the Israelis brought some of it on themselves.."

"Doesn't affect us? Morty, do you remember back to the 1967 Six-Day War?"

"Sure, I was in high school then. Some of us cut class to go to a teach-in at George Washington University. It was funny—some of the same professors who were against the war in Vietnam wanted the United States to do something to help Israel. Turned out Israel didn't need help, not of those professors, or the U.S." He laughed again.

"The day of miracles is over," Marcus said, "it's bad planning to count on them, anyway. The point about '67, for American Jews, was this: Didn't you walk a little taller, with your back a little straighter, than you did before? And didn't non-Jews react to you in a more positive way than they had before?"

Halpern paused. "You're right. My friends stopped telling me jokes about Jews and started telling them about Arabs. But I didn't think about the cause-and-effect."

"I'm telling you, Morty, if not for Israel the place of the Jew in America and our way of life here would have been less assured, less comfortable—more like my father remembered it just before and after World War II. What we took for granted from 1967 through the early '90s may yet turn out to have been the golden age, the exception to the rule. Hence the wave of antisemitism in Europe five years ago. In cutting Israel down, the world has been cutting the Jews down—as a group, if not as individuals."

"Okay, that's what your woman rabbi preaches. But what does it do for us, for your reelection, other than serves as a big distraction?"

Marcus knew that Halpern hated distractions, especially in politics. He suspected his friend was right about the effect on his own campaign later of focusing on Jeri Levi now. So he said, partly to convince himself, "this is politics by another means. Morty, I'll worry about the next campaign when it comes."

"Okay, Jonathan, I'll do it. But only because you insist. Worrying about the next campaign when it comes might damn well be too late. You've never doubted Halpern's rule number one, at least up to now: The campaign never ends, it's always election season, and you can never raise too much money. Especially not when Steve Silvers is out there already."

"Touché. But right now Rabbi Levi is our candidate."

"I said I'll help. But it's a mistake, Jonathan. You can never raise today's dollar tomorrow. And Mona likes it less than I do. 'Appalling,' I think, was the nicest thing she said about it."

Now it was Marcus' turn to laugh. "Maybe so, but Mona is going to get Rabbi Jeri Levi a full-scale local media blitz, all the radio and TV talk shows, more print coverage and a decent office to work from, with a secretary. At the same time, we'll need to build up a national speaking circuit for her. If she continues to catch fire, a nation-wide media blitz, a book, a Website and video tape."

"You're talking about a two-year, full-blown promotional campaign," Halpern said.

"Exactly," Marcus responded. "But Morty, I want it done—or at least well underway—in six months. You and Mona have to come back to work full-time for my campaign no later than next spring. I really haven't forgotten about the whiskerless Mr. Silvers."

"Jonathan, tell me the truth: You having an affair with this woman rabbi?"

"You still don't get it. Look, I want to make her into the Jewish Billy Graham. Lord knows we need one!"

"So you're having a spiritual affair with her. Even worse! Like a monk in love with a nun, and they never even hold hands. Well, you'd better not forget Silvers. He nearly beat us the last time."

Two days later Congressman Marcus took a telephone call in his Capitol Hill office from Jeri Levi:

"Congressman, a character named Morton Halpern came to see me this morning. He brought another person with him—a creature, really—a hard-bitten woman with coal-black hair, eyes and dress to match, who sat in my house drinking coffee non-stop 'because I'll wait to smoke until I get outside'. From what I could gather, you've appointed them to run my life."

Marcus laughed. "Better yours than mine, which is what they have been doing the past 20 years or so. At any level other than presidential—and maybe even that—they're just about the best in the business."

"And what business is that, real estate liquidations?"

"Even better, politics. Halpern is one terrific fund-raiser, and Mona Margolis is my 'advance man,' maybe the best. Don't let the first impression put you off; she gets results."

"Jonathan, just one thing: What, exactly am I running for?"

"Jeri, I'm not sure. I think it might be queen of the Jews."

"Why did you send them to me now?"

"Because after your second rally, after the riot, I promised Jerry O'Malley I would get you the staff you need."

"Jonathan, don't be elliptical. The staff you think I need to do what?"

"Jeri, what you're doing is important—more important than anything any of the so-called American Jewish leaders most Jews can't name have done in the past generation. I'm not sure I can define it exactly, not yet, but I know it's vital for you to reach the largest audience possible, as quickly as you can."

"Suppose I agree with you. It certainly would fit with one of these recurring dreams of mine…"

"What?"

"Never mind. If I agree, who is going to pay for all this? Neither WBLS nor I have the cash, and if these people are the pros you say they are, they must come at a hefty fee."

"Don't worry," Marcus said. "Morty Halpern will raise more than enough to cover expenses, including his and Mona's. So you don't object to speaking in other cities, doing the media bit? It has a way of eating up your time, your private life. You could go up as fast as Kitty Dukakis or Geraldine Ferraro, for example, and down and out just as quickly. A lot of pressure is involved. Like Hillary, you'll find out just how tough you are. And it'll be harder on you, plagued as you are by a moral sense."

"I appreciate your concern," Rabbi Levi said, "but you needn't worry. Ever since I left Or Kodesh—or it left me—I've felt a call to reach a larger audience, to take the word as far as possible. Your helping me, like Jerry O'Malley's helping me, is no accident."

The door to Marcus' private office swung open. Felicia Sanchez swung in. She pointed to the clock and then to her copy of his daily schedule card. He glanced at his own card on the desk in front of him. He was twenty minutes late for a meeting with some constituents, an elderly couple named Franks.

"Rabbi, I must go. I'm late, as always. I'm not sure myself how I came to be so all-fired interested in you. Maybe it's time for guerrilla politics. Our enemies have been stalking us through the underbrush for years."

"All right. I accept your help, gratefully. Just one thing: that witch in black does not get to take me in tow. I'll decide in the end what I'll do, and won't do, and when."

Felicia Sanchez was standing over him now, hands on her hips—talk about a distraction—one foot tapping impatiently.

"Of course, of course," Marcus said into the telephone. He swore the same thing to himself at the start of each campaign. And before the race was a week old Mona Margolis had him up by six and on the go 'til midnight—to the right places, at the right times, saying the proper things to the necessary people.

He put down the phone, stood and impulsively gave Felicia Sanchez a peck on the cheek. It surprised both of them.

"I should sue you for sexual harassment," she said, pretending displeasure, "'creating a hostile workplace environment'."

"For a peck on the cheek? Now that would be hostility."

"For making me wait so long," she smiled. To herself, Felicia Sanchez thought, men are so slow. Of course, in today's anti-romantic environment, subtle signals may be too subtle. Even for an intelligent congressman.

The Franks. Marcus remembered their letter, one of the saddest of the tens of thousands of constituent letters, faxes and e-mails he had received in his time in Congress. Years in which he felt like a social worker-confessor almost as frequently as a legislator. For many writers their representative was the last resort, last hope to repair private worlds which, for whatever reasons, were collapsing about them. Marcus knew the sorrow often masked by daily life.

"As you may know, we owned the carryout torched during the riot at Rabbi Levi's sermon," the Franks' letter stated. "We are Holocaust survivors. We came to America in 1949, when we were still in our teens. We got married—it was an Orthodox ceremony in Baltimore, Isaac's cousin Morris paid for it—and went to work in the grocery in Arlington. After a few years, with a loan from Morris. we bought it."

And so the story went. The couple lived in the apartment over the store and prospered to the extent that they could afford a small house a few miles further out in Falls Church. They joined Or Kodesh Congregation and waited for children.

Years passed, but the children never came. By the late 1970s the area around the grocery had been transformed beyond their recognition. Their customers now were primarily Hispanics, blacks, Indochinese. "Our store was broken into so many times we no longer could afford insurance. Worse, we were robbed three times, three times at gunpoint. Like the Nazis, except each time by a person of another race.

"Two times the police made arrests, and one time the no-good actually was convicted. It didn't matter; he was back on the street after a little while. And each of them would return to the store to taunt us, to frighten us."

The Franks gave up their Falls Church home and moved back into the apartment above the grocery to keep better watch on things, to be human burglary alarms. But the change only heightened their nervousness; their health began to decline. Finally, the fire and the letter to Marcus.

"Dear Congressman, we have lost our business. We wanted to sell for a good price and to retire, but now we'll sell just the property, probably at a discount. We no longer feel at home here and don't want to go to Florida, where we know nearly no one and where there's also a lot of crime. We believe we would be safer in Germany, in a familiar culture, and would like your help. Many Jews are moving to Germany now, especially from Russia.

"Can we receive Social Security and our other money saved for retirement there? Will we need special papers? Do we have to give up American citizenship? We don't want to, unless it's absolutely necessary.

"We are sorry to trouble you, but at least in Germany we'll be able to speak our first language on the street as well as at home, and, so we are told, the police come when you call them."

He had re-read the letter several times. Each time it made him furious—not with the Franks, but with himself and his colleagues. What the hell had we let go wrong here?

*   *   *

Alexandria, Virginia (October 1, 2007)—"Get a seat on a U.N. plane, then!" Madeline Marcus commanded her son, Jeremy. "It's made me sick with worry, you over there in a war zone all these months. Now Ben Gurion Airport's been reopened and you can get out. I insist that you do so! Jeremy, you listen to me, I'm your mother!"

"Mom, please. Calm down," Jeremy said. How many times had the two of them had this argument, he thought wearily? It was always the same, except that his mother sounded even more upset. "Sivan and I..."

"I'm tired of hearing about this Sivan! You're my son and I want you home, now! Besides, if she really loves you, she'll come with you, like I did your father."

Jeremy Marcus tried another tack. "I don't know what the news there is saying, but it's not so easy to get out of the autonomous Jewish zone, as they call it now. Officially, we're still under curfew after the latest 'terrorist' attacks on the Republic of Palestine. The U.N. planes are only for the international peace-keepers–if that's what you want to call them–and private people, especially Jews, can't get on them. Not officially, at least, and I don't have the money for bribes."

"Bribes?"

"I wouldn't leave without Sivan."

"Sivan, again! Jeremy, I told you, this is making me sick. Now you listen to me: You don't need to pay bribes. You're a congressman's son. Use your father's influence…."

"I'm sorry mom, but without about $35,000 per person, that influence is rhetorical. But I'm not leaving, at least not without her and not until we see what happens at the trials of Prime Minister Sarid and General Simon Tov. And besides, I…" Jeremy hung up the telephone while he was talking, a trick he'd learned from his father. It ended unproductive calls without unduly upsetting the disconnected party.

Madeline Marcus dropped the receiver with a clump. Tears rolling down her cheeks, she pounded the tabletop with her fists, simultaneously angry and fearful. She scratched absently at the spots along her jaw. Not so long ago they had been fiery scales but now, thanks to her new medication, they were smooth, light skin, surrounded by barely noticeable rust-colored stains.

And then she thought of it, of him. A man in her debt. He could pay whatever bribe was necessary–two, if Jeremy insisted. He could write a $70,000 check from his personal account without blinking. In fact, it was just the sort of gesture that, made publicly, appealed to him. She dried her tears, composed herself and dialed an unlisted number.

Two hours later Madeline Marcus, naked except for a unbuttoned man's shirt, stood behind sheer curtains of a room in the Four Seasons Hotel on the edge of Georgetown and looked down onto the bustle of M Street. He watched her from behind, still in bed and stretching contentedly. She wasn't that bad, he thought, now that she had her rash under control and had dropped a few pounds. That smoking, incessant as it was, really did depress her appetite. Her butt and thighs still had too much fat on them, he admitted–but she was a middle aged woman, after all, and so many of them carried extra pounds. Unlike himself, who ate his whole wheat toast dry and still played squash a couple times a week, she abused herself, as she so often reminded him. Taking that into account, she still had a waist line, still had those impressive breasts, which by themselves aroused him, plus an attractive if hard face and, when she was in the mood, a tempting, passionate mouth. But all that was secondary. Primarily, she was the wife of a man with whom he had not, until now, settled a score.

"Okay," he said. "You told me on the phone it was urgent. Besides this, what did you mean?"

She turned to face him, letting the shirt hang open. She knew that inflamed him, and she wanted to drive down the businessman in him before she made her request. So it was with satisfaction that she watched his eyes stare at her chest, saw his worm of a penis stiffen and begin to grow back into something useful. God, she thought, if I could only get rid of this headache and concentrate. I need to handle this just right.

She bent down and snuffed out her cigarette in the ashtray on the lamp table next to the bed. She half-turned so his face could stare straight at her pubic triangle, the hair still, incredibly, strawberry blonde after all these years. "I want," she said as if it were the most ordinary thing in the world, "for you to write a check to me, or maybe just to cash, for $70,000, and I want you to...."

Her left hand shot up to her temple. "Ooh," Madeline Marcus said softly, an expression of almost detached surprise on her face. And she crumpled, lifeless, to the floor.

He was out of bed and immediately bending over her. He knew she was dead. His father-in-law had died the same way, standing about that close to him, a decade before. Cerebral stroke, no doubt about it. He yanked his shirt off her—he had to pull twice, her body had collapsed over her right hand—dressed in fresh clothes from the closet, and wiped or gathered anything that might have his fingerprints on it, a matchbook, a wine glass. He turned the Do Not Disturb sign above the knob, pulled the door locked behind him and stepped away from disaster.

At the elevator door he admired once more the Four Seasons' logo stamped into the sand of a burnished brass ashtray canister. Such a tasteful, temporary and intentionally superfluous touch. Superfluous, and perfect for it, he thought.

An hour later, before catching a flight home to Chicago, he used a pay telephone to call the hotel. "I've been trying to leave an urgent message for Mr. Bailey in room 415," he said. "Would you please take it up to him personally?"

"Of course, sir," came the reply.

"Thank you." Once again, he prided himself on having stuck to decisions made long ago; never take a woman to his Washington apartment, never use his own name at the Four Seasons.

*　*　*

Washington, D.C. (October 1, 2007)—Jonathan Marcus sat staring out his window, looking once again from the Cannon House Office Building across Independence Avenue, over a corner of The Lawn, the green quadrangle of grass, flower beds, hardwood trees and concrete walks, at the Capitol itself. It was, he thought once more, the most perfect public building he had ever seen, anywhere in the world. Except for a cathedral or two, inspired and yet limited by their ecclesiastical purpose, it was perhaps the most perfect building in the world, of refined esthetics, practical purpose, grandeur that was not haughty but dignified, a structure truly embodying an exalted yet humane ideal for the conduct of practical affairs.

Yet for practical affairs, his were a mess, he considered, self-mockingly. If you're so good, so insightful, so judicious, Congressman Marcus, what of your own life? What kind of building would represent that? What about your wife, the unfailingly difficult, touchingly needy Madeline? What about her alter ego—in your own mind, at least—Felicia Sanchez? Jeremy, your son whom you tacitly encouraged to remain on a battlefield, a battlefield for which he is manifestly untrained? Your grad school daughter, Jane—how did she ever get a name like that?—intelligent, reserved, remote. And this Sivan? Jeremy's infatuation? Soulmate? Can you help them? And what about the Jewish people, dying before your eyes? What about America, your country, and the dry rot within, epitomized but hardly caused by the boy president, Johnston, and his weather woman wife? What the hell good are you doing about any of this, Congressman Seatwarmer?

The telephone rang, bringing him back to the moment. "Jonathan," said Felicia, "the District police are on the phone, for you personally."

"Thanks," he said flatly, uncertainly, as the call was put through.

"Congressman Jonathan Marcus?"

"Yes."

"This is Detective Arno Haynesworth, D.C. Police. Can you meet me at the Four Seasons Hotel?"

"When?"

"As soon as possible."

"Why?" Marcus said, his stomach tightening.

"It's your wife, sir."

If it was possible to be stunned but not surprised, that was Marcus' state. Suddenly, he registered everything about his wife's recent behavior—her remarks, attitude, appearance—that he'd been too busy, too removed, self-blinded, to have credited before. And, insulated for the moment by this sudden realization, he knew, with an odd detachment, that Madeline was dead.

Marcus left the office, putting on his suit coat as he went. "I'm going to the Four Seasons," he called over his shoulder as he opened the outer door to the hallway.

"Jonathan," Sanchez asked, concern in her voice, "do you want me to come with you?"

"Yes," he croaked out the word, his throat constricted by pain and passion, "but you can't. This I have to do myself."

In room 415 of the Four Seasons, standing next to and in the shadow of Detective Haynesworth—a black man of such proportions that he seemed more a structure than a mortal—Marcus watched evidence technicians fuss about Madeline's body. A photographer snapped pictures from a variety of angles his wife—had it been but a few hours earlier—would have ferociously forbidden. Emotional detachment still shrouded the congressman. The sight of her strawberry-blonde pubic hair, exposed now to the clinical gaze of strangers, took him out of the present, erasing for a second years, decades, and with them gone so too his wife's faults, his own disappointments. It left instead not just memories of their strengths, but even better, of a once mutual fondness, of common hopes. A smile of remembrance crossed his face. He saw Haynesworth scrutinizing him, and the smile vanished.

Marcus tensed, realizing the detective's suspicions. Madeline was naked, lying on her right side on the floor. Without the animation of life, without her perverse vibrancy, that powerful if negative energy, she already looked smaller and older than he thought right. Ironic, how her skin was so much smoother than it had been for so many years. Had it made her happier, he wondered. The new medicine worked, and for what it cost, it should have.

He recalled again that peculiar scene just before the Home Builders' fund-raiser, when she arrived at the house face flushed, calling him Johnny and saying she felt better than okay, she felt fine.

So she had been having an affair. He did not feel betrayed, not really. Their feelings for each other, whatever mutual respect or at least sympathy might still have survived, did not include affection, let alone passion. Maybe she had wrung a bit of happiness out of her depression.

And maybe you're thinking that just to make yourself feel better, less guilty. Were you really so free of responsibility for her unreasoning agitation? Marcus was arguing with himself again. A bad sign, a sign of his own doubt and depression.

"What was she doing here? Do you have any idea?" Haynesworth asked.

"I don't know, detective."

"Do you think she was having an affair?"

"I know she was acting a little strange lately, a little manic, but only quite recently, and I didn't know why—other than that our son is stuck in what's left of Israel and it weighed heavily on her."

"Not on you?" Haynesworth's tone was pointed.

"Of course," Marcus replied, as evenly as possible. "Only Madeline seemed practically irrational about it. Or maybe not irrational, but obsessively maternal."

"No signs of violence, detective," said one of the technicians. "We'll know more from the lab tests."

Haynesworth's posture relaxed a little. "Of course," he said. Turning back to Marcus, he asked about the rust-colored stains visible on Madeline's body. The congressman sketched his wife's history of skin problems, explained about the new medicine, the warnings regarding possible side-effects, his wife's aversion to petroleum jelly. "The dermatologist cautioned her about the risks. And lately she'd begun to complain about headaches. Still, we just assumed the odds against serious risk were quite high…"

"High, but not impossible," Haynesworth said. "So it could have been natural causes?" Marcus thought it was a leading question.

"Possible? I suppose. But that still wouldn't explain what she was doing here, at lunch time on a Thursday afternoon."

"This might," the lead technician said as they finally lifted Madeline Marcus' body onto a stretcher. In her right hand was an expensive gold and diamond cufflink. Etched deeply into it was the monogram HH.

"Any idea whose this is?" Haynesworth asked.

"Oh yes," Marcus said softly, almost whispering. "Yes, I know."

A suspect, Haynesworth mused.

The list, Marcus thought. Hesh Hestin's membership and donor list for the American Israel Political Affairs Group—60,000 names for Jeri Levi's first national direct mail solicitation, for the beginning of a new, national Jewish organization, for the establishment of Jewish Palestine's American hinterland. Did Madeline know she was still helping him, in spite of herself, Jonathan Marcus wondered, uneasy at his own obsession.

* * *

Jerusalem (October 3, 2007)–"I will not tolerate anymore of these attacks!" Yacoub al-Masri shouted. "Jewish bandits will not be allowed to disturb the Jerusalem caliphate!"

"We call them bandits, they call themselves freedom fighters," Fahd al-Husseini responded. Fatima al-Masri looked at him, her eyebrows arched, her face drawn into an expression of exasperation. Al-Husseini, personal security chief to the caliph, stared back at her, their eyes locked.

Yacoub al-Masri, self-annointed caliph of Greater Palestine, continued standing on the balcony of his large study, which also served as his office and command center. He gazed south over Jerusalem. Completing the palace Jordan's late King Hussein had left unfinished at Shueifat– its concrete skeleton left untouched, outline of an alternate reality, for 40 years after the 1967 Six-Day War–marked the physical and symbolic crowning of his own efforts after the War of Arab Unity. From its high ramparts, finished in a neo-Ottoman style, he truly was master of all he surveyed.

Or nearly all. Of course, there were still the Jews, subdued but not submissive. And there was the civil government of Mahmoud Terzi. Terzi, al-Masri knew, continued to delude himself that as president of the United Arab Republic of Greater Palestine he actually was in charge, rather than convenient window-dressing for al-Masri himself.

Some feet away from his wife and his senior security aide, al-Masri remained with his back to them. "I care not what the U.N. says. It sided with the Jews in the early days, and has no right, not even after helping us all these years, to lecture us now. Sarid and Simon Tov must be tried, and executed. Publicly. If that does not stop the Jewish bandits, we will insist that the United Nations rescind its obviously failed peace-keeping mandate, and finish the job ourselves!"

"My husband," Fatima said soothingly, moving toward him. "Isn't it just as likely that if we hang Sarid and Simon Tov the Jewish terrorists will increase their attacks, like we did in the old days? Then the U.N., using that as a pretext, will say there are not enough peacekeepers in Palestine and send in more. All this will obstruct your great work of rebuilding the caliphate and reuniting Arab Islam."

Yacoub al-Masri said nothing. But as his wife drew near he growled. His sixth sense, Fatima reminded herself; forget it at your own peril. Al-Masri still did not turn to face her, but ordered her to halt. "Do not touch me!" he commanded as she stretched her arm toward his shoulder. "I am concentrating. We must break the Jews' will. Then they will be defeated finally and their terrorism dwindle away. You say we must do it in a way that does not bring us more problems from the U.N., from the United States and the rest. But the U.N. is a paper tiger, as we learned years ago in Lebanon, Bosnia and Iraq. We can drive out the U.N. with attacks of our own, which we will blame on the Jews. Remember Beirut, Somalia, Rwanda? International peace keeping forces are short of breath, especially when opposition is *samud*, steadfast.

"So the trial will take place at midnight. Tonight. The executions will be held at dawn. Do either of you have anything to add, anything helpful?"

"If they are to be hanged," Fatima said, "don't let CNN or the other networks cover it. We can tape it ourselves, edit it as necessary, then give them our copy, with our message. Remember how badly the decapitation of the reporter Pearl played in the West, America in particular?"

"Those were amateurs!" al-Masri thundered. "But you are right, Fatima. A sanitized hanging is what the Western media wants, but is still a little too delicate to ask for. However, if we give it to them, they won't be able to restrain themselves from showing it, again and again. Very good, my wife. Very good. Now you both may leave."

As soon as his wife and al-Husseini were gone, Yacoub al-Masri returned to his desk and, using his intercom, called for the Council of Sages to assemble as a judicial panel, in the palace courtroom. "Bring the prisoners from their cells," he added. "And summon their lawyers. Invite the peace keepers to see that all is in accordance with law, our law."

Islamic law. As interpreted by me, Yacoub al-Masri, caliph of Jerusalem and greater Palestine. Soon to be caliph of Greater Palestine and Syria. Leader of the Arabs, leader of the Muslins.

*　*　*

Alexandria, Virginia (October 3, 2007)–Madeline. Hesh Hestin. Jeremy. Felicia Sanchez. Meir Sarid. Yacoub al-Masri. President Johnston. Felicia Sanchez.

Jonathan Marcus could not sleep. His thoughts, like the thousand drunken monkeys in the brains of Charlie Chan's irritable Occidentals, leapt from branch to branch of his near-conscious mind and back again, never stopping long on any one limb. Unable to rest, Marcus got out of bed. It was 2:15 a.m. To hell with it, he thought, I'll do it. I should have done it years ago. He got out his appointment book, looked up a number, took a slip from a pad of paper next the kitchen phone, wrote down the number and padded back to the bedroom, leaving the slip next to his clock. He set the alarm for six a.m. and got back in bed. Having resolved to act, Marcus felt more at ease and his mind clearer–enough to let him sleep until morning.

"Hello?" came the drowsy, warm voice at the other end.

"Felicia, this is Jonathan. Did I wake you?"

"Jonathan? Yes, but I was going to get up in a few minutes anyway. Why are you calling now?"

"Felicia, I want to talk with you. Can we meet somewhere, for breakfast?"

She heard instantaneously that he had lost his habitual inflection with her, that of professional collegiality, of boss to loyal assistant. Of the office and day-time. This was a new tone, that of one uncertain man speaking at dawn to a woman he needed.

Momentary silence. Marcus felt his pulse quicken.

"Certainly," she said. "Where?"

The tight muscles in his face relaxed, his grip on the phone eased. "How about the Hotel Washington? It's on the way for both of us, and they serve the best oatmeal in town at the Sky Terrace."

"Oatmeal?" Felicia Sanchez laughed. "With brown sugar, walnuts and raisins?"

"Exactly," Marcus said. "I'll see you there in an hour." Long after he and Madeline had stopped going there together and other newer, more fashionable places intervened, the thought of the Sky Terrace brought back pleasant memories.

Marcus drove into the District from Virginia, on U.S. Route 50 past Arlington National Cemetery and the Marines' Iwo Jima statute. Quickly across the Theodore Roosevelt Bridge, the well-proportioned white marble colossus of the Kennedy Center on the left, the magnificence of the Lincoln Memorial to the right. The Potomac River flowed wide and dark; light reflected from the city's official buildings and memorials cast an aura combining familiarity and power, symmetry and order. On such mornings it seemed to him that life, his life and that of those dear to him would, like this monumental tableau, go on forever. It was an illusion, he knew—as Madeline's death, as the Pentagon, in his mind's eye forever scarred, testified—but almost tangible, one of the forces that drew people from across the country and around the world to and kept them in Washington.

He glimpsed an encampment of street people, all men, mostly black, with their battered shopping carts and little mounds of possessions covered by plastic sheeting among the trees around the steam grates near the Einstein sculpture at the National Academy of Science. A few blocks east, at Constitution and 19th Street, three police cars had a new white-and-gold Ford Expedition pulled up across the curb and half on the sidewalk. The driver of the SUV, his door shut and window up, appeared to be screaming at the cops. Marcus could hear nothing but the oppressive bass throbbing of the man's music system, a feeling more than a sound, pounding through his own windows. Several of the officers drew their revolvers, and the passenger door behind the driver flew open. Two girls, probably no more than fifteen or sixteen, in miniskirts, tub tops and platform heels, darted from the Ford into traffic just behind him on Constitution.

So many possibilities, so little sense, Marcus thought as he passed the Ellipse, instinctively glancing left across the expanse of trees and grass toward the White House. So little sense in so many places. I've got to do better, this time, he told himself. Two long blocks past the Commerce Department, with Washington's Monument rising on his right, and Marcus turned left onto 14th Street and into a parking space, a half-space actually—construction or street repair around the hotel seemed perpetual. The tail of his new Pontiac Bonneville SSE ("Never campaign in a German or Japanese car, even if they're built here," Morty Halpern insisted; "and never campaign in an old American car, it makes you look out of touch," Mona Margolis added) protruded into the next space. He hoped his congressional plates would protect him from a ticket.

The Washington was an old hotel whose renovations could not keep pace with the building and rebuilding nearby at the showy J.W. Marriott and the restored, reinvented Willard, "hotel of presidents." But the Washington held a trump card for Marcus nevertheless. From its 12th floor Terrace, a porch-like affair under a big green awning, one could sit, drink in hand, commanding the

Treasury complex across 15th Street below, a bit of the White House grounds just beyond and much of important and self-important Washington to the west and northwest. The Terrace afforded a clear view—albeit through anti-terrorist Plexiglass—along Constitution Avenue and the Mall to the Lincoln Memorial, the State Department and out across the Potomac to Alexandria and Reagan National Airport, the Pentagon, and Arlington.

They arrived within minutes of each other, before 7:30 a.m. Only a few business travelers sat at scattered tables, although the Terrace would fill within a half an hour. They both ordered oatmeal and coffee. Marcus added wheat toast and orange juice, Sanchez half a grapefruit. Occasional joggers jousted on the sidewalks below with office-bound government workers. The morning sky brightened unevenly, with low clouds threatening rain. The air was humid, close, which Marcus didn't mind—it aroused him to sleep with the windows open on balmy nights, weather that had driven Madeline to the coolness of a basement sofa bed.

After they had ordered, he looked directly at Sanchez. "Felicia," he started, "Madeline's death and this police investigation have forced me to do what I should have done anyway but had been avoiding. My job, as usual, depends on re-election, and this time it'll be tight, I know that. Jeremy's in danger—along with the rest of the Israelis, or whatever they are now—and this administration clearly is not up to the job, even without the Chinese rattling their missiles over Taiwan. I need to make some decisions, and I want to make them with you."

"Me, Jonathan?" It had taken him a long time, she thought, almost too long.

A gust of wind pushed aside the enveloping humidity and blew the napkins off their table. It also tossed back Sanchez thick black hair; Marcus stared, captivated.

"Yes, you, Felicia."

"Are you certain? You know me at the office, on the job. Do you know I have a temper? That I'm religious? That I love raw onions and hate cats? That I can't bear a man who doesn't pick up after himself?"

"Dogs it is," Marcus said. "I have a temper, too. The question is," he asked, thinking of Madeline, "do you hold a grudge?"

She laughed. "I've been told I'm forgiving to a fault."

"Whom do you pray to?" he asked, quietly.

"To God." He had been afraid she would say Jesus. "And you, Jonathan, do you hold a grudge? Do you pray? I know you well, but even after all these years maybe not well enough."

"A grudge? Well, I've learned to admit when I'm wrong, so not as many as I used to. Yes, I pray... not every day, but more than before."

"Well, that's a start. Jews are supposed to pray three times a day, aren't they?"

"Yes, but not all of us know that."

The gray, low-lying clouds had darkened and gathered into a squall. Lightning cut the sky, backlighting the nearby buildings. Thunder exploded quickly after. As if to punctuate their conversation, big, cold drops of rain began to strike the awning over the outer reaches of the terrace. Wind blew the rain in underneath, and in no time it was not just a few drops but a deluge. They moved back inside, to the bar area itself, under the permanent roof. There they watched the awning sag with water that then ran off in sheets.

At a new table, their food in front of them, Marcus took Sanchez's hands in his.

"Felicia, I want you. I need you."

"I know, Jonathan. But do you love me?"

"Yes," he said, his voice husky with emotion. "Without reservation."

"You waited almost too long," she said softly, firmly, and kissed him.

He responded, in a full, lush kiss of passion and commitment. Marcus felt desire, relief and promise surge within him. And from a corner of his consciousness, a sardonic voice whose wisdom he'd learned to respect long ago, even when it told him things he didn't want to hear, said, Well, old man, you're still alive. In fact, she's saved you....

Some moments later, as they rose from breakfast, Marcus caught sight of the television over the bar. "Wait a second," he said to Felicia. "And, as you can see," the announcer intoned, "the former prime minister and former defense minister of Israel, Meir Sarid and Binyamin Simon Tov, were executed today in Jerusalem. The men were hanged at dawn in the plaza before the Wailing Wall in the Old City, reportedly after a midnight trial by the Council of Islamic Sages, presided over by the Caliph of Jerusalem and Palestine, Yacoub al-Masri.

"Sarid and Simon Tov were charged with directing, from their jail cells, the recent campaign of terrorism against the Arab Islamic Republic of Palestine. Both had proclaimed their innocence. But they refused to recognize the legitimacy of what they called a kangaroo court, and would not defend themselves.

"Nevertheless, they were represented by counsel. U.N. observers did monitor the proceedings. The United Nations did not have time to decide whether or not to object to the sentences, but had urged a stay of execution while it reviewed the case.

"Palestinian President Mahmud Terzi said he had urged leniency, that is, life imprisonment, but in this case responsibility rested with the Sages, who tried the men for blasphemy rather than treason. The White House has promised a statement tomorrow. Our correspondent, Winifred Hassan, said Palestinian security forces are on alert to deal with any terrorism by the Zionist underground using the executions as a pretext.

"This videotape you are watching of the sentence being carried out was provided to CNN by Palestinian Television...."

Marcus and Sanchez stared dumbfounded at the screen. "A statement tomorrow!" Marcus was livid. "We can't wait for tomorrow!"

They were gone, hand-in-hand, as rain continued to pour off the Sky Terrace awning.

* * *

Washington, D.C. (October 4, 2007)–Hesh Hestin was not happy. Not all of his money, his connections, his expensive K Street lawyers had been able to free him from jail. Jail, with the kind of human crud he had only imagined before. Crud and worse, but real. Another night of this and the man who once bragged to fellow AIPAG board members that he was "the savviest political player in the United States," the man who beat a thin-skinned secretary of state in tennis and then made sure a Washington Post Style section columnist knew about it, the man who suspected God–if He existed–might have chosen him to lead the Jews, might just loose his mind in this filthy place. And now he was being taken upstairs, against his will, to the visitation cell.

"Someone to see you, Mr. Hestin," the guard had informed him.

"Who, my gouging lawyers?"

"No, a man who says he's an old friend, Congressman Marcus."

"Don't want to see him," Hestin had replied.

"Ordinarily, you probably wouldn't have to, him being the husband of the dead woman you were screwin' and all…"

"I wasn't screwin' any dead woman!" Hestin exploded.

The guard smiled. It was always like this. He loved baiting the high-and-mighty, when they came under his control. The bigger they were, the harder they fell. The only thing he couldn't figure was how a jerk like this Hestin could be a multi-millionaire and he himself was still a prison guard. Must be inherited money, he told himself.

"So you say," the guard replied. "Makes no difference. Since Congressman Marcus was the dead lady's husband, you see him. Detective Haynesworth says so."

Haynesworth. Hestin cursed to himself. That giant was nothing but a dumb policeman. Big, stubborn and stupid. If this were Chicago, I'd have his job, and his hide. Holding me as a material witness to a possible homicide. Hell, he knows it was no homicide!

"Hello, Hesh," Marcus said dryly. Haynesworth sat a few paces off, watching both men closely but saying nothing.

Hestin glared through the metal screen but kept silent.

"I said, 'Hello, Hesh.' If you've got any brains left–not to mention any sense of shame–you'll speak to me. And" said Marcus too softly for Haynesworth to hear clearly, "answer my questions."

"If I had any sense of shame? You're the son-of-a-bitch who ignored Madeline, made her so unhappy…"

"If I were you, asshole, I wouldn't yap about things beyond my knowledge," Marcus hissed. Then, quietly again, he added, "I'm prepared to tell Haynesworth to let you go, that I agree Madeline's was a natural death–but only if you give me the AIPAG membership list, complete, no questions asked–and nothing ever said about it. Just call the executive director and tell him to do it; he's your puppet anyway. We know it if the press doesn't. Then you get out."

"You got no leverage, Marcus, as usual." Hestin laughed spitefully. "They've got to let me out today. That's what my lawyers say."

"Not if I press kidnapping charges. The drugs Madeline was taking impaired her judgment. She was going to break it off with you, but you forced her to that hotel room, and kept her there. How's that sound? We can keep you here at least for a few more publicity-filled days. That's what my lawyers say."

"You son-of-a-bitch!"

"Gentlemen?" Haynesworth inquired, rising from his chair and moving toward the two. These puffed up Jews, he thought. I wonder what the hell kind of deal they're cooking up now, for themselves over the law? If they was brothers, they'd be at each other's throats, literally, not figuratively in this bloodless, heartless way they do...

"All right," Hestin whispered. "It's yours."

*　*　*

Falls Church, Virginia (October 5, 2007)—"Jeri, I want to thank you for officiating at Madeline's funeral. I know you've been very busy."

"It's alright, Jonathan. I wanted to be here. Are you okay?"

"Emotionally? I suppose so. I mean, our marriage died a long time ago."

"I'm sorry."

"Still, it's strange. Even with the bad, and there was so much of that, she was part of my life. We had children together, were partners, after a fashion, for years," Marcus said.

They both fell silent. Finally, Jeri Levi said, "You're right, you know. I have been busy—thanks to Morty Halpern and that Mona Margolis. Do you know that I was on 'Good Morning, America' last week?" She put it as an accusation.

"Among commercials, station breaks, introductions, 'outros,' sandwiched between a slovenly rock singer and a woman with forty-seven cats. I barely had time to make clear I was not a 'Jew-for-Jesus.' The lovely co-hosts had trouble grasping that a Jew might proselytize, even among fellow Jews. Anyway, your precious Mona," here Rabbi Levi shook a finger in Marcus' face, "called it 'seven golden minutes of free air time'."

"Free air time, on network television? Morty's schedule for you must be on track."

"The six-months-to-stardom thing? Please, Jonathan..."

"Don't be dismissive, Jeri. This is how we're going to help save the Jews, save Israel."

She looked at him closely. "Jonathan," she smiled, "this town isn't big enough for both of us to have a messianic complex."

"No problem," he said. "You're Jeremiah. I'm merely Baruch, your scribe."

"The Jews tried to kill Jeremiah," Rabbi Levi reminded him.

"Yes, but he lacked your charm—not to mention your advance team and your rising ratings."

Six thousand miles away, another funeral was taking place. In attendance, along with tens of thousands of other Jews, were Israel Miller and Uri Eshel. In disguise, they listened as the new "chief rabbi" of the autonomous Jewish district of the Arab Islamic Republic of Palestine said Kadish, the ancient, universal Hebrew prayer of mourning.

"Yitgadol vyitkadosh, shemay raboh... Magnified and sanctified be His great Name in the world which He has created according to His will. May He establish

His kingdom during your life and during your days, and during the life of all the house of Israel, even speedily and at a near time.... Let His great Name be blessed forever and ever to all eternity."

The "chief rabbi"—an obscure yeshiva leader named Bar Kochba Blum, approved by the Arab military governor—read without emotion. It did not matter. The Kadish, not a remembrance of the departed but homage to the God of the living made even in grief, had been chanted by religious and non-religious Jews in Israel and the diaspora for millennia, its words still Aramaic, not quite Hebrew.

Asserting their right to grieve, to pray as Jews if not govern themselves as Jews, tens of thousands supplied the emotion the rabbi lacked, responding almost defiantly:

"Praised and glorified, exalted, extolled and honored, magnified and lauded be the Name of the Holy One, blessed be He; though He be high above all the blessings and hymns, praises and consolations, which are uttered in the world...."

"Seeing all these people, all these Jews, I think perhaps a Jewish state is still possible," Miller whispered to Eshel. "But first, we'll have to get rid of the kapos like this 'chief rabbi'. There're always some willing to be kapos, aren't there?" he said, using the term for Jews pressed to serve as ghetto and concentration camp guards over fellow Jews.

"Yes," said Eshel. "And they haven't all worn uniforms or worked for Germans. But this particular rabbi is not what you take him for. I knew him from before the war...."

Eshel did not trust Israel Miller's judgment anymore. The war, the death of his wife, accumulated stress and sheer old age seem to have undermined even this indomitable figure. Sometimes the pauses between the other man's sentences, the gaps within his spoken thoughts, made Eshel wonder. The years of two packs of cigarettes a day, the drinking—understandable, and he lately had given up the smoking. But had the arteries hardened? Had, perhaps, there been silent ischemia, undetected "little strokes"? Was Miller, now well into his 70s—as Rabin had been when he had stumbled badly, stubbornly into Oslo—too old for executive authority? Shamir, Peres, even Sharon—too many stayed too long, too far past their prime in Israel's sclerotic multi-party parliamentary democracy. In Miller's case, Eshel was not certain, so he held back. Regardless, Miller had no immediate need to know that Rabbi Bar Kochba Blum's yeshiva in Mea Shearim was Magen Israel's Old City outpost.

Instead, Eshel scanned the crowd and the landscape. What had been one of the last open stretches on the beach north of Tel Aviv and south of Herzliya after the high-tech development bubble of the '90s had been turned into a mass grave. It was one of four required after the fighting stopped. One near Haifa, one outside Jerusalem, one along the road from Beersheva on the southern approaches to Tel Aviv, each with 50,000 to 100,000 bodies. More Jews were buried on this particular site, with the sun-splashed blue Mediterranean just to the west, war-damaged mid- and high-rise apartments and offices of Herzliya and Ramat HaSharon to the north and east, than were present for the services. Under international pressure, and with an eye to public relations and foreign aid, Yacoub al-Masri had agreed to allow the bodies of Meir Sarid and Binyamin Simon Tov to be interred here, according to Jewish tradition, and to permit–finally–a formal Jewish memorial service for the many thousands fallen in the War of Arab Unity.

"May there be abundant peace from heaven, and life for us and for all Israel.... He who makes peace in His high places, may He make peace for us and for all Israel: and say ye, Amen."

"Amen!" The word was a roar.

How can we repeat those words now?" Miller muttered.

"How can we not, and still not surrender?" Eshel asked.

"This time they knew, everyone knew, and still they didn't help us, didn't even help Meir and Binyamin." Miller nearly choked out the words.

"They knew last time, too, soon enough," Eshel said.

The pair walked back to their bus, two old men in the work clothes of kibbutzniks, camouflaged by the slowly departing throng. Miller was becoming argumentative; the funeral had not so much subdued as enraged the old man, rekindling the old will to triumph, the emotion which, by the time of what had been called "the peace process," had seemed passe among so many Israelis, among so many Jews.

As they neared their bus and the crowd began to disperse, both men were quiet. They knew Mahmud Terzi had his agents, Jews and non-Jews, wherever Jews gathered and they did not care to be overheard.

Eshel was thinking of an article he had written long ago. In it he had argued that the Jews made two false and dangerous assumptions after 1945. The first, that the non-Jewish world understood the Holocaust as its tragedy, its responsibility. But it had not. Rather, it compartmentalized the Shoah as a Jewish, or Jewish-Nazi event, separate.

Second, Jews assumed that because something so evil, so unprecedented, happened to them once, it could not happen again–that, in Yael Dayan's words, "the world would not allow it." They denied that the Holocaust, having happened, became not just warning but also precedent.

So Jews, Israelis in particular, behaved as if the post-colonial mass murders in Sudan and Chad, the communist mass murders in China and Vietnam and the Cambodian autogenocide, Bosnia, Rwanda and a dozen other outrages did not relate directly to them, did not–if their own strength failed–presage the nature of the next Arab-Israeli war. They took comfort, especially the intellectuals among them, in the abstraction of "man's inhumanity to man," avoiding the possibility of the re-crystallization of man's inhumanity to the Jews.

Now, Eshel understood, instead of inoculating human conscience against a repetition, this generic, neutered view of the Holocaust paved the way for a second destruction. So here we are, he thought, barely four million Jews now, crammed into our big open-air ghetto, from Haifa to Tel Aviv to west Jerusalem–our "Jewish autonomous district"–awaiting the next blow.

Well, not only waiting. There was, he consoled himself, Magen Israel, the Shield of Israel, the underground–which would make al-Masri and Terzi pay for this funeral. If only we could get some help, more ammunition, more weapons, more communications equipment, more people. Where, Uri Eshel asked himself again, were the American Jews?

As they reached the bus, Miller turned back to the long, low sandy hillock under which one hundred thousand bodies lay. "Look," he said, tugging at Eshel's arm. He struggled with the word. "Look!"

Eshel turned back and saw it too, a scene from Dante. The dune, stripped of mourners now, rippled. The soil heaved, slowly, soundlessly, like a dry geothermal mud pot.

"The bodies," Miller whispered. "The decomposing bodies. So many in so little space. The gas erupts to surface. They say it was like this at Auschwitz and Babi Yar. The earth cannot quite hold all its Jewish dead."

* * *

Kibbutz Nof Benjamin (October 8, 2007)–"We need to retaliate," Aharon Tabor said. "For the sake of Jewish morale. The murders of Sarid and Simon Tov must not go unavenged."

"Yes," Uri Eshel replied, "we must bolster morale. But if we stage an attack, or a series of attacks, the Arabs will–of course–round up Jews, innocent and guilty, jail them all, torture most, murder some. And what will that do for morale, for our ability to recruit and organize in the future?"

"What do you suggest?" Tabor challenged.

Eshel and Israel Miller had undertaken, after the burials of the former prime minister and defense minister, a personal canvas of all the Magen Israel cells. Miller had Tel Aviv, Jerusalem and the corridor between; Eshel was responsible for everything north of Tel Aviv through Haifa. The cell at Kibbutz Nof Binyamin, headed by Aharon Tabor, ranked as one of the underground's best. Eshel did not want to waste it in inactivity, but he feared needlessly exposing it.

"Bombings, small arms attacks, these make noise but are self-defeating. When the Palestine Liberation Organization did the same, it galvanized the Arab world and forced the West, which hated the inconvenience, to pay attention. If we adopt the same tactics, we'll just play into al-Masri's propaganda about what bloody diehards we are. The old double standard persists. Therefore, we've got to do something that gives us leverage, which strikes at the enemy's morale," the older man said. "Something that hits al-Masri's sense of invincibility, his belief and that of his followers in his own historical inevitability.

"We know from the Shin Bet's psychological profile updated not long before the war that he is a classic borderline personality, maybe even schizophrenic. We also know that his is the charisma that holds together the Arab Islamic Republic of Greater Palestine and the alliance between Palestine and Syria-Lebanon. He is the magnet that attracts the people, if not the regimes, in Iraq, Saudi Arabia and even Egypt. We must keep the pressure on him, and intensify it. In this initial stage of our struggle we must make Yacoub al-Masri begin to doubt, begin to doubt himself."

"Fine. But how—have him kidnapped by a dozen psychologists?" Tabor was irritated. He knew Eshel was right, but did not see what profitable action led from the older man's insight.

"I think," Eshel replied in an oddly detached manner, "it is time for those around Yacoub al-Masri to begin to disappear."

"Kidnapping?"

"An organized campaign. Quiet at first, the knowledge of it spread word-of-mouth through the Jewish community. Partially revealed as it grows, to cause doubts about al-Masri's grip over things among his own people and among the Americas, the Europeans and so on. Eventually, we'll make examples of a few in retribution for Sarid and Simon Tov. The rest we'll keep as hostages, for leverage, both against al-Masri and his regime and to manipulate outside powers as mediators, even suppliers. We'll be like Hezbollah in Lebanon in the '80s."

"Why do we want foreign intervention?" Tabor asked. "It's always compromised our independence, or failed us outright before."

"We don't want it to succeed," Eshel explained. "We'll use it to buy time, time to continue strengthening the underground for the general uprising."

"What do you mean, general uprising? I thought this underground was defensive, just enough to keep us all from being massacred, kind of like the Druze militia, speaking of Lebanon. We haven't got a prayer of waging a successful open war against Palestine and its allies."

"Not now, but when the time comes maybe Palestine and its partners will be at each other's throats, and we'll have secret reinforcements," Eshel said.

"I'm not a child," Tabor replied. "If you've something specific in mind, please say so."

"I can't, not now. But that's what happened in 1948, more or less—six thousand rifles for three times than many men, at the beginning, against five Arab armies."

"The post-Zionist say it wasn't like that…"

"The post-Zionists were anti-Zionists, and it was like that. I've seen enough of the primary documents, and interviewed enough of the participants, to know. It was like that, alright. Once my own father and a company of Haganah men, about eighty in all, with eleven working rifles among them, took a hill defended by three or four hundred Arabs. Of course, it was night, and they had the element of surprise, but that's how it was done…"

"Okay, okay. But this isn't 1948. Or 1967. Not even '73…"

"I know that," Eshel said shortly. "I've taken that into account, young man. It'll either be much worse, or much better."

* * *

Jerusalem (October 29, 2007)—Chief Rabbi Bar Kochba Blum stepped off the sidewalk and into the gutter of the street, to let the Arab policemen pass. The rabbi's students, in a row behind him, did the same, a line of black-hatted, black-coated analogs, their side curls and untrimmed beards giving them an ancient, surreal look. The rootless luftmenschen of a Chagall painting come to earth. The police lieutenant, who remembered these anti-Zionist Jews from before the war, acknowledged Blum and stopped to speak.

"One of my men is missing," the lieutenant said, frowning. "Have you seen anything of the Zionist bandits?"

"Nothing," Blum replied. "But if we do, I will call you immediately. Your missing man—what does he look like, and what is his name?"

"Actually, he is not one of my men—he is the commander of police in eastern Jerusalem, Colonel Barghouti. He is nearly six feet tall, a little stout, dark hair, balding, no glasses."

"This is most distressing, lieutenant. I will notify you immediately if I hear of anything. You can rely on us."

"I know, rabbi. Thank you." Still frowning, the Arab police officer led his men down the street. Barely half an hour before, Col. Barghouti's car had been found near the old Mt. Scopus campus of Hebrew University, now Sheik Yassin University. The driver, unconscious and apparently drugged, slumped behind the wheel. A body guard, his temple crushed from what might have been a karate-like blow, lay half in, half out of the vehicle. Of the colonel himself, no trace.

This unnerved Lieutenant Atallah abu Atallah. If the Jewish bandits could grab his boss, they certainly could take him. And from the rumors that raced through the Arab police force, abu Atallah understood that his commander was not the only senior official of the Arab Islamic Republic of Greater Palestine who had disappeared within the last twenty-four hours. The gossip—usually a more reliable source than the government-controlled media—claimed that half-a-dozen people had vanished, including Yacoub al-Masri's half-brother, the minister of defense himself. That, if true, would trouble the caliph greatly. And what began by troubling his superiors ended by troubling Lt. abu Atallah.

"Look sharply, men," he barked. "The smallest thing could be important."

Rabbi Blum watched them go. Then he nodded slightly to his students and they resumed their slow but purposeful walk back to the yeshiva. In the middle of the little column, two of the seminarians assisted a third who, obscured by his overlarge coat and the big black hat pulled low across his head—moved on unsteady legs.

The sun had not yet risen over the Mountains of Moab that morning as the rabbi had led his students to the narrow little intersection near the university campus. His hands were clasped behind him and his head was bowed, as if he were arguing with God again and the latter, by not answering, burdened the rabbi with his own questions. Since the final Israel-Palestinian settlement—the final one before the war—an Arab flag had flown over the ground he and his men trod. To international applause and prizes for peace, Jerusalem—City of David, physical and spiritual heart of Judaism and the Jewish people for more than three thousand years—had been sundered.

Blum and his companions halted at the amphitheatre. In this place in 1925, at a ceremony in the presence of Martin Buber, Albert Einstein, Sigmund Freud and other dignitaries—including Christians and Muslims as well—Dr. Chaim Weizmann inaugurated Hebrew University. He pledged that the rock-strewn ridge, with its commanding view of the Old City below to the west and across the Judean Desert down to the Dead Sea eastward, one day would support a school the equal of Oxford or Cambridge, Harvard or Yale. Weizemann's dream, proclaimed a generation before the rebirth of the state of Israel, had become a reality, and been so for half a century.

Ironically, it had been that same half century during which intellectuals from the liberal arts and law faculties of Hebrew University—derided by Israel's first prime minister, David Ben-Gurion, as "the professors"—warred with and progressively undermined the Labor Zionism of Israel's founders. Their students, dominating, suffocating the second generation of Israeli academics, journalists, writers and artists, eventually did the same to the national-religious Zionism of Ben-Gurion's rival, Menachem Begin. "The professors'" victory of a denatured Jewish universalism over replanted Jewish nationalism was the prerequisite of Palestinian Arab success, yielding as it did the anchorless secular Israelism, the delusion of the bright young men of Oslo. John Maynard Keyes had been right, Blum mused; theory counts. If even the most unlettered are the unknowing pupils of long-dead ideologists, imagine the vulnerability of self-conscious intelligentsia.

The sun began to crown the sere hills with rays of pink. A few miles east into what had been wilderness Blum could see the rubble of Ma'ale Adumim. One of the biggest of the original post-1967 Six-Day War settlements, it had been authorized by a Labor government to strengthen Israel's control of its capital against attack from the east and to help reassert, as Israel Miller liked to say, the Jewish claim to the core of biblical Judea and Samaria, "the estate of our fathers."

The chief rabbi of the autonomous Jewish district of the Arab Islamic Republic of Greater Palestine glanced at his watch. "It is time," he said softly to his men, and waved them into position.

"Ready?" he asked a few second later.

From all corners of the intersection opposite the amphitheatre to the west, still not touched by the fiery sun rising up over the rift valley, came the whispered response: "Anachnu muchan." We are ready. A second later, the Arab police commander of eastern Jerusalem had driven into view.

"I cannot eat this food!" Yacoub al-Masri roared. "My brother is missing, the police colonel for half of al-Quds is missing, four other senior people in my government seem to have vanished, and you tell me to be calm, to eat. By Allah, you have water in your veins, Terzi!"

"Yacoub, please," Prime Minister Terzi began.

"Caliph!" al-Masri shouted. "You must address me as your caliph!"

The prime minister glanced at Fatima al-Masri and at Fahd al-Husseini, chief of security. Fatima returned Terzi's look and nodded. There was, she realized, nothing to be done now but humor her husband and, having humored him, try to isolate him. She had seen these spells before, and this one, she knew, would get worse before it got better.

"It has been nearly six hours since this rash of kidnappings, undoubtedly by the Zionist bandits...."

"Not really bandits, the Jewish underground," al-Husseini corrected.

"Fahd, do not, I repeat, do not interrupt me," declared Caliph Yacoub al-

Masri, spiritual leader and political mentor of the Arab Islamic Republic of Greater Palestine and tens of million of believers beyond its borders. "I'm warning you all: your jobs are to heed my orders, not dispute them.

"Now, as I was saying, it has been half a day since the kidnapping and we know nothing more than we did this morning. This lunch wasted my time. By the time we meet for dinner, I want facts, I want answers! If we can't cope with this first action by the Zionists, you can bet there will be more. Pinpricks at first that don't blunt our power but do challenge our control and make us look ridiculous. It's psychological warfare, and over time, could weaken our hold on our own people. The destiny of the caliphate is too important to be upset by a handful of reactionary Jews—or the failure of Palestinian officials to do their jobs.

"So, I demand solid information on the whereabouts of those seized; a plan for uprooting this Zionist underground before it goes any farther; a schedule for getting the U.N. observers out of Palestine and the subsequent liquidation of the Jews, and a plan for absorbing Syria-Lebanon into Greater Palestine under the direct rule of the caliphate.

"Don't look at me like that. We started on all this, but got delayed. It should have been finished long ago." With that, Yacoub al-Masri strode from the room.

"We got started on it, all right, then someone's idiotic plan to try and then execute Sarid and Simon Tov disrupted everything, extended international supervision and delayed our consolidation of power. Meanwhile, oh great caliph, how much longer do you think you can spend money we don't have?" al-Husseini muttered after al-Masri's departure.

"Fahd, quiet!" Fatima breathed. Prime Minister Terzi looked at the other two, his eyes wide. "Is he like this often?"

"It is a phase. He has been like this before, and will settle down, like before. I am sure of it," Fatima said.

"How long?" the prime minister persisted.

"Days. A week at most," she lied. In the beginning, when she had first known him, Yacoub's angry, manic states passed that quickly. But not anymore. In fact, he had been in one since the premature end of the War of Arab Unity, deeper, more volatile, longer than any she had ever seen. And it frightened her. Not that she would ever let Mahmud Terzi know.

Terzi, one of two suspicions confirmed, gathered some papers and prepared to leave. As for the other suspicion, he did not expect the truth about it from either Fatima or al-Husseini. Smart as they were separately, Terzi thought, together they must be fools. "I will call before I return at dinner. We can share information then."

"Good," al-Husseini said, escorting the prime minister to the door. When he was gone, the chief of security turned to the wife of the caliph. "Great," he said, his voice on edge. "It's not enough that Yacoub is working against himself, against us, now Terzi thinks he's going to play his own games. Did you see his face when you looked at me?

"We've got the U.N. monitors on our backs. We're almost out of money, and the rumblings in Damascus, Baghdad, Riyadh and Cairo are getting worse. Perhaps it is time the price of oil increased, significantly."

"And perhaps it is time Yacoub went on one of his retreats," Fatima said. As she spoke, she stepped toward al-Husseini. Fearfully, passionately—and quite briefly—the cousins embraced.

In another wing of his palace, Yacoub al-Masri stared out a window south over Jerusalem. The clear, bright sun glistened under a high blue sky, the Jerusalem stone facades of the buildings showing subtle hues, sometimes golden, sometimes rose, suddenly mixed with and overcome by an almost blinding white. A few wisps of cloud floated far above. Comfortably warm in mid-afternoon, the city air would turn chilly at sundown, cold in late night darkness. In another few weeks this brief fall, of comfortable days and bracing nights, would give way to the rainy season—to winter—its squalls, dampness, chill winds punctuated by a succession of bright, dry, crisp days.

Nature was, as it should be, reliable even in its unreliability, Yacoub al-Masri thought. But man, man was another story. By their tone of voice, their incompletely concealed expressions and poorly camouflaged body language, his wife and al-Husseini let the caliph understand that they thought him out of touch, perhaps even a bit mad. Yet he knew that of all of them—Fatima, Fahd, Terzi and the rest—only he held the Arab Islamic Republic of Greater Palestine together, only he inspired the Muslims of Syria, Lebanon and beyond. They all needed him more than he needed them, and Yacoub al-Masri knew that they knew that as well. And if, so far, he'd let Terzi live, his motive had been utilitarian, not humane.

His long legs stretched before him, crossed at the ankles. He reclined, hands clasped behind his head, resting against the high back of the chair. A strong, well-proportioned man, taller than average, his face arresting if not classically handsome, only the premature gray streaks in his hair showed the strain al-Masri shouldered as he tried to force history itself.

So the Jews think they can wound me with their pitiable little underground and a few hostage-takings? he thought. Can they still underestimate me? A smile crossed al-Masri's face and his gaze lost its focus as he began to daydream:

It was a few years after his escape into Jordan, after the start of the New Palestine Islamic Army. He lay on a cot in a small, sparsely-furnished room near the center of Damascus. Dawn was but a suggestion on the eastern horizon. Nevertheless, he already was fully awake, refreshed by the comparative luxury of four hours' uninterrupted sleep. Like a fusion reactor, al-Masri seemed to gain energy the faster he expended it. That he had in common with great conquerors through the centuries, from Alexander to Napoleon. Of course, Alexander was dead at 33, Napoleon at 45. Yacoub al-Masri had been conscious from the start of time running out.

Ever since the creation of the New Palestine Islamic Army he had been a man in motion. The Israeli defeat of the Palestine Liberation Organization in Lebanon, paradoxically, had opened opportunities to him, in Lebanon, in the Gaza Strip, and the West Bank. At first too small to be a priority of Israeli intelligence, or even the Jordanians or Syrians, he chose carefully, recruiting quality over quantity. Some of his several score of new followers were men with a little college, even degrees, searching for an answer to the Zionists' ahistorical success. They found it in al-Masri's blend of basic Sunni teachings, fired with the examples of the mujahedin in Afghanistan, alloyed with the zeal of Ayatollah Khomeini's Shi'a teachings in Iran, and made contemporary with the social-economic critique of leftist Palestinian Arab nationalism. Less egocentric than Libya's Qaddafi, at least early on, clearly more pious than Arafat, Yacoub al-Masri by his appearance, speech and deeds drew people to him, especially young people, those of high school and college age. And since a majority of Palestinians were under eighteen—while a majority of the Jews were over thirty—this was a large, energetic potential audience.

Sometimes as graduate student, sometimes as seminarian, occasionally as revolutionary or Islamic holy man, he moved through Beirut and south Lebanon, through Damascus, Amman and even the Arab towns and cities of Israel's Galilee, through Judea and Samaria. He had many names, many disguises. Men did not always know what he looked like but more and more they knew his words and honored his deeds.

"Sleep well?" The boy, son of his host this past night, regarded him with awe. The boy stood in the doorway of the room, and though he held al-Masri's breakfast tray, dared not enter.

"Yes, thank you. Please come in and put down the tray."

The boy did so, then stepped back, but not completely out of the room. "My father says you will do it."

"Do what?" al-Masri asked absently, picking carefully from a pile of rags as he dressed.

"Bring the revolution we have heard about all of our lives but never seen."

"In'shallah," al-Masri replied. God willing. "Your father is a good man. Listen to him. And," he said, a finger to his lips, "do your best to forget everything that has happened here this day. Never speak of it, understand?"

Al-Masri's sudden vehemence frightened the boy, and he backed out of the room. His father, a small businessman, had supported the Sunni Muslim Brotherhood against the heretical Alawi regime of Hafez al-Assad—until 1981, when Assad destroyed the Brothers' stronghold in Hama and 15,000 people with it. Now the merchant helped provide the small but necessary amounts of cash required by the New Palestine Islamic Army.

Three months had elapsed since al-Masri last relaxed in his uncle's villa in Amman. Moving through Jordan, Syria and Lebanon, with occasional excursions into Egypt and Saudi Arabia, along main roads and unpaved tracks, crossing and re-crossing his own path, he rarely slept in the same place two consecutive nights. Often, with the exception of a half-hour here or an hour there, he did not sleep at all. Leader and emissary of the NPIA, sometimes working with the Brothers, sometimes with Arafat's al-Fatah, slowly co-opting the Palestinian Family Jihad, al-Masri drove himself to the limits of endurance.

"We are," he reported to the boy's father late the night before, "forging the Brotherhood, zealous but politically dull; the youthful, devout but erratic Family Jihad, and some uncorrupted cadres of al-Fatah into the instrument that will liberate first all of Palestine, then Jordan, and finally Syria itself."

"I hope so. One more defeat will kill me—one way or the other," the merchant had said. "But a word of advice: liberate the Syrians first and the others will follow; free the Palestinians and Jordanians without Syria, and you'll still have nothing, nothing that lasts, anyway."

The remark had angered him. Any criticism angered him. But he was wise enough to learn first and settle scores later. Now as he listened to the Syrian capital awaken, he reminded himself of the tightrope he must continue to walk: subsume the contradictions between religion and ideology, between the veteran survivors and new recruits, absorb and smother the intra-Palestinian and inter-Arab battles among his followers and within his own personality. Be the vessel that held the internecine fury, storing and concentrating it until time to pour it out on the Zionists, on the Jews.

Give me the power, al-Masri prayed, and I will fulfill Your will. Send Your power through me, and I will return the people to You as in times before.

Like a true revolutionary, he did not wait for the masses. As his Soviet instructor in south Lebanon had made clear, the masses rarely rose by themselves, in time. Insufficient class consciousness, capitalist monopolization of information. Hence the historical necessity of the revolutionary party and the dictatorship of the proletariate—actually, as he argued with his instructor, over the proletariate. But as the young Yacoub al-Masri taught himself even then, his New Palestinian Islamic Army and its jihad was the real ideology of revolution, and Muhammad himself had been the ultimate revolutionary. Al-Masri would embrace Western technique but not philosophy. He would not fail like Nasser, Qaddafi, or Saddam Hussein, and he would not be limited in the Arab world like the Persian ayatollahs. He would blend the Arabism of the former with the Islamic power of the latter into one unstoppable force. Marx would not be imposed over Muhammed once more, to the detriment of Islam. This time the ummah, the community of believers across all borders, would use Western means to defeat the West, and overturn its Jewish, imperialistic outpost, Israel. Then, he promised himself as he had many times before, the Arab-Islamic world could be reunited, restored as the hub of civilization, under a new and great caliphate. Such was Yacoub al-Masri's dream of a total jihad, and it had sustained him.

In Damascus, in Amman, Beirut, Riyadh and Cairo, the authorities suspected. Their multiple intelligence services, mukhabarat secret police who watched over other secret police, were virtually omnipresent. The dictatorship over the proletariat became, in Middle Eastern lands, the post-colonial Arab police state over the Arabs. The regimes frequently manipulated some of the better known terrorist factions, even those ostensibly opposed to them, as necessary for purposes of state. Nevertheless, virtually was not literally, so al-Masri could operate in that shadow land between the two, between subversive and informer. He did not stage terrorist raids for transitory headlines, but organized, proceeding warily, building an infrastructure.

Small cells formed the core of his organization, with single contacts between them. Arrest and interrogation, standard Syrian torture—crushing the genitals, red hot skewers forced up the rectum, eye-gouging—could not jeopardize more than a few individuals at a time. Organizational counter-measures, including the requirement that new members assassinate political, religious, military or other rivals in the manner of the fidawi recruits of the twelfth century cult of the Assassins, complicated secret police attempts at penetration. Regardless, al-Masri took care this morning, as he did every morning, to avoid the snares he knew had been set.

"Your wardrobe suits you?" the merchant asked.

Fingering the foul-smelling rags, al-Masri replied, "Excellent."

"Hardly befitting a descendant of the Prophet," the man added.

"Is that what they say now?"

"Some whisper it, in Damascus, at least."

Al-Masri's face remained impassive, but he smiled inwardly. The claim he had instructed his NPIA aides to circulate was taking root already. "Well, people will talk. Still, it is a compliment, of course. In any case, the costume is perfect— and, thankfully, not permanent."

Moments later a limping beggar of indeterminate age shuffled through the alleys and side streets toward the central bazaar, the teeming Damascus shuk. There, among farmers from the countryside with their produce-laden wagons and trucks, urban peddlers with cheap housewares of every sort, and hordes of shoppers rich and poor, he would meet his lieutenants.

Around him the produce of local peasants and contraband from the Far East—stereos, computers, tape players, calculators, cameras, and always radios and television, as if there was something to hear, something worthwhile to watch— competed for the shoppers' money. There even were illegal video tapes, pornographic, political and religious on shelves next to each other. The Saudi-made "Kill the Jew" and the German produced "Koncentration Kamp Kommando" were both popular, almost as much as the videos of Western lesbians having oral sex. Compact discs, smuggled through Lebanon, reflected nearly every musical taste. Bargain hunters, from the rag-clad urban poor to the fashionably dressed wives of senior government officials and leading merchants, who arrived in chauffeur-driven Mercedes, mixed but did not merge.

Al-Masri disliked this disordered, godless diversity. It unsettled him, reminded him of the West, of the influences he sought to extirpate. It reminded him of the Israelis, of Georgetown University.

I will not think of that again, he swore to himself once more. What I did was right. It was necessary. She was a devil, sent to test me. And I passed the test. I am certain of it. Certain.

The beggar moved slowly on through the marketplace. No one spoke to him except by prearrangement. After nearly an hour of wandering from stall to wagon, from wagon to booth, of apparently unsuccessful alms-seeking, he entered a tiny store selling brass utensils and decorations.

"Your stock is always the same," he said to the vendor.

"No—are you blind as well as a beggar? We have added several new pieces, as if you could afford them. Look over here: they are bright and strong."

"I see that now. Too bad you are right—I don't have the money."

"Nor I the time. Out with you now, don't bother me again!"

So it went in three other stalls. After an ostensibly aimless ninety minutes, al-Masri was satisfied. His perilous excursion had been worthwhile.

He squatted at the corner of a building near the edge of the shuk, beggar's bowl in his outstretched hands. Passers-by tossed but a few coins into it. Their lonely metallic clank reaffirmed for him once again that the poor, pious man could not live under these heretical Arab regimes. And would not have to forever, he told himself.

A paramilitary policeman stopped in front of al-Masri. The militia man knocked his rifle butt hard onto the walk, next to Yacoub's leg. "I've been watching you, old man," he said in the rough, rural accent of northern Syria. "You've squatted here long enough. Move along, and don't bother people."

You've watched me, but you have not seen me, al-Masri thought. He rose as if unsteady, claiming his footing. Then, not daring to glance back at the militia man, plodded away from the market–like a turtle through a field, barely noticeable on his way, in the direction he had meant to go all along. Interesting, he mused, how unpopular governments mistake obedience for loyalty, until too late.

The policeman did not worry al-Masri. The sight of a man known to him as an informer for the mukhabarat, the secret police, did. But the agent had fixed his eye on a luckless peasant, his American videos–smuggled through Lebanon, like much of Syria's real economic activity–poorly hidden among his cucumbers, tomatoes and onions. With a twinge of regret, more for the piquant smell of cumin-spiced lamb sizzling on a charcoal brazier than the peasant, al-Masri turned into a tight, refuse-strewn alley. Potent hashish fumes, borne on a wayward breeze, filled his nostrils. Behind, at the edge of the bazaar, the tempting aroma of fresh pita bread, baking in a dozen tiny outdoor earthen ovens, lingered.

Breaking the spell of the marketplace, he pushed on through the alley, turning soon into a second, then a third. And then the rag-clad beggar disappeared through a metal gate into a small courtyard. An hour later, in an adjacent neighborhood of small but respectable homes, a young man in a business suit, carrying a briefcase in one hand and a small suitcase in another, entered a waiting taxi. The driver could well have passed for Syrian himself.

"To the airport, please."

"Where are you headed?"

"Cairo."

"On business?"

"Always."

"And how was Damascus?"

"Better this time. The brass has improved."

"You are in the market?"

"For good brass, yes."

"I'm told the brass is much better in Egypt than it used to be."

"It's about time."

Egypt in those days, the early Mubarak years, was the Nile, the army, half-a-million new mouths to feed annually in a population of 40 million, and incipient anarchy. A rising Islamic fundamentalist movement was determined to suppress the Coptic Christian fifteen percent of the county–descendants of the indigenous, pre-Islamic, even pharaonic Egyptians. An intellectual class resented the peace with Israel but depended for its life-style on the infusion of American aid money that came as baksheesh for that peace. And a coterie of senior government officials, drawn from and bolstered by the military, simultaneously modernizing the army with U.S. support and freezing relations with Israel to regain Arab legitimacy. In such an Egypt, where holy warriors already had assassinated Anwar as-Sadat, al-Masri had room to work—and plenty of domestic competition that disdained upstart Palestinian holy revolutionaries.

Saudi Arabia, where Fatima taught Arabic literature to women's classes at King Khalid University, presented its own obstacles and opportunities, as she explained to him during one visit. Her women students, in practice if not theory often beneath notice of the male authorities, made excellent sources, able to gather information from all levels of society merely by being attentive in their daily affairs.

"The Saudis are fools, taken with their wealth but anxious at their shortcomings. They have tens of billions of dollars worth of American, British and other Western-made weapons, but only two little armies, each to watch the other, neither able to absorb the military purchases.

"There's a comic-opera secret police called the Committee for the Propagation of Virtue and the Suppression of Vice—good for detecting religious back-sliders but not much else—and a separate royal guard, once mostly Pakistani, now Egyptian, to keep an eye on the secret police and protect the ruling clan.

"There are literally thousands of brothers, sons and nephews with patents of nobility, each wanting to be in the cabinet if not on the throne. They make their money in 'business,' skimming 'commissions' on every sale, import, export and construction project in the kingdom. If it weren't for oil, they'd all be mullahs, majors or petty sheiks.

"Meanwhile, a third of the population, if not more, is non-Saudi, laborers and managers. These Arabs of the peninsula—like feudal European aristocrats—do hate to get their hands dirty. And each foreigner harbors some grievance for the way he or she has been restricted and assigned second-class status. Here as invited guests, they remain unaccepted, regardless of salary.

"As to foreign policy, the Saudis continue to pay billions in protection money to Syria, the Palestinians, Iraq, everyone but the Americans, whom they dupe, selling overpriced oil, posing as an ally but in reality a weak protectorate. The Saudis even fear the Yemenis, with whom they have an old, bitter border dispute involving oil lands bigger than Palestine. There are more Yemenis than Saudis, probably, and they're a tougher people."

"But perhaps less ambitious. So what are our opportunities?" he had asked her.

"Among the Yemeni tribes, good—so long as we work quietly, not seeming to imitate Sultan Qabos of Oman as a outside meddler. Among the Saudis, not so good, unless we have senior Saudi adherents."

"I thought you were working on that?"

"I am," she said, flashing a smile she meant to be mischievous but that only infuriated him. "Prince Turki, whose oldest daughter is one of my students, is especially active in al-Ikhwan al-Muslimi. He thinks we are just the Palestinian offshoot of his movement. Let him think so; when the time comes, maybe Saudi Arabia will transform itself faster than Iran did in the month between the Shah and the ayatollah."

"In'sallah. I am weary of these pointless little parties they feel compelled to throw, wherever they are. And the alcohol they drink, while pretending not to. I am weary of the whole corrupt house of Saud, its thousands of parasitic retainers and its hypocritical pose as guardian of the two Holy Cities."

"They're classic nouveau riche, seeking to buy acceptance and demonstrate their modernity," she said, "but trapped by their need for traditional legitimacy. Don't worry–they and their money will be useful to us... if we can build momentum elsewhere first. The Saudis are congenital followers."

"We will meet in Amman when the school year ends?"

"Of course. Do you have any doubts?"

No, Yacoub al-Masri thought, not about our plans. But sometimes about you, my wife. You are a woman, yet you carry yourself like a man, you think like a leader. I wonder if you truly can be any man's follower, even mine. Yet I doubt too that I can succeed without you. It was, he felt, a weakness in himself.

Slapping his cheeks to sting away the lethargy, Yacoub al-Masri came back to himself, looking south over Jerusalem and remembering his wife. Yes, she was still a pillar to him. And by being one, she reminded him that even he was incomplete, flawed, weak.

"Hello," he said, speaking by intercom to the offices of the Islamic Sages, whom he had installed in grand suites in the palace. "Ask the khadi to come see me."

"Yes, caliph," replied the voice at the other end. "Shall I tell the judge what you wish to see him about?"

"Martial law," Yacoub al-Masri said.

Fatima al-Masri, Fahd al-Husseini and Mahmud Terzi each did a poorly-concealed double-take when the caliph brought the khadi with him to their dinner that evening. Al-Masri waved aside attempts to update him on the Jewish underground. It was just as well, al-Husseini though, since there was precious little to add to their disastrous noon-time meeting; the kidnappers had issued no demands, made no communications of any sort, in fact. No useful witnesses or other leads had been turned up, not even any bodies recovered.

"Carry on, I know you'll do your best," Yacoub al-Masri said airily. "I've been talking with the sages, with the judges of the High Sharia Court this afternoon," he said, referring to the ranking Islamic law court in the United Arabic Islamic Republic of Greater Palestine. "I believe it is time for me to renew my understanding of sharia, to cleanse my soul in preparation for the last battle with the Jews. So beginning this evening, I am going on retreat for a month or two. I will be, of course, basically incommunicado during that time–although I might consult with you individually as necessary."

"Yacoub," Fatima began, her pleading tone telegraphing her intent to dissuade him.

"Please," he said, interrupting. "Do not waste your time arguing against this. I feel the need for renewal. You yourselves know that I have done this before and that we all have profited from it it."

"Yes, but..." Fatima began again.

"No buts," her husband shot back. "There will be plenty to do. I know the

United Arab Islamic Republic of Greater Palestine needs more money. We will get it from the Japanese and Koreans. I know there is grumbling in Damascus, Cairo, Baghdad, and even Riyadh. So we will quiet Mr. Rifaat Habib. His example should do wonders in the other capitals. The plans already are in place, you need only to implement them." With that he smiled once more and then, with great appetite, dug into his meal. The others, after a moment's hesitation, did likewise. In silence.

Part IV

Jerusalem (October 29, 2007)–"When will I see you again?" Fatima al-Masri asked her husband after dinner.

"Soon. Don't worry," Yacoub said softly. "Meanwhile," he added, rising to address al-Husseini and Terzi as well, "regarding the Asians and the Syrians–it's time." Then he turned his back on them and, with the khadi at his heels, walked from the room.

"I know he can be difficult," Fatima sighed. "He has been under strain since the jihad was stopped and we had to grant the Jews autonomy. Last night he asked me if I thought that adding Egypt to the republic would enable us to compel the Americans to do as we please.

"I said it might, if the Egyptians joined us, which I thought doubtful. That angered him–and he insisted than the Americans, Jews, and maybe the Russians, if not all three working together, had bugged the palace."

"He knows we sweep it daily for listening devices, other than our own," al-Husseini put in.

"Yes, but he thinks your security people have been infiltrated by our enemies," Fatima answered. Al-Husseini felt a chill; perhaps Yacoub had infiltrated his own security agencies, and was separately listening to them.

"This madness–and that's what it appears–is becoming known. I've heard that some of our own troops joke about him, call him Yacoub al-Qaddafi."

"Such behavior must be stamped out!" Fatima shouted at Terzi. "Yacoub is, as we all know, irreplaceable. Without him there is no Arab Islamic Republic of Greater Palestine–or anywhere else, no Arab-Islamic movement beyond our borders that looks to us for direction. And this is not madness," she insisted.

"Then what would you call it?" Terzi asked, with a hint of a sneer.

"Occultation," Fatima said firmly.

"What?" Terzi demanded, uncomprehending.

"You're not really as pious as you like to appear, are you? Occultation—disappearance, religious or mystical, but still a tool of leadership. Like the vanished imam of the Shi'a, like the mahdi for whose return the dervish dance and the rest of us wait," she said. "Like the visiting Musa al-Sadr in Libya in 1978—who Qaddafi probably killed but whose example inspired the Lebanese Shi'a and so has never died. Disappearance with the promise of triumphant return."

"Spare me the lesson," Terzi said. "It sounds more like the Christians' second coming. In any case, it's from the religion of old, passive men. Tell me about the politics of this 'occultation.'"

"Passive? Like the Hezbollah in Lebanon, or the Hamas fighters prodding you onward? Musa al-Sadr may be unknown to many, but Ayatollah Khoemini wasn't. Neither was Sheik Yassin, nor bin Laden. And neither is Yacoub al-Masri! If it is revolution you really want, Yacoub will lead it." It was Fatima's turn to sneer.

"Both of you stop it, please," al-Husseini said at last. "We agree that for us politics, religion and revolution are part of the same whole. So let us use this retreat of Yacoub's. Let us present it to our advantage. To the gullible West, it will be proof of Yacoub's saintliness, like Gandhi meditating in his ashram. To the faithful we will hold it up as a sign of Yacoub's purity, his legitimacy. As for the unreliable, we will seize this opportunity to clean house while the caliph is engaged in 'higher matters.'"

"Now you're making sense," Terzi said. "There already are too many separate, competing security agencies, too many deputy ministers of this, that and the other thing freelancing, acting like they're in charge. Give me two weeks and I'll have things in order. With your approval, of course."

"Of course," al-Husseini said tightly.

"Both of you remember this," Fatima said. "We must maintain unity and the appearance of unity to the outside world—and to the Jews. Whether Yacoub is gone for a week, a month, or longer, we must be seen to be in power and exercising power at his direction, as if he were still at work. And," she hesitated, "we must take care that nothing leaks, nothing that suggests Yacoub is not himself, that he has become erratic, weakened. It is not true, and it would undermine us as we try to get the cash from the Japanese, the Koreans and the others, and quickly."

For some time after Terzi left, al-Husseini stood next to his cousin. She was agitated. He became aware of her scent, some sweet fragrance from a shampoo or perfume combined with the smell of her body, the sweat on her skin. He felt himself aroused. He turned to her. "Let us pray," he said, in a strained voice. They did.

Later, al-Husseini asked Fatima how long she thought they could keep Yacoub's absence from government hidden. "Not long," she said, "but it must be long enough."

"It will be only days before foreign diplomats and reporters hound me for appointments, interviews with Yacoub, photo opportunities at the least. Even those friendly to us, and there are many, won't be brushed off lightly, or repeatedly, not without starting to suspect something," he replied.

"Well, we will just have to make certain this 'disappearance' does not last long," Fatima answered, as much from hope as conviction.

"Speaking of diplomats," al-Husseini resumed, "I'm told they are beginning to gossip about us. About you and me, I mean. If it gets back to Yacoub, his rage will know no bounds. And if it gets out, it could undermine our authority."

"I wish," Fatima said, barely audibly, "that the gossip were true."

Al-Husseini stared at her. She returned his gaze for one brief moment, eyes on fire. Her own voice strained, she said, "But our struggle is greater than any individual." Then she turned and strode out, but not before he saw the muscles of her jaw sag.

"I know," he said to the door closing behind Fatima. "But I cannot accept."

Sympathetic ambassadors and Western correspondents were not the only ones gossiping about Fatima and al-Husseini, not as lovers so much as "the caliph's keepers." The Central Intelligence Agency; Russia's remodeled KGB, the Federal Protective Security Service; Britain's MI-5; the remnant of the Jews' Mossad and their colleagues and competitors across the globe speculated on which of a dozen diseases al-Masri must suffer from to send him into hiding this way. But none guessed the extent of his self-removal from daily affairs of the Arab Islamic Republic of Greater Palestine. They did not grasp the thoroughness of the "regency." Fatima, al-Husseini and Terzi, through manipulation of their own media, plus the bounty paid informers who denounced to the mukhabarat those slandering the caliph, kept al-Masri's popular image largely intact. For the moment. "It is frightening," al-Husseini said to his cousin one night. "Yacoub sometimes reminds me now of Idi Amin when he was our guest in Riyadh years ago and I, as a young Fatah security officer, was in charge of his 'escort.'"

"I know," replied Fatima. "Yacoub's zeal for Islam and for Arabism has led him to greatness. But his magnificent obsession, this new study to prove to the world the superiority of Islam over Judaism and Christianity, is a terrible diversion—one that might undo everything."

"We still need him," she added. "Our grasp on power, without him, is uncertain. We must manage him without alienating him."

"And must keep the Asian cash coming if we're to avoid bankruptcy—we've expanded so far so fast," al-Husseini said.

His hand reached toward hers. She touched his, then withdrew. She is only part conspirator, al-Husseini admitted to himself. She also is still part wife.

Only months after the great jihad, after he had assembled a united Arab state of Jordan, western Palestine including half the Galilee and most of the Negev, and had vanquished the Jews almost as thoroughly as Saladin had the Crusaders, Yacoub al-Masri lived as a semi-recluse. Occasionally seen on videotaped broadcasts or heard on prerecorded radio addresses, the caliph—whose holy influence, thanks to his 'occultation', extended beyond Palestine into Syria, Lebanon, Saudi Arabia, Iraq and Egypt, busied himself writing a comparative commentary on the Koran, the Hebrew Bible and New Testament.

"This will be even more important than forging the Republic, than crushing the Zionists," he informed Fatima, al-Husseini and Terzi one evening in December. "My commentary, God willing, will be the beacon the Arabs use to cut through the darkness of Christianity, the way our knives and rifles cut through the occupation of the Jews. Christ will be seen in his true light, like Moses, a messenger who paved the way for Mohammed. Then all will worship Allah and our victory will be complete! I correct myself–this work is not more important than forging the Republic... it is the capstone of the construction. The Jews, and the other non-Muslims, non-Arabs–the Copts, the Maronites, the Berbers, the Kurds, the Druze, the Ba'hai, the Alawi–will convert. Or else. Then, with the help of the millions of Muslims already there, Europe too, and finally America itself."

He had tapped the purest source of the zealot's power: he now believed his words were God's. For every finished video tape or radio broadcast a dozen false starts had to be erased. The smallest thing, from faulty equipment to a technician's appearance, could set al-Masri off. And the moment he departed from his script, the day was lost to disquisitions, declamations, ranting. Fatima and al-Husseini learned they must control the entire process; an iron grip was required to minimize chances that the caliph would slip from a brief "state communique" into an endless tirade "in the name of Allah, the merciful, the compassionate... "

Every miscue, every delay, no matter how minor, al-Masri blamed on "the Jews, the cursed Jews!" In his mind they were everywhere, paradoxically more threatening after their defeat than before. He planned a great massacre, "something on the order of the Mongol invasions" of the thirteenth century, he explained, to "cleanse" the rest of Palestine. No doubt he already would have attempted it but for the presence of U.N. observers and international "peace keepers" in the autonomous Jewish district. He forced himself to wait; authorization for UNFORPAL–the United Nations Force in Palestine–was due to expire in less than five months and the Russians, Chinese, and French, over half-hearted American objections, were insisting that it was too costly and no longer needed. As it was, many Jews, especially young women of marriageable age, already were disappearing. Like in the old days. The days before the Zionists, when the good Jews knew their place, in the mellah–the Jewish quarter–where no synagogue could be as tall as the lowest mosque.

The Japanese plan, which al-Masri had approved before making his retreat, proved successful enough at first. The Arab Islamic Republic of Greater Palestine's allies, in particular Iraq and Saudi Arabia, controlled nearly all of Japan's petroleum sources. This was especially so after Iraq's de facto annexation of Kuwait and the Saudi's benevolent take-over of the United Arab Emirates, both mimicking Syria's absorption of Lebanon.

Tokyo had been informed shortly after the War of Arab Unity that its government and giant industrial concerns henceforth would use the new Bank of Arabia as their prime commercial bank. Loans, deposits, bond issues, inter-bank and international transfers all would take place on terms favorable to Palestine, which with Iraq and Saudi Arabia controlled the institution.

"Should Tokyo hesitate, let alone refuse, the chain of oil tankers that stretches one every three hours from the Straits of Hormuz to the port of Nagasaki will snap!" al-Masri had declared. "And what is good for Japan is good for Korea and Taiwan. The economic centers of the Far East must be our patrons."

Tokyo, Seoul, and Taipei did not dawdle. Soon the large, free Asian economies were as dependent on Palestine and its partners in the Bank of Arabia for financial services as they were for fuel. But this revenue—large as it was for al-Masri's country of ten million, his empire of twenty five million, had its limits. In the Arab Islamic Republic of Greater Palestine, even more than in Iraq and Saudi Arabia, grandiose construction, military and social welfare plans consistently ran over budget and beyond schedule. "Everyone is getting rich—on paper," Terzi had informed him once, "but few of our people can afford necessities. New cars litter the streets of Nablus and Hebron, as well as Baghdad and Riyadh, thanks to a surplus of dealers and dollars but a deficit of spare parts and mechanics. New villas, with satellite dishes, pop up like mushrooms all over Ramallah and Jenin, and even in Gaza City—but the sewers are backed up and the roads crumbling. Everyone has a video tape player, a computer and a cell phone, but despite martial law there are bread riots. Our growth has come too fast, without consolidation."

Al-Masri glared at him. "Never speak ill of Islamic Palestine!" he shouted, his face red, contorted. Then, more in control of himself, he added, "I am the leader, you are the executive. If problems exist, I expect you to solve them." That's why I had your dosage lowered, he told himself.

Sure, I'll just wave my magic wand, Terzi thought. To al-Husseini and Fatima he pleaded. "Such imbalances, to be expected in a thrown-together little empire such as ours, nevertheless could threaten our stability."

"Do threaten it," al-Husseini corrected. "But without Yacoub's active, daily involvement, we cannot correct the problem at its source. Too many people with a little authority behave too independently. Frankly, too much baksheesh, too much protexia," he admitted, using the Arab word for graft, the Hebrew for "who-you-know."

"Then we must get more money from the Asians," Fatima asserted.

"Without Yacoub's endorsement?" al-Husseini asked.

"He insists he cannot be disturbed. His writing is going too well, he says."

"I'm afraid we're overreaching," al-Husseini warned. "Just as OPEC's oil price escalations in the '70s forced the West to learn to conserve, to find additional energy sources, this… extortion—that's what it is, really—will force some kind of reaction. Japan, Korea and the Taiwanese are no less proud, and, in the long run stronger, than we."

"Do you have an alternative?" she challenged.

He did, but dared not utter it.

"Tokyo and the others have the money, but not the military reach. As the world learned with the Afghan war, only the United States has that, and the Johnston administration gets less inclined to use it every day," Fatima said. "We must have the money, now!"

"I wish I could be sure this will work," Terzi said. "But I can't. I've dealt with those people for years, and I tell you they have too much pride for this."

In fact, within days of receiving their notice of a twenty-five percent surcharge from the Bank of Arabia, the governments of Korea and Taiwan had sent senior officials to Tokyo for an emergency meeting. Historic enmity submerged by the present common threat, they soon formed what they called the Triple

Alliance and began to develop a coordinated response. For the first months of its existence, the alliance remained unknown even to the intelligence agencies of friendly countries.

*　*　*

Alexandria, Virginia (January 3, 2008)–Rabbi Jeri Levi had refused to watch the hanging of former Prime Minister Meir Sarid and Defense Minister Ariel Simon Tov on television, or the repeated videotaped replays. But the killings, as final punctuation to the War of Arab Unity, had greatly affected her work. Those American Jews who had been on their way out of Judaism–shedding their heritage, changing their names, hurried to complete the metamorphosis, to reach a post-Jewish haven. But other Jews were galvanized by the executions. They reasserted themselves, began to rebuild communal life on a more assertive footing. Many flocked to her ministry. Emotionally battered but unbeaten, this saving remnant saw in Levi its leader.

Even before the war, Congressman Marcus' support of her work began to bear results. Morty Halpern raised the money and Mona Margolis arranged the bookings. Jeri Levi learned to be at home in airports, television studios, Jewish community centers and synagogues all along the East Coast and beyond. Her reputation spread quickly from metropolitan Washington throughout the shrunken but still-operating network of national Jewish agencies and their speakers' bureaus.

Interviews and stories in the remaining Anglo-Jewish press led to general news media coverage. She turned up on network news programs and a spate of syndicated television talk shows–on which the hosts invariably tried to relate to her as a feminist or New Age cleric instead of as a neo-traditional Jewish revivalist. A collection of her sermons was selling nearly as well as the organic-cooking-for-mental-health and ghost-written celebrity autobiographies that choked the best-seller lists.

A cover story in Hadassah, a Jewish women's magazine, led to a two-page spread, with photographs, in People. This circulated also in the Jewish autonomous district of Palestine. Her Internet web site registered thousands of hits per week, many from overseas. Rabbi Jeri Levi had become a demi-celebrity herself, her organization a cottage industry of Jewish renewal.

Nevertheless, her reception in the U.S. Jewish community–more accurately, in the Jewish communities–was mixed. She spoke mostly to people who found themselves in the reaffirming third of diaspora Jewry. To the speeding assimilators she sounded obsolete, foolishly sentimental, dangerously high decibel; to the "religion only" Jews–many but by no means all Orthodox–she appeared as a national zealot, an old-fashion secular Zionist abusing a believer's vocabulary, a woman doing man's work.

But in her book, her sermons and interviews, Jeri Levi insisted, as Solomon Schechter had a century before her, that one could no more separate Jewish nationalism from Judaism than one could the farm from the farmer. "A faith,

Judaism, articulated in a language, Hebrew, rooted in a land, eretz Yisrael, populated by a people, the Jews," she repeated until others began to reiterate the ancient truth as a new mantra. "A healthy diaspora can exist only as an extension of a strong Israel, and subsequent to it. A strong Israel is central to Judaism and the Jews. It can draw from the diaspora and inspire the diaspora, but dare not feed it at its own expense," she insisted.

"And the purpose of the Jews, to be not a light unto the nations but the light necessary for human redemption cannot be accomplished unless the Jewish people itself is living as the Chosen People, as a Kingdom of Priests on its Holy Land. Not that this will be abnormal, or paranormal, but instead it will emerge, in practice, as completely normal, at last. It turns out, to bring Herzl to his proper conclusion, the Jewish state is not that physical place in which Jews will lead 'normal' lives like any other people, but the place in which the theory of Judaism will be normalized, and normally practiced, for the good of all."

It seemed obvious, after 4,000 years of Jewish experience and in accord with the plain teachings of the Torah. Of course, other Jews fought her bitterly, especially the diaspora rabbinic establishment. To plain Torah teachings it responded with Talmudic digressions, with midrashic emendations—subtle, stimulating, but ultimately diverting. It could not be otherwise, given rabbinic Judaism's exilic roots and long history as the necessary but not sufficient balm of the Jewish people in its nearly two millennia of defeat, dispersion and self-effacement.

Rabbi Levi's followers came to be labeled (first by Time magazine, derisively), as neo-Zionists. Levi found the connation dubious, implicitly attempting to separate the religious and national halves of the same whole. Regardless, her influence, and the number of her followers, mushroomed.

Jeri Levi learned that she could live with the notoriety. She was winning, in fact already had won, that larger congregation she had been seeking after Or Kodesh. As she kept traveling, talking and writing she wondered how she would lead her new flock, where, and what God had in store for them.

*   *   *

Kibbutz Nof Benjamin (February 22, 2008)–Aharon Tabor was walking unaided. He limped, but not badly. "All things considered, you've made a miraculous recovery," Shoshana told him. The pair strolled along the beach at the edge of Kibbutz Nof Benjamin in the early evening darkness. Most of his fellow kibbutzniks still had yet to see Tabor following the battle against the Syrians, and he was damned if he would advertise his resurrection to the Arabs of the adjacent village of Gizr a-Zarka.

"I feel much better," Tabor replied. "But there's an ache in my leg, where I'm sure the shattered bone did not mend properly."

"It could have been worse," Shoshana said, her arm squeezing his waist.

He smiled at her. "Anyway, walking helps me regain muscle tone."

They moved on, unspeaking, for a while. The breakers from the Mediterranean crashed rhythmically, almost hypnotically, along the beach.

"Stop!" Aharon commanded in an urgent whisper. A few paces ahead of them, coiled at the edge of a sea grass clump, lay a viper. "Probably sleeping," said Shoshana. "They like the warmth of day to move around in."

"They like it, but they don't require it," Tabor answered.

Notwithstanding the holstered 9 mm. automatic pistols each of them wore, they gave the snake a wide berth. "That reminds me," Shoshana said, "what are we going to do about the People's Progressive Party?"

"The 'Canaanites?'" her husband asked.

"Yes," Shoshana said. "I hear that they're trying to set themselves up as the 'sole, legitimate representative' of the Israeli people and negotiate with the Arab Islamic Republic of Greater Palestine."

"Negotiate what?" Aharon Tabor inquired.

"An 'autonomous Jewish cultural homeland,' but without any municipal, civil—without any governmental—authority. A return of the Jews to dhimmi status under the Muslims… 'protected people' with religious privileges but no enforceable rights. I think it's a dodge to undermine support for Magen Israel among the amcha, the grassroots people, claiming we'll only 'bring more bloodshed in the name of the obsolete dream of Jewish nationalism,'" his wife responded.

"And who's leading this? Wait, don't tell me—Shulamit Dayan and Ehud Ramoni?" Aharon Tabor mentioned the two leaders of the self-declared "post-Zionist, post-Jewish, Canaanite progressive party." Both had served in the last Knesset.

"You got it," Shoshana said, "the 'best and the brightest of the beautiful Israelis'."

"They survived the war?" Tabor asked.

"Yes," Shoshana said, "probably as guests of Mahmoud Terzi."

"You can't be serious,," Aharon challenged.

"But I am. We think they offered themselves to the Palestinian Arab leadership after the last Knesset session as peace-makers, mediators, whatever."

"To sign the surrender, you mean," Tabor cut in.

"Their leaflets and posters have appeared all over the Jewish autonomous area," she explained. "They're calling the Jewish district 'the world's largest ghetto,' implying it's not worth fighting for, and suggesting we endorse those Arabs who want to help Jews 'return to the lands of our origins,' that is, 'resettlement' in Europe and the Middle East."

"You're not serious," Aharon said.

"Absolutely," Shoshana added. "According to Dayan and Ramoni," she went on, "we're post-religious Jews and post-Zionists Israelis. They don't see that these are contradictions, or that they also would rule out our 'return' to Europe, since they make us residents of a 'Jewish cultural homeland' and simultaneously cancel our presence here as non-Zionist post-Jews, or whatever. So really we should float in the air, people without a land.

"But they have that covered, too," she concluded. "No one said they weren't facile. They insist that as Hebrew-speaking Canaanites, we are really just another tribe of Arabs, and—under those terms—deserve to assimilate here."

"Then why aren't we entitled to our own 'Arab' state?" Aharon Tabor asked angrily. "This stuff is dangerous. It's what corrupted the Israeli intelligensia, eroded general Israeli morale–and the rigor of Israeli generals–from the 1970s on, the religion of the secular, liberal arts professoriate that found even Ben-Gurion too right-wing. It's why Rabin negotiated with the Palestinians as if they held all claims to legitimacy, acquiescing that 'Hebron is a Palestinian city' and all that abasement and appeasement. We might just have a chance here, of holding on or even regaining what we've lost, with clarity and unity, with confidence in the rightness of our cause–but not unless this 'Hebrew Canaanite' intoxication isn't stopped!"

"How?" Shoshana asked, urgency in her voice.

"Cut off the snake's head," Tabor said grimly.

They looked at each other, then walked on in silence.

* * *

Washington, D.C. (March 2, 2008)–Representative Jonathan Marcus and Rabbi Jeri Levi sat in the former's office with eight other people, including leaders of several major American Jewish organizations, or what had been major Jewish organizations. The Arab Islamic Republic of Greater Palestine had communicated a proposal through the Peoples Progressive Party of the Jewish autonomous district. The party, which asserted that it spoke on behalf of the approximately four million Jews remaining in Palestine, proposed that Palestine and the United States cooperate in their resettlement. Many would come, of course, to the United States, some would relocate to Western Europe and others to Canada, Australia and perhaps New Zealand. A sizable number would remain in Palestine as "Jewish Arabs." A quota for Orthodox Jews who insisted on remaining in Jerusalem could be discussed.

"Those in our government who take the proposal seriously–and most don't– are hesitant," Marcus said. "There's no room in the budget for refugee resettlement on such scale, and, of course, given the current wave of antisemitism, such a flood of Jewish immigration might be political dynamite."

"Socially, too," said Ron Goldblatt, head of the small but wealthy American Jewish Committee. "Although the F.B.I. puts the number at only seven, according to our figures there were nineteen murders–including four lynchings–last year directly attributed to antisemitism."

"Our figures show twenty-one," interjected Melvin Wolfman, veteran head of the Anti-Defamation League. He and Goldblatt had been rivals for two decades, and neither saw any reason to stop now.

In addition to Marcus, Levi, Goldblatt and Wolfman, those present included Morty Halpern; Sylvia Weinberg, who had left Or Kodesh to rejoin Rabbi Levi; Mickey Teitelbaum, Marcus' staffer on the Middle Eastern affairs subcommittee; Beatrice Gottleib of Hadassah, Mervin Adelstein, current chairman of the still-active rump of the Conference of Presidents of Major American Jewish Organizations; Felicia Sanchez, taking notes; and former Adm. Chester Wingate Fogerty, now Marcus' pro bono military affairs adviser.

Marcus perched on a corner of his desk. Jeri Levi sat in a small, standard congressional issue green leather armchair. The others occupied similar chairs or slumped in the spongy, dark green leather couch or sat on secretarial chairs wheeled into the crowded office.

"What do you mean, our government is balking?" Adelstein wanted to know.

"The Johnston administration blanched at the suggestion of up to two million Jews suddenly arriving on the national doorstep as a way to bring final Middle East peace. Not just the murders Mr. Goldblatt mentioned, but the fire-bombings of several dozen synagogues, looting of Jewish businesses, attacks on Jewish students on campuses across the country. Our psychological shield, Israel, was kicked aside, so we're perceived as vulnerable once more. And perception is everything in these matters.

"However, according to hints from the First Lady's office, if there is no cost to the taxpayer, something might be possible for a somewhat smaller number of immigrants."

"You mean we have to ransom our fellow Jews privately?" Rabbi Levi asked.

"Something like that. Remember the 'trucks-for-Jews' proposal the Germans floated during World War II? This time the president's wife seems to be saying, 'Okay, we'll admit some of the Jews, most on temporary visas, but only if private funding, accommodations and other support can be arranged,'" Marcus explained.

"So what's left of the American Jewish community must literally become its brothers' keepers for what's left of the Israeli Jewish community?" Levi responded.

"Basically, that's it," Marcus said.

"And if this fails?" wondered Bernice Gottleib.

"We don't know. After all, this has been cast as a trial balloon of the Jews, or at least some of the Jews, in the autonomous Jewish district. It is not, officially, a proposal by the Arab Islamic Republic of Greater Palestine," Marcus said.

"No, but al-Masri would not have let it go this far, not through his official channels, if he weren't interested in our response," said Teitelbaum.

"Speaking of al-Masri, we haven't heard much of him lately, have we?" Levi asked.

"No—but he's heard of you," Teitelbaum said.

"What do you mean?" Marcus asked.

"I'm told that when the international edition of People, the one with the story on Jeri as 'the Jewish Billy Graham' arrived at Ben Gurion—I mean, Sheik Yassin—Airport a while back, the censors flipped," Teitelbaum said. "All copies of that issue were confiscated and burned. Usually they just cut out the offending articles or pictures—you know, starlets in bikinis, stories about non-observant Muslims—that sort of thing."

"So the Jews really are Prisoners in Zion, now that Zion is no more," Jeri said.

"Excuse me," Fogerty broke in, "but it seems to me that if Jews are still committed to surviving as a people, your goal should be strengthening those in Palestine, figuring out how to reinforce them, not considering some defeatist evacuation."

"That's why I asked you to join us," Marcus said. "You have the expertise, and, I must say, some recent experience along these lines...."

"Well, I do have an idea or so," Fogerty admitted. "But I think it's more appropriate that you all get your concerns on the table before I toss in my two cents' worth."

"We have to strengthen American Jewry, don't we, before we can help the Israelis?" Rabbi Levi asked.

"On that premise I invited Mrs. Gottleib, Mr. Goldblatt, Mr. Wolfman and Mr. Adelstein," Marcus said. "Anyway, we don't seem to have the levers anymore to influence events in the Jewish autonomous district."

"Besides," said Gottleib, more as a lament than as a statement, "it will be many years, if ever, before Jews are sovereign again in Palestine."

"With all due respect, I disagree," Fogherty said. The others, silent, stared at him. "Look, there are still more than four million Jews living pretty much where the same number of Jews lived when Israel was a sovereign little power sitting out the '91 Persian Gulf War, inconvenienced by but not in existential danger from Iraqi Scuds. That is, most of them in the 'L' 75 miles long north-to-south, and 35 miles west-to-east, and ten miles wide, from Haifa to Bat Yam south of Tel Aviv and east up to Jerusalem. Unless I miss my guess, in that Jewish heartland they've got plenty of small arms and probably a para-military organization or two. Not a bad base at that end, I would say.

"Now here, and you all know better than I, you've got several million committed Jews. Whether it's one, two, or three million I don't know, and it probably doesn't matter. You've got critical mass–if you get, or provide–compelling leadership.

"So that's sufficient at this end, with organization and planning. As to leadership, I suspect you're it, or you wouldn't be here today. So it'll be up to you to carry the ball. Sometimes," the admiral added, thinking of his own career, of Simcha Horowitz, and of this Rabbi Levi, "events mold the man. Or woman."

"What makes you so sure about the Jews in what was Israel, their weapons and militia?" Marcus asked.

"I'd rather not say," Fogerty replied. He was thinking of the letter his wife had received from Mrs. Horowitz not long ago, a letter about gardens and vines, foxes and hares–on first glance. On second reading, an allegory about grapes and spies, dry bones and a nation reborn. A concise, coded intelligence report. "However, given that the Israel Defense Forces was largely a citizen army built on an active reserve, and the army did not so much surrender as melt away with the truce, I doubt there's a Jewish house without its small arsenal of pistols and light automatic rifles, grenades and who knows what else. And, I hope you'll pardon me, given the Jewish penchant for starting organizations..."

"Starting, if not properly maintaining," Marcus interjected. "Two Jews, three synagogues..."

"Yes, so I assume at least two armed Jewish undergrounds," Fogerty said.

"But how do we connect?" Adelstein wanted to know.

"When the time comes, I doubt that'll be a problem," the admiral said. "First priority, it seems to me, is deciding what you mean to do. Is it to reestablish a free, Jewish state? If so, act quickly. It will be easier to do now, in the next year or two, than later, when–if–the Arab Islamic Republic of Greater Palestine eventually consolidates its position. The contras, with U.S. help, never let the Sandinistas get an iron grip on power in Nicaragua. That's what the Jews of Palestine have to do to al-Masri and his people. Contest, overtly or more often covertly every edict, every move. Guerrilla warfare without the war, or at least without much of it, without provoking great reprisals, at first.

"So the Jews in America have to get organized to help that effort, and quickly. And by the way, whatever you do along the lines of organizing, establishing networks and viable new institutions here to help the Israelis will redound to the renewed vigor of the American Jewish community."

"So the short run is the long run," Jeri Levi said.

"That's how it looks to me," Fogerty replied.

"Are you saying that the remnants of the just-defeated IDF can, in a year or two, take on the Arab armies, and win? Without an air force?" Marcus said.

"I am. Or at least, that its best chance to do that is in the near future," Fogerty responded. "As for an air force, a small one will do–given the element of surprise. And I think I know where to find it. You all put together an organization here to help the Jews in Palestine, and let me worry about air power."

"I'll admit I don't understand, or see the logic in, everything you've just said," Gottleib remarked. "But admiral, you've given me the first real hope I've felt since the War of Arab Unity. I have to ask, however, why do you care what happens to the Jews in Palestine, or even here? Care so much to get involved like this?"

"I am a Christian, a born-again Christian. I pray for the peace of Jerusalem. That's Jerusalem the physical and spiritual capital of the Jews, not al-Quds, not Aelina Capitoliana, not any other Jerusalem but David's city," Fogerty said matter-of-factly. "I believe that the Second Coming of my Savior awaits the ingathering of the Jewish exiles in Zion. This dispersion, if you consider it that, can only slow things down. So I'm interested for my own sake, my own faith and what it says to the world. I also believe, as the Old Testament teaches, that the Lord will bless those who bless Israel.

"Besides, you could say I've always sided with the underdog, at least with the deserving underdog. My father taught me that might does not make right, that right makes might–but sometimes needs a little kick to make it work. It seems to me that much of the Arab-Israeli conflict really has been an Arab conflict with the Jews, over not tolerating them as free and equal people on their ancestral land. And I don't like intolerance."

"That's good enough for me," Gottleib said.

"I'll second that," Marcus added.

For the next few hours, the small group worked to sketch a structure to resurrect Jewish sovereignty in eretz Yisrael and rebuild an organized Jewish community in the United States that rested on peoplehood, nationhood, as well as on religion. Rabbi Levi's nascent organization, in possession–via Marcus–of the American Israel Political Action Group's membership list, bolstered by the hundreds of thousands of names and addresses on the Hadassah lists and pirated portions of the membership rolls of the Orthodox, Conservative, and Reform movements became the kernel of a new umbrella group. Potential donors, activists, educators and polemicists were identified. Means of outreach and substantive programs were outlined. That evening in Congressman Jonathan Marcus' suite in the Cannon House Office Building the ten of them drafted the blueprint for a salvation machine and put it into motion. They finished around midnight, writing a statement announcing the birth of the American Jewish Council or U.S. Kehillah, a quasi-official association open to all Jews who paid a nominal fee. Jeri Levi would announce it on her next WBLS broadcast, now widely syndicated and heard around the country and the world by satellite radio and Internet–partly to preempt any similar attempts by other de facto groups.

"Remember," Fogerty advised, "welcome support and participation from all quarters, but make clear you are going ahead regardless. Hold the reins yourselves. Stick together–there'll be white-knuckle flying before you reach your destination–and whatever else, lead!"

When they finally were alone, Sanchez asked Marcus, "Well, what do you think?"

"I think," he responded, holding her lightly about the waist, "the Jews are damned lucky to have a Gentile like Fogerty on our side."

"What about me?" she asked, looking inscrutable.

"I think I'm damned lucky–no, not damned, blessed."

* * *

Kibbutz Nof Benjamin (March 12, 2009)–Spring arrived in the Jewish autonomous district with extraordinary rains. Wildflowers of purple, crimson and white decorated the Galilee hills. Late oranges and grapefruit–in the groves not bulldozed during Israel's post-Oslo economic bubble or leveled in the War of Arab Unity–remained to be harvested along the coastal plain of Sharon. Even the dun-colored hardpan of the northern Negev strip still part of the autonomous area showed thin green cover punctuated by brilliant, low-growing wildflowers. After the winter rains water flowed, briefly, along every otherwise dry northern gully and southern wadi, leaving subterranean sources to feed the springs and hidden pools of the wilderness.

A few Jews went out to farm small holdings in the western Galilee, near Haifa. A few cared for a small portion of the once-productive lands in the settlements between Tel Aviv and Beersheva, land rapidly returning to the stony desolation of pre-Zionist days. Two-thirds of the territory, one-third of the industrial and commercial capacity, nearly ten percent of the people–including a third of the standing army and its leadership–such had been Israel's losses in the war.

Yet within the confines of the Jewish autonomous area, daily life continued in many ways almost as before. Tel Aviv, Haifa, and western Jerusalem were still Jewish cities. Millions of Jews went to work or school in the morning and returned home at night. Their standard of living was lower, their freedom circumscribed, but they were still there. For the fourth time in twenty-seven hundred years, in a phenomenon unknown to any other people, a Jewish state had lapsed but the Jews of eretz Yisrael endured.

Except for the crater where the southern wing of the communal dining hall had stood and the roofless shell of the gymnasium, Kibbutz Nof Benjamin looked much as it had before the war. A few of the old cottages with the red tile roofs remained, relics of a '50s picture post card, among more modern buff-colored masonry mini-apartment blocks. The children's houses, the clinic–built with poetic justice on Roman ruins–the barn-like laundry and general store still dotted the low ridge three hundred meters from the Mediterranean shore. Pine trees shaded the walks and gravel and asphalt lanes circled the perimeter as before. Workers gathered the last of the citrus and avocadoes. Volunteers from the States and elsewhere–prohibited by the truce but smuggled into the autonomous area nonetheless–stretched wire cables to hold young banana trees upright. Veteran kibbutzniks continued to supervise operations in the plastics and lithography plants, although the onerous export fees now went to the treasury of the Arab Islamic Republic instead of the Israeli bureaucracy. Children still climbed mulberry trees outside the kindergarten buildings and a few ponies grazed on the lawn next to the auditorium.

The mood of the village had evolved from desolation in the weeks immediately following the war through sullen resignation to–in this spring of exquisite natural beauty–something more. Like every such settlement, Nof Benjamin had its cell of Magen Yisrael. Like some others, it also had a core of the People's Progressive Party. Members of each lied to, and spied on, the other.

Aharon Tabor, fully recuperated but still in hiding on his own kibbutz, both lead the Nof Benjamin cell of Magen Yisrael and served as a senior member of the underground's national leadership. He read again the message on the scrap of paper in front of him. It had been flashed from a small ship offshore the previous night and copied by the watchman on his station atop the water tower.

The tower itself told much of the story of the kibbutz. A fifty-foot high concrete cylinder, it was one of the first permanent structures erected at Nof Benjamin in the 1940s. It did double duty, storing precious water and serving as observation and defense point in the waning days of the British Mandate for Palestine and in Israel's 1948 War of Independence. Damage from the machine guns of a straying Syrian fighter in '48 had never been repaired. It reminded each generation of kibbutzniks of where and who they were.

With the relative calm after the '56 Sinai campaign and the arrival of national television–one government-controlled station broadcasting seven hours a day–in the late 1950s, the observation post was dismantled. A communal antennae replaced it. Extension of the national water carrier from Lake Kinneret a few years later ended the tower's original role.

But when P.L.O. terrorists from Lebanon began probing the coast, attempting night landings in rubber dingies in the '70s, a successor to the original observation post was installed. The water tower became a watch tower once more, with a regular army detachment on duty. After the evacuation of Judea and Samaria as part of the Oslo II agreement with the Palestinians, the IDF reassigned the observation unit fifteen miles east to border patrol. So the kibbutzniks themselves–in some cases sons and daughters, or even grandchildren of the original guardians–reassumed the watchman's role.

To start and finish each shift they scaled the side of the tower, using steel rungs embedded in the concrete as footholds, carrying their equipment up and down on their backs. They continued now not as the IDF but as members of Magen Yisrael. And, fearing a possible cut-off by their Arab overlords, the kibbutz resumed storing water in the tower as well.

"One hour after dark, swim to the islands. Two men in a small boat will be waiting. They will transfer you to the yacht 'Athene.' In Cyprus, claim ticket at Nicosia airport. Name, D. Pearl.

"In Rome, as N. Diamond, change planes for Washington. Friends of New Israel will meet you at Dulles International. Identification and tickets will be provided. Take care—airports in Nicosia and Rome are watched."

By whom, Tabor wondered. Al-Masri's men, Jewish spies for the PPP, the Cypriots or Italians, even the Americans? Whoever, he would be careful.

The message memorized, Tabor folded and refolded the scrap of paper, then tore it to pieces, dropped the remnants into an ashtray and burned them. He dumped the ashes into the sink and ran the water.

It was late. In less than forty-eight hours he would be in the United States for the first time in more than a decade.

During the fall of 1994, Tabor had studied aqua-culture, lectured on Israeli fish-pond farming at the Scripps Oceanographic Institute in California and made speeches across the state on behalf of the Jewish National Fund. The size and variety of California had astonished him. It was like Europe, many different terrains and climates, different cultures and languages, different ethnic groups and races. Yet unlike Europe, it claimed to be just one state, albeit a big one, in a much larger national union.

This he found hard to understand. "Californians seem to have little in common except moving away from their pasts—and maybe each other—and an expectation of participating in an ever-growing economy... as if economics ultimately can be divorced from culture," he had written his father, Ambassador Yehuda Tarbitsky. "Are Americans fooling themselves about their nationhood?" he asked. "If California is an example—and they say here that California is the rest of America ahead of schedule—the United States is not a country, but the remains of a benevolent empire."

If California as a whole was perplexing, the Jews of Los Angeles County, where he spent considerable time, were a revelation. There were over half a million of them, enough to tip the Arab-Israeli balance back in the Jews' favor. At first he thought their places were not in the San Fernando Valley or even the more distant suburbs, not in Hollywood or Beverly Hills or Brentwood but in the Galilee, the Sharon, the Negev, even in Judea and Samaria. They were Jews but felt little personal tie to Jewish land. Having moved to California from all over America, from all over the world—including tens of thousands from Iran and Israel and Latin America—they did not see Israel as a homeland so much as the old country, even if they'd never lived in it. After speaking before a few J.N.F. audiences, he understood how determined they were to avoid such knowledge, to avoid the ancient concept of a people with a land of its own. They were Jews, alright, but for most of them that was a religious—no, spiritual—or cultural term, no longer ethnic and certainly not national.

"Southern California is like Washington, D.C., only less humid," his father had replied. "The only places Jews appear to have survived outdoors long as Jews seems to have been Israel and Ethiopia. Chew that over."

On this trip climate would be among the least of his concerns. His surreptitious departure was necessary since the few remaining commercial flights from Sheik Yassin International Airport were not for Jews, unless they had special permission from the authorities. As far as he knew, the authorities thought he had died in the war, and he meant to keep it that way, at least for now.

Aharon had said little to Shoshana about the journey. Knowledge might implicate and endanger her should Arab police come with questions. He had confided in his father however. It was a habit he had tried to break, and failed. Tarbitsky, now seventy-eight, had engaged in more than a few perilous operations of his own, for the pre-state Haganah and for the Israeli government after independence. His early career in the security section of the Foreign Ministry was the stuff of best-sellers, which he declined to write. His way of preserving his reminiscences had been to impart them to his son. Besides, Yehuda Tarbitsky also was a Magen Israel member.

"What do we know of this organization, Friends of New Israel?" the old man had asked his son.

"A good deal. Several of its representatives already have been here, and information comes by other means as well," Aharon replied. "The war changed the American Jews even more than it did us. For many our defeat provided the excuse they needed, maybe without admitting it, to assimilate, just as the earlier 'heroic Israel' had held them to a spiritless Judaism. But for others, it gave birth to a new determination, a new national feeling. Some of these Jews started Friends of New Israel, and they are not just marginal people, but men and women of some standing. They say they can help us reconquer the land."

"Reconquer the land?" Tarbitsky scoffed. "Where were they when we could have used their help–conquering the land in the first place, and hanging onto it in the second? How do they plan to help–with a few smuggled pistols? This isn't 1948. Tell them we'll do well to hold onto what we have, like the Druze in Lebanon. What dreamers are in charge of these fools?"

"Admiral Chester Fogerty, for one, the man who sent the Sixth Fleet against the Arab ships during the war. And Congressman Jonathan Marcus for another. Not to mention the woman rabbi, Jeri Levi."

"Win Fogerty? He's not even Jewish," the old man snorted. "And a congressman who never was a committee chairman and one woman rabbi who nobody outside metropolitan Washington has ever heard of? Good people, sincere people–but leaders? I doubt it."

"Maybe you shouldn't–they've already sent us one shipment of new Swedish assault rifles, mortars and plenty of ammunition, along with some American electronic surveillance equipment, and have promised more in the near future. Oh, did I mention one million dollars in emergency money–for bribes and so on?"

The old man looked at his son, eyebrows arched. Aharon Tabor knew that pose: behind the superficial skepticism, his father was intrigued. So he continued:

"And there's more to it than those three, I'm told. There are other leaders and already tens of thousands of members. Friends of New Israel is the main faction in the U.S. Kehillah, the new council the American Jews formed. So these three people do not work alone."

"Kehillah? You're not telling me that the American Jews finally put themselves under a central authority, one with some teeth, after all these years of every man his own president, every woman her own chief rabbi? Anyway, I thought kehillahs died with emancipation, with the end of the ghettos," Tarbitsky said flatly.

"Well, perhaps this is a new era, and the old models don't help much. In any case, the Friends seem to have some money, and access to heavy weapons. That's why I'm going."

"Heavy weapons? Not just guns and grenades?"

That's what they said. We'll see."

Feeling hope lighten his old heart, if briefly, Tarbitsky clasped his son to him and simply said, "Go with God." It was the first time he had used that word out loud in half a century.

That night, an hour after sundown, Aharon Tabor, dressed in a wet suit and carrying flippers, scrambled up the bank of the last fish pond, across fifteen yards of open beach, and into the light surf. Then he strapped on his flippers. He saw the headlights of the Jeep belonging to the Arab coast patrol about a half-mile off. He could imagine the .50-caliber machinegun mounted on the hood. After all, he had driven the same Jeep, when it belonged to the IDF and its mission had been to keep Arab terrorists out, not Jewish patriots in.

The flippers would help him cut through the persistent undertow a half-dozen strokes offshore. Except for that hazard—which a swimmer of strength could manage—the 100 meters to the small islands opposite Nof Benjamin should be uneventful. He had swum it countless times as boy and man even after the rocky protrusions, breeding grounds for migratory waterfowl, had become a national bird sanctuary. Supposedly off-limits to humans, it had always been a special, if somewhat uncomfortable place for young kibbutzniks, and for more than a few foreign volunteers, pursuing their own mating rituals.

On the other side of the little islands, hidden by them and enveloped in darkness, a rubber dingy bobbed in the choppier waters of the open sea.

From atop the water tower a pair of eyes aided by infrared night vision binoculars followed Tabor's progress. Shoshana had appropriated the Israeli-made optical device (a half-generation more advanced than those much-prized by the Americans during the 2002 war in Afghanistan) from the Magen Israel arsenal. Knowing her husband's inclination to keep secrets from her when he thought it was "for her own good," she outflanked him, for she knew equally well his inability to keep secrets from his father. Given the old man's fondness for her, prying was too strong a word.

She too had swum to the island, first with girlfriends long ago, later with Aharon. She held her breath as the patrol moved down the beach. From the Jeep a small spotlight swept over the sand. As the beam touched the small waves, she saw the eerie phosphorescence of her husband's wake. The patrol moved on. Shoshana took a deep breath, envisioned Aharon skirting the islands, and began climbing down the tower.

"That's far enough," a voice commanded just as she dropped the last few feet from the final rung to the ground.

Shoshana turned. Facing her was Ehud Kenaan, his 9 mm. automatic pointed at her stomach.

"What were you doing up there?" he demanded.

"Drop the gun, Ehud!"

It was Jeremy Marcus. He too held a pistol, this one trained on Kenaan.

Kenaan whirled.

"Fire!" a voice barked from the shadows.

Jeremy did, surprising himself and jumping with the gun's retort. Kenaan collapsed.

"Why, Ehud, why?" Shoshana Tabor asked, bending over him.

His words were hoarse, coming with difficulty. "I got tired of fighting. I had to get you to stop, too."

"People's Party?" It was Yehuda Tarbitsky, who had stepped from the darkness.

"Yes," Kenaan gasped, and died.

Shoshana Tabor, Jeremy Marcus and Yehuda Tarbitsky stood silently for a moment. Then Tarbitsky said, "I would have handled the gun myself, but I'm not sure my heart would have stood the waiting."

"When I said we would have to cut off the head of our enemy within, I didn't know I would recognize it as a friend," Shoshana said. Then she put an arm around Jeremy, who was trembling in a cold sweat.

*　*　*

Alexandria, Virginia (September 18, 2009) – "We have much of the nucleus of the force I envisioned when we first discussed this project."

"None of us then really believed it was possible," Jeri Levi said. "Chester, we're in awe of what you've accomplished already."

"Thank you, rabbi, but I'm afraid this has been the easy part," the former admiral said.

Once authorized by the U.S. Kehillah, Fogerty had assembled his own small staff of former military officers. Some had gravitated to the new Jewish community headquarters in suburban Washington even before the admiral began setting up operations. Fogerty and his people became the unofficial, unpublicized recruiters for a new Israeli air force, one that of necessity would have to be based outside of Israel, at first.

"But still, how do we equip and transport our... our forces?" Jonathan Marcus wanted to know.

"All right. Until now I've not shared this with anyone, except for Captain Silverman, who's functioning more or less as my executive officer. It's part of my adaptation of Col. Samuels' plan. Remember at our first meeting nearly two years ago, right after the War of Arab Unity, I said that once we had the personnel we could get the materiel? What I meant was this: the Sixth Fleet—my old command—still patrols the Mediterranean, even if in reduced numbers, given the Bush-Clinton-Bush cuts and now the Seventh Fleet build-up opposite China. In another few months the people we've already identified and pulled strings for in Naval personnel will have finished staffing key parts of the fleet, from command level to pilots. Often this is simply happening through normal assignment and rotation. Sometimes we help it. By early next year we'll have one carrier support group—most importantly the 80 or so combat aircraft of a major carrier—in position."

"To do what?" Marcus asked.

"To support a general rising in the Jewish autonomous area. If we catch the Arab Islamic Republic of Greater Palestine by surprise, particularly if they are facing problems elsewhere, we can win. Three days of sustained action should be enough to tip the balance, and I think—first by secrecy and then by dissembling—we will have them."

"Fantastic," said Marcus. "Utterly fantastic. And at least as plausible as the idea that in 1948 a few thousand Haganah rifles, some half-tracks, a couple of World War II surplus planes and converted ships could defend the infant state of Israel against five Arab armies."

"Well, those Arab armies weren't too well equipped themselves, and—suspicious of each other just like the Syrians and Iraqis, Egyptians and Saudis mistrust each other now—not well coordinated. Still, they had the edge in numbers and hardware, but not in morale," Fogerty noted.

"In any case, requisitioning the battle group ought to compensate for the kehillah's expenses in absorbing Jewish immigrants. Call it poetic justice," Levi said.

Fogerty's plan for the Sixth Fleet was the most ambitious, most bizarre of the kehillah's many ventures. But a number of them revealed daring, vision and enthusiasm little seen in the American Jewish community before the War of Arab Unity. In fact, ever since Gorbachev's release of Soviet Jews in the late 1980s, and the Oslo Israeli-Palestinian "peace process" of the '90s, American Jewry had been divided and demoralized, deprived of its two unifying but emotionally cost-free causes. After the resurgence of anti-Zionism and antisemitism following the destruction of the World Trade Center and attack on the Pentagon, it had been stumbling.

However, now it had its own popular cable television network, featuring a nightly half-hour news program including Rabbi Levi's daily commentary, and a host of less visible but compelling activities and institutions. Broadcast from the council's own studio in Washington by cable and satellite across the country, the nightly news combined religion and politics. It expanded the precedent set earlier by Jeri's WBLS radio show. Nearly one million Jews watched Jeri Levi regularly; most of them, having long-since abandoned CNN and the other networks with their inveterate anti-Israel bias, tuned in a half-hour early to catch the kehillah's news.

Other network offerings included Jewish cooking and quiz shows, exercise and meditation, even history and Hebrew instruction. The telecasts were slick, substantial, and—on the cable outlets that carried them in the nation's top dozen major markets, home to the vast majority of American Jews—popular. Barely a year old, the network, extended over the Internet, had become the new central nervous system of the resurgent remnant of U.S. Jewry.

Less glamorous institutions provided the muscle. A chain of halfway houses for refugees on their way back to Judaism from cults and simple assimilation had sprung up. Synagogue life too evinced a rebirth of sorts; many large, established congregations had split and withered after the war, but portions of them regrouped as followers of Rabbi Levi. These One People congregations appeared in all parts of the country, in urban, suburban and small town settings, anywhere a consistent minyan could be found. Often led by young charismatic rabbis and lay people previously on the fringes of Jewish organizational, monied life, or drawn from the Chabad Lubavitch and Aish HaTorah movements, these outposts provided a new Gush Emunim, a new bloc of the faithful. From kehillah headquarters in Alexandria a new web of synagogues and family service agencies was evolving into a smaller but stronger American Jewish community.

"I can't believe it myself," Levi said, looking at the charts. "Barely two years after the earthquake that shattered the Jewish world, we have two hundred thousand children studying a full curriculum in kehillah-affiliated schools."

"What is really mind-boggling," Marcus added, "is that the schools are self-sustaining. No tax dollars at work. A lot of people are making real sacrifices—extra jobs, foregone vacations and new cars, that sort of thing. Who would ever have believed that most of us would have submitted, voluntarily, to a five percent 'tax' to support the council's work? We've revived the official self-taxation of medieval European Jewish communities and gotten away with it!"

"We've 'gotten away with it' because the community has revived itself," Jeri Levi said.

"And that one million or so, that is your real American Jewish community. I say this as description and as a caution," Chester Fogerty put in.

"Don't worry, Chester, it'll be enough," Rabbi Levi answered.

"Jeri," Marcus asked, "how are your children?"

"All right now, I guess," she replied, slowly. "My bodyguards eventually had to grab them from Hal. You know he'd taken them on a visitation and refused to return them. They're confused, and more than a little angry with both of us. Still, I think they enjoy being with their mom—and don't understand their father's new, open anti-religiousness. Still, I wish their mother had more time to be a mother…" Her voice trailed off.

After his defeat in the fall, 2008 elections, Jonathan Marcus devoted nearly all his time to Rabbi Levi and the kehillah. His political and communal ties, built during more than two decades in Congress, spanned the country. His original role in setting the rabbi on her path toward leadership had forged a bond of loyalty between them.

But loyalty was not love. That Marcus had found with Felicia Sanchez. It had blossomed—more precisely, erupted—immediately after Madeline's death, sustained by roots planted long before. Although he thought of his late wife at times with sadness, sympathy and regret, he had realized years earlier that he would one day have to escape his failing marriage before spiritual exhaustion became physical. He had never forgotten the warning given by D. H. Lawrence: One cannot cheat on life, especially not on the heart. That was months before he had asked Sanchez to breakfast at the Hotel Washington.

Marcus lost his seat in an election decided by less than two percent of the votes, four thousand out of more than two hundred thousand cast. Morty Halpern had told him it was coming. Ten days before the balloting he had walked slowly into the district office, shooed out the gaggle of aides and hangers-on and shut the door behind him.

"Jonathan, we're through."

"Morty, you've told me half-a-dozen times in half-a-dozen elections that we were in trouble at this stage of the game, and we always cross the line ahead."

"Not this time. I didn't say we were in trouble. I said it's over. And we've been together too long for me not to be able to read that amateur poker face of yours," Halpern said. "You knew it before I walked in here."

"Maybe. Let's have it all now," Marcus answered, planting his big forearms on the desk.

"This week's tracking poll confirms the previous two. You haven't moved a point since late September. And this time, unlike before, we didn't start with fifty-five percent. We peaked at forty-six. Silver's dead even, the difference being that he started at thirty-seven on Labor Day. He's moved up a point a week since. With a four percent margin of error, you could be as low as forty-two, he could be as high as fifty. Even if we split the maybe ten percent still undecided, he's got the momentum. He wins."

"Are you sure?" Marcus said, prodding Halpern to unload every bit of bad news. "I could be at fifty, he could be stuck at forty-two. We'll run all out these last ten days–money's no problem, is it?–and sneak back in for another encore."

"Jonathan, we're out of bucks, at least out of big bucks for a last-ditch media buy. And Silver's already bought up most of the remaining time for a television blitz that's gonna roll over us the last weekend."

"Okay, you don't have to say you told me so. I spent too much time–and directed too much money–to launch the Levi project. I took the race for granted when Silver showed us two years ago he was dangerous. All right, it's true. But we've got a week and a-half left. Plenty can happen–and I'll bust my butt to make sure it does."

Both of them know it wouldn't make any difference. Unless Steven S. Silver, Stevie on the campaign trail, was indicted before election day for child molestation or smoking in public–virtually the only remaining sins in American civic life–he was going to replace Jonathan Marcus in Congress. Congressman Stevie Silver. Marcus let the words slip through his brain. They sounded ridiculous.

Silver, a mediocre business lawyer chosen two years ago by Arlington County Republicans more because of his bilingual fluency in Spanish and English than for any professional or political accomplishments, surprised both his backers and Marcus with his campaign acumen. He held the incumbent's reelection margin to fifty-four percent. This was a warning signal, since conventional wisdom held that any seat retained by less than fifty-five percent could be taken by a strong challenger. The designation of a "marginal" incumbent drew challengers like Los Angeles does runaways.

With his toussled hair, former fashion-model wife, two small children, one dog and one kitten (the latter redeemed from the animal shelter just before the campaign), Silver proved extremely telegenic. What was unsuspected was his insatiable appetite for campaigning. Well before the Republican primary–a wealthy retiree in favor of the gold standard and government-subsidized scholarships for all engineering majors always contested the nomination–Silver surfaced everywhere throughout the district. He talked to anyone who would listen. He did not just hit the malls, supermarkets, bowling alleys and senior citizens centers, but suspended his law practice and began canvassing door-to-door. By the time the election in 2006 was over, everyone in the district felt they knew Steven Silver ("Just call me Stevie!") even if they were not prepared, not yet, to send him to Congress.

In that campaign Silver and his handlers isolated the political weakness of Rep. Jonathan Marcus. His name was too familiar, his face oddly unknown and no longer young-looking. A whole new generation of voters–including not just blacks but also Hispanics and southeast Asians–peopled his district and Marcus held no automatic attraction for them. As for the older voters, one had responded to Marcus' personal solicitation by saying, "Sure, I'll vote for you. That guy we got in there now never comes around no more." A bit pedantic, likely to tell voters what was good for them rather than what they wanted to hear, with his seniority as much a handicap as a help–"he's part of the problem, not the solution," Silver repeated endlessly–the twenty-year incumbent was vulnerable. When campaign 2008 started, twenty-four hours after election day 2006, Silver was ready.

He went house-to-house, smiling pleasantly. His television commercials, which started airing ten months before the balloting, hammered at "an incumbent whose first concern is the International Relations Committee, not northern Virginia." No one could call it anti-Israel, let alone antisemitic. After all, Silver himself was Jewish. Marcus could hardly capitalize on the fact that Silver's Jewishness was casual, a twice-a-year vestige when it came to worship, bolstered by a limited Yiddish vocabulary recalled from long-gone grandparents and leavened with a fondness for shellfish. To make an issue of that would have been to take sides against a third of the congressional Jewish caucus, and many of Marcus' own contributors.

The challenger ostentatiously addressed what his polls told him were the concerns of African American, Hispanic and Indochinese voters in the district. His rhetoric was borrowed directly from campaign focus groups. Silver, a self-described "pragmatic populist," did not know any blacks, Hispanics or Indochinese on a personal, social basis. But no matter. Did the polls say they wanted more money for education? Then he did too. Less rigorous enforcement of immigration laws? Then he too favored "sensitivity." Easing of welfare reform? "The carrot is always preferable to the stick." Did they favor mass transit subsidies? Then so did Silver, even if he never rode a bus or took the subway. By no coincidence whatsoever, his campaign staff reflected closely the demographic mixture of the district. Success, the challenger believed, was a matter of fine-tuning, of proper calibration, of what he called "political tweaking."

Unlike Marcus, Silver never lectured questioners at town meetings on the distinction between earned income and taxpayer-supported "entitlements." That did not make good video. And like a successful rock musician or Middle Eastern terrorist, Steve Silver understood good video.

Of course he supported a strong defense, family values and—especially when speaking in a synagogue—aid to Israel. "Don't we all? But hey, I'm for peace, not war. I'm for conciliation, not confrontation. Being an activist means never dodging moral considerations. Being a politician means seeing the gray areas, in which all people—except fanatics—live. So we aid Israel, and Palestine, and Syria, Egypt and the rest, buying time to help them learn to live with each other. Right? And anyway, I'm running for Congress, not Knesset!"

His slogan? "Energy, not memories." People applauded.

Marcus ignored Silver at first, seeing him as a lightweight. He scorned his opponent's calls for "action, not reaction" and "compassion, not compulsion," as cliches or worse, empty doggerel. But when Silver caught him in the polls, Marcus lashed back. He dismissed his opponent's claim of "new ideas" and focused on Silver's nearly total lack of accomplishments. Silver—and editorial writers from the Alexandria Packet to The Washington Post—criticized the incumbent for negative campaigning and appearing out of touch.

And Morty Halpern was right. Some of the dollars siphoned to Jeri Levi in the past were subtracted by Marcus' donors from their contributions to his race. Silver also, thanks to a special court-ordered redistricting, had more new, unaffiliated voters to mine than Marcus was used to dealing with.

When it was over, nearly $5 million had been spent to elect just one of the 435 voting members of the U.S. House of Representatives. The winner, Congressman-elect Steve Silver, had not read a book on history or economics since his days as an undergraduate. He was, however, devoted to The Post's Style section and Cable News Network. In him the public had a thoroughly modern solon of wide, flat horizons with a solid grasp of video production values, principles of public opinion sampling and the attention span of an unruly junior high school student. Steve Silver didn't know Yalta from yogurt, Orwell from Motherwell, halacha from halavah. But he did know—to the last digit—the names of all his contributors of $100 or more, what interested his benefactors and what names and faces went together. He had spent years going in and out of Washington for candidates' schools at the Republican National Committee headquarters on the Hill, for fund-raisers and related activities, but had never visited the National Gallery of Art or seen a show at the Kennedy Center, except to take his children to a production of "The Nutcracker" one December.

Silver, Marcus thought, tried to reflect the electorate, while he had tried to lead it. Elections usually turned on one of those two approaches, he knew. When voters had courage, they looked for leadership. When they had appetite, they sought affirmation. In that sense, American campaigns always had been a gamble between regression and redemption, secular morality plays for the political peasantry and its clerics.

Felicia Sanchez and Jonathan Marcus had been packing the books, papers, autographed pictures and other mementoes in the congressman's office; counting his days in the Virginia legislature, there were artifacts of thirty years in public life. In a few days they would move across the Potomac. Marcus planned to work full-time on the kehillah, ostensibly as Jeri Levi's counsel. Sanchez insisted on serving as his executive assistant. It had been her decision, and he was glad.

"What Israel, or the Jews of Greater Palestine, need," she had said, standing from one of the boxes and stretching, "is an equalizer. From what you've said, and what I've seen, alliances between small and larger countries don't help the junior partner much, not in the long run."

"Historically, that's right, certainly for the Jewish state. From the deal between Judea and Egypt against Babylonia or with Parthia against Rome to the alliance with the French in the '60s against the Arabs and Soviets–not to mention the 'special relationship' with the United States–these connections all pushed a little country further out on a limb than it could, by itself, afford to go. In the end the limb proves brittle."

"The Bible calls Egypt the 'weak reed,' I remember," Sanchez said.

Marcus stared at her.

She smiled mischievously at him. "My mother read the Bible, and read from the Bible to us kids, quite often."

"What else do you remember?" he asked, quizzically.

"Oh, like Admiral Fogerty, to pray for the peace of Jerusalem, and that those who bless Israel will be blessed... among other things." Turning serious again, she continued, "But the question, Congressman, is how a tiny state can protect itself from bigger enemies, with recourse only to its own forces?"

"You won't be able to call me that much longer. The new Congress'll be sworn in right after New Year's."

"And we'll move on to other things. Maybe even more interesting than one more term in the House," she said. "Meanwhile, can you answer my question?"

She was a wonder, he thought. He and Madeline had not held a playful, provocative conversation the last five or six years of their marriage. "Well, history again provides a clue: How, for example, did Alexander and an otherwise insignificant Macedonia conquer the world, and in a few years at that? With surprise and superior technique–the maneuverable phalanx. And with superior motivation, like the nearly defeated French, inspired by a girl, Joan d'Arc, going on to victory."

"How can Israel regain that edge?" Sanchez mused.

Both were silent for a while. Then she said, "Have you seen the revival of the musical 'Gypsy'? There's a character, one of the strippers, named Miss Electra, and she sings 'You gotta have a gimmick, if you want to get ahead.' Israel's gotta have a gimmick, something its enemies can't match."

Marcus, staring at his briefcase, picked up the phone and called an old colleague from the Science and Technology Committee who now served as dean at Massachusetts Institute of Technology. Then he called a man he knew not only as a minor contributor to his own campaigns, but also as a former giver, now disillusioned, to the United Jewish Appeal. "Beryl, this is Jonathan Marcus. I want to ask you for another contribution–not for me, but for something much bigger. And believe me, if this works out, you'll get more bang for your buck than you can imagine!"

As he put down the receiver, Marcus felt Sanchez circle his waist with her arm. "What was that about?" she asked.

"You gave me an idea. About a gimmick, an equalizer," he said earnestly.

"And you've given me one." She led him through the half-packed boxes to the green leather sofa against the wall. "I don't think we've gotten nearly as much use out of this as we might have," she said, pulling him down to her.

A few weeks later some of the brightest Jewish students, technicians and scientists known to the kehillah began receiving stipends to pursue applied physics and micro-engineering research at major American universities. Among them were a handful of refugees from the Technion in Haifa and Weizmann Institute in Rehovoth. Thanks to the generosity of Beryl Hochberg and a few of his friends, they began working on the second of the kehillah's two secret projects. The first, "Operation Flotilla," involving the U.S. Sixth Fleet, was nearing fruition. "Operation Slingshot," given the background of those involved, showed signs of catching up.

* * *

Rishon Lezion (October 2, 2009)–"Damn! We've got to get to Jerusalem tonight, regardless of the Palestinian police," Israel Miller exclaimed. "It's imperative the executive committee meets, and that we communicate with the others before the Magen Israel mission in America ends!"

"And it's dangerous as hell to travel now. You know that," Uri Eshel replied. "Ever since the killing of that double agent at Kibbutz Nof Benjamin and the Magen Israel crackdown on the People's Progressive Party, the Arabs and the PPP have been working together–kind of like the 'saison' in 1944 when Haganah men hunted Irgun and Lehi members for the British."

"God, will we ever stopping fighting among ourselves, stop fighting ourselves?" Miller sighed, his weariness bone-deep. Then, a little more firmly, he said, "Uri, it doesn't matter. We simply must be in Jerusalem tonight."

"I know." It was Eshel's turn to sigh. "I'll make sure everything's ready."

Israel Miller barely noticed his quarters. He registered little of the mundane anymore. At each step along the route of retreat and defeat he had buried his feelings deeper inside himself. The sorrow he felt the day he and Judith had been exiled from their home in Ramat Eshkol, the anger and anxiety that struck with the siege of Jerusalem, his bereavement at Judith's death, the despair at surrender, none of it registered consciously anymore. Miller was no longer a man, or just a man, but a type; in the darkest hour for himself and the nation whose name he carried he had vowed his people's ultimate resurrection. Eshel noticed that the former deputy prime minister now talked to himself, aloud and frequently. Not as one deranged but as two aspects of one powerful personality, the intellectual and the psychological, the mind and the heart, in profound debate.

In a basement in Tel Aviv, in a high-rise overlooking Haifa or in some village loft on the edge of western Jerusalem, the flying headquarters of Magen Israel orchestrated the resistance. Ever-changing externals were not disorienting, Eshel had decided. It was the ectoplasmic internals, the mental certainties of half a century turned to quicksilver that buffeted him and the rest of the underground leadership. Was he disoriented by such change? Could he rely on his own judgment anymore?

In preparation for the night journey to Jerusalem from Rishon Lezion, a large suburb of Tel Aviv in which they now hid, Miller washed, trimmed his heavy gray beard and drank yet another cup of coffee, thick with sugar and milk, and smoked yet another cigarette. False fuel for the fugitive's life; it had all become normal. The United Arab Islamic Republic of Greater Palestine honored him with a quarter-million dollar price on his head. Phantom sightings of Miller occurred at least weekly—many of them planted by Magen Israel members to confound police.

To preserve its status as "the sole, legitimate representative of the Jewish people in Israel," granted by the last Knesset, Magen Israel now pursued a ruthless struggle against the People's Progressive Party. But the PPP considered itself the pragmatic voice of post-Zionist Israel. After all, it had grown from a fragment of the honored Israeli intelligentsia, from a kernel of the left wing of Israel's founding Labor Party and its allies in the far-left Meretz Party, those who—using Yitzhak Rabin's premiereship in 1992 and after as their Trojan horse—spearheaded the Oslo process with Yasser Arafat and the Palestine Liberation Organization. Like most strife between brothers, its unseen roots as deep as the strife between Joseph and his brothers, between Cain and Abel, the clash between Magen Israel and the PPP was intimate and brutal. And both alternately aligned with, and against, groups of Jewish religious extremists. Such factionalism made penetration by the Arabs or their Jewish agents possible, although not particularly easy.

Fahd al-Husseini had proscribed all the Jewish groups, although a tacit exemption applied to the PPP. Membership in "any organization advocating or working for Jewish nationalism, apart from tolerated religious communal activity," was punishable by imprison or death. In practice, the former often resulted in the latter.

"Moving day," David Ben Melech reminded Miller as he removed the older man's empty cup. "Today a shaggy, bearded and bespectacled scholar from Rishon Lezion becomes a well-groomed, contact lens-wearing pensioner in west Jerusalem."

"Contacts again? You know how I blink and squint with them. They make me more conspicuous than my glasses," Miller complained. He was accustomed now to the clothes of laborers, pensioners and rabbis, he wore dentures that made his face puffy, dental caps that left his smile gaping, even dyed his hair different colors. Forged documents attested to four different identities. But he could not abide contact lenses.

"Well, if you'd had laser eye surgery before the war," Ben Melech said goodnaturedly, "and taken ten years off your appearance—say, made you look like a young 68-year-old—we wouldn't be having this conversation now. Anyway, we're not going to a costume ball. To the best of our knowledge, no one possess a picture of you, taken in the last fifteen years, without a beard and glasses. Minus them, your face becomes whoever we say it is."

David Ben Melech, an electrical engineer, was the son of Menachem Melchior, last in an innumerable line of Scandinavian rabbis, and Rachel Luzatto Melchior, a jewelry designer whose family fled to Turkey after the

Expulsion from Spain in 1492 and had made its way to Jerusalem by the eighteenth century. His story had been repeated countless times during the war: As a soldier at the front he survived while his parents died in the rubble of their apartment building. The artillery shells that blasted it caused some of those muffled explosions that punctuated the debates of the last Knesset.

Ben Melech joined Magen Israel even before the final ceasefire, and did not return to Jerusalem, not immediately. What the hills and caves of Judea and been to the Maccabees in the early years of their revolt twenty-two centuries before, the dense urban landscape of Israel's three metropolises became for the provisional government and Magen Israel commanders. Clandestine experiences accumulated layer by layer until, for Ben Melech, his previous settled existence seemed like a long-ago accident.

"Tonight, if the executive committee approves, we contact the units in Iraq, Lebanon, Egypt and Yemen?" Yitzhak Ben-Ami—whose name, literally, meant Isaac, son of my people—asked Eshel.

"Yes. And so we must be in Jerusalem for the night," Eshel replied.

"I don't like it. Even one night with so many of the committee members and a portable short-wave transmitter in the same place is risky," Ben-Ami said. Eshel nodded his agreement, but added, "Risks taken and survived look like opportunities seized."

At the beginning the Arab authorities had imposed a dusk-to-dawn curfew on the Jewish territories. Later, in response to an American request allowed to pass the U.N. Security Council, the curfew had been liberalized. Over Fahd al-Husseini's vehement opposition, Yacoub al-Masri magnanimously contracted it to 9 p.m. to 5 a.m.

For night travel, the underground sometimes used vans and cars modified to resemble official police or emergency vehicles, as the Palestinian Authority had used ambulances in the fighting of 2000-2002 to transport gunmen and ammunition. Nevertheless, such movement was avoided whenever possible, since it jeopardized both personnel and equipment.

Shortly after curfew a white van with the black, red, green and white emblem of the Arab Islamic Republic of Greater Palestine sped along the side roads parallel to the Tel Aviv-Jerusalem expressway. Ben Melech—David, son of the king—and Ben-Ami wore the uniforms of the Palestinian police, olive drab fatigues, maroon berets with stylized golden eagle insignia, brown combat boots and belt. Ben Melech sat in the front passenger's seat, a vintage Kalashnikov assault rifle between his feet, an updated map in his hands. Ben-Ami drove, a new machine pistol across the console between the front seats, and glanced frequently into the rear view mirror.

In back, Israel Miller lay on a padded bench built into the side of the vehicle. His eyes were closed and covered with a forearm to shut out the lights at occasional intersections. Even the soft contact lens Ben Melech had procured proved an ordeal for old and tired eyes.

On the opposite bench sat Uri Eshel. He felt the automatic pistol tucked inside the waistband of his trousers. What an odd way for a history professor, eligible for retirement, to spend the evening, he thought. Then again, he corrected himself, not so odd for a Jewish professor of Jewish history.

Ben-Ami radioed the police checkpoint on the outskirts of Jerusalem. His fluent Arabic helped clear the way. "We will be waved through," he informed his compatriots, "especially since one of the 'Arabs' at the checkpoint on this shift is a member of HaMagen."

"We're getting better organized all the time," Eshel muttered.

"Yes, but one of those at the checkpoint might also be from the PPP, able to recognize you on sight, even with your new sideburns and moustache," Ben Melech said.

"Quiet, everyone!" Ben-Ami ordered.

"What is it?" Ben Melech whispered urgently.

"Headlights… someone's been tailing us for the past few kilometers and now they're closing in."

Ben Melech scooped up his AK-47. Ben-Ami's right hand slipped from the steering wheel, found his pistol and flipped the safety off. In the back both older men were wide awake now. Eshel handed his automatic to Miller and flipped up the bench-top. In the storage bin beneath was a weapon that resembled a large-bore sawed off shotgun with a conical charge protruding from the barrel. A Vietnam-era rocket-propelled grenade launcher, it was more lethal than a half-dozen shotguns and, like the Kalashnikov, typified Magen Israel's eclectic and laboriously assembled arsenal.

A police car overtook them, its blue lights suddenly flashing, its siren wailing. Ben-Ami was waved toward the shoulder of the road. He eased off the accelerator.

"I count four of them," Ben Melech said. "Two in front, two in back. Even, and we have the element of surprise."

Eshel and Miller pressed themselves against the sides of the vehicle and simultaneously tried to peer through the windshield. "Should we let Yitzhak talk to them, play the game out?" Eshel asked.

"Too uncertain," Miller snapped. "We don't know what they know, why they stopped us. We must assume they're in touch with their headquarters. We might have just seconds to finish these four."

"Right, but if so, this van's too hot to drive to Jerusalem," Eshel replied.

"So we've got to kill them and take their car," Miller said

Although it was too dim to see Miller's expression clearly, Eshel thought he heard of hint of relish in the old man's voice.

For some reason, perhaps lack of experience, or to block an escape attempt, the police car pulled off in front of Ben-Ami. Two Arab officers already were getting out. Suddenly, he flipped his headlights to bright, shining at the officers and into the other vehicle. As he did so, he and Ben Melech leaped out, firing. The two men out of the car fell. The pair inside struggled out of the front seat, returned fire and ran for cover in a rocky field. Eshel took aim with the grenade launcher and fired. The fleeing police pitched up into the air like giant rag-dolls.

Miller yanked open the back door as Eshel climbed out the sliding side door. Quickly they unrolled canvas tent-halves and carried the bloody remains of their necessary victims back to the van. The battle itself had ended in less than 15 seconds. Eshel, amazed at the accuracy of his shot and even more at the steadiness of his nerves during the fighting, realized now that his whole body shook. He saw Ben Melech standing over Ben-Ami.

"He's hit."

Ben-Ami, moaning in pain, bled from a shoulder wound.

"Damn, this slows us down." It was Miller.

They bandaged him quickly.

"Why did they stop us?" Miller asked.

"The plates." Ben-Ami said weakly.

"What about them?" Miller's voice was distant, distracted.

"The plates on this police car are green. I noticed it as they passed. Ours are white. They must have made a snap change again, to isolate stolen vehicles before we could make new copies or steal some originals"

We are not as ubiquitous as we pretend, Eshel thought. What else do we not know that we must? He barely managed to control himself as he fired a second grenade, this one into the fuel tank of the van. As the police car headed toward Jerusalem an angry orange ball of fire receded in the distance.

"Radio the checkpoint, tell them it's an emergency—we were attacked by Jewish bandits, we've got a wounded man and are going straight to the hospital."

Ben-Ami, speaking with difficulty, relayed the message in Arabic. "We'll wave you through, came the reply. They'll be waiting for you at Ayn Karim."

Ayn Karim, formerly Hadassah Hospital at Ein Karem, retained much of its Jewish staff. However, administrators appointed directly by Yacoub al-Masri ran it, and insisted that it be called by its new name, Suleiman Medical Center.

Ben Melech slowed the police car at the checkpoint on Rechov Herzl—now Izzedin al-Qassem Boulevard—at one of the western approaches to the city. Almost every night Jewish children pulled down the new street signs, as they did throughout the Jewish autonomous district. And every morning Arab municipal authorities saw to it that they were replaced. Occasionally, a child would be caught and beaten, jailed or worse. Still, the street corner struggle continued.

Sent through the checkpoint, the occupants of the auto could not relax, not yet. Magen Israel operated several "safe houses" in apartment buildings in western Jerusalem, not far from the B'inyaneh Ha'Omah convention center. The center now housed a display celebrating the life of Yacoub al-Masri and another highlighting the glories of the United Arab Islamic Republic of Greater Palestine, but otherwise remained little changed and little damaged. They soon found the building they sought, and the specific apartment, a unit fortified with reinforced and sound-proofed doors and walls and equipped with a secret exit to the unit directly below. Inside a paramedic injected Ben-Ami with morphine and sutured his wound.

In a corner a short wave transmitter stood ready. Ben Melech had decided it was safer—if because older, less common and more arcane—than Internet connection to remote laptops or satellite telephones. Miller, Eshel, and four other men— two senior commanders from Jerusalem, one from Tel Aviv and one from Haifa— stepped into a small sitting room. Behind closed doors they argued about the advisability of diverting some of Magen Israel's limited supplies to Iraqi Kurds, anti-Saudi Yemenis, Lebanese Christians and Egyptian Copts. After more than an hour of heated argument the vote went four-to-two against, with Eshel, Rabbi Blum and the Tel Aviv and Haifa commanders in the majority. But since Miller was one of the two in favor, the decision was approved.

God, I believe I'm coming to loathe my old comrade, Eshel thought. He is becoming a tyrant and I am going bankrupt, not the least bit certain anymore that there is justice or that it will be done by or for us. There is only blood and more blood. He shook his head, as if to clear it from a nightmare.

Employing prearranged frequencies, the radio operator sent short wave signals from the low Judean peaks of Jerusalem hundreds of miles northeast, to the Zagros Mountains on the border between Iraq and Iran. There the Kurds, descendants of the ancient Medes and of all peoples the closest, genetically, to the Jews, waited. And north to Lebanon, where in the Christian heartland above Beirut the Maronites, descendants of the pre-Arab Phoenicians, listened. Southwest to the Nile Valley, where the Copts, descendants of pharaonic Egyptians, heard. And southeast to Yemen, where ancient tribes of the Sheba known to Solomon hoped to reclaim their oil-rich lands from the upstart House of Saud. Among each were agents of Magen Israel, some Jews, some Israeli Druze, Christians, Circassians—Middle Eastern minorities who knew that the Zionists, for all their shortcomings, were preferable to the Islamists, reactionary revolutionaries who proclaimed the theology of power.

"I'm getting nothing," the short wave operator complained, listening to the static that answered his messages. "Wait, there is something!" Quickly, a weak signal became audible, and as they jumped about the dial, the reports came in:

The Kurds, as usual, harried Iraqi troops, "but the U.N. guarantees have become a joke. We need anti-aircraft weapons badly. Stingers...."

The Copts repeated their appeal for small arms and ammunition—not so much to fight Egyptian police and military but for defense against the gunmen from al-Ikwan al-Muslimi, the Muslim Brotherhood, and from the even more violent al-Ga'amah.

In Lebanon, the Christians, especially the Maronites, who had long ago abandoned hope they could reestablish the dominance they enjoyed as late as the early 1970s, concentrated with new clarity on survival.

And in the Arabian peninsula, Yemen's new leaders searched for any assistance whatever against the expansionist, U.S.-backed Saudis who for decades had refused to demarcate the border between them and forcibly claimed Yemeni territorial and mineral rights.

If hardly friends, the Jews at least could have timely allies, if only they could cement the deals. That had been a guiding principle of Israelis from Ben-Gurion through Shamir, until Rabin dumped Palestinian "collaborators" in the West Bank and Gaza Strip in favor of Arafat and the P.L.O. in 1993 and Barak did likewise to Israel's south Lebanese clients to appease Hezbollah seven years later, inspiring the second intifada. Israel Miller revived that principle, as both tactical necessity and strategic advantage.

"We're short of the same stuff ourselves, what little we smuggle in," Jerusalem replied. This bad-mouthing was true only in part. Magen Israel received small but significant amounts of weaponry from outside, directly from Scandinavian arms merchants and indirectly from the Kehillah through Friends of New Israel. But there definitely was no surplus. And seeking to prevent a Palestinian crackdown, the Jewish underground did not want to be recognized as a bigger threat than the Arabs already perceived.

Israel Miller listened to all the reports and requests. He decided to provide each group with enough to make it effective when the time came. "We are going to need them. When we rise, they must also, and prevent a consolidated Arab counterattack against us."

"It's plausible, but I doubt it's probable," Eshel said, repeating an old objection. "The historical record is not encouraging."

"We've had this debate, Uri, and you lost," Miller asserted. "Besides, we're going to make new history. Again." To the radio operator, he barked new instructions. "Contact Tabor in Washington, by latest code. Tell him his new friends must make four special deliveries, within the next ten days. And don't worry about the cost."

"Hey, where's Ben-Ami?" Ben Melech asked, looking around. Eshel realized too that he had not seen the wounded man for some time. A quick search of the safe house showed him missing.

Believing himself mortally wounded, Ben-Ami had decided on a final mission. While the commanders had closeted themselves in debate, he convinced one of the younger Magen Israel members on duty to help him. He left this note:

"We Sephardim know what you Ashkenazi deny. Our enemies live in a different mental world. For us the year is 5771, for the Christians, 2009. But for the Muslims, it's only 1431. We will not reason them into accepting us anymore than they will convince us of the date. Whose birthday do the Egyptians still celebrate, Sadat's or Nasser's?"

Like the believers who occupied the Grand Mosque in Mecca in 1979, like the smiling Shi'ites who brought down the American embassy and U.S. and French marine headquarters in Beirut and Israel's command center in southern Lebanon in 1983, like the Iraqi-supported fundamentalists who came within a couple of concrete pillars of bringing down the World Trade Center in 1993, or the followers of Osama bin Laden who blew up the U.S. embassies in Kenya and Tanzania in 1998 and nearly sunk the destroyer U.S.S. Cole in 2000 and finally did destroy the Trade Center and hit the Pentagon in 2001, like the scores of Sunni suicide bombers who struck Israel as lethal accompaniment to negotiations with Arafat and blasted the front off Union Station in Washington in 2005, Ben-Ami turned politics to religion to war. It is often thus, when fanaticism arises after passion is blocked.

With help, he loaded the Arab police car with explosives. It was, after all, his last request, one last attempt by a frustrated modern to bridge the gap, to communicate with those on the other side, still in feudal self-isolation. Most of Jerusalem heard the explosion as he drove the cruiser up to the front door of Palestinian police headquarters.

* * *

Jerusalem (October 5, 2009)–Fahd al-Husseini was stunned. Apart from a few routine arrests, brief military trials and summary executions, Yacoub al-Masri denied his request for all-out suppression of the Jewish gangs. "It is not necessary," he had said grandly. Speaking to a command council including his wife Fatima, al-Husseini, Mahmoud Terzi and a few others, he informed them that "my code explaining the unquestionable superiority of Islam over Judaism and Christianity is nearly finished. In a few weeks, I will introduce it to the world in such a way that its truth cannot be denied. This will instantly and complete demoralize the Jews of the autonomous area and their American supporters. In fact, I anticipate that most of them–certainly most of those in the autonomous area–will convert to Islam, especially the more devout among them. I see now that trying to destroy Israel and the Israelis was a distraction when the Prophet's true path for them–and peace be upon him–conversion and absorption, was always before our faces." Terzi stifled a laugh as the caliph left the room, but then demanded "what the hell is he talking about?" of the remaining council members.

"I'm not sure," Fatima said, "but he speaks of this 'code'–which he tells me, compares Islamic law to Jewish law and Christian practice and determines that the others are 'immature' versions of the former–as if it will be recognized like the Ten Commandments."

"If he makes a fool of himself, and us, we'll be weakened both here and elsewhere," Terzi fumed. "Must we stop him? Can we?"

"I don't know," Fatima said in a far-off voice. "But," she added, speaking more directly, "this is not our only problem. Intelligence reports unexplained military activity in Japan, Korea and Taiwan."

"Perhaps this is directed at China, given its continued belligerence?" al-Husseini suggested.

"It could be, but Korea and Japan appear to be taking the lead."

"Are any of the Asian tigers behind in their fees to the Inter-Arab Bank?" Terzi asked.

"Of course not," Fatima said. "But if they were planning something, they would not likely telegraph it by withholding payment."

Terzi glared. He couldn't be sure, but he thought Fatima was being sarcastic with him again. "What if the Japanese always meant to lull us into complacency?" she continued. "They, like we, are a proud people, a clever people with a long memory. And remember, the truth is the Japanese, Koreans and Taiwanese mastered modernization, building institutions, developing technology, exporting brainpower to American and Europe in ways we Arabs did not. Somehow they learned to beat the West at its own game, even using a democratic system foreign to them. We did not. Pan-Arabism substituted for secularization. Pan-Islam substituted for development. While the Asians copied the West, improved and innovated, we fought and then bought. If not for the oil, we could not have done that. If we are to succeed, we must be honest with ourselves and stop seeing the outside as we want it to be and see it as it is...."

"This is getting us nowhere!" al-Husseini erupted. "The Jews blow up our police headquarters in western Jerusalem–no doubt inspiring the neo-Zionists everywhere–the Japanese and their allies might be preparing some sort of...

something, and you engage in amateur sociology. Meanwhile, we sit here as Yacoub prepares to regale the world with his esoteric theology!"

"It's not esoteric!" Fatima nearly shouted.

"Okay, sorry. I know that. I believe it," al-Husseini retreated. "But I also know we could be headed for big trouble."

"You're headed for trouble, all right," said a voice in another part of the palace, listening through headphones to the command council via one of the tiny, sensitive microphones that had been stitched surreptitiously into Fatima's brassieres. "Yacoub does not like traitors, and when I play this tape, he'll know you are all about to betray him, that the only one he really can trust is me." A long and joyless laugh followed.

One step the caliph had allowed his security minister to take after the bombing was to proscribe all overseas travel by Jews. Ben-Gurion International–Sheik Yassin Airport–now was closed completely to Jews, even for humanitarian travel. So were the ports of Haifa and Ashdod. Movement overland through eastern Jerusalem to Amman, from Tel Aviv to Cairo or Haifa to Beirut, previously treacherous, now was impossible.

Jews caught overseas by the new order could accept involuntary exile or return illicitly. Aharon Tabor chose the latter. "It was easy, actually. I just flew from Washington to Stockholm and then worked my way back on a freighter, with the papers of a merchant seaman. There are more than a few well-placed, low-profile Jewish business owners and managers. I walked out through the dock-yards with my forged stevedore's identification and then, using a fake ID card for the Jewish autonomous area, took a bus back to the main gate of the kibbutz."

"This won't help tourism," Yehuda Tarbitsky said, managing a weak joke. "Instead of being gone three weeks, it was nearly seven months. I hope you got what you went for."

Much as he had derided the idea as a fool's dream, the old man too had begun to hope–since he could not pray–that the diaspora might succor the Jews on their own land. It had been the other way around, spiritually even more than physically, when, in his prime, he had been a diplomat representing the free Jews to the newly-prideful American diaspora. But he had watched, from the war in Lebanon through the first and second intifadas, as much of American Jewry in particular separated itself from a beleaguered, seemingly violence-prone Jewish state, so that by the War of Arab Unity it was nearly mute.

"You cannot believe what the Americans have done," his son was telling him. "With additional Russian and Ethiopian Jews, and Israelis caught out of the country–several hundred thousand altogether–they've constructed in just a few years virtually a state within a state. Over one million proud, positive Jews. And not all of them are Orthodox, by any means."

"Good," Tarbitsky interrupted. For him the distinctions and dissensions were old, but hardly irrelevant. He blamed rabbinic Judaism for opposing rather than fusing with early Zionism. This weakened the Jewish national movement, stunted its growth in pre-state Palestine and, indirectly, intensified the Holocaust by delaying the rebirth of a Jewish state and refuge. And–as he now saw with the benefit of years–the rabbinic-Zionist split also reinforced the secular Zionists' anti-clerical, anti-Jewish bent while maintaining rabbinic Judaism's galut orientation, relapsing into a diluted universalism in place of reborn religious nationalism. So the rabbis' children died powerless, and Zionists' offspring either moved to America or, in Palestine, worshipped the cultural offspring of Marx and modernity empty of Jewish animation.

"... The Jews in the Kehillah take their religion and their Zionism seriously, as parts of the same whole. Hell, now they voluntarily tax themselves—no more schnorr machine with its dinners and professional campaigns is necessary. And they run a television network more interesting, more balanced, more Jewish than Israel Broadcasting ever was!"

"That wouldn't be hard," Tarbitsky commented.

"Most convincingly, they do something we did not succeed in doing here—and we had the intention and the natural resources. Remember that survey that showed nearly one-fourth of Israeli school children did not know what Yad Vashem was, than nearly one-third did not know the origins of the terms Judea and Samaria? Such a thing could never happed with the students of the kehillah schools."

"Okay, you've convinced me. They will survive, like the majority that stayed in Babylon. But what about us?"

"I don't think all those young Jewish men enlisting in the U.S. Navy expect to protect Miami from Cuban invasion. I spoke with Admiral Fogerty himself," Aharon said. Fogerty was now a legend in what had been Israel—one of the Righteous Gentiles. "I believe him when he says that they are nearly ready to help us liberate our land."

Yehuda felt his heart race. The irregular beat that flared occasionally during his last years at the foreign ministry had returned. But he was excited. If his son—no romantic, at least no more than necessary to live as a Jew in Israel—counted on the Americans, maybe he could too.

"I hope you live to see it," he told his son.

"You will live to see it, abba," Aharon replied. You must, he added to himself. God owes you at least that much.

Next morning at Haifa port the Greek freighter Apollo 14 finished unloading its shipment of Swedish industrial goods. Battered Mercedes and MAN cargo trucks—remnants of the fleet that once crowded Israel's busy, hazardous highways—ground their way up from the piers, through the razor-wire topped chain link fence and past a final, perfunctory check by the gatemen. Once outside, the vehicles began a slow climb up the Carmel into the heart of the city, transmissions and engines complaining at every turn and stoplight.

Not all the trucks followed the routes listed on the bills of lading presented to the Arab harbormaster. Nearly half the small convoy melted away down residential side streets before ever reaching the city limits and the roads south along the coast or north and east into the Galilee and Jezreel Valley and the United Islamic Arab Republic of Greater Palestine beyond. Their drivers, Arab-looking, Arabic-speaking Sephardim—whose families had been driven from ancestral homes in Arab lands in 1948 and after—proceeded to other destinations. Dispersed to half-forgotten warehouses and garages, their cargo was transferred hurriedly to smaller private trucks, vans and even cars bearing the license plates of the Jewish autonomous area.

Within minutes of one such transfer, several crates of Swedish-made assault rifles, mortars, grenade launchers and ammunition—just one more example of that country's unswerving commercial neutrality—were on their way to the Magen Israel depot at Nof Benjamin. So were harvested the first fruits of Aharon Tabor's American visit.

"And the people rejoiced throughout the land, when they heard the word of the Lord," said Yehuda Tarbitsky, as much to himself as to those around him, when the shipment arrived.

"Abba," said Aharon, "I never heard you quote Scripture before."

"Was I? Perhaps what you call Scripture is to me a half-remembered phrase from childhood that has everything to do with our present, not our past. 'And the Lord shall drive all those nations out of your way'...."

"Exodus?"

"Deuteronomy," the old man said flatly. "Not that I'll ever believe God told it to Moses. No, it was written by your ancestors—shepherds, farmers, warriors, poets—centuries after Exodus. 'Be strong, be brave, for you are to bring the Israelites into the land which I promised them; I will be with you.'" Tarbitsky finished, looking into his son's eyes. "But it was written for you."

Other waiting groups also saw the deliveries as godsends. A transport plane, bearing the markings of a Belgian air freight company, left Stockholm and after refueling in Vienna, landed at Ankara. There crates identified as drilling equipment were placed onto skids affixed with parachutes and loaded into a military transport with fresh NATO markings.

Late that night the transport lifted off and headed east. Just before dawn the pilot strayed into Iranian air space south of Lake Urmia near the point where the borders of Turkey, Iran and Iraq contend. Thousands of feet below, in a mountain valley above the old Kurdish city of Mahabad, he spotted a signal beacon. Out of the payload doors slid the palettes, soon canopied by yards of billowing nylon. The plane banked sharply and moments later was safely back over Turkey.

As the crates thudded to earth Kurdish fighters, a Magen Yisrael agent among them, raced to collect the precious cargo. Quickly they loaded light arms and ammunition, medical supplies, communications equipment and, most important, anti-aircraft rocket tubes onto Jeeps captured from the Iraqi army, onto donkeys and even onto their own backs. Similar scenes were played in Lebanon, Yemen and Egypt. Sometimes the shipments came by air, sometimes by sea or overland, but always with the help of Magen Israel and the Kehillah. Across the Middle East, in mountain fastness, trackless desert, Nile Valley cotton fields, Lebanese hilltops and Jewish cities, secret bands of determined men and women, minority descendants of ancient peoples, waited and grew stronger.

*　*　*

Alexandria, Virginia (November 29, 2009)—Rabbi Jeri Levi felt faint. She reached for the armchair in her study and half sat, half collapsed into it. She rested for some

Total Jihad

moments, her forehead propped up with her right hand. As the weakness passed, she looked around the room, focusing on familiar objects. She was alone, and took time to compose herself. She could deny it no longer; the others were right, she had been working too long, too hard. It was time for a break.

For three years, since her separation from Hal, Jeri Levi's life had whirled like a dervish. Like some singular, benign tornado she had whipped through sundered, shrinking American Jewry. And though the redemption she had been instrumental in achieving seemed nearly miraculous, Rabbi Levi took little personal pride in it. Fully conscious of her individual self, she simultaneously felt that her course had been charted from without, or perhaps better, by a higher power from within.

Whatever its origin, the great Jewish revival—similar to the enthusiasms and the resistance the American Methodist Awakening provoked two and a-half centuries before—had cost her personally. She had aged a dozen years in the past four-plus. Her face, still attractive, was no longer youthful. Now devoid, or rather beyond sensuality, it shone with an almost otherworldly beauty. Silver-gray streaks gleamed from her luxuriant, previously raven-black hair. She had come to resemble physically the symbol her task made of her.

And now she was tired, spent. Rabbi Jeri Levi just wanted to go away for a week, or maybe two, and lie unthinking under a tropical sun.

Deliberately, like an old woman not sure what the next step might bring, she moved back to her desk. She drew herself up, assumed an authoritative posture, and buzzed for Sylvia Weinberg.

"What is it, Jeri?"

"Sylvia, that vacation you've been talking about. Let's book it. Two weeks in the Caribbean?"

"Done. Been done for weeks. How's Curauco sound? There's a small Jewish community, with the oldest synagogue in the Western Hemisphere, still in operation—with sand covering the floor, to remind you of forty years in the desert. A few families going back three hundred years and more to Dutch colonial times. Plus children and grandchildren of Holocaust escapees, a few Israeli refugees, a displaced American or two. You'll have plenty of people to talk to—if you want to talk at all. I just have to confirm flight times."

"Who planned this behind my back?"

"We all did. Jonathan, Admiral Fogerty, me—everyone. Even security is prepared."

"Good. I'm ready to go."

Threats against Jeri Levi, against the Kehillah and its leaders, had been a weekly occurrence in the beginning. They had tapered off in the aftermath of the War of Arab Unity. Following the initial lethal outburst of antisemitism, when Jews once more were recognized as vulnerable, as fair game, public attention drifted elsewhere. With the Arabs victorious, and the Jews apparently self-absorbed, they no longer seemed so attractive a target. In America's open, polymorphous culture, with its superficial ethnicities and sectarianisms, scapegoats came and went. Gay, feminist, born-again Christian, Hindu, Libertarian, Social Democrat, white supremacist, Nation of Islam? Want fries with that? Only race really mattered, and even that—given the closed loop of official black and brown leaders and political-ly correct followers—had evolved from a question to be answered to a condition to be endured.

Attacks against Jews had dropped to two or three a week—not enough to engage law enforcement, quite enough to keep the Jews—at least those not organ-ized through the Kehillah, anxious and in their place.

Regardless, security remained a preoccupation for Friends of New Israel, as Kehillah headquarters was known. In charge was Rabbi Chaim Wise, a stocky young Chabad-Lubavitcher who'd been a Tae Kwan Doe karate instructor before becoming ba'al t'shuvah. Jeri Levi rarely traveled without Wise and a fellow mar-tial arts expert, an ex-Brooklyn yeshiva teacher named Joe Caro.

"Remember," Wise told her as she packed for the trip, "your wig and sun-glasses."

"I hate those things," Jeri said. "Rabbi goes Gidget. You at least could have gotten me some quieter frames."

"Wouldn't have been hip," Wise replied.

The following Sunday a blonde woman with upswept waves, wearing punk sunglasses and carrying a leather travel bag over her right shoulder, got into a dark blue Chevrolet sedan. She was accompanied by two husky, bearded men in black fedoras and suits that matched the color of the car. One put two suitcases into the trunk while the other opened the back right passenger's door for the woman. Both men climbed into the front seats, one to drive, the other in the front passenger's seat.

Inside the car, the passenger in front opened his briefcase and withdrew two machine pistols. He handed one to the driver and kept the other at his side.

A block away another man watched through binoculars. When the Chevrolet pulled from the curb to begin its drive to Dulles International Airport twenty miles to the west, the man put down his binoculars, turned the key in the ignition of his Nissan Pathfinder and moved out to follow. As he did so he spoke into a cell phone.

"Convoy forming. Take the lead at Seminary Road."

Heavily-inflected English came back to him: "Affirmative." With it, another sports utility vehicle, an older Izuzu Rodeo, pulled from a sidestreet and soon passed the Nissan. The two SUVs did not crowd the Chevrolet, but Rabbi Wise, a graduate of more than one course in pursuit-and-escape driving, realized quick-ly he was being tailed. He accelerated, changed lanes, then braked and turned.

"Get down rabbi, we've got company," Wise barked.

Caro punched an auto dial number in his telephone, said "We've got a tail, just east of the Seminary Road/I-395 ramp. Backup, and call the cops." Then Caro reopened his briefcase and laid out extra ammunition clips.

In the Rodeo, three passenger—two in back, one in front—brought subma-chine guns up from the floor. In the Nissan, three other men already gripped their weapons.

The sedan managed to put a red light between it and the pursuing vehicles. Not that it mattered—both SUVs rammed through the red light, the second caus-ing an oncoming car to swerve onto the sidewalk, the driver laying on his horn and screaming curses, to no avail. "Forget the airport! Circle back to the office," Rabbi Levi commanded. "And call the cops again!" But before Wise could spin the steering wheel the Rodeo, its front bumper reinforced for just this moment, shot forward and smashed into the Chevy, driving it into a utility pole. The crash of metal and glass erased any response to the rabbi's instructions. In the Rodeo, a dark-skinned young man, dazed from the airbag inflation, managed to disengage himself from his seatbelt. Behind, the Pathfinder braked hard and three ski-masked men leaped out, firing at the Chevy. Rabbi Wise slumped over the wheel, dead, his head and upper body shattered by multiple wounds and marked by large and ugly red blotches.

From the backseat, Joe Caro squeezed off a burst from his machine pistol. The force of the rapid-fire rounds sent one attacker sprawling onto the pavement and doubled over another just feet from the Chevy. Then more gunfire sounded from outside the car. Caro, slammed across the seat into the body of Wise, moaned in a slow, deep protest and slid to the floor.

As if in a stroboscopic dream, a clump of frames followed by a frozen pause, then another bit of fast-forward action, Jeri Levi was seeing everything in vivid detail, reaching, reaching impossibly slowly it seemed to her, for the revolver in her purse. Too late. She screamed as two men yanked her out of the wrecked, blood-spattered car. Pinioning her through the armpits they half-carried, half-ran with her back to the Pathfinder, now waiting with its doors opened, just behind the Chevrolet. Crouched behind storefronts and parked cars, stunned witnesses peeked out.

One of the attackers waved his gun in their general direction, fired it into the air, sending them ducking, and shouted, "Allahu akbar!" He laughed without humor, fired a second burst, shouted "Beirut! Kabul! New York! Washington! Jerusalem!" and as his compatriots flung Rabbi Levi into the Nissan, climbed in behind. The Pathfinder, crammed now with six men and Rabbi Levi, roared off, leaving behind the intersection of sudden carnage.

Someone jabbed a hypodermic needle into Jeri Levi's arm. She had no time to struggle. But as she plunged into unconsciousness, she was quite certain someone said, "Now you can go to the airport, Jew whore!"

When she came to, Rabbi Levi found herself handcuffed and bound at the ankles. Someone gave her a sip of water. It tasted like bitter metal. She tried to speak, to ask a question, but dumb lethargy blanketed her and she slept again.

The second time she awoke, hours after a dream of fire and death, she realized she was on an airplane in flight. They allowed her to use the toilet. Who were they? A man with a long, wide-bladed knife slashed the thick construction tape binding her ankles. She shuddered as he jerked the blade up to her knees. Watching her reaction he brought his face close to hers and smiled. In his silent smirk one could hear the scraping of bones.

She staggered back to the lavatory. Several times she leaned hard on the seat-backs for support. Her arms and shoulders ached from their angry handling. Due to the after-effects of the anesthetic, she could urinate only with effort and con-centration.

However, her mind began to clear. She understood what had happened and resolved to remain in command of her spirit if nothing else. She might be a prisoner, but she would not behave as a prisoner. Pale and drawn, Rabbi Levi returned to her seat more steadily than she had left it. They handcuffed her again but left her legs free.

"It is foolish to bring her like this," one of her captors said to another. "We should have shot her on the street with the other dogs." He was utterly indifferent to the fact he was speaking English and she could understand every word.

"I agree. But Yacoub has plans and we do not question them. He insisted that the woman be taken alive, and well."

The pair glared at her, a murderous hatred in their eyes. "He has a use for her, of that you can be sure." Again she heard the laugh of death.

Nevertheless, the news that her life was not in immediate danger helped calm her. That her captors acted for Yacoub al-Masri she already had guessed. That he would number her days and determine their purpose filled her with loathing.

Why did al-Masri want her, Jeri Levi wondered. As a surety against action by the Jews of America? Were their plans known? If they were not, then she had been seized for another reason, but what? Her brain fuzzy again, her body exhausted, she slipped once more into sleep.

She awoke as the plane touched down with a slight jolt. Someone thoughtfully had fastened her seat belt. Her wrists remained shackled.

Rabbi Levi stared through the window at the modern concrete terminal, the flowers and palm trees, the outlying orange groves and apartment buildings. She had been here before, several times: Ben-Gurion International Airport. Only the sign over the terminal's main entrance read, in large Arabic letters and smaller English ones, "Sheik Yassin Airport. Welcome to Palestine." There was no Hebrew.

She was blindfolded for the forty minute ride to Jerusalem, then walked, her eyes still covered, through a large building, up stairs and down long, echoing corridors. Finally, she heard a door being unlocked and opened before her. Quickly she was pushed through. She started when someone grabbed her arms.

"Quietly now. I am merely removing the handcuffs. When I leave you may take off the blindfold." A woman's voice, good but strongly-accented English. Then the woman's footsteps out the door.

"Welcome to the Arab Islamic Republic of Greater Palestine. Welcome to Jerusalem–al Quds." Jeri Levi wheeled to see who stood behind her. He rose from a chair and stood over her, smiling. She tried but could not stifle a gasp.

"So you recognize me," Yacoub al-Masri said, his voice not unpleasant. "I know we have caused you great inconvenience, but you will be well cared for while you are here."

They can kill me but they cannot defeat me, Rabbi Levi concluded after an instantaneous debate with herself over how to react. "Inconvenience?" she shouted. "You murdered two of my friends, kidnapped me and call it an 'inconvenience'? I pray you will be so inconvenienced."

She felt the hard slap almost before she saw it coming. A look of contempt replaced the polite smile. "Bravado will gain you nothing. Your behavior will determine how difficult your conditions are. Bavakasha," al-Masri said, using the Hebrew for please.

He stepped to the door, opened it and turned to her. "There is much for you to read and review here. You must prepare yourself." With that he closed the heavy door behind him. She heard a lock click. She tried the knob, but it stood motionless.

Jeri Levi turned to look at her cell. It was an odd one, a large suite of richly-appointed rooms. Thick Persian carpets, their intricate weavings a kaleidoscope of oriental patterns and colors, covered much of the floor. An ornate wooden and brass chandelier–with dozens of small electric bulbs–blazed from the center of the ceiling.

Near her was a table with matching heavily worked wooden chairs. Beyond was a small sofa and large floor cushions in a living-room arrangement. Further away, around a corner of the L-shaped main room, was a large bed, a chest of drawers, dressing table–with cosmetics–and bench. A tall bookcase separated the two areas. Inspecting it she found, to her amazement, a copy of the Hebrew Bible, a siddur or daily prayer book, and a complete 32-volume set of the Babylonian Talmud. Maimonides' Mishneh Torah stood nearby. Also shelved were copies of The Protocols of the Learned Elders of Zion, The King James Bible and Louis Farrakhan's The Secret Relationship: Jews and the Slave Trade.

Alone, on the top shelf, stood a new copy of the Quran. Bound in white leather, gold letters cut deeply into the grain and printed on vellum pages–Arabic on the right-hand, English on the facing left–it was of incalculable worth as an objet d'art alone.

"What the hell is this, she thought, Theology 101–Beginners' Mistakes? Tearing herself from the bookcase, she walked to the one large window. It over-looked a courtyard. Fluted, pointed arches repeated themselves in a square about 90 feet on a side, three stories high. Her suite was on the top floor and faced south-westward. For the first time in her life she would look toward the setting of the sun, not its rising, to pray toward Jerusalem, toward Har HaBayit–Temple Mount. She let the fine damascene curtains fall shut in front of the window, where a decorative wrought-iron grille served as bars nonetheless.

Next to the bed stood a large trousseau. In it she found a variety of clothes, all in Arabian-accented European styles, some with labels of European makers. She tried on an embroidered shift of rich, dark cloth and golden thread, a morbid fear clutching her heart. Yes, it fit perfectly! Someone had prepared for her arrival with intimate premeditation.

Off the bedroom area was a small bathroom. A pale pink marble countertop and glazed ceramic wall tiles sparkled at her. The fixtures in the gleaming porce-lain sink were polished brass. Thick, wide towels hung on brass rings and fragrant soap lay in a china dish. The luxury, even opulence of her swaddling cell made it plain that whatever al-Masri had in mind went well beyond simple kidnapping. Again dread crawled out of her mind and across her skin as she tried to imagine what that might be.

The inventory completed at last, she washed and fell into bed. Only then did she notice the closed circuit television camera mounted high in one corner, sweeping relentlessly to-and-fro, a tiny red light winking every ten seconds beneath the fisheye lens. Even the hypnotic scanning of the camera did not push her into sleep. A firm knock at the door and the sound of the lock being turned interrupted her tossing.

A woman stood there, a man on either side of her. She stepped across the threshold while they remained motionless. The woman deposited a large bowl of fresh fruit, breads and cheeses on the table under the chandelier. Suddenly, Jeri Levi felt a ravenous hunger, an appetite suppressed by the events of the previous twenty-four hours.

"I am to tell you that everything will be kosher," the woman said, before closing and locking the door behind her.

Kosher materially, not in spirit, thus invalidating the fact, Rabbi Levi disputed her silently, kosher actually meaning in order, as ordained by God. Whatever, she thought to herself, as her children would say. Her children; would she ever see them again?

Jeri sat at the table and reached for the bread. As she did so, she saw the envelope among the fruit. Heart racing, she opened it. "Eat well. You have two weeks to prepare for the disputation. I believe you will find everything you need here. You will be able to request other references if you desire. Remember, the world awaits the outcome." It was signed, in Arabic and English, Yacoub al-Masri, Caliph of Palestine.

Disputation! Now she understood. She did not believe, but she understood. Rabbi Levi had been seized, her companions murdered, and she flown half-way around the world so she could debate theology before a religious court that must inevitably find against her or judge itself guilty. She would be punished for having had the effrontery to be who she was, to have had visions and led Jews.

In medieval times disputations had been an elevated means of Jew-baiting. Often taking place in lands tainted by the Inquisition, disputations featured well-known Jewish community leaders or religious scholars, forced to defend their faith against the implied superiority of the "one true Church" before prominent lay and clerical figures–often Jewish apostates who twisted Torah and Talmud to please their new masters. Church authorities simultaneously acted as advocates of Christianity, prosecutors of Judaism and judge and jury. The verdicts of these courts, whose duties included bolstering public commitment to and observance of Catholicism, were meant to root out heretics and make examples of the stubborn, hateful, perhaps Satanic Jews. They had an economic side as well; after the Jews lost, the entire community paid damages, sometimes its property being forfeited.

Regardless of their preordained outcomes, disputations often provided stimulating intellectual and social theater, such as in the brilliant performance of Rabbi Meir of Granada in 1448. In that case, spoken of in Iberia for centuries, the only answer the bishops could make to the rabbi's incisive comparison of the trunk and branch beliefs was to burn him at the stake. As a result of this and similar show trails fought to a draw even before prejudiced courts, the Jesuits commissioned On Refuting the Jews, instructing the faithful on how to deflect Jewish arguments countering Christianity's claims to have superceded Judaism. This

216

work remained necessary and in print until Popes John XXIII and John Paul II acknowledged that, for Roman Catholics at least, Judaism did continue as the living word of God. Islam, of course, had yet to undergo its own Reformation or Counter-Reformation, to find its own John XXIII or John Paul II. It had yet to even recognize cogent arguments against its insistence on not only supremacy over both Judaism and Christianity but also its holy manifest destiny to replace them, so its scholars had not conceived of the need of a work of refutation, other than polemics justifying the otherwise anti-Islamic acts of suicide bombers.

Now al-Masri meant to stage a similar production with her in the supporting role as captive antagonist. The idea was ludicrous, she thought. And given the events of the previous day, deadly earnest.

She stared at the sacred and profane works in the bookcase. "So much depends on the outcome," al-Masri had warned. That she doubted. Would they free her if she "won"? Of course not. Al-Masri could no more admit a persuasive ratiocination for Judaism over Islam than he could discuss with the pope the virtues of ecumenicism. For such as he there were no virtues in compromise, heterogeneity. To the al-Masris of this world, all diverse humanity was free, free to agree with him. Words like dialogue and pluralism connoted temporary weakness on the part of believers, the compromises they facilitated to be overturned as quickly as possible, like Muhammad's truce with the tribe of al-Qurish, like the treaty of Hudabiyah. Like Arafat's accords with Rabin and Peres, Netanyahu and Barak.

Jeri Levi thought of Chaim Wise and Joe Caro dead on Seminary Road in Alexandria. If my last days are to be spent in forensics, I will be ready, she decided. Finally, she ate. In spite of herself she admitted that the cheese, bread, fruit and the small crock of lentil soup packed beneath the bread was delicious.

The next morning, after a surprisingly restful sleep, she found a breakfast of diced cucumber, tomato, onion and dill salad, small rolls and butter, yogurt and fruit, and tea waiting on her table. She showered, ate, and then began to prepare. Finding paper and pen, she wrote out a request for more texts, beginning with Hitti's History of the Arabs and Patai's The Arab Mind. That should annoy him, she thought, resolving to practice a little psychological warfare on al-Masri even before the debate. Insane, he could perhaps be unhinged if the disputation did not unfold according to his necessary script. Then she began leafing through the Chumash, the Five Books of Moses, for some of the many references to the oneness, unity and universality of G-d, the G-d of Abraham, Yitzhak and Yakov–the Jews against whom al-Masri warred, but from whom his religion borrowed the self-same concepts. She started with the Decalogue itself: I am the Lord your G-d and you shall have no other gods before me," with which al-Masri could only agree, and finished with the "Alenu" prayer and its reiteration of the biblical injunction and promise that "... And on that day the world will know that G-d is one and His name one; Because the Torah shall go forth from Zion, the word of the Lord from Jerusalem." Not Rome, not Mecca, but from Zion's holy mount.

Of course, al-Masri would expect just such an opening and try to co-opt it, appearing to accede to her argument but then insisting that Islam, as the "final revelation" had begun at Sinai, continued on the Cross, coming via Mohammad and the Quran to complete and supersede both Judaism and Christianity. He would

claim that they were immature preliminaries to Islam, necessary but hardly sufficient and no longer justified in any case. At that point, she planned to led him
across the pitfall of his assumptions, forcing him to stare at the monotheism of the
Israelites–simultaneously universal and particularistic, something that non-Jews
certainly could, as Christians and Muslims, accept, but that Jews need not, in fact
must not move beyond. So says the Lord your G-d who brought you out of Egypt
to receive My Torah and be My people. She would demonstrate the internal
integrity of the Hebrew Bible, complete in itself, needing neither that which al-
Masri might concur was the elaboration of Jesus nor–here he would object ferociously but defensively–skewed restatement by Mohammad. Further explication
only dimmed its lapidary brilliance, she would argue; G-d having made his eternal revelation at Sinai needing, as omniscient Creator, no subsequent revision,
editing or expansion of His remarks. If anything, the New Testament and Quran
were more like talmudic tractates for Gentiles than succeeding scripture to the
Torah. "Proofs" to the contrary ostensibly based on Torah foreshadowing were
theology driven by historical, political, martial, demographic exigencies, not cor-
rective revelation.

That is what I will tell them, Rabbi Levi said to herself, that and the fact that
Muhammad, in the Quran, himself makes clear that G-d's promised land belongs
to the Jews for all time. I will argue this case to al-Masri's face–for as long as he
can bear it. Let him try to refute me. He wanted a disputation… very well, I'll give
him one!

Part V

"Thus says the Lord God: 'Behold, I will take the children of Israel from among the nations, whither they are gone, and bring them into their own land; and I will make them one nation in the land, upon the mountains of Israel, and one king shall be king to them all…. And the nations shall know that I am the Lord that sanctify Israel, when My sanctuary shall be in the midst of them for ever.'"

—Ezekiel, 37:21-22, 28.

Alexandria, Virginia (November 29, 2009)–Jonathan Marcus learned of the abduction from a news bulletin. A roving television crew, monitoring police radios, arrived on the shoot-out site simultaneously with the cruisers and ambulances. Scenes of technicians loading the remains of four human beings into body bags interrupted soap operas across the metropolitan region. This, of course, irritated many viewers. One reporter, trapped as usual by compelling videotape and lack of specifics, spoke in sensational generalities, promising "more information as it becomes available…." Then the on-screen carnage evaporated and scheduled programming returned.

Regardless, it had been enough. Jonathan Marcus recognized the Chevrolet sedan. He had arranged the lease himself. Only recently Marcus had suggested to Chaim Wise that they replace it with something bullet-proof or even armor-plated.

On his way to the Friends of New Israel offices he prayed that a ransom demand had been received. But he doubted it. This kidnap-murder was political, not commercial. He punched Fogerty's number on his cell phone.

"Chester, have we heard from the kidnappers?"

"No," the admiral answered, "and my guess is we won't. These perpetrators are motivated by ideas, not money."

"If so, we don't have it in our power to offer a ransom," Marcus said. He hung up, wondering how whoever killed Chaim and Joe knew Rabbi Levi's route and schedule.

Marcus expected to find the office in a woeful frenzy, but he was wrong. Fogerty was asking questions and issuing instructions firmly and calmly. The most obvious changes were the weapons. Now the security people carried them openly.

"How can I help?" Marcus asked.

"We want you to serve as interim chief–and especially to deal with the press.

The birds of prey already have begun to descend. They traced the car's plates. We had to promise a press conference ahead of the evening news shows before they would clear out. Will you handle it?" Fogerty asked.

"Of course," Marcus said. "But I won't presume to substitute for Jeri except as co-chair with you and the rest of the leadership."

"Fine," said Fogerty. "Now, this is what we know, or rather, suspect. According to witnesses and our own sources with the police, the men who murdered Rabbi Wise and Mr. Caro 'looked Middle Eastern.' One apparently was screaming something about Beirut and Kabul. Could be fundamentalists in general, the U.A.I.R. in particular."

"What's the motive?" Marcus asked. "If al-Masri wanted to do away with Jeri," he hesitated as he saw Fogerty blanch, "why kidnap her? Obviously, they had the chance to kill her right there on the street."

"Maybe they want to make an example of her in some other way," said Ron Goldblatt, the former American Jewish Committee official now also working full-time in the Kehillah leadership. "Maybe they want to interrogate her first. It's possible they could be onto us. We know that a few of the smuggled arms shipments— thank God no more than a few—have been intercepted."

"Make an example of her? You mean like Meir Sarid?" Sylvia Weinberg interjected, her voice querulous.

"Perhaps… but it would be more difficult with the rabbi. For Sarid they claimed to act under international law, that gelatinous fiction, finding him guilty of 'crimes against humanity' because he insisted on leading a 'Zionist colonial regime in genocide against the Palestinian Arab people.' Putting Rabbi Levi, a civilian and non-combatant by any definition and a kidnap victim on top of that, on trial—publicly—would expose them to international opprobrium…" Fogerty said.

"Might expose them," Felicia Sanchez qualified.

"And there could be a related problem," Marcus said. "A leak, here. How else did they know Jeri's itinerary?"

There was silence in the room as the small group of people searched each other's eyes and their own suspicions. Finally, Marcus said, "we've got to collect as much information as we can. Whatever we tell the press has to have our spin on it. We're too close to the endgame to appear uncertain now."

The Kehillah tapped intelligence sources in a almost a dozen countries, including the United Arab Islamic Republic of Greater Palestine. Official and unofficial links, Jews and non-Jews, motivated by money, belief, love, jealousy, revenge or some combination plugged into sensitive information. From London, Paris, Damascus, Jerusalem, Tokyo, Seoul, Washington and elsewhere rumor, fact, secret and headline trickled back.

A surface calm had descended over the diplomatic world following the War of Arab Unity. Fogerty called it a phony peace, comparable to the phony war between France and Germany in 1940. There was, he insisted, a cauldron of intrigue bubbling below the surface. The Russians, with a renewed sense of nationalism and of their own power over the former Soviet "near abroad," had poked their fingers through Armenia and Azerbaijan, Turkmenistan and

Kazakhstan back into the Middle East. In Tehran, a power struggle had grown increasingly bitter between what The Washington Post called the "pragmatic radicals" and the "radical radicals." From Jerusalem itself came rumors, so persistent that they might contain a germ of fact, that al-Masri himself no longer ruled on a day-to-day basis, delegating authority to Mahmoud Terzi. Some claimed al-Masri was terminally ill, others that he was drug addicted, insane, or under house arrest. Most startling of all, Magen Israel agents in the Far East turned up traces of an alliance between Japan, Korea and Taiwan. Details were sketchy—but records in U.S. Naval Intelligence, scanned by Kehillah computer hackers, referred to at least one large-scale amphibious military maneuver carried out by this triple alliance. And reports of anti-regime restiveness in Syria, Iraq, Saudi Arabia and elsewhere in the region turned up frequently. The alliance with Caliph al-Masri's greater Palestine, while popular on the streets, grated among the bazaaris and the elites. But of Jeri Levi herself, not a single hard fact. None, except the absence of Jason and Deborah from school the day before, and Hal Levi's failure to report to work each of the past three days.

After the press conference that afternoon, Fogerty pulled Marcus aside. "Jonathan, I don't want this to sound heartless, but something bigger than Jeri's kidnapping is up."

Marcus stared at Fogerty, challenging him to continue.

"I know she's been the mainspring of everything we've done, but I feel this in my bones: the Middle East is about to erupt again. The Jews of Israel must be ready, and we've got to accelerate all our efforts on their behalf..."

"Without wasting time looking for Jeri?" Marcus interrupted, accusingly.

"That's not what I meant, and you know it. See here, I believe the woman's a saint, I really do."

"I'm sorry, Chester. I know."

"But look: if there's a Jewish rising, and it's successful, Jeri might turn up. If it's not, and al-Masri does have her, she's probably finished anyway," Fogerty said.

"And so are the rest of us, one way or the other. Okay, what do we do?" asked Marcus resignedly.

"Get Operation Slingshot into place. Immediately!"

"We're not quite ready, you know that. With so little time, it's a hell of a stretch," Marcus replied.

"Haven't the Jews always been history's longest shot?" Fogerty asked, with the merest smile.

*   *   *

Kibbutz Nof Benjamin (December 24, 2009)—Aharon Tabor could not believe it. Word had come through Magen Israel in Jerusalem that not only were Kurds downing Iraqi helicopters with U.S. Stinger anti-aircraft missiles but that Yemeni "irregulars" were doing likewise to Saudi fighter-bombers. Maronite Christian forces in Lebanon had blown up a Hezbollah poison gas factory with powerful incendiaries. Egyptian Copts fought pitched battles with Sunni Muslim extremists. On their own, Berbers in Algeria proclaimed self-rule. The curtain was rising ahead of schedule.

But were the Jews of the autonomous district of Greater Palestine ready? He thought not. The Arabs remained strong and well-motivated. If they had any weakness, it might be the now-erratic leadership of Yacoub al-Masri. But tantalizing though the rumors were, Tabor could not be sure. He discussed it with his father.

The old man looked out the dining hall windows that covered the entire western wall of the building. He took in the sweeping panorama of fishponds, kibbutz gymnasium and tennis courts, the path between the ponds to the beach itself, the same beach on which PLO terrorists landed thirty-one years before to begin the infamous Coast Road Massacre–39 civilians butchered, family members on a company outing–their murderers praised as "heroes of the resistance" by Arafat to the end of his life.

It would be three months before the last of winter's rains and chill winds left the Carmel coast, before the Mediterranean would transform itself from a roily gray sea into a seemingly limitless pool of sparkling blue-green water. But one day in mid-March scudding packs of low dark clouds would give way to isolated wisps of white vapor high over the sea, confectionary tracings in a luminous blue sky. On that day each year Tarbitsky would know that winter was gone. No rain, no raw wind would visit again until late the following October. Even in his most childish–or, better, childlike–dreams, which came frequently of late, he did not imagine heaven to be more beautiful than the scene beyond the dining hall windows on such a day, a Chagall-like vision created by the art of seeing.

Tarbitsky doubted he would sit here to witness another such day. He admitted to himself what his son affected to deny: I tire too quickly anymore. The climb up the gentle hill from the beach trail leaves me laboring for breath. When I sit to rest afterward I can feel my heart pound. Before I was old; now I am weakening, the systems shutting down.

"So the Kurds say they are ready. They have said the same thing many times before. They always fight bravely. Then, divided among themselves even worse than Jews, betrayed by erstwhile allies–Russians, Americans, us–they always loose. As for the Christians and Druze in Lebanon, more oil and vinegar, and whatever chance they might have in unity, they turn on each other and among themselves, even as the Sunnis and Shi'a recombine with yesterday's enemies. We'd do better to cut off our own hands than to rely on the Lebanese. The word Levantine means what it does because of them. Same for the Yemeni. How many people have tried to use them, only to end up like them, defeated by their own stubborn cunning, insisting in defeat on what might have been?"

For a while the son sat still, saying nothing. He too gazed out over the ponds, the island bird sanctuaries and the relentless breakers. A small gray patrol boat rode the horizon. After more than three years it still surprised him to realize that these boats were keeping Jews in, not plying the coastal lanes as they had once done to keep terrorists out.

"I don't know, abba. I really don't. But it will be a great battle. Will it be like Bar Kochba's doomed revolt against Rome, or like the Maccabees' successful one against the Syrian-Greeks? We can only go forward because if we don't the Arabs will crush us completely the moment they think they can get away with it. And at least we have allies this time."

"Sure. And Judea had allies too, or thought it did. Egypt would counter Babylon, Parthia would deter Rome. The pharaohs' mummies lie in foreign museums, only historians remember Parthia, only the Jews remember Judea," the old man said. "Some of us, anyway. Besides, you of all men should know there are no great battles, only necessary ones."

The son looked at his father. Tears threatened to blur his vision. "Some necessary ones are great. Whatever happens, I feel as if the Bible has opened again, and we Jews are about to write a new chapter."

"My son, the Bible has been open again since 1917, and we Jews have written an entirely new book. That's what all the fighting has been about—whether the world would allow this new scroll to become Scripture. Now your generation will finish the last verses. I do not expect to see them completed. I pray that you will. This God who does not exist, this Adonai, this 'I Am That I Will Be' changing verb of a God whom the world would have rejected long ago but for the brilliance of Moses His interlocutor and Solomon the author, King Josiah the redactor and Nehemiah the collator, demands so much from his Jews...."

Aharon Tabor did not contradict his father.

* * *

Jerusalem (December 26, 2009)–Fahd al-Husseini was uncharacteristically late. Fatima al-Masri met with the United Arab Islamic Republic of Greater Palestine's chief of security, and with its president, Mahmoud Terzi at least daily. Together they made the political decisions that directed the course of the republic. Having absorbed Jordan, been linked closely to Syria and Lebanon and subsumed the Jewish autonomous area, Greater Palestine was a peculiar Austro-Hungarian empire of the Near East. These three—with a handful of others whose silence was enforced—held the secret of the caliph's absence. Or so they thought.

As for al-Husseini and Fatima al-Masri, the cousins' passion for each other smoldered but did not blaze. This was due more to Fatima's sense of dread at her husband's towering rages than to al-Husseini's implacable commitment to duty. Their infrequent embraces alone had shocked them both, nearly overpowering their combined urge to self-preservation.

They knew about the kidnapping of the woman rabbi. Husseini's sources early on confirmed the anxiety the incident incited among the American Jews and even many of those in the autonomous areas. Fatima was troubled that Yacoub had perpetrated such a bold stroke under their noses at a time when they assumed he was under their supervision. They increased their efforts to infiltrate his own cadre of loyalists and palace guard, as, they realized, he already had done to theirs.

"Whatever is happening," Fatima said to Terzi, "Yacoub seems content, as he has for months now, to remain a virtual prisoner of himself. He lives in his spacious but spartan quarters on the third floor—opposite the woman rabbi's suite and one corridor from my own apartments. But I hardly ever see him. And he sees our children even less."

In fact, al-Masri was obsessed with his disputation. He poured over Islamic texts, talked late into the night with bearded, black-robed clerics, weathered men with strange, bright eyes. Spiritual relatives of those Sunni clerics who formed the Muslim Brotherhood in Egypt in the 1920s, they also were the political cousins of the sages who presided over Khomeini's torture chambers, who inspired Beirut's kidnappers, Sudan's new slave masters, mentors to Osama bin-Laden and Afghanistan's medieval Taliban oppressors, Algeria's throat-slashers and Palestine's smiling terrorist bombers.

Al-Masri wrote furiously, ate little and seemed to sleep less. Each time Fatima saw him the fervid gleam in his eyes shone brighter. He is like a candle that flares highest just before it gutters and dies, she thought. I loved this man once, and I'm still loyal to him. But he both pushes me away and boxes me in.

Analogies to Qaddafi seemed appropriate now. The older the Libyan got, the greater his power, the more isolated, eccentric and ego-centric he became, dressing in designer robes and his face oddly tightened, as if by some aberrant combination of surgery and injections. Al-Masri too became grander—at least to himself—and more detached, more volatile.

There was a knock at the door. She and Terzi turned at the sound. "You're late," Fatima said, expecting al-Husseini. Opening the door, she came face-to-face with her husband.

"Yacoub, what a surprise. We didn't expect you."

"I'm quite sure," he said, gliding into the room. "As to what I'm doing here, are not these my wife's quarters? Mr. President, you are excused. We wish to be alone."

"Certainly," Terzi said, stepping out. As he did so, he thought he saw fear on Fatima's face.

"Of course I didn't mean you don't belong here, Yacoub," she said to her husband, making an effort to appear composed. "It's just that you surprised me, having been away so long. And we expected Fahd for a meeting."

"Of course," al-Masri said evenly. "I know I bear some of the blame. My work drives me and keeps me away from you. Nevertheless, it is for the good of us all, for the good of all the world.

"I have replaced Fahd as head of security. We will not be seeing him again." Al-Masri add this last, just as evenly as he had his apology. "As to President Terzi, he is ill, his medication has begun to provoke allergic reactions, and I do not think he has long to live. In any case, both of them were conspiring against me. Against us," he added, with emphasis.

Fatima realized that her own fate was being determined. She listened intently not only to her husband words, but also to his tone, and scrutinized his expression, searching for any useful clue as to how to respond.

"I do not fault you for spending so much time with al-Husseini and Terzi, for thinking that this time the political Yacoub, the man of action, was gone for good, replaced by the holy Yacoub. But did not the Prophet, blessings be upon him, teach that religion and politics could never be separated, that the latter was only part of the former? They are united in the will of Allah.

"You assumed I was mad..."

"I only..."

"Don't deny it! You did, despite the fact that such a thing is impossible in one chosen to lead his people in true faith. You took it on yourself, mistakenly, to hold the nation together. I do not fault your intention. But what you tired to do, and the way you tried to do it, was subversive regardless. Besides, it was beyond a woman's ability, especially a woman of insufficient faith."

"But Yacoub, I..."

"Stop! I am speaking. Whereas I sought to use politics for religion, you meant to use religion for politics. And your... assistant... he could never have been more than a glorified policeman, couldn't you see that? While I, I am caliph!"

He paused, then turned his back on her. After a moment he began to pace. For a time he seemed to forget her presence altogether.

"Do you know that I have the rabbi, the American, here in the palace?"

She knew, of course, but gaped nonetheless, more at the non sequitur than its substance.

"All the while you thought you were watching over me, I was monitoring you. For every one person in this palace in your pay there are two devoted to me. I let you run the country for me. I needed time to prepare for our greatest battle, my disputation with this Rabbi Levi. When I defeat her, on live television, the world will see the undeniable supremacy of Islam over the false Jews. Then I will present my great commentary. We shall offer the Jews of the territory the choice of conversion or the sword. Thus we will put an end to them, the continuing humiliation of abiding their autonomous territory, and their religion, while gaining numbers, land, strength and respect ourselves!"

"After that," al-Masri raved, his eyes bulging, his chest swelling with breath, "it shall be the turn of the Christian infidels and their pope. I have devised a perfect plan to capture him as well! The Crusades will end at last with one victor— me!" He laughed, his head jerking up and down with the violence of his emotion.

The laughter ceased. He seemed to come back to himself. Looking directly at his wife, al-Masri asked softly, "Well, am I mad, or is this brilliance?" Fatima understood. Her husband, this manic depressive, was irretrievably gone. This was no Napoleon returned from Elba. No, this time the pragmatic revolutionary, the political genius, the patient executive, was lost forever, extinguished in the febrile brain of the zealot with whom he had coexisted until now. And, she knew, an inappropriate response to a zealot's question could mean death.

"Your concept is brilliant," she said firmly, with the conviction of an actress. She strove to seem sincere; Yacoub used to be able to smell evasion, dissembling, like a dog sniffing fear. "However, there might be flaws in the details."

"For example?"

"Do not show the woman rabbi live on television. Tape the disputation and release it serially. The world will snap it up as if it were live, but taping allows you to control everything that is seen. We can obliterate her best arguments, emphasize your own."

"You are much like she is," al-Masri replied, "women with a man's sense of authority, but not a woman's sense of place. She refused an offer to do this on tape if she could not control the editing of her own portions. I almost killed her then, but Allah inspired me. We are going on the air live—but at the end, when the judges rule that I have prevailed, naturally, she must either convert or die! Either way Islam wins. But, I must say, you were trying to be helpful."

Fatima al-Masri had bought herself, and the government of the United Arab Islamic Republic of Greater Palestine some time.

Jeri Levi grew accustomed to delays in starting the disputation. What was to have begun two weeks after her abduction was now two more weeks overdue, postponed three times. She found she had been looking forward to it, to the change and, to be honest, the excitement. She forced herself not to look beyond it.

Rabbi Levi had maintained a strict study schedule. Morning prayers, then she read from breakfast until lunch, with only short breaks to refocus. In the afternoon she made and collated notes, taking her pre-dinner walk in the courtyard, under escort, then showering. After supper, evening prayers were followed by a review of the day's research. The only semblance of communication she received from outside the palace came by radio. But the set in her room was locked on an Arabic station. Rabbi Levi did not speak Arabic.

Sometimes she thought the disputation would be like the radio broadcasts, signifying nothing for those who did not already understand, did not already believe. Nevertheless, it had become the center of her mortgaged life and she anticipated it eagerly. She already had argued for and won the privilege of walking in the courtyard. For half an hour a day she moved briskly about the enclosure. Much as she resisted the feeling, the palace, at least parts of it, was becoming familiar if not homelike, the atmosphere somehow almost warm. She even came to see her silent, black-robed female guards as dependable if uncommunicative companions. The two fatigue-clad soldiers who trailed the women trailing her also seemed to lose their threatening mien as they filled their assigned roles in her routine. It was, she recognized, the hostage syndrome, the human impulse to draw near the potent, threatening authority figure, of hoping to elicit sympathy by feeling sympathy. Like Patty Hearst in the Symbionese Liberation Army, like the Jewish left in praise of the Palestinians from Oslo to the al-Aksa intifada. Hers was the individual parallel to the behavior of threatened nations, the psychological reaction of the "well-treated" kidnap victim.

She inhaled the fresh air deeply, like a euphoric. She marveled at the sky like a landscape artist surveying a favorite setting under ideal light. The exercise time too soon ended, as always, alone again with her books and her thoughts and fears, Rabbi Levi wondered how much longer this would last. Once or twice she fantasized about rescue, but only once or twice. She knew that elements of Magen Israel must be only a few miles away, in battered western Jerusalem. But even if they knew where she was, which seemed unlikely to her, they hardly could be expected to jeopardize the rescue of a nation for that of an individual. Once she decided not to cooperate, to force al-Masri to stop this absurdity and kill her now, or let her speak directly to her people, to her children. But then she heard a voice, or rather comprehended it, commanding her to go on. Perhaps it was just her own subconscious.

* * *

Washington, D.C. (January 3, 2010)–"The work started in the labs at M.I.T., Virginia Tech, Cal Poly and elsewhere almost as soon as the Kehillah was formed has, with a final push, come close to fruition," Chester Fogerty was explaining to the group's executive committee. "Right now agents are on their way to Damascus, Cairo, Baghdad, Tehran, Amman and Riyadh, to London, Moscow, Paris and Berlin to put 'Operation Slingshot' into place. If they don't succeed, even a victorious rising by the Jews of Palestine could be rolled back again by big power diplomacy or regrouped Arab strength."

"What about Washington?" Ron Goldblatt asked. "No 'Slingshot' site here?"

Fogerty chuckled. "Yes, Washington too. We've got to be evenhanded to reach a comprehensive Middle East peace, don't we?"

When Felicia Sanchez had pointed Jonathan Marcus' attention to the Jews' need for an equalizer, something more specific, targeted, more flexible than conventional nuclear weapons, Kehillah researchers had gone to work. The concept was simple: In medieval Europe warring states often exchanged royal hostages– not infrequently heirs to the throne–to be held for years at a time as surety against treaty violations or surprise attack.

The same principle, but suicidally expanded to exchange entire populations of hostages instead of selected political guarantors, underscored the Cold War's MAD–mutually assured destruction. Although MAD prevented nuclear war between the Americans and Soviets for forty years, it ironically provided the umbrella under which a multitude of conventional proxy battles and wars could be, and were, fought–from Malaysia, Korea and Hungary through Cuba, Vietnam and Angola to Nicaragua and Afghanistan and including, in part, the Arab-Israeli wars.

Israel's conventional nuclear arsenal had, by the early 1990s, lost much of its deterrence. The more advanced Arab and Israeli strategists recognized it as an empty threat, one that could not be employed to save Israel but, given Jewish practice and international diplomacy, could be used only to punish radical Arab or Islamic states for obliterating Israel, not deter them from doing so. Only anti-missile defense really could supplant MAD. For Israel, equivalent retaliation for nuclear attack would be much like Samson pulling down the Philistine temple onto his immediate tormentors and himself, and could only signal the end of Israel, the survival of many of its enemies. This was true long before former Iranian President Ali Akbar Hashemi Rafsanjani said in 2001 that one or two Islamic bombs could destroy all Israel, while Israel's total retaliation could destroy only ten percent of dar al-Islam. And when he suggested the exchange would be worth it, the response from Europe, from North America was… silence.

No, for true deterrence something both more concentrated and unanswerable was required, given the Jews' utter inferiority in territory and population. Exchange was the wrong word, Marcus understood, although the concept of hostage was exact. Israel would have to deploy a threat as dangerous as a nuclear strike, but one its enemies understood as much more likely to be used. So not long afterward some of the best scientific brains known to the Kehillah went to work on the solution. Now this gift, this modern surety for a peace of unequals not everyone might desire, was ready. It might have been available even earlier, Marcus smiled to himself, if as many Jews of his generation had gone into the hard sciences as had entered law, journalism and the arts, into engineering instead of arms control. A mind is a terrible thing to waste, he reminded himself.

"From Dulles International Airport eleven people, not all men, not all Jews, but all familiar here at Friends of New Israel headquarters, have begun journeys that collectively should put the world on a new strategic footing," Fogerty was saying. "They will usher in a new equilibrium, and with it an era of true Jewish equality. Or so we pray."

The travelers carried identical oversized briefcases. Lining each was an ultra-dense plastic developed as part of Slingshot to spoof airport metal detectors. When opened, the cases revealed only a fraction of their total contents. Packed between the lining and core, in spaces the size of a large cassette recorder, were miniaturized neutron bombs. If activated by cellular signal, the device would emit a flash of lethal radiation over a radius of more than half a mile.

"The existence of the weapons is not to be revealed until the rising in the Jewish autonomous area is well underway, and then only by private diplomatic contacts. If it proves necessary, a demonstration will be made in the most appropriate target city," Fogerty explained.

He read the abhorrence on the others' faces. "Do you accept that a world in which a Jewish nation cannot survive should itself survive, intact?" he asked them.

"No," Marcus said. "But where is the justice in holding civilians—unknowing civilians—hostage? Doesn't that lower us to the level of the Arab terrorists?"

"Think clearly, Jonathan. Terrorists murder civilians for political gain. They go on terrorizing to enforce those gains. We will not hurt anyone, and certainly not preemptorally, unless someone acts to hurt us. We won't demand anything of anyone else, other than to be left alone. And we will demand that only of those who by commission or omission already have harmed us."

"But why a bomb in Washington, or even London? At bottom, hasn't the United States always been Israel's ally, and Great Britain, if not a friend, at least after America the world's beacon of democracy?"

"Jonathan, you know Great Britain no sooner adopted the Balfour declaration than it began backtracking. The whole history of Mandatory Palestine from the late 1920's through 1948 was one of British evasion and duplicity, of pandering to the Arabs and keeping Jewish would-be immigrants out. Though many sympathetic words followed for decades after Israel's independence, they weren't supported by policy.

"As for the United States, in truth the record is mixed. Yes, America was the first country to recognize the new state of Israel—and then immediately joined with the other Allies in slapping an arms embargo on it. U.S. policy forced Israel to retreat from the Sinai in 1956 with no lasting gains. Washington replaced France as Israel's major military backer after 1967, but wouldn't let it crush the encircled Egyptian army in '73. It supported Israel—and Egypt—with tens of billions of dollars after they made peace in '79—but forced Israel to let Arafat and the PLO depart Beirut intact in '82. It forged high levels of military and intelligence cooperation with Jerusalem throughout the '80s, then forced Israel to sit out the '91 Persian Gulf War, eroding its deterrence against the Arabs, and played a more sophisticated version of the same game in the war against terrorism after September 11, 2001. Speaking of Jerusalem, the United States never moved its embassy from Tel Aviv to Israel's capital, so why would most other countries?

"Without the United States, Israel would have been abandoned to a hostile world. With it, Israel was prevented from ever decisively defeating even one of its Arab enemies."

To that, Marcus only muttered, "I know."

Fogerty carried his point. Within forty-eight hours the word traveled back to Washington eleven times: "Slingshot loaded."

But there was still no trace of Hal Levi or the children. "I think we have the leak," Sanchez said at one of the planning sessions, which by now had blended one into the next as an endless blur. The others looked at her, the women comprehending, the men blank. "Jeri was going on vacation, right? She certainly told the kids, and somehow Hal learned enough from them to fill in the blanks."

"Even so, it's a long way from an embittered ex-husband to what happened on Seminary Road," Marcus said, testing her.

"Not so far. Have you talked with Hal Levi recently, or rather, heard him talk to Jeri, or about her? The man was not just embittered but enraged. I think he sought revenge."

"You're saying he managed to make contact with Islamic fundamentalists, with al-Masri's people?" Marcus asked.

"Maybe, but more likely with go-betweens, with intermediaries. Yacoub al-Masri—who might be crazy but certainly has been brilliant—probably had some already in place, awaiting an opportunity. And for Hal, the prospect of uncontested custody might have tipped the scales."

"Absolutely," Sylvia Weinberg chimed in. "I've watched that man for years; the more Jeri established herself as a rabbi and then as a leader, the more he changed from friendly and outgoing to cold, even nasty and introverted. I think Felicia is right."

"If you're correct, does knowing this help us, or help Jeri?" Marcus asked.

"Well, for Jeri's sake we've got to find the children regardless," Sanchez replied.

"Excuse me," a staffer interrupted. "The Asian fleet has cleared the Straits of Malacca and is steaming north by northwest."

Fogerty looked quickly around the room. "This is it," he said. "Let's go."

The admiral dispatched instructions through the Kehillah network within the U.S. Navy, which then originated what seemed even to senior naval officers like formal orders. Off the Azores the captain of the nuclear-powered aircraft carrier Eisenhower opened his sealed instructions. They had come by diplomatic pouch, borne by the naval attache at the embassy in Madrid, an officer named Revson. Odd, the captain thought, but not unheard of, and these were unusual times. The Eisenhower and its battle group of destroyers, missile frigates and other ships—core of the U.S. Sixth Fleet—reversed course and steamed back into the Mediterranean. As the Asian armada powered westward, the Eisenhower's flotilla headed east.

Around the globe the latest petroleum surplus had been worked down by a combination of production decreases in the United States and Russia, increased demand from many industrializing former Soviet and newly-developing third world countries and by periodic withholding by the Organization of Petroleum Exporting Countries to boost prices. The East Asian tigers—Japan, Korea and Taiwan—languished under the terms through which they were required to do business with the United Arab Development Bank. Japan's traditional, and costly, 45-day petroleum reserve was down to three weeks.

In the Kremlin, desperate Russian leaders could not revive domestic oil production—once higher even than Saudi Arabia's but ruined by decades Communist and post-Communist mismanagement, shoddy equipment and outright neglect. Militant Islam unsettled the countries of their "near abroad," from Azerbaijan to Kyrgizstan, and varying forms of Islamic extremism radiated through Chechnya from Iran, Pakistan and Afghanistan.

In the United States, President Johnston had been reelected with little more than one-third of the popular vote. The rest had been scattered between a lackluster Republican whose slogan—"Vote for me, I'm not really a reactionary"—proved too clever by half; an independent Hispanic flat-tax, pro-gun, pro-abortion Libertarian; and the black feminist Green Party nominee. Congress, while not as clearly divided, split into factions across the ideological and special interest spectrum. So Johnston, while not yet a lame duck, wielded surprisingly little influence.

"I don't know why there's such division. Even the party's congressional leaders openly disrespect me," the president lamented. "They laughed at my proposal for a $100 billion tax hike—called it too little, too late."

"Look," the First Lady replied one spring night in the Lincoln bedroom (she still hoped to see ghosts during intercourse, anticipating ethereal spasms), "for that bunch it doesn't matter what you do; not being a 'real' Eastern intellectual or Western radical, being a Midwestern bumpkin, you'll never be one of them, you'll always be too conservative. Anyway," she added, nibbling his ear lobe while sliding his hand onto her breast, "you might be too early sometimes, but you're definitely not too little."

The president just moaned.

*   *   *

Jerusalem (January 5, 2010)—Moscow maintained an interested silence on the movement of the Asian fleet. Senior officials throughout the Johnston administration, reading planted e-mails and authentic sounding cables, assumed that other senior officials had dispatched the Eisenhower's battle group in response. After all, it was the prudent thing; they would have done it themselves. At the palace in Jerusalem, Yacoub al-Masri placed a file containing a report on the Asian ships in a drawer in his large, polished mahogany desk. It lay there, prints of American satellite photos and all, untouched as he made final preparations for the disputation.

With al-Husseini disposed of and Terzi gravely ill, al-Masri's word went unquestioned inside the palace. Doubted, but unquestioned. Fatima strove to appear both loyal and helpful. Nevertheless, she understood the menace in her husband's cold correctness toward her.

Late one blazing night–the dry, sand-filled, super-heated chamsin blowing in from the Arabian Desert made Washington's oppressive summer humidity seem comfortable by comparison–Jeri Levi answered a knock at her door. Unused to visitors except the warders at their regular hours, she felt a stab of fear. She watched as the door opened silently; she came face-to-face with a woman she recognized only from news photographs.

"Please," the woman said, stepping in and closing the door. "We have little time. The surveillance is off for a few moments; nevertheless, speak softly.

"I am a prisoner here as much as you. You may believe that as you choose. Has Yacoub confided to you how long he expects this... this disputation to last?"

Utterly surprised at Fatima al-Masri's appearance, not to mention her words, Rabbi Levi answered guilelessly: "Not exactly. But I have the impression it will take several weeks, perhaps a month. Why?"

"Then that is how long we have to save ourselves, and our children, in our own ways," Fatima said, as much to herself as to Jeri. "Would it surprise you to know I don't hate you? That I have no ill feelings toward you whatever? In fact, I admire you. I hardly agree with you, but I think that you are, perhaps, a woman much like myself."

"Yes," replied Jeri Levi. "In other circumstances, I think I might enjoy getting to know you–but what do you mean, our children?"

"You haven't realized, you poor woman, that we both have been deserted by our husbands? Mine left me not even for the revolution, our revolution–for the revolution, for Greater Palestine he would never would have indulged himself with your kidnapping and this disputation," she spat the word, "but left me he has for this occultation and vision of himself as the mahdi.

"And your husband–this I do not understand at all, perhaps some inbred obsession with the personal–abandoned you not for a cause, not for another woman, but the mean revenge of stealing a mother's children from her."

Jeri gasped.

"Yes," Fatima said, "he was the source that made your kidnapping possible, and he has the children here."

Jeri's hands pressed hard against her mouth.

"Our only chance, I think, is for you to go through with this damned debate as best you can, buying me time to save Palestine–even if I have to negotiate to do it. Fate has made us partners, I believe."

With that, she whirled and disappeared beyond the locked door. Jeri Levi stood rooted, staring at the closed door. Our children! What did she mean?

She staggered as much as walked to a chair. Had that really been Fatima al-Masri, or an apparition? *Am I beginning to crack under the accumulating stress?* Jeri Levi asked herself questions the answers to which she could not be sure. Absently, she reached for some fruit in the basket on the table, and brushed a piece of paper. When Jeri saw the note she shuddered again, just as she had the first time she read it.

"Tomorrow we begin. Soon you will be almost as widely known, although not so loved, as I. I urge you to get some sleep so as to be fresh in the morning. Then we begin to write history, together. Al-Masri."

* * *

Tel Aviv (January 5, 2010)–Jeremy Marcus jotted down the jumble of words and numbers, compared them to a computer-generated table before him and leaped out of his chair. He handed the scrap of paper to Professor Eshel in the Magen Israel command center in Tel Aviv, where Marcus had been transferred to keep him out of sight after the killing of Ehud Kenaan. Eshel read the seven words, reread them and embraced the boy. On the paper was written, "Ships moving from east and west. Prepare."

The two of them compared the code to the table a second time and virtually danced about the room. Ever since Magen Israel had been alerted to the formation of the Asian fleet and the start of "Operation Slingshot" commanders had been on duty around the clock in the basement communications center. There, beneath an old North Tel Aviv apartment bloc, Eshel now grabbed a secure telephone. He called Israel Miller.

"HaShabat Herutanu approaches," Eshel said. The former deputy prime minister of the former state of Israel, now a stooped old revolutionary with a price on his head, felt his pulse quicken. The Sabbath of freedom was coming

* * *

Jerusalem (January 6, 2010)–After breakfast her usual companions, augmented by several new guards, accompanied Rabbi Levi from her apartment cell. They walked through long corridors and descended by elevator into the heart of the palace. When the doors opened Jeri Levi found herself in the midst of a large, sophisticated television studio. Al-Masri's remark about their impending notoriety came back to her.

A door opened in the glass-enclosed control booth suspended eight or nine steps above the studio floor. Al-Masri himself came down, his stance and manner that of a supremely self-satisfied man.

"Welcome," announced the deep, mad voice. "As you can see, all is ready. It is time for us to take our places and begin." He gestured to a barely elevated set which, to Rabbi Levi, approximated those used on American television for political debates. Two lecterns stood a few feet apart. One bore a large, burnished emblem of the sword, palm and crescent moon of Islam. On the other was a small, flat Star of David. Behind al-Masri's podium was a full-color panorama of the Grand Mosque at Mecca. It depicted the sacred Kabaa, the shrine of the ancient extra-terrestrial stone—an object of veneration even before Muhammed's revelation— toward which all Muslims turn in prayer, in the center of its expansive, multi-tiered white courtyard. Tens of thousands of believers, all in white for the annual haj, filled the open space of the great shrine in the city closed to infidels. Behind her own podium Rabbi Levi saw an artless sketch of the ruins of the Western Wall in Jerusalem, showing Judaism's holiest physical site after the intentional neglect following the executions of Sarid and Simon Tov there.

On the set at the cameras' left were two rows of throne-like wooden chairs. On the far right, over her left shoulder as she would stand at the podium, was a large screen for projection of visuals. Her eyes lingered on the chairs. For the jury, no doubt—and me with no preemptory challenges, Rabbi Levi thought.

"The arena meets with your approval?" al-Masri asked, his smile that of a gambler offering his own deck for inspection.

"No," she replied. With effort she kept her voice even. "I have some experience in television myself, as you probably know. The symbolism here is unacceptable. If we are going to have a disputation, Caliph al-Masri, then we must begin at the same starting line. I will not say a single word until the picture of the Kotel is replaced by one showing how it looked before," she paused and stared at al-Masri, "and the magen David on my podium is the same size and luster as the crest on yours. The extra elevation of your podium also is unacceptable. You certainly are a tall enough man without it, so you don't need it...do you?"

The veins in his neck and face bulged. She thought for a moment that he might strangle her, if he didn't have a stroke first. Then suddenly he seemed to relax. He laughed and she thought it almost sounded genuine, almost engaging. In an instant he was all charm and courtesy again. Such was the power of his own idea—this disputation—over him that he forced himself to behave as she persuaded him was proper.

"You are right," he conceded. "No doubt some of my staff has been overzealous. But we must be fair." Crew members went to work on the changes immediately. Meanwhile, al-Masri, already at his microphone, gestured to Rabbi Levi to move to hers.

"Excuse me," she said, continuing to stand in the middle of the studio floor. "We will be broadcasting live, right?"

"Right!" he snapped, showing exasperation.

"Excellent," she said, trying to project a confidence she did not feel. Nevertheless, it gave her pleasure to provoke him, in displaying her apparent self-control superior to his. And she hoped to goad him into over-reaching, into a bad, perhaps self-destructive performance. The Islamic sages who now occupied the double row of chairs on the set gaped at her effrontery.

Sound and light checks complete, the emblem changed and the backdrop replaced by a photo mural of the Kotel, the disputation began at last.

Each opened with the obvious. Al-Masri claimed that the Jews treacherously betrayed Mohammed soon after joining the Prophet in his fight against the pagan tribes of Arabia. Mohammed recognized the Jews' sacred, albeit incomplete, role as a people of the Book. But they, in turn, stubbornly rejected the revelation of the Quran as the fulfillment, the crown of both the Old and New Testaments.

Rabbi Levi annoyed those in the studio by occasionally quoting from the Quran in support of her arguments, including, of course, Mohammed's confirmation of the Jews' status as a holy people. She stunned them by citing the preeminent medieval Islamic historian Ibn-Khaldun in favor of the Jews' right to the holy land. The weeks of intense study, in which she felt she had reviewed much of what she had learned in seminary and since, had not been wasted.

She insisted that there was no Old Testament, only the Hebrew Bible, God's Torah, His eternal word to mankind, complete in and of itself. The prophetic intimations of a future messiah referred neither to Jesus nor Mohammed but to the Jewish people as a whole and to those who might arise from within it, descendants of the House of David, as messengers of God. These pious, anointed leaders would neither proclaim nor conquer but exemplify. The messiah's message would signal the dawn of the age of redemption, on earth, and the revival of the Davidic dynasty, not a new religion or caliphate.

Mohammed revised the Hebrew Bible as much as he wrote a new Islamic one, she suggested, tailoring it for the unlettered tribes of the Arabian peninsula once he saw that the Jews would not flock to him. Hence the change of tone and teaching toward the Jewish tribes midway through his book. But the Jews did not so much turn against him as he had abandoned them, spurring his followers to attack their early allies in a new war of expropriation. Earthly plunder as much as the promise of eternal bliss motivated those first mujahadid—holy warriors, Rabbi Levi asserted.

In the face of such blasphemy al-Masri and the jurors restrained themselves with difficulty. The caliph lyrically recited Mohammed solitary desert searchings, his communing with Allah and his divinely-inspired vision. Distilled, this became the Quran, the last and greatest book of revelation, of religion, philosophy, politics and behavior for all mankind. Did not the fact that possession of this heavenly knowledge—and nothing else—enabled Mohammed and a few relatives and companions to inaugurate Islam, gain tens of thousands of adherents, then millions of converts, and conquer half the world, all in a few decades certify it as holy writ? How could anyone look on such an unprecedented accomplishment and say that it was not divinely ordained—unless Satan controlled his or her tongue?

"How," Rabbi Levi rejoined, "could a merchant believed by most scholars to have been unable to read, produce a holy work so close in many of its tenets, personages and plots to those of Judaism and Christianity. Does not the text itself suggest much borrowing? And, in direct comparison of texts, does it not read like borrowings based on what he had heard and inevitably distorted—through omission of his own teachers and human forgetfulness—of the first two monotheisms?"

Did Mohammed not know of the Jews and their beliefs from his own travels? Was it not also the caravan routes—not only his lonely desert visions—that were the source of his new system? And if such copying was necessary for Islam's foundation, necessary to beat down the prevalent pre-Islamic paganism of Arabia, then why not return to the source itself, to Judaism? As Islam has a close but not syn-

onymous system of kashrut, the hallal practices for meat, for example, and a rec-
ognizably parallel system of law, sharia roughly tracking halacha, why not return
all the way? Mohammed only ordained that Muslims face Mecca in prayer
instead of Jerusalem after he realized the Jews would not join him; isn't it time for
the Muslims to rejoin the Jews? We are agreed that there is but one God, that
Adonai and Allah are the same; in that case, perhaps Muslims, like Christians as
branches off the trunk of Judaism, should recover their common roots as Jews.

"You will cease coupling the name of the Prophet with that of Jesus!" the chief
juror ordered her. "We note and overrule your bald attempt to diminish the former by tying him to the latter."

"As you wish," she said politely. "But another basic question remains: Why
did Islam, like Christianity, have to be propagated, have to be enforced by the
sword, protected for centuries by the power of the state? Judaism survived despite
oppression of the sword, despite governments of men, in spite of Pharaoh, Caesar,
Czar, Fuhrer, Commissar and all such. In which could the hand of man be seen
more clearly, in which the work of God? Why was it that, when Frederick the
Great asked his philosophers for a proof of God, they answered, 'The Jews, sire.'?
The Jews, sire—not 'the Christians,' and not 'the Muslims.'"

Why was it, she challenged, that alone of the three Western monotheisms,
Judaism did not insist that non-believers were condemned to earthly and otherworldly punishment? How could such confidence, especially from such a small
people, be anything other than providential? Judaism's universal message was to
be acknowledged by all, but voluntarily. And its key points—the Ten
Commandments, charity, mercy, righteousness—were so acknowledged. It was
Judaism that had wrought the revolution in the human heart. So why was it that
the universal claims of both the cross and the crescent had to be enforced first,
embraced after, and those of "infidels," even monotheistic "unbelievers" denied?

Al-Masri counterattacked. If indeed the Jews were God's chosen people, why
did he chose to permit such devastation to befall them? Perhaps their miserable
history, from the Roman dispersion to the German purges and the ultimate holy
verdict of the War of Arab Unity demonstrated on which side Allah walked. "If
this God of Abraham and Moses so loved his Jews, why are there so few of them?"
he taunted. "The tiny people of Israel, as you call them, against the global family
of dar al-Islam, the world of Islam; does this not show where primacy lies, how
Allah intends to spread his word, and how much punishment the Jews deserve for
their corrupt behavior, for betraying Allah and his prophets?"

"There are at least two problems with that argument," Rabbi Levi responded
evenly. "First, it is an appeal to the sword for an historical verdict; it is not an assertion of faith in an ultimately unknowable God. It is too easy, might makes right.
How much harder to persevere, when the earthly score often seems to be against
you. If we Jews have been punished, then does not that make our adversaries—
make you, Caliph al-Masri—an instrument of our God? And if we have been punished, perhaps it has been for not being more Jewish, for not having kept the
mitzvot, the commandments of our God regarding the Chosen People on the
Promised Land, more fully? If we would follow the Torah more closely, and more
of the exiles of Am Yisrael, the people of Israel, return to eretz Yisrael, the land

of Israel, would you, sir, be vindicated—or subsumed? That you won a great victory in the War of Arab Unity cannot be doubted. That we can see in it the final wave of the hand of God is, at the least, open to question. All the conquerors of the Jews are gone, from Assyrians and Babylonians, Greeks and Romans, to Crusaders, Cossacks, Nazis, and Communists—all gone. If God's plan is for the Jewish people to spread His message for the redemption first of this Chosen People and then through and with it all mankind, then perhaps you've drawn incorrect, premature conclusions."

"The court will not tolerate such rancor and arrogance!" the chief juror interjected, raising his voice.

"It is the judgment of history, and history's God, Adonai who is Allah," al-Masri said softly. "And as you well know, for us—who as Muslims are completed believers, just as Christians are completed Jews and Jews brought God to the pagans—religion and politics merge. And history, Allah's deeds, is their record. Is that not what the Jews brought to mankind, as the historian Paul Johnson taught, that the Jews discovered God who manifests Himself through history?" He smiled at her in self-satisfaction.

Jeri Levi was startled. Al-Masri might well be a fanatic, but that did not prevent him from being both broadly read and occasionally subtle. She tried to regroup.

"That is almost a Jewish way of putting it. We are not so far apart about God, about Allah, as the chief juror might think. But as for Jews and Muslims, or better Judaism and Islam, we differ sharply over who, or what, is the Lord's subject and what His object."

Now it was al-Masri's turn to be startled. "What do you mean?" he asked, sounding sincerely curious. It was as if this last remark entered his mind through a space unprotected by the shell of fanaticism accumulated over the previous four decades. She seemed to have caught him momentarily off-guard, engaging a man, not a self-proclaimed caliph. If he was manipulating her, setting a trap, it was a superb performance.

"Just this," she said, taking a chance, and answering his question in kind. "If you expect Jews and Christians to accept Mohammed and Islam on your terms, then why can't Mormons, as Mormons—to pick one of several examples—expect you to accept Joseph Smith, the angel Moroni and the Book of Mormon on their terms? To you the Quran is the final revelation—but not to them. So to Christians only their New Testament completes the Torah, which to Jews is eternal and complete, requiring no further divine texts."

"Because," al-Masri thundered, the caliph returning, "these later ones are false prophets, about which we were warned. It is Mohammed and the Quran that are true and final! It is the will of Allah!"

"Inshallah," the jurors intoned.

"Perhaps you are right," Rabbi Levi said. "But you see, you are now again arguing faith, not facts or rather, not history. And faith, in the end, is a matter between God and all his people, not for you nor I nor anyone else in this studio or watching us to enforce. Only God. When we act according to God's will, that is faith, our own faith; when we compel another, than is aggression. Did not the

Prophet himself, peace be upon him, teach that Allah permits people to believe in Him according to their own understanding, and that there will be more than one path for that understanding?"

"You have the right words, but you twist their meaning!" It was the chief juror once more. "Take care, woman, that you do not serve Satan!"

"Thank you," Rabbi Levi said, bowing slightly and offering an even slighter smile to the chief juror. "I will take care, as we all must."

Turning toward al-Masri again, she said, "Do you not believe that 'if He desires any good for thee, none can repel His bounty?' Of course you do. So if Allah leads you through Islam, inshallah, it is His will. And if God leads me through Judaism, im yertze HaShem, it will be His will. But if you compel me, or I coerce you, that is not religion, that is theft, theft of another's mind and will. And God, Allah, forbids stealing."

"Not so," insisted al-Masri. "We are not speaking of mundane robbery, but of holy war. It is the duty of the Muslim to extend dar al-Islam, the world of Islam, to dar al-harb, the world of war. And if we fall as shahid, as martyrs in the fight, we are assured that Allah rewards us in paradise. As the Prophet said, 'When Allah has decreed concerning a servant that he shall die in a certain country, He also gives him an errand there.' You, rabbi, ignore the central element of predestination, of humans carrying out Allah's will. We did not simply conquer with the sword–then and now–in jihad, but we did it as God's will, your God as well as ours, as you say."

"You say predestination, but we insist that God gave man free will," Rabbi Levi countered. "As the Torah states, God told Moses–whom you know as Mousa– to make clear to the children of Israel, in his summation to them, that 'I have set before you this day the blessings and the curse, good and evil, life and death, therefore choose life.' That means we have fundamental choices to make in this life, that they involve our individual decisions between good and evil, life and death, God's word and Satan's deceptions. If human beings are not free to choose between good and evil, then we are never mature, never adult and therefore not responsible for our actions. Man's free will cannot contradict God's omniscience; God sees our journeys whole, but we as limited humans must take one step at a time.

"As for God's will, does not the Quran say, 'Pharaoh sought to scare them [the Israelites] out of the land [of Israel]: But We drowned him together with all who were with him. Then We said to the Israelites: 'Dwell in this land. When the promise of the Hereafter comes to be fulfilled, We shall assemble you all together.'? In fact, does not the Quran echo the Torah, in that the Promised Land belongs to the Chosen People so long as we keep God's covenant? 'And when Mousa said to his people: "O my people, call in remembrance the favor of God unto you, when He produced prophets among you, made you kings, and gave to you what He had not given to any other among the peoples. O my people, enter the Holy Land which God has assigned unto you, and turn not back ignominiously, for then will ye be overthrown, to your own ruin."' So the Quran says it is the duty of the Jews to be better Jews in the Land of Israel, not to leave it."

"You can make that argument from the sacred text, of course," al-Masri said, "but are you not obligated to complete the plain meaning–that failure to follow Allah's will, as the corrupt so-called Jews, descendants not of the ancient Israelites but of the Khazars and other exilic, non-Semitic people, have failed, must result in your overthrow, 'in your own ruin'?"

"I do not think so," Rabbi Levi replied. "First, there are Semitic languages, as Hebrew and Arabic are so closely linked, but there is not one Semitic people. Today's Palestinian Arabs are most definitely not the descendants of the Biblical Philistines, a sea-faring people from the Aegean and Black Sea region who, like the Jews, were defeated by the Babylonians at the end of the seventh century B.C.E.–but unlike the Jews, then disappeared as a people from history. Nor are today's Palestinian Arabs the direct descendants of the Canaanites–the Moabite, Edomite, Jebusite and others the Torah speaks of. The people of those vanished cultures might have left their genetic legacies–much in common with that of the Israelites–but of their cultures, of their peoplehood, nothing.

"Yet the Jews are both the physical descendants of the children of Israel who left Egypt with Moses and their culture, Judaism, the direct continuation of the original monotheism established by their ancestors. That's why more than 90 percent of all Jewish men today–whether from Indianapolis or India–who claim to be Cohanim, descendants of the priesthood, of Moses' brother Aaron, the first high priest, show a common genetic marker on the male side that first arose roughly 3,200 years ago. That why the 2,000-year-old copy of the Book of Isaiah as seen in the Dead Sea Scrolls is identical with that we read today, and undoubtedly consistent with the oral tradition that preceded it for seven centuries, from Isaiah himself speaking the word of God to the kings and people of Israel."

"No," al-Masri said flatly. "The false Jews, the so-called Jews, instruments of British imperialism and Bolshevik atheism, became Zionist tools to dispossess–temporarily, like the Crusaders–the true believers from this holy land."

"Is it not illogical to believe that Zionism was simultaneously a capitalist and communist plot, a Western, Christian assault on Islam and the Arabs–widespread and wealthy with oil–on behalf of the few and downtrodden Jews? Is it not better to say, with the Quran, 'And thereafter We [Allah] said to the Children of Israel: "Dwell securely in the Promised Land. And when the last warning will come to pass, we will gather you together in a mingled crowd."?' God–Allah–will decree the Day of Judgment for all of us. Until then, He has given eretz Yisrael only to b'nai Israel."

Yet again the chief juror interrupted: "Do you deny that Allah has set his believers, the Muslims, to extend dar al-Islam until it encompasses His whole world?"

"Even if Allah sent the Muslims to holy war on His behalf, it could not have been to deprive the Jews of their just inheritance. Nowhere does the Quran dispute the claims of 'Banu Isra'il,' the children of Israel, to the 'blessed land' that Allah promised their forefathers. As it is written, Allah commanded Ibrahim to leave Mesopotamia and go to 'the land' promised him and his offspring, 'the land which We have blessed for the sake of the entire world.' It says so plainly in Sura 21, verses 71 and 81.

"And referring to the Exodus, the Quran also states, does it not, in Sura 10, verses 90 to 93, that 'We prepared for the children of Isra'il a safe abode,' a mubasa'a sidqeen, so important it is written that way just this once in the entire Quran, 'and provided them with all good things'?

"Is it not the Quran faithfully reflecting the Torah? 'Then God once more reassured Abram: "I am the God who brought you out of the Chaldean city of Ur to give you possession of this land,"' as it says in B'resheit, Genesis. And later, as Abram has become Abraham, literally, the father of the nation, 'I will give to you and your descendants after you, the land in which your are now only an immigrant—the whole of the land of Canaan—as a possession for all time, and I will be their God.'

"This promise is reiterated literally dozens of times, and applies only to the Jews. Does not the Quran echo the Torah faithfully?

"Caliph al-Masri, distinguished scholars, even if Allah wants you to rule the world, or the rest of it, He clearly means for the Jews to live freely in our own land, certainly the more faithfully we live as Jews. And since the Quran never mentions Jerusalem, and the name Al-Quds—the Arabic contraction for the Hebrew ir kodesh, the holy city—was unknown in the Prophet's time, but the Torah refers to Jerusalem as the Jews' holy city on more than 70 occasions, and as Zion many more, it is clear what the position of the Jews should be, indeed must be, here in eretz Yisrael."

"No!" shrieked another juror. "This she-devil lies by telling the truth! When the Prophet, blessings be upon Him, said, 'Then Mousa said to his people: O you people! Remember Allah's grace toward you when He sent you prophets and appointed kings unto you and gave you that which was given to no other people on the earth. Enter the Holy Land that Allah has assured you in writing,' He meant 'until the time of the Muslims and the final revelation.'"

"With all due respect," Rabbi Levi said, "I have been quoting what you say is the final revelation. Sura five, beginning with verse 20, which you also have just referred to, clearly notes God's grant to Moses and his people legal title to the Holy Land, 'the gift bestowed on no other people on the earth,' a people that God allowed to have their own kings over them, that is, to be sovereign over themselves. This is the final revelation on that matter, according to the Quran itself."

The sage, whose face and gone from pink to purple, collapsed into his chair. Al-Masri, who had been standing with a quizzical expression on his face, now stuttered almost incoherently. Before he could form a sentence, Jeri Levi said evenly, "Great Caliph, isn't it so that in the spirit of the holy Quran, the true believers also must be truthful believers?"

"You are henceforth forbidden to cite the Quran!" al-Masri thundered. "Confine your citations to your Torah."

So ended the first disputation. It turned out to be the first and last televised live, regardless of al-Masri's promise. He and the jurors decided among themselves that Rabbi Levi had proved more formidable than anticipated, and would from now on require editing. But the damage had been done. By holding her own, if not more, in a telecast seen—although not rebroadcast—throughout the United Arab Islamic Republic of Greater Palestine and beyond, and across the Jewish autonomous region, Jeri Levi had struck a hammer blow at Palestinian morale.

She also bolstered that of the Jews.

In conceding now to videotaped installments, Rabbi Levi was playing for time. But having done better than she could have hoped in the first round, she gambled that some additional gains might leak through even the censored segments.

As the disputants moved deeper into their arguments, the rhetoric grew more esoteric. Al-Masri moved from Quranic citations to the Hadith or traditional reports compiled about Muhammad and his teachings after his death. Rabbi Levi progressed from the Torah to the Talmud and even later Jewish works. To her surprise, she found herself increasingly at ease, even enjoying the event. Over the next two days, it became apparent that al-Masri, although well-versed, was not particularly nimble. He could declaim but not really debate. He can play theological checkers, she thought, but not chess. Should have stayed in politics, old boy, she told him silently.

And she played on the jurors just as she did on al-Masri. By modulating her voice, precisely choosing her facial expressions and vocabulary, she provoked them emotionally as it suited her, eliciting surprise, shock, anger, confusion, apprehension almost at will. However they edit this, she thought, the medium will be the message, and countless Arabs, men and women, will see a Jewish woman unafraid and giving as good as she gets, even if the substance of my remarks is reduced to the merest sound bites. The only thing she could not gain, of course, was the assent of the jurors or al-Masri. In the context of disputation, she was both captor and captive.

Not only on televisions throughout the Middle East, but via cable and satellite in Washington, Moscow, London, Paris and elsewhere, the disputation drew keen audiences. "What the hell is this?" President Johnston demanded, watching one segment. "Damned if I know," the secretary of state replied, making a mental note to fire his director of intelligence and research, who had been blindsided by Rabbi Levi's kidnapping and subsequent reappearance on the televised disputation. What the hell is this, indeed, the president wondered aloud to his wife.

"Why dear," she told him evenly, "it's the Arab-Israeli war. It's the Muslims versus the Jews—and by extension, versus the Christians. Even I understand that. I never should have written your papers for you in grad school."

At the Friends of New Israel headquarters they knew exactly what the disputation meant. So they monitored the pace of the debate and made ready. In the Jewish autonomous area of Palestine, the leaders of Magen Israel did the same.

"The Asian fleet is just outside the Straits of Hormuz. The Americans are less than two hundred miles east of Jaffa," Fatima Tlas al-Masri said aloud to no one but herself. "And what are we doing about it?" she continued, knowing the answer. "Nothing,"

If few dared to question Yacoub al-Masri before the disappearance of al-Husseini, before the tragic death due to illness of Mahmoud Terzi, then no one even raises an eyebrow now, Fatima thought. Everyone is busy, pretending to be hypnotized like Yacoub and his holy jurors by the disputation. It is as if these fleets do not exist.

Fatima's life as an aide to her husband the caliph was circumscribed. This was as Yacoub intended, no doubt. However, she still retained a small personal staff and access to her husband's quarters. Occasionally he asked for her counsel, although she suspected he did so only for appearances sake, or perhaps to lull her into a false sense of security. As discreetly as possible, she still gathered information.

Her husband's obsession with the disputation reinforced her belief that he was irretrievably mad. Only an insane man would spend his time in such juvenile play while dangerous matters of state accumulated. Only a leader out of touch with reality would deny the perils he and his nation faced. She looked at Yacoub and saw Marcos in his last days as ruler of the Philippines, leading the sycophants in applause for his wife's singing in home movies, or Ceaucescu, insisting until almost the last—and forcing Romania to do likewise—that his semi-literate wife was the world's leading scientist. Or Peres, at the height of the second intifada, complaining that Barak would not give Arafat "a day without funerals" so the latter could resume "negotiations," as if Arafat did not require funerals, Arab and Jewish alike. Denial, backed by the yes-men if not the assassins of a palace guard, had undermined many a once-great ruler, she knew. And denial had become Yacoub's touchstone.

But what portion of his madness was cunning? By appearing to restore their old relationship was Yacoub testing her, tempting her toward a misstep? Did he hope to force her to drop her own disguise?

She had always loved him, and loved him still, somehow. Whereas the poor Jewish woman—the female rabbi, how curious—had been abandoned by her husband, Fatima knew the bond still holding her to Yacoub and him to her would never be broken. He might kill her, yes, but discard her? Never. And yet she despised the way his passion for, what, godliness? had overwhelmed his passion for her.

Whatever the truth, Fatima felt she must act. And given Yacoub's elimination of Fahd and Mahmoud, she must act on her own. Fact and rumor came to her in the same hushed tones. She heard of Yacoub's file on the Japanese financial scheme and intelligence estimates of the military preparations of Tokyo and its two allies. Palace gossip held that he had not even looked at it, boasting of ignoring such "mundane matters" while the great disputation unfolded.

"We know the Japanese," she had warned al-Husseini in what turned out to be their last conversation. "Their acquiescence in our financial blackmail was suspicious, their practice of smiling at all Middle Eastern oil states and then playing them off against each other—like Iraq and Iran during their long war, selling to both, buying their oil in turn at below market prices and alienating neither—quite a performance! What the Soviets used to do with arms, the Japanese have done with trade."

Whatever was in Yacoub's folder, she had to see it. If he would not save the still-uncemented empire they had built, she must.

The night of the fourth installment of the disputation, Fatima managed to enter her husband's study undetected. She locked the door behind her and clicked on one small lamp. By its dim light she began rummaging through the contents of Yacoub's desk. She remembered from their underground days his habit of sandwiching important papers between layers of ordinary, unrelated documents and leaving them in a mislabeled folder to hide them from whomever it was he suspected at the moment. But he always did so in reverse alphabetical order. So it was with little effort that she found a one-page summary on the size, direction and capability of the East Asian fleet, in the middle of a folder marked "Finances" in his bottom right desk drawer, the one with the hanging files. Also in the folder were aerial photographs. A second folder produced the full report.

Fatima sucked in a deep, surprised breath when she read it. She had no idea the Japanese—with Korean and Taiwanese support—had rebuilt a modern, offensive navy. The paper confirmed what had seemed obvious to her: a pincher by the industrialized nations, Japan and its partners from the east, the Americans, no doubt with British and German, if not French or Russian support, from the west, to recolonize Middle Eastern oil countries, or at least the oil fields. And subordinate the United Islamic Arab Republic of Greater Palestine, if necessary. It would be 1956 and Suez again, with perhaps the opposite outcome for Arab independence, she thought.

Setting aside the summary and the photos, she automatically sat down in Yacoub's chair and began reading the entire file. Later, deep in concentration, she became conscious of something, or someone else, in the room. As she started to swivel in the chair to look, a powerful hand clamped itself over her mouth. A strong arm encircled her from behind.

"Yacoub said you would come, eventually. He is always right. He wanted to present when you condemned yourself, but was too busy with the woman rabbi. So he sent me."

The words ended in a mirthless laugh. Fatima recognized Khadoumi's voice. If there were any deficiencies in her husband's psychosis, any lack in his brutal deviousness, Khadoumi filled them. Or, she thought, induced them.

Her Westernized professors at Bir Zeit had taught her a word for ones like him—sociopath. She remembered wondering why Arabic lacked a similar word. Certainly the vocabulary was rich, poetic, but where were the labels, the clinical warnings for those whose insanity was not singular but plural?

Fatima tried to shock Khadoumi as he had shocked her, to deter him. "Listen!" she struggled to shout through the hand cupped over her lips. Khadoumi eased his grip slightly. "Do you know what is in here, Fawzi? Proof we are going to be attacked! Yacoub has got to read it, now! We must tell him! Help him...."

Khadoumi never hesitated. "Yacoub told me you would speak like this. And he told me to answer you this way," he said, driving his big fist hard against her temple. In the instant before the explosion in her brain, Fatima quite clearly heard the cracking of her own skull.

Hoisting her limp form as if it were a sailor's duffle bag, Khadoumi carried Fatima al-Masri, more than first lady of the United Arab Islamic Republic of Palestine, actually one of its co-creators, out a side door of the study and down flight after flight of stairs. Under the television studio, in the sub-basement hardened against penetrator if not thermobaric bombs, was a row of cells. Khadoumi deposited Fatima, blood beginning to congeal around her wound, onto a cot in a small, cement-wall square with a solid metal door. Then he telephoned Yacoub's quarters.

Uncharacteristically, the phone rang and rang before being picked answered. "What is it?" the caliph shouted. His voice sounded high and he swallowed half his words, like a man panic-stricken.

"I did as you said," Khadoumi stuttered in reply, taken aback by the tremor in his leader's voice. "Your wife is in her cell. She is unconscious and needs a doctor."

"Many will need doctors. The Japanese are landing at Abu Dhabi, Ad Doha and Al Manamah. They are seizing the southern shore of the Gulf! Should I continue the disputation, or lead the resistance? This is so... uncalled for!" Al-Masri, who seemed to Khadoumi to be talking to himself, hung up.

Fawzi Khadoumi let the receiver dangle. A rush of exhiliration swept over him, surprising him. The sound of fear in the caliph's voice, a sound he had not heard in thirty years with Yacoub al-Masri, freed him as a shattered manacle frees a slave. The sound told him everything had changed, and his instincts took command. He was free, all restraints were gone. Now there was no cause to bow, no need for fealty, even to Yacoub. The structure was crumbling. In chaos he could indulge himself.

Fawzi Khadoumi did not know and would not have understood that many leaders–Stalin in the face of Hitler's invasion, Rabin for a time before the Six-Day War–broke down temporarily when confronted with their most fearsome tests. Such men regained self-mastery in time but Khadoumi, a true foot soldier of his era, longed for the liberation of anarchy. He resonated to it, like the Nazi storm troopers 70 years before whose marching song proclaimed, "We are the new men, come not to build but to destroy!" The self-imagined new men, those throwbacks to pre-civilization, the curse of the twentieth century, pre-cursor to post-civilization in the twenty-first.

Now he could do exactly as he wished. Every mean and vicious impulse, large or small, could be gratified. And because it could be, should be, must be. Khadoumi moved off toward Jeri Levi's prison suite. Even on the plane back, when he had cut her bonds–before that, on the street in Alexandria–he had wanted to kill the Jewish bitch. Now he would, and properly.

* * *

Jerusalem (January 11, 2010)–In western Jerusalem, in Tel Aviv, Haifa, Kibbutz Nof Benjamin and the rest of the Jewish autonomous area, in the mountains of northeast Iraq and the alleys of east Beirut, among the Copts of the upper Nile and the remaining Jews of America, the anticipation, already unbearable, seemed to intensify. In the command post of Magen Israel, at the headquarters of the Friends of New Israel, they knew that the ships of the Triple Alliance–after delaying some time in a show of maneuvers in the Indian Ocean–had moved through the Straits of Hormuz. Satellite reconnaissance showed that the fleet had split into three task forces and that these were steaming toward the capitals of the oil-rich sheikdoms of the United Arab Emirates, Qatar and Bahrain, respectively. All three were small, lightly if expensively defended sites. But no one was sure if landings were planned, and if so, that they would meet with success.

It did not matter. Fighting erupted spontaneously in Jerusalem, sending armed Jews storming out of apartments, offices, cellars and attics, some swearing like the Maccabees of old to reclaim what was theirs. It began with Jeremy Marcus and a few colleagues. Dispatched from the Tel Aviv command center as part of the general alert, they had been manning an observation post barely one hundred meters from the Old City Wall and Jaffa Gate. Several, like Jeremy, were by now seasoned members of the underground. Others were even younger, dedicated but untried hangers-on.

From a sand-bagged storage room in the Mamilla Mall just north of the King David Hotel, they looked across to the Ottoman walls of the Old City, some portions of them standing on the foundations of King Hezekiah's walls that had resisted the Assyrians. The King David itself loomed as a darkened hulk. It had metamorphosized into the headquarters of the United Arab Islamic Republic of Palestine's secret police. Into the once-grand, history-burdened block, many members of Magen Israel, or suspected members, and Palestinian Arabs out of favor with the regime had disappeared.

But Ben-Ami's car bomb the year before forced the mukbarakat to relocate, and repairs to the ponderous pink tetrahedron never got finished. The observation post occupied by Jeremy and the others was a new and critical position for the Jewish underground in Jerusalem. From it they watched as the upper curve of the sun broke over the parapets of the 500-year-old fortification, starkly outlining David's Tower and the Jaffa Gate.

"What the hell is that?" Jeremy exclaimed, peering through binoculars at a section of the wall just north of the gate. "I don't believe it! There's an Arab on top, in keffiah and combat fatigues. And he's holding a person, a woman, whose hands and feet are bound!"

"Let me see!" shouted several of his companions at once. One, Yehuda Israeli, another Magen Israel veteran, took the glasses. He stared intently, focusing, squinting. "God! It's a woman alright, or what's left of her."

Jeremy Marcus watched through his sniper scope. The man on the wall pulled a knife from his boot. Jeremy nosed his rifle—a 20-year-old M-16 carbine still favored by the underground for its adjustable sights, compactness, and ease with which recruits unfamiliar with firearms could be taught to use it proficiently—out a window of the observation post. Sighting through the high-resolution scope, he aligned the cross-hairs on the middle of the man's torso. He was still squeezing back the trigger when the shot echoed across the valley. Khadoumi wavered for an instant, then toppled backward into the Old City. The woman, still bound, teetered forward and fell off the outside of the wall, landing in shrubbery 30 feet below on the landscaped mall just north of Jaffa Gate.

For a second that was eternity the carbine's crack went unanswered. Then the sounds of dozens of skirmishes throughout Jerusalem opened. They quickly grew into the roar of one battle as Jews sought to retake the city, all of the city. Seconds later the word was radioed to Tel Aviv and the rest of the Jewish autonomous area: "We are fighting throughout Jerusalem. Kol mat'chilim!" All begin!

Total Jihad

With news of the fighting in Jerusalem and confirmation of the landings in the Gulf, planes from the Sixth Fleet–standing just off the horizon in the Mediterranean–streaked from the carrier decks. Retired–cashiered–or not, Admiral Chester Fogerty's instructions were followed. The War of Restoration was on.

Insurrection, informally coordinated, expanded too in the Christian and Druze sections of Lebanon, in the mountains and remote valleys of Kurdistan, in armed clashes between Copts and Muslim fundamentalists along the Nile, between Berbers and their masters in Algeria. It amplified the battles on the beaches of the emirates. Suddenly, across much of the never monolithic Middle East, Arab overlords were on the defensive. Suddenly, the United Arab Islamic Republic of Greater Palestine was fighting for its life, without prospect of immediate help, and without the charismatic leadership of the one man responsible for assembling it in the first place.

In northeast Jerusalem, in the caliph's palace, Fatima al-Masri lay comatose, her brain hemorrhaging. The metal door to her cell remained locked. Her husband stood at his podium in the television studio floors above, parsing theological minutiae in front of an empty control booth, pausing every few minutes to scramble back up to make sure he caught his own performance rebutting the she-devil Levi on video tape.

In the palace's situation room, lieutenants of al-Husseini, Terzi and al-Masri himself fought to exert authority over other underlings, a rabble which, having been chosen for traits of blind obedience and brutality, rather than ability, had survived the caliph's successive purges. Fatima had consider them a useless lot, like Arafat's cronies in the old PLO.

But one of them, Issam Abayat, rose to the occasion. If only I can get out of here and resurrect the old leadership, the surviving veterans of the Palestinian Authority and the Hashemite senior civil service, he thought. The former were experienced if corrupt, the latter cold but efficient bastards. If I just mobilize them, we will still have a chance, a good chance.

But the caliph's aides were not ready to let him leave, not until they finished arguing over who should do what, when, and who deserved what rank. Like survivors of the Yemeni cabinet meetings of the 1970s, the victors in the Popular Front for the Liberation of Palestine's factional gatherings in the '80s, like the Islamic Jihad executive committee sessions of the mid-1990's, the participants placed on the table in front of them not note pads and pens, but their machine pistols. It would, Abayat knew, fingering the small five-shot Captain's back-up pistol in his inside suitcoat pocket and sweating under his Kevlar body armor, be a long debate with a quick ending.

*　*　*

Jerusalem (January 11, 2010)–"Ever since Israel was dismantled, conventional wisdom held that we could not reestablish a Jewish state without an air force. And since it was assumed we could not build one under such close control, then it followed we could never revolt successfully. Of course, as the modern world has proven repeatedly, never is of short duration," Professor Eshel noted in his log of the first day's fighting.

"The Eisenhower carries almost ninety planes and helicopters, equivalent to a fifth of our combat air force after the European Union revised the Mitchell Commission recommendations. Small, but enough for now, enough for adequate air cover for Magen Israel units to overrun nearly every police station and Arab military strong point within the Jewish autonomous area. Even enemy artillery on the western slopes of Judea and Samaria was suppressed if not silenced, thanks to the planes and cruise missiles and guns of the Sixth Fleet. If tomorrow goes as today, we should regain most of 'Israel proper,'" Eshel finished writing.

It is a big if, he thought to himself. Is it possible the Eisenhower and its carrier battle group could fight a rogue war for a second day, without being interdicted by the authorities in Washington? He doubted it.

"The markings have been changed?"

"Yes," a voice crackled by satellite phone from six thousand miles away.

"The pilots have their instructions?"

"Yes. Everything is ready," came the distant reply.

"At daybreak, then. We can't afford to be late."

Fogerty removed his headset. "Ladies and gentlemen, I think we've done just about all we can from this end, at least those of us knowledgeable about Operation Slingshot and the Sixth Fleet. It's time for us to go. To those who remain, you know what to do, and why. Carry on. If I might paraphrase, ever so slightly, Yasser Arafat–may he continue to rot in hell–it is a counter-revolution until victory! And thank you all for everything. God bless you."

As dawn broke the second day, two planes from the United Arab Islamic Republic of Palestine attacked the Eisenhower, or tried to. Their German anti-ship missiles, by way of Iran, were intercepted by Israeli-designed, U.S. Navy-modified Harpoon missiles. Although fighters from the carrier went after the two intruders, the planes managed to escape.

"Washington, we've been attacked," the captain radioed.

"Continue patrolling in force," came the reply from the Pentagon executive briefing room, "the tank." "We understood you were under attack last night. Reply to hostilities as necessary. The Kennedy battle group will reinforce you." As the late Col. Abner Samuels had suggested, and Admiral Fogerty devised, rogue signals had convinced the Defense Department that the Eisenhower's initial involvement had been defensive, in reaction to attack. By the time events were sorted out, the War of Restoration ought to be over.

Now Fogerty, along with Jonathan Marcus, Felicia Sanchez, and several other original members of the Friends of New Israel were on their way to Greece, where they would change planes. Meanwhile, the plans they had helped formulate three years earlier continued to be executed.

"Casualties?" Israel Miller asked Eshel at the end of the second day's fighting.

"Light so far. Many of our troops have the body armor we developed and the Americans upgraded in the '90s. We had exported so much–including to the

Palestinian police–that there was not nearly enough during the War of Arab Unity. But since then, the underground has been manufacturing it clandestinely. Of course it cannot protect against rifle fire, but it greatly reduces the danger from pistols, grenades and shrapnel."

"In Jerusalem?"

"Fierce fighting again today, but we're on the offensive."

"Arab reinforcements?"

"No sign yet. Fighting is subsiding at the three Gulf landing sites. The Japanese and their allies seem to be moving to control nearby oil fields. From Lebanon and Kurdistan, the reports are harder to verify, but it sounds like more heavy fighting. There's some poetic justice too–the Kurds apparently are using poison gas, with the Iraqis on the receiving end this time."

"Armor?"

"In that respect, we've taken a great leap backwards. You know we sabotaged many of our own tanks and armored personnel carriers at the end of the last war, just so the Arabs would find them useless. They've managed to repair some, but not enough to be decisive. And we managed to keep a few hidden, which we've retrieved. But over all the lack has been in our favor, especially as the United Arab Islamic Republic kept most of the Jordanian equipment it inherited near the borders with 'fraternal' Syria and Iraq, just in case."

"And of al-Masri?" Miller asked.

"Not a sign. It's incredible."

"Or a miracle. What about the woman rabbi?"

"Jeri Levi? She's in intensive care, but the doctors think she'll live. They just don't know if she'll walk again," Eshel said.

"Okay. Tomorrow we move from small-unit tactics to company and battalion-sized operations. By this time tomorrow night most of the land inside the pre-1967 borders–excepting the Syrian-occupied areas around Lake Kinneret and in the eastern Galilee–needs to be ours, plus much of the western half of Judea and Samaria."

On the third day of the War of Restoration, the Jews continued making gains. But the cost was rising. They took most of the Arab garrisons that ringed the autonomous territory and pushed along the main roads to the interior of western Palestine. Larger enemy forces were encountered, with greater firepower and determination. Planes from the Sixth Fleet, many now operating from airstrips around metropolitan Tel Aviv, began running low and fuel and ammunition. The number of sorties had to be curtailed. In Tulkarem and Qalqilya in particular, Arab cities that pinched Israel's coastal waist, that had been breeding grounds for suicide bombers earlier in the decade, house-to-house combat continued in darkness.

"Although al-Masri remains invisible, a former mid-level official, Issam Abayat and what's left of the old PA-Jordanian elite are back in command. Arab leadership might not be inspired, but at least their performance now is dogged, and stiffening by the hour," Eshel reported to the ad hoc executive committee of Magen Israel on the third night. "Thanks to the Japanese, Koreans and Taiwanese, we remain almost a secondary news story. That's good; had video tape, mini-cameras and satellite dishes existed in 1948 to film the Arab refugees on their way out, or our planes launching in '67, we never would have been allowed to found the state in the first place or defend it later."

"Be that as it may," Israel Miller resumed, "for the past seventy hours nearly the whole of the Jewish autonomous area and immediately adjacent Arab sectors of the United Arab Islamic Republic of Palestine have been one great battlefield. Much of the combat, especially in Jerusalem, has been door-to-door. We and the Arabs have fought pitched battles over intersections, depots, radio and television stations, power plants, even hospitals. Destruction is everywhere.

"And although the Syrians occupy much of what was eastern Galilee and the northern Jordan Valley, the Arabs of Palestine see no reinforcements. So after three days we're poised to break into central eretz Yisrael. But we too will get no reinforcements, neither men nor materiel, certainly not in the next few days when they might be decisive. We will stand or fall on the efforts of the Jews here on the ground, as always. Therefore, I put to you a fateful choice:

"We have six hours to daylight, six hours to catch our breath, resupply the units—as much as possible—let the men grab an hour or two of sleep. The first day we had surprise, yesterday we had momentum. Today the fighting was tougher, more even. Our people and resources are strained. If we're going to succeed—to create facts on the ground not only the Arabs but also the 'international community' will be hard-pressed to reverse—we must do so tomorrow. Yet we cannot do everything without risking everything. We must try to regain the Syrian-occupied Jordan River Valley, so that's where the planes will strike. But as for most of the Negev, and even the Gaza Strip and its extension to Ashkelon, I propose we forget it."

The room was hushed.

"I propose instead that we try to rewrite—correct—history and so finally clarify if not limit our conflict with the Arabs. In 1948, Ben-Gurion first ordered the Haganah to abandon the Negev for the defense of Jerusalem. When western Jerusalem was secured, he put the choice to the war cabinet of the provisional government: Judea and Samaria or the Negev? With the Arab Legion holding at Latrun and elsewhere along the coastal plain and the Haganah badly strained, the cabinet split, a bare majority for the Negev. Ben-Gurion warned his colleagues they were laying the seeds of future trouble, but he abided by the vote. So from Beersheva to Um Ras Ras—Eilat—the Egyptians were dislodged. But barbed wire ran through Jerusalem and Jordan occupied the eastern part of the city, along with Hebron, Bethlehem, Ramallah and Nablus, the spine of our ancient patrimony. Only then did B.G. begin to insist that the future of Israel lay in the development of the Negev. It became the arid consolation prize for losing Judea and Samaria.

"For two decades we made the best of that expedient, because we had to. Ironic, considering that hundreds of thousands of Jews had fought in the Allied armies only a few years before '48, and only a couple more regiments then would have changed everything, maybe even made the first Arab-Israeli war the last.

"But we did what we could. And the Arabs fled from Jaffa, Haifa, Tiberias, Safat and elsewhere. We threw them out of Ramle and Lod and few other places. But it was our right, the right of military necessity and national survival. We could not live as free men anywhere without our own land somewhere; we could not live as the Jewish people without the Jewish land.

"In '67, we gained the Jewish heartland, but found it home to another people, and not just another people, but a competing nation that still meant to deprive us of the coastal plain, the Galilee, and the Negev. Thinking time was on our side, that the Arabs would come to their senses and see the value in cooperation and coexistence, we waited for them to make a deal, for Dayan's famous phone call that never came. The Arabs, with a sense of time as millennial as ours, a higher birth rate, perhaps a greater passion—or lower empathy—and therefore higher pain threshold, thought they could outwait us. Especially if they pursued a war of attrition called terrorism, accompanied by a relentless psychological war intended to make the world—and us, eventually—believe they were the victims, we the aggressors. So they wore us down while we imagined we had 'decided not to decide,' and later that we were 'strong enough to take risks for peace.' Even with 200,000 settlers in the territories, even with one million recent immigrants from the former Soviet Union, we could not tip the balance—not without another one million free Jews from the United States, France, England, Canada who never came. Weary, we convinced ourselves we were visionaries for peace and gave the Arabs, especially the Palestinians, nearly everything they demanded. Nearly forty years later, we submitted to Brezhnev's dictate, and 'liquidated the consequences' of our victory in 1967, submitted to the 'three no's of Khartoum' in disguise but got no lasting peace in return.

"Of course, the flawed peace quickly became the breached truce, and the broken truce the next war. But this time, once more and probably never again, we have a chance to put things right, to redraw not just the map but the geographic and psychological reality on which it can stand. This time the Jews must have the Jewish heartland!"

The silence was broken by Eshel. "Very neat, Israel. But didn't we agree less than a decade ago to get out of the Jewish heartland, to give up the 'West Bank,' all two thousand square miles or so of it, because there happened to be two million Arabs—mostly Muslims—living there? And don't more of them live there still?"

"I know I'm old, Uri, but I'm not stupid. Look at the options: to move south into the Negev probably means war with Egypt, something we're hardly prepared for, even with a couple score planes from the carriers. We can't afford that, and if we don't attack, we might be able to negotiate the return of Beersheva."

"Negotiate Beersheva?" David Ben-Melech asked.

"Signal Egypt through Washington that we have no intention of moving south of the city. They give it back, we recognize Egyptian sovereignty over most of the Negev. They've always wanted that land connection to the Middle East, even when they haven't demanded it."

"What do you mean 'most'?" Ben-Melech wondered.

"We'll need a small corridor just south of Beersheva to the southern end of the Dead Sea so Gaza can connect directly to Jordan, to 'Palestine.' The Palestinian Arabs must feel they've gained something important as well as lost something important. That's why I'm also proposing a corridor from Jordan through Jericho to Ma'ale Adumim, including Bethlehem and Ramallah but not Ramat Rachel or Beth El."

"Ma'ale Adumim?" Ben-Melech was incredulous.

"Yes," Miller said. "We'll retain sovereignty over unified greater Jerusalem, but they'll rule themselves next door. For reasons old and new, we need the biblical borders, 'from Dan to Beersheva,' or as close as demography lets us get. Besides, by going east another twenty miles to the Jordan River, except for their 'Jerusalem corridor,' we keep our supply lines short and we gain terrain necessary to guard our costal population centers from surprise attack. To change the requirement of always being a nation in arms, of having a huge reserve establishment always partially mobilized, our 'rear' areas only a few miles from potential invasion routes, we must move eastward.

"We need the highpoints of Judea and Samaria, not as observation outposts in a fictitious 'demilitarized zone,' not as isolated settlements in Arab Palestine, but as integral, settled parts of Israel proper. We dare not limit ourselves to the densely-populated coastal ghetto, with the Galilee as heavily Arab and the Negev as mostly empty appendages. Tomorrow we must seize the high points, then declare a ceasefire and offer to begin negotiations."

"But what about the West Bank Arabs?" Eshel asked again.

"Uri," said Miller wearily, "would you please stop saying 'West Bank?' Might as well call it Canaan. I get your point. The answer is that those Arabs under our jurisdiction at the end of the fighting will be given a choice: full citizenship in a Jewish state that will respect their religion and culture but expect their full participation in the social and civic life of the country. No more schools separated by ethnicity, just as we would not do for Sephardi and Ashkenazi Jews, Russians and Ethiopians. As citizens, Muslims, Christians, Druze, Circassians, Baha'i, Jews–all equal. No disbarment from military and other national service. Hebrew as the only language of commerce and government, not Arabic, not Yiddish, Russian or English. Full integration of Muslims and Christians into a state with a Jewish majority, Jewish civic culture. The end of irrendentist Palestinian Arab nationalism at war with Zionist Palestinian Jewish nationalism."

"You can't decree such an outcome. It didn't work in Bosnia, for but one recent example, and the Catholic Croats, Eastern Orthodox Serbs and Bosnian Muslims were all Slavs," Eshel said. "Do you really think it can work here?"

"No. But I do think that the twenty percent of our Arab population that is Christian and Druze can be assimiliated, more or less, in a democracy that is 85 or 90 percent Jewish. I don't expect the majority of Muslims, however, can or would accept this offer. Islam hasn't separated mosque and state yet, let alone legitimized equal rights for women or minorities. So I don't expect them to settle for individual equality and minority group status under Jewish rule. But if they resist passively, we'll overcome and rebuild the Jewish state anyway. If they resist actively, we'll be forced to expel them next door to Arab Palestine."

"Ethnic cleansing? It'll mean yet another war, and demoralize the Jews to boot," Eshel said.

"Not if we first sincerely try to integrate those who want to be integrated. No more separate and unequal, like the Arab sector used to be," Miller said. "And don't forget, a Jordan-Palestine with a corridor up to, and generally free access in eastern Jerusalem and a corridor connecting with the expanded Gaza Strip just might lead to long-term mutual stability."

"You're rolling a lot of dice at once," Ben-Melech said.

"Yes, but that's always been the Zionist condition," Miller said, "rolling a lot of unpredictable dice simultaneously—but at least having the dice in our own hands to roll. Besides, if we have another choice, I would like one of you to propose it."

*   *   *

Kibbutz Nof Benjamin (January 11, 2010)–During the first two days of the War of Restoration the Magen Israel unit of Kibbutz Nof Benjamin under Aharon Tabor won two small but significant victories. It freed an important section of the shore-hugging Tel Aviv-Haifa expressway from Arab police and reestablished a Jewish stronghold on the southern end of the Carmel range. Such was the nature of the terrain that in accomplishing these breakthroughs it moved barely two miles inland from the shoreline kibbutz and less than four miles to the north and four miles south. From the police station on the crest of the old winery and resort village of Zicron Yaacov–reoccupied at the price of eight members of the kibbutz–they could still look down from Carmel onto their own homes.

Nevertheless, by rushing up the heights they greatly strengthened the Jewish position south of Haifa and at the northern tip of the Sharon Plain. Just to the east lay the steeper, more imposing interior flank of the ridge with the Plain of Meggido at its foot and the route to the northern Samarian interior. From long before Solomon established a cavalry garrison at Meggido in roughly 950 B.C.E. to General Allenby's World War I victory there over the Turks–following biblical blueprints–this area at the fringe of the Jezreel Valley had been the battleground of kings. And in the hills above the Prophet Elijah had called on his God for the heavenly fire that defeated the priests of Ba'al, much to the annoyance of the Israelite King Ahab and the fury of his Phoenician queen, Jezebel. It would be a battleground once again.

While the ad hoc committee discussed the Negev offer to Egypt, Tabor's men had six precious hours. Weapons had to be cleaned, vehicles refueled, men fed and an hour or two of sleep stolen. From ten that night to three the next morning, Zicron Yaacov was quiet save from some troops preparing for morning. They would be joined by a nearby unit and be in battle again well before dawn. Following radioed orders, units all over Israel were to be advancing eastward before daybreak.

Restless, Tabor left the command post. Years before this building, a low, pleasant masonry residence in the late Ottoman style, had housed Israel Defense Forces psychologist Reuven Gal's institute for the study of war, peace and society. Despite the fighting, and its most recent use as an Arab arsenal, the building was intact. Tabor walked south through the village–which in the late 1990's had become a favorite with Israel's newly affluent and overgrown with villas, bougainvillea vines and sport utility vehicles–to the Rothschild Gardens. The gardens were now a shattered stand of pines. Shells from the Sixth Fleet had silenced an Arab anti-aircraft battery just above the graves of Baron de Rothschild and his wife. From a point between two broken rows of evergreens Tabor looked westward at the clump of buildings that was the center of Nof Benjamin. It was dimly lit by a handful of screened lights, a wartime precaution. To the south and north were Arab villages so different they highlighted the arbitrariness of the label Palestinian.

The southern town, Gezir a-Zarka or "Blue Bridge," was quiet. It usually had been so in the days before the War of Arab Unity. Before the intifadas. One of the poorest places in Israel, it was a settlement of black Sudanese—African in appearance, Arab in language and dress, Muslim by religion. The first residents of Gezir a-Zarka had been imported by the Turks at the turn of the previous century as indentured servants. They dug pottery clay from malarial swamps and remained clannish, wary in dealings with outsiders, Jewish or Arabs. The Turks prized them for their upper Nile immunity to swamp-bred fevers. But neither the Turks nor the neighboring Arabs mingled much with their dark-skinned co-religionists.

When the first kibbutzniks drained the swamps—the Turkish pottery works by then a grass-covered hillock in the middle of what became cotton fields—the residents of Gezir a-Zarka turned to coastal fishing, cotton-growing on their own thin strip of arable soil and husbandry and crafts. The village's subsistence economy did not check its population growth, especially after Israel established a regional health clinic nearby.

Just north of Nof Benjamin, in a cleft of the western slope of the Carmel range where the newly-expanded four-lane road from Yokneam penetrated to the sea, lay the village of Furedis. There lighter-skinned Arabs, many only three or four generations removed from Syria, had little contact with the Muslims of Gezir a-Zarka. Furedis—"Paradise" from Farsi through Arabic to English—had its own vineyards, which sold to the winery in Zicron, its own tomato fields and grapefruit orchards and, like Gezir, flocks of wide-ranging goats. But the residents of the village—whose population, like that of Gezir, grew faster than Nof Benjamin's—tended not to poach in the fish ponds of the kibbutz. So they had even less contact with the Jews there than the kibbutz's nearer neighbors of Blue Bridge. Regardless, living no more than four miles apart from north to south were three groups of Palestinians—the Sudanese; the Jews, themselves hailing from a dozen countries; and the Syrians of Furedis. Unlike Gezir a-Zarka, all was not quiet between Nof Benjamin and Furedis.

After the War of Arab Unity the police station had been relocated to Furedis from Zicron Yaacov so the Arab constabulary could keep watch over the Jews on the hill, at Nof Benjamin below, and—to tell the truth—the black Arabs at Gezir a-Zarka. To the inhabitants of Furedis, who previously had to humiliate themselves by seeking police protection from the Jews at Zicron, the little station bedecked with poster-sized photographs of Ya'acoub al-Masri and Mahmoud Terzi and banners proclaiming the renaissance of the Arab-Islamic nation symbolized their newfound status, their reclaimed identity.

When word of the Jewish revolt jumped from the radio and television at the Furedis station, the police and their auxiliary—most of the town's young men, a militia formed from the former Fatah Hawks and Tanzim and the Iz'zidin al-

252

Qasem armed wing of Hamas–prepared to counterattack. Unwilling witnesses to Jewish autonomy, as their parents and grandparents had been first cowed and later resentful citizens of a Jewish state, they now coveted Nof Benjamin itself. Led by police jeeps, a caravan of private cars, mini-buses and "technicals"–Japanese pickup trucks with heavy machineguns mounted in back, popularized first in the civil wars of Chad and Somalia–they headed for the kibbutz entrance on the first day of the fighting. Teenagers hung onto the sides of trucks, brandishing old Kalashnikov assault rifles Arafat's police had sworn to the Israelis not so many years before had been confiscated. At the kibbutz gate they ran into the Nof Benjamin Magen Israel unit on its way out.

Although outnumbered, the kibbutzniks–many veterans of more than one war and most armed with modern equipment smuggled in from the Friends of New Israel–savaged the force from Furedis. It was not that the Arabs lacked valor or that these Jews possessed a special martial flair, simply that the latter were better organized, better trained and better led than the former. And from great battles like Nelson's victory at Trafalgar to small ones like this, organization and leadership, not sheer size or even individual heroism, carried the day.

Rocket-propelled grenades and anti-tank weapons in the hands of Tabor's men left the remains of the village caravan littering a kilometer-long stretch of the old, two-lane coastal road at the western foot of the Carmel, just outside the main gate to Nof Benjamin. In less time than it takes to steep a strong cup of tea the only land battle for the kibbutz in its sixty years was over. Three kibbutzniks were dead, seven wounded. Twenty-five villagers lost their lives, twice that many fell wounded. As the battle ended, a plane from the Sixth Fleet bombed the Furedis police station, reducing it, a restaurant on one side and the town hall on the other to a debris-filled crater.

An half an hour later the vehicles from the kibbutz were parked in the tiny town square. Furedis waited, sullen, grieving and fearful as a detachment of Jews moved into the main street. Periodically fighter-bombers, previously from the Eisenhower and now based at small strips just north of Tel Aviv, shrieked low and loud across the village, scenting some target inland near Tiberias, intimidating the people of Furedis and similar villages as they went. From behind scores of shuttered windows angry eyes peered between the slats at Adi Aronson, a young kibbutznik, as he dismounted from his jeep. Two Magen Israel members were ripping posters of al-Masri and Terzi from nearby buildings. Through a bull-horn Aronson issued instructions:

"All pistols, rifles, grenades and any other weapons and ammunition must be brought to the square within three minutes. All those captured in the attack on the kibbutz will be held as prisoners of war. The rest of you have thirty minutes to gather your belongings. Your are to tie white flags to the aerials of your cars and other vehicles and take the road northeast past Yokneam to Nazareth.

"After we retake Nazareth we will compensate you for your property here. In thirty one minutes we will begin demolishing Furedis. If you had not attacked us, you would still be living here. Anyone who resists, anyone who conceals a weapons, anyone who interferes will be shot."

Shots were fired from a nearby building. Aronson and the driver of his jeep fell dead. The rest of the Magen Israel detachment returned fire, blasting at the two-story masonry residence from which the shots had come. Heavy machinegun fire and rocket propelled grenades slammed into the building. Then a squad stormed the house, tossing in grenades first, firing submachine guns as they crossed the threshold. The explosion that lifted the roof off the building also destroyed what remained of the spirit of Furedis. There was no further resistance.

Tabor, through Aronson, had decreed special treatment for Furedis because of the attack its men had perpetrated on Nof Benjamin and because it abutted an important junction on the costal expressway. There the main road intersected with an important secondary route running toward the Jezreel Valley through a gap in the Carmel. He assumed, correctly as it proved, that news of Furedis would spread through other nearby Arab villages and ease the task of his over-extended little force. In reality, Magen Israel units in the area were too few for either an all-out offensive into Samaria or occupation and police duty along the coast, let alone both. Fortunately, the example of Furedis proved salutary in the handful of Arab Moslem towns scattered along the southern Carmel. In the few Druze hill villages the Jews' advance, coupled with news of the revolt by their Lebanese brethren, helped offset recent trends toward "Palestinianization" and rekindle the old alliance between two minorities of Greater Palestine, Druze and Jews, which had abided for more than forty years after Israel's founding.

By the time new orders came, as Tabor returned from his walk through the Rothschild Gardens, his Magen unit supervised, if it did not actually hold, nearly all the territory in a swatch eight miles wide and running inland nearly ten miles—more than halfway to the old green line.

"No!" Aharon Tabor barked when he heard the first of the new instructions. "This could jeopardize everything!"

"What is it?" Avigdor Hammer—Aronson's replacement—asked, agitated in his new position and by his superior's own agitation.

"Headquarters wants us to attack Nablus, to take Mount Ebal, tonight! Barely one hundred men, with no armor, against a large fortified base, on the top of a mountain! I know it well—it used to be ours. It sits above a city of 140,000 hostile Arabs. What we should do is bypass Ebal, seize the Jerusalem-Damascus road on both sides of the city and the wadi highway leading east to Dhamiyah bridge, get reinforcements, and try to choke Nablus into surrender. Old man Miller must really have lost his mind this time!"

Hammer was staring at Tabor when the radio crackled again. Unit Nun Bet would be joined by seven helicopters, including two gunships, from the Eisenhower. Welcome as the additional troops would be, the helicopters would boost the unit's firepower and mobility beyond calculation. Hammer watched his commander's expression soften.

"And your tens shall be as hundreds, your hundreds as thousands," Tabor mumbled.

"A prayer?" Hammer asked, skeptically.

"Apparently a promise—at least for tonight."

Calling his other two deputy commanders together with Hammer, Tabor told them to ready the troops for the helicopter assault. "Have them in the gardens at 0300. We're going to take Mount Ebal!"

Five helicopters, carrying about 60 of his men, would follow the two gunships. The rest of the unit plus those flown into Zicron from Tel Aviv by the choppers, would meet at the foot of the mountain after an hour's ride overland. Then they would fight their way up to join those landed on the summit.

At 0300 seven helicopters buzzed down into the open space in the center of the gardens. A popular tourist stop until the last war, the area once resembled the lush, well-manicured formal grounds of a French chateau. In fact, it was the final resting place of the Baron Edmond de Rothschild and his wife, Sophie. The baron, a nineteenth century patron of Jewish agricultural colonies in Palestine, underwrote much of the original cost of Zicron Yaacov—in memory of Jacob—and Rishon le-Zion—first in Zion—its wine-making sister-city south of Tel Aviv. Rothschild acted after it had become clear, in the 1880s, that philanthropy alone would not suffice to replant the Jews on their native soil. Instead, Jewish immigration accompanied by investment—first in vineyards and citrus groves, later in industry—was found to be required to lay the foundation of both economic and spiritual self-sufficiency. It was a lesson that diaspora charities would have to relearn a century later.

The doors on five of the helicopters slid back, disgorging Magen Israel members from greater Tel Aviv. While they joined several dozen kibbutzniks in land transport, Commander Aharon Tabor and three score of his men clambored aboard the choppers. Escorting them would be the two Cobra gunships, lethal wasp-like machines capable of sudden darting and diving maneuvers, of stinging with guided rockets and machine cannons.

The Magen Israel commander from Tel Aviv briefed Tabor: "Two fighters will make spoofing runs on the missile batteries above Nablus just before we go in. Two others then will unload their bombs. We'll fly in skimming the peak, just behind the bombers. You'll jump off on the west and north side of the mountain top. The gunships will cover the landing and drop flares behind the mountain to the east. That should light up the outpost for the assault. The defenders will be visible to us but we'll be coming out of the darkness at them."

"When we captured these gardens," Tabor said, gesturing at the blackened trunks and burnt lawns about him, "we found floodlights set up along the perimeter. Mount Ebal—and all the other West Bank anti-aircraft missile sites—probably will have perimeter illumination as well."

"If so, the gunships will take care of it."

Tabor felt satisfied. But satisfaction as to the technical arrangements did not dispel his fear. He already had cheated fate at least three times in battle, and felt that Aronson now had died in his place. What subconscious premonition had kept him from making the announcement in Furedis himself? Yet, looking at the American helicopters and the Magen Israel men fresh from Tel Aviv, glancing a last time at the lights of Nof Benjamin no more than two miles below to the west, he experienced a transcendent feeling of balance, an exquisite rightness.

"Kadima!" he shouted, climbing into the lead chopper. Forward!

Forward, for the third time in four days his men were following him into battle. The helicopters rose, the rotors' wash beating back the remaining evergreens. The airborne war chariots moved east, passing almost immediately over Megiddo and the ruins of the stables for the horses that pulled King Solomon's own battle chariots.

All along the one hundred-plus miles of irregular front from Kiryat Ata east of Haifa in the north to Kiryat Gat inland from Ashdod in the south, similar scenes were enacted. Inside his concrete bunker Captain Mustapha Ali, commander of the garrison on Mount Ebal, heard the fighter-bombers as they made their runs on his position. He had been expecting them. His men were under orders to use their remaining missiles with care. At the beginning of the Jews' insurrection they had fired every time a blip appeared on their radar. Ali believed that one of the two planes they hit was their own. Most of his missiles were American surface-to-air models from the middle and late '80s, unsophisticated compared to the countermeasures carried by the newer planes. Since the high command had not expected a Jewish rebellion, especially one with air cover, his requests for newer anti-aircraft weapons had been ignored. A good pilot, in a well-maintained craft, could beat his surface-to-air missiles four out of five times.

Ali and his men knew they would not be resupplied, let alone reinforced, in the near future. News from the Gulf, still considered the primary front by other Arabs, had not encouraged the Palestinians. Reports of uprisings among the Druze and Christians in Lebanon, Kurds in Iraq, Copts in Egypt, Yemeni against Saudis and, opportunistically, Berbers in Algeria added to the gloom, since Iraq and Saudi Arabia used them as pretexts for not aiding the Palestinians immediately. The Syrian were busy on the Tiberias-Kiryat Shemona line and in Lebanon. Even when the Egyptians suppressed the Copts—Ali thought it matter of when, not if—he expected little from them. They were the French of the Middle East after all, utterly unreliable, diplomatic courtesans. As the French were the Saudis of Europe. Regardless, the most dispiriting was the silence from Moscow. A former noncommissioned officer in the Jordanian army, he had been chosen on the strength of his leadership ability and intelligence to train under Russian advisors. The advisors themselves had been trained by Lt. Gen. David Dragunsky, a Jew who helped lead the Soviets' old Anti-Zionist Committee. Ali could visualize the resurgent Russian nationalists looking for a Middle East wound to poke, calculating what profit might accrue to them from the triumph of the United Arab Islamic Republic of Palestine, and what from its defeat.

In learning to distrust the motives of all his would-be patrons over the years, from the Russians to the Iraqis, from the Americans to the Israelis, Capt. Ali learned to rely only on himself. One thing the Europeans and Americans had taught him—let your beliefs rule your heart but logic your mind. Then, when time to decide, combine, not separate them.

A devout Muslim, he had concluded that the Israelis, having lost the passion of their religion, could no longer defend themselves against enemies they rationalized but did not understand. So they signed treaties with Arafat and the PLO, with Arafat and the Palestinian Authority, with Jordan, with Egypt and others, always giving away, giving up their own positions, their own land, land won with their own blood. This was not the behavior of people dealing in reality, unless they had a national death wish. But al-Masri and his followers, full of dreams of Islamic glory more than one thousand years old, seemed impatient to die—or at least leave death strewn in their wake—as they tried to force history to conform to their fantasies. Preoccupation with an imagined past left them prey to an onrushing future. One thing the Israelis had done, even when no longer self-assured, was meet the modern world, at least meet it technically, meet it materialistically. This al-Masri apparently could never do, and so he and his followers had to have been surprised by the Asian invasion and the well-organized rebellion of these post-Israeli Jews.

As captain of a single garrison, Ali did what he could, continually improving the already formidable fortifications of Ebal. His command post occupied the ruins of the altar of Joshua, the one Moses—Mousa, to Ali—ordered erected two millennia before the Prophet Mohammed himself brought the final revelation. Now deep trenches, lined with rock from the alter and topped by sandbags and concertina wire, bunkers with their machinegun slits barely showing above the mountain's crest and nearly buried missile launchers attested to Ali's seriousness and foresight.

Below Ebal to the south lay Nablus. Only a regular military force of some size—several thousand men with tanks and armored personnel carries—could capture the city with its armed and hostile population, its crazy-quilt of narrow streets running up the lower slopes of Ebal and Mount Gerizim. And even then, as the Russians found in Grozny, or the Jews in Jenin, for example, only after days of close-quarter, high-casualty fighting. The Jews did not have such forces, not now, Ali knew. Some of the Israel Defense Forces tanks that survived the War of Arab Unity became al-Masri's; many slowly rusted in the armories of his politically-appointed commanders, maintained by poorly trained technicians.

In any case, Ali expected the Jews to go around Nablus, over it, attacking his position instead. He kept his men on alert, patrols circling the base of the three thousand foot dome, sentries posted on its sides.

Ali had read accounts of the Jewish irregulars' successes against such positions, like Castel outside Jerusalem, in 1948. Not the emotional reports of the Arab armies as amended and "corrected" by later polemicists, but the official military histories of the Jews themselves. I will not make the mistakes of my predecessors and underestimate the enemy, he told himself upon taking command two years before.

But Churchill's maxim that the mistakes of World War I would not be repeated in World War II—entirely new ones would be committed, applied to Ali as well as to most military men regardless of nationality. His defense of the mountain assumed that his enemy would strike by land, by scaling the heights. After all, they had no helicopters.

"Achari!" Tabor screamed as the choppers swooped up the mountainside and hovered at the crest. After me! He leaped out, his men following. He chose to land inside the enemy compound, not outside the fortified perimeter from where he would have had to fight his way in. The gunships had done their work. The floodlights Ali had planted were largely destroyed. Flares dropped by the helicopters illuminated the outpost from behind the defenders, anticipating the rising sun.

Nevertheless, machineguns and grenade launchers firing from concrete rein-forced pillboxes and the well-protected trenches immediately pinned Tabor's company to the earth.

"Can we outflank them?" shouted Avigdor Hammer.

"There is no flank! This is a mountaintop. We have to get forward, enter the trenches, and roll them up!"

"Suicide!" Hammer yelled into his ear.

Tabor, grim-faced, nodded almost imperceptibly. Then he barked an order into his walkie-talkie. Instantly the attackers concentrated their fire on a ten-meter-long section of the closest trench. RPGs fired at almost point-blank range smashed into the concertina wire and tore out large chunks of the roof of the near-est bunker. Hand grenades landed all about this section. Suddenly, for several seconds, the attacking fire raked left and right. Half-a-dozen men, Hammer in the lead, dashed through the gap in the center, through the shattered wire-and-sand-bagged defense, and leaped into the trench.

In the next fifteen seconds, before their number was reduced by four, these six cleared a portion of the defensive line and silenced the remaining machine-guns. More Jews poured into the breach in Ali's lines. Slowly they worked their way along the outer connecting trenches. The combat, often hand-to-hand, cost Tabor nearly half his force killed or wounded. But evacuation, even if he ordered it, was impossible. The helicopters were gone on other missions. The men could either fight to take the mountain or try to fight their way off. Already on top, the choice was victory or death. Or maybe victory and death, Tabor thought.

Slowly, orderly, the surviving Arab soldiers withdrew to the inner ring of trenches and the central bunkers. The well-practiced maneuver impressed Tabor. This deadly enemy was worthy. His losses, first to the gunships, then to the ground assault, also were high. For two hours the post atop Ebal, measuring less than five acres, was the universe and hell itself for two hundred and fifty men, almost evenly divided between Arab and Jew. They struggled, flesh and blood, muscle and bone, spirit against spirit, locked in a desperate combat. A man would suffer a ghastly wound while the one next to him passed through the same fusillade unscathed. A wild shot, perhaps friendly fire, would tear off the top of one man's skull while a carefully aimed round fired by a marksman would go wide of its human target. One side crawled forward, the other inched back. The attackers, joined by their comrades who had moved up the bitterly defended slopes, closed in.

Just after dawn, Captain Ali ordered that a white flag be hoisted over the command bunker. He had prepared for this moment too. Tabor, wounded in the shoulder, sent two men to receive the surrender. As they entered the bunker Ali bowed slightly and squeezed the detonator concealed in his right hand.

The center of Mount Ebal erupted like a volcano. Concrete, rock, dirt and the mangled remains of human beings flew outward in a mad rain of destruction. Tabor, bandaged and resting in one of the captured outer bunkers, understood immediately. The command bunker and the ground around it had been booby-trapped.

Soon after the helicopters returned, free for the moment from their multiple missions of ferrying troops to Jenin, onto Jebel Hureish, Bet El, on Ba'al Hazor and a dozen other strategic sites, ancient and modern crossroads, heights and towns throughout Judea and Samaria. On Ebal they found twenty-seven of the Jewish attackers dead, thirty-two wounded; total casualties half the force. With the explosion of the command post Arab losses were even higher.

"Magen Israel unit Nun Bet will not fight again in this war. It can't," Tabor said before he let them give him a morphine injection. Morphine, Hammer thought, as indispensable to modern warfare as bullets. Almost as an afterthought, Tabor asked, "how is it going?"

"Like it went here," a medic with an American accent told him. "We're winning. For that you can thank the pilots, the ones who've survived. That and the fact that the Palestinians apparently hadn't had time to put together much of an air force, even with the Jordanians, and neither the Syrians nor the Egyptians helped them. But we've been chewed up badly. A lot of good men are dead."

"There won't be another offensive then," Tabor mumbled, fading into unconsciousness.

None were needed. Capt. Mustapha Ali had not been the only Palestinian commander fighting without hope of resupply or reinforcement.

In Washington, President Johnston had been watching the Asian invasion of the Gulf closely. "Blind trust or no," he said to the first lady, "this is serious. Most of our stock is riding on the outcome of this invasion."

"If you'd listened to me when it came time to appoint the secretary of defense and the secretary of state and put some political loyalists in there, some people with loyalty and savvy, we might not have been blindsided," his wife snapped. "But no, you had to court the Washington establishment, the original three-hour lunch-and-a-seminar crowd, the bloviators and Washington Post editorial board. But I repeat myself. Oh no, you had to play statesman and appoint an M.I.T. professor and a Wall Street lawyer. One techno-nerd and one brass-initialed brief case, two Foxhall Road addresses, combined I.Q. of close to 400, probably, but not a political brain, or ball, between them. Guys who, with all their smarts, all their money, would still strike out in an Indianapolis singles bar. No wonder we've been flying dark in the Middle East...."

"Don't Monday morning quarterback me, Sue Ann," said the exasperated president. "Just give me one usable suggestion for today."

"Okay, here it is: Get that damned mutinous Sixth Fleet under your personal control—you are the commander-in-chief, aren't you?—and fix things, fix 'em good, so it looks like you were in charge of the fleet all along, not the other way around. Send those ships to reinforce the Seventh in the Indian Ocean, steam into the Gulf and take charge from the damned Nips! Thank them, and their Korean and Taiwanese friends, for their help, but make clear we're in charge now. They'll get all the oil they need, but through a joint venture with us. Use this whole thing, this... I don't know what, global riot by a bunch of Jews and Orientals... to reimpose order and not coincidentally our control of the oilfields. And either co-opt the Russians or kick 'em out, too!" She paused, cocked her head in thought, then added, "Look, the silver lining here is thick: the Arabs, those experts in energy extortion, will finally be back in their place. I mean, without the petroleum deposits they happened to be sitting on, the world would have heard little from them and thought about them even less."

"Done," President Johnston said. He did not ask the first lady for her views about his Jewish problem. He did not want to start a conversation that might force him to reveal what the director of Central Intelligence had told him at yesterday's morning briefing: the Jews were demanding to be left alone with their conquests, or reconquests, threatening massive retaliation with some secret weapon if they weren't. The agency chief informed the president he had reason to believe the Jews were not bluffing.

So it was that on the fourth and final day of the War of Restoration the Jews lost their navy. But of the approximately 140 planes and helicopters from the Eisenhower and Kennedy that had been committed to the fighting, a little more than 100 had survived; of those, 50 now were based on Jewish soil, "undergoing repairs."

"It's enough, barely," Uri Eshel told Israel Miller, "even if they are nearly out of fuel and ammunition. The enemy can't be sure of that, and can't be sure there aren't more. But it is well-aware of the superiority of our pilots and command and control operations. I think the air is ours, if by default, for the next few days at least."

"Should be sufficient," Miller said. "The secret talks with the Egyptians are going well. And the Russians—even before being informed of Operation Slingshot—agreed, as their ambassador in Jerusalem put it, 'to let the Jews keep this barren crumb of property they insist on coveting.'"

Issam Abayat also had looked to the Russians. He had done so with hope, but not much expectation. So when Moscow virtually ignored the latest Jewish-Arab war in favor of horning in on the Persian Gulf land-rush, demanding oil concessions of its own in the Kuwaiti-Saudi Arabian neutral zone as the price for accepting the East Asian-American condominum in Bahrain, Qatar and the United Arab Emirates, Abayat was not surprised. And when the Americans agreed, provided their own newly-enhanced special relationship with Saudi Arabia—in which a large garrison of America troops would "safeguard" remote oil fields indefinitely—was not disturbed, he understood that the Palestinians were alone.

"It's amazing," Eshel was saying, "but after four days of fighting the war might be over. And we've won."

Barely ninety-six hours after Jeremy Marcus squeezed the trigger back on his M-16, the leaders of Magen Israel stood knotted before a large wall map of the Middle East that hung in the Tel Aviv basement still serving as their headquarters. It seemed premature to reoccupy the Kirya in south-central Tel Aviv, the old Israeli "Pentagon" with the ruins of the giant concrete telecommunications tower that used to watch over the Near East for hundreds of miles in all directions. On the map and nearby charts of north, central and southern Israel the course of the war had been plotted.

"According to our people in U.S. intelligence, the Americans and Japanese and their allies hold most of the old U.A.E. and all of the peninsula of Qatar and the island of Bahrain. A joint U.S.-Russian force is arriving to 'protect' Kuwait and the Kuwaiti-Saudi Arabian neutral zone. The Americans are increasing their presence in Saudi Arabia. The United Arab Islamic Republic of Greater Palestine's alliances with Syria and Lebanon, and with Egypt have disintegrated. Damascus, Baghdad and Cairo once more go their own sovereign ways, competing as before for a remnant of Arab hegemony.

"In the past twenty-four hours, local Palestinian commanders seemed to be fighting mostly on their own, and mostly on defense. Except for one brief, nearly incoherent television broadcast at the start of the war—in which he urged his people on to martyrdom in the great struggle against Rabbi Jeri Levi and her blasphemy, Yacoub al-Masri has not been heard from. In fact, his muddled speech and ragged appearance probably helped spread anarchy in Palestine, not contain it."

"Neo-colonialsim in the Gulf, Palestine as a backwater. The 'good old days'?" Miller mused.

"If we're deft enough to enforce them," Eshel said.

"Whatever, we need the breathing room," David Ben-Melech said. "We're exhausted. The whole Jewish autonomous area, or maybe I should say new Israel, is out of gas, figuratively and literally."

Nearly one-quarter of its fighters had been killed or wounded. Most of its materiel had been expended. About one-third of its vehicles—trucks, jeeps, vans, buses, armor cars, a few tanks and artillery pieces brought out of hiding, and the appropriated planes and helicopters—had been destroyed or badly damaged.

"But how is morale?" Miller asked.

"Great," Ben-Melech said quietly. "Profoundly great."

"Then we'll be all right," Miller answered.

"Yehiye tov," Eshel added. It'll be good. "There are no really large Arab infantry or armored forces on this side of the Jordan River able to mount a concerted counter-attack, other than the Syrians above Lake Kinneret. But they're about to get an ultimatum they won't be able to refuse. Still, we might have only a few days not just to bandage ourselves but also to improve our geographic-demographic situation as much as possible, maybe do what we should have done in the months immediately after the Six-Day War: create some new realities we really can live with."

The Magen Israel executive committee, acting with the authority of the last Knesset, did just that. The announcement was made at noon the following day over the radio of what had been, six days earlier, the voice of the underground. Suitable television studios had not been repaired and staffed yet. At the microphone was David Ben-Melech. Israel Miller decided that his tired old voice was not what the citizens of the fourth Jewish commonwealth in three thousand and a few odd years should hear this day. Eshel was privately elated that Miller—still savvy but increasingly erratic—had ruled himself out. And Eshel, ever the analyst, knew that he too belonged to a generation whose time, whose times had passed, finally.

So it was that David Ben-Melech, literally David, son of the king, a young member of the last Knesset, a senior figure in Magen Israel, went on the air as acting prime minister of the new state:

"Shalom. Brothers and sisters, Jews of our ancient and new nation, we are reborn. Today, after three years of slavery, we once again have escaped, passed through the wilderness, liberated ourselves, defeated Amalek and reclaimed our land. In the name of the executive committee of Magen Israel, legal successor to the former Knesset of the State of Israel, I proclaim:

"By the authority of the Jewish people victorious in a just cause, the new state of Judah–land of the Jews–is hereby established. It will be a Jewish republic, influenced by the Torah, governed under a civil constitution to be written by a publicly elected assembly. Hebrew will be the one official language, Jerusalem again will be our capital. Until the constitution is written and approved in a plebiscite and elections held for the new Knesset–all this to be completed in the next twelve months–the executive committee will act as provisional government. I have been chosen the new chairman and acting prime minister.

"The borders of Judah will be fixed at the old border with Lebanon to the north, include the escarpment but not the plateau of the Golan Heights to the northeast, follow the Jordan River south from the Yarmuk to Jericho, west to Ramallah, southeast to Ma'ale Adumim, southwest to Bethlehem, southeast to the northern tip of the Dead Sea and south into the Arava. At Hatzeva it will run west to Sde Boker, then north through Revivim and Ofakim to the northern outskirts of Ashkelon. 'From Dan to Beersheva, from the Salt Sea to the Great Sea,' these are our covenantal boundaries, as best we can fix them, maintaining our historic rights, Jewish majority and security while minimizing future Arab grievances.

"Nablus–that is Shechem–and Hebron–that is Kiryat Arba–will be open to Jews but autonomous cities of Arab Palestine, which, confederated with Jordan, should include the Jericho corridor, the Gaza Strip and the central Negev. The southern Negev, including what was Eilat, will be transferred to Egypt.

"Judah stands ready to welcome all its people from their dispersion. We do not demand the return of the exiles, but only the exiles' return can finally assure the success of both Judah and the Jews, the continuity and flowering of Judaism in our generation and the next. This success, which will enable us at last to be the 'light unto the nations' as foretold in our holy book–which is holy to half the world–is required not only for our own destiny but for the dawning of redemption in this too often dreary, brutal world.

"Jews, we need you here. This is your place. Our past has shown once again what a weakness for all of us is the absence from our own soil of so many of us. And you need to be here, to become your fulfilled selves. Israel as a refuge failed. Judah as a renaissance will succeed. Sit no longer by the waters of Babylon and weep, or tarry by the flesh pots of Manhattan and Bel Air. Let your eyes behold, as we always have prayed–and your hands contribute to–the rebuilding of Zion. Not 'next year in Jerusalem,' but now.

"Am Yisrael chai! Baruch HaShem! The Jewish people live! Blessed is the name of God!"

The stillness blanketing the Jewish autonomous area–now Judah–during the broadcast lasted another moment. Then, as the realization of what had transpired set in, people poured into the streets of the cities, the squares of little towns and the centers of the remaining moshavim and kibbutzim. They were shouting, singing, dancing and laughing. They were embracing, weeping and praying.

About two hours later an earthquake rumbled along the ancient but still active fault line underlying the Syrian-African rift, the Jordan Valley and Dead Sea. Like the quake of 1927, it measured between 6.0 and 6.5 on the Richter scale and its epicenter was in roughly the same place, about twenty-five miles northeast of Jerusalem. Like the quake of 1995, which caused considerable property damage in Eilat and elsewhere in southern Israel and resulted in a handful of deaths, this temblor too caught geologists off guard. Unlike those twentieth century earthquakes, but in company with the one of 1837, it caused thousands of fatalities and widespread devastation.

Modern buildings not damaged by the latest fighting also withstood the quake, especially those built on limestone and dolomite rock that underlay western Jerusalem. But the innumerable war-shattered structures, especially older ones built on chalk and even rubble fill from layers of earlier construction–like much of the Arab sectors of eastern Jerusalem, the casbah of Nablus and other old Arab towns and villages in the Samarian highlands –suffered heavily. So did a few Jewish structures in and around Jerusalem, the legacy of the ill-advised, short-lived "fast building" code and its bribery-compromised inspections highlighted by the Versailles wedding hall collapse of 2000.

Curiously, a fissure opened across the Temple Mount, itself composed of man-made fill gathered over millennia. Running east to west the earthquake crack passed a few yards north of the Dome of the Rock. The beautiful Muslim shrine survived undamaged, except from some dislodged ceramic tiles and shattered glass, although damage to the historic al-Aksa mosque (previously St. Catherine's Byzantine church) was extensive. The crevice north of the Dome of the Rock measured nearly fifteen feet wide and forty feet deep. At the bottom, laid bare for the first time in thousands of years, rested the foundation stones of the Second Temple.

On the eastern edge of Mount Zion a section a the Old City wall collapsed. Coincidentally, it was the portion that contained the Golden Gate, bricked up by Muslim authorities centuries earlier, undermined by illegal excavations of the Waqf in the late '90s. Jewish legend had held that when the messiah arrived, he would enter Jerusalem through that portal, on the back of a white donkey. Christ, familiar with his people's folklore, purportedly passed into the city for the last time in just such a manner. Much later, the Muslim conquerors–themselves cognizant of Jewish and Christian beliefs that they both appropriated and subordinated– blocked the Golden Gate with stone and mortar. They imaged that such a material obstacle would demonstrate to the Jews the futility of continuing to await their messiah, God's anointed human messenger who would herald the inauguration of the renewed Jewish kingdom and its Davidic dynasty, required in preparation of the kingdom of God on earth.

The quake electrified both Jews and non-Jews. For even the most secular of the former it seemed a divine omen, transfixing all Jews just as the liberation of the Western Wall did in 1967. Then even the skeptic had thronged with the pious to the Wall, singing and dancing, weeping and laughing if not praying at the long-forbidden site. This time the response touched the same spiritual chord, but more deeply. This time the hand of man was nowhere to be seen.

The militant secularists, those Israelis who had styled themselves Hebrew Canaanites, not or no longer Jews, were sullen, silent–those who had not left the country altogether for the cafes of Paris, Rome and even Berlin, for the galleries of New York and the beaches of Los Angeles. The anti-Zionist religious Jews, who had celebrated Israel's defeat and collaborated—at least a few—with al-Masri's regime, were discredited. It was left to the modern Orthodox, to the Masorti Conservative Jews and Zionist Reform Jews, with traditional Sephardim among them, to re-center Jewish religious peoplehood, to reform the national chorus, echoing the solitary holy man who prayed under Ben-Melech's office window each morning: "And the Mount of Olives shall be cleft in the midst thereof... Yea, you [mountains] shall flee like you fled from before the earthquake, As in the days of Uzziah king of Judah." The whole country resonated to the quake long beyond the after-shocks.

For many Muslims, especially the older, more devout followers of the Brotherhood and the lesser-educated rural dwellers, the earthquake came as a rebuke. It sealed the Jews' victory with an apparently heaven-sent imprimatur. The next morning the bridges across the Jordan River to the east and the leading to them were choked with Palestinian Arabs fleeing the renewed Jewish state. Ben-Melech's promise of extraterritoriality for the two biggest cities meant little to those outside them, and to those outside the Jericho corridor or Negev Bedouin. The flight swelled as neighbor spread contagion to neighbor, each hasty departure stimulating another, paralleling the Arab flight of 1948.

Nevertheless, other Palestinians were more than ready to keep fighting. Members of the Palestinian army, veterans of the 1987 - 1992 and 2000 - 2002 intifadas—alumni of Arafat's Force 17, the Fatah Tanzim militia, Hamas' Iz'zidin al-Qasem 'military wing,' assorted gray-haired PLO gunmen—were still more than ready to battle the Jews. But in the chaos without al-Masri's leadership, with the Jews on the offensive, with many of their families and friends decamping across the Jordan River, against wild rumors like that of the new poison gas that killed only Arabs but spared Jews, they could not do it effectively. Bitter fighting continued for days, but in increasingly isolated pockets, dwindling in number.

Two days after Ben-Melech's proclamation some West Bank thorns in the old green line, like Jenin, Tulkarem and Qalqilyah, were virtual ghost towns. In nationalist-minded Nablus and fundamentalist Hebron, nearly all the residents stayed put, glowering amid the ruins and waiting for the Jews.

The partial Arab evacuation was a counterpoint to the new wave of aliyah, the first real mass movement of Jews to Israel since the influx from the Soviet Union and republics of the former Soviet Union in the late 1980s and early '90s, and Operation Solomon from Ethiopia in 1991. Previously, large-scale Jewish migration to Palestine, to Israel, came as a result of persecution elsewhere. Jews with little or no choice—refugees—returned to their ancestral homeland out of necessity. This was, perhaps, a necessary movement, but a psychologically negative and therefore reversible one. Hence the emigration of roughly half a million Israeli Jews in the first fifty years of statehood—ten percent of the Jewish total. But now, finally, waves of Jews came not to escape oppression but mainly to find a unique, an ultimate opportunity to participate in, to help shape, the long-delayed Jewish renaissance. This positive motivation was unlikely to be reversed by any countervailing human force. In this rush, small as it began, of free and comfortable Jews, Zionism at long last was validated.

One day after the fighting stopped crews finished repaving the cratered main runway at Ben-Gurion International Airport–the name reclaimed with so much else. The day after that the planes of immigrants, the olim–those going up the altar, up to Jerusalem, up to Mount Zion–began landing.

"Two days ago we had half-a-dozen flights with a couple hundred olim each," the acting minister for absorption reported to David Ben-Melech a week after the war. "Yesterday we had fourteen, about six of them 747's with close to five hundred people each. Altogether more than 4,500 people–in one day! Why, we hardly ever got that many in one year from the United States and Canada together!"

"Is that where they're coming from?" Ben-Melech asked.

"Most of them, sure. Where else are there than many Jews left? But we've been getting immigrants from France, Britain, the Ukraine, and Argentina," the minister said. "Many of those coming from the States are Russians, the ones who went to America in the late 1980s and '90s. I never thought I would live to see it, but we're getting more immigrants than we can handle. The big tent we set up in which to process them–the terminal still needs major repairs–is crowded and sweltering, a cross between a circus and a sauna. Best of all, no one seems to mind, too much. It's a carnival all right. Many of the immigration people are working overtime, voluntarily, just so they can be part of it.

"Anyway, I need another runway to handle more planes. And another temporary terminal to handle the people, and more transport to get the people to absorption centers in Tel Aviv, Jerusalem, Haifa, Beersheva and wherever else we're going to be sending them...."

"Don't forget Jenin, Tulkarem and the other abandoned Arab towns and villages in the western Samaria hills," Ben-Melech interrupted.

"Right," the minister said, "but that reminds me. A lot of those places are heavily damaged. The ministry of housing and construction seems to be lagging. I mean, with some flights already backed up in airports around the world we've got to hustle. We've got to accommodate all the Jews who want to come home, don't we?"

The acting prime minister and the acting minister of absorption began to laugh, deeply and uncontrollably, like schoolboys at a joke their teacher could not comprehend. Their laughter turned to tears and still they continued. They were in that moment as happy as it is given to men to be.

* * *

Alexandria, Virginia (January 18, 2010)–The Washington headquarters of the Friends of New Israel was nearly empty. So recently the headquarters for diaspora Jewry, now suddenly the rear echelon for the Jews of Judah, the remaining personnel spent most of their time coordinating travel, housing and other arrangements for tens of thousands of emigrants. Jonathan Marcus had received word of

Ben-Melech's proclamation shortly before it aired. He used the Friends' satellite and cable networks to reach the audience left by Jeri Levi. After Ben-Melech's address appeared over Friends of New Israel facilities, Marcus added a few lines of his own:

"As many of you know, I served more than 20 years in the U.S. House of Representatives. It was a high honor, a calling I am proud to have answered. But the events of the past four years have amounted to another calling, to the extent my own involvement matters. A new chapter, a new book of Jewish history, world history has been written, is being written. It's our history, and to help complete it I must go home to a land I have never lived in, but from which my earliest Jewish ancestors came.

"This decision is not lightly made, yet it is not a difficult one. I trust many of you will join us. N'sayah tova, have a good journey."

In the weeks that followed, a saving remnant of North American Jews, like their grandparents and great-grandparents, prepared to cross the Atlantic to a new, strange country in which they nevertheless could live as free people, as proud Jews. Only this time the route would be from west to east and the new land would be one foreign to their eyes but not their hearts. The new host culture, while sometimes anything but seductive, would not be alien. This time they would put down roots in their own soil rather than pollinate the vineyards of other lands. After two thousand years of multiple personalities, of living the sage's words about being "a Jew at home and a man in the world" they were about to heal themselves.

From 1880 to 1920 nearly four million Jews had abandoned the misery of Russia, Poland, Lithuania and other parts of Europe for the freedom, the tolerance of the West, mainly that of the United States of America. It came to pass in the months immediately after the War of Restoration that nearly four hundred thousand Jews left North America for Judah. Joining the four million Jews still left in eretz Yisrael, they began to fill the waste places and repopulate the towns under reconstruction in the Galilee and northern Negev, the empty Arab villages of western Samaria. Flesh was beginning to be put back onto dry bones.

Among them were Jonathan Marcus and his wife Felicia Sanchez Marcus; Admiral and Mrs. Chester Fogerty, at ease among and honored by the citizens of Judah; Sylvia Weinberg, who decided that "the beach in Tel Aviv is as good as the ones in Florida to retire to." They came together, most of them, with Jeremy and Sivan Marcus and their newborn son, Mordechai, to comfort the Tabor family at Nof Benjamin.

A day after Aharon had won a seat to the constitutional convention, Yehuda Tarbitsky had died. The old bull, the last of the kibbutz's founders, had willed himself to stay alive to witness the final triumph. Desire kept a failing heart beating just that long.

So it was that on a bright, dry day in March, several hundred kibbutzniks and guests overflowed the small cemetery at the southern end of the ridge between the Mediterranean and the mile of fields stretching to the Carmel. Inside a low fence, under a ring of evergreens, a knot of family and close friends stood at the grave.

Close behind them, a large group of old colleagues, acquaintances and strangers mindful of Tarbitsky's stature also paid tribute. Entitled to a military honor guard and rifle volley in salute, Tarbitsky had left instructions forbidding any weapons. Instead, the soldiers stood rifleless, in clean fatigues, at silent attention next to the simple wooden coffin dictated by Jewish tradition.

Aharon offered the eulogy: "My father, who saw or felt all of our battles, wanted no shooting, even in ceremony, today. He asked instead that we all chant the mourner's kadish, loudly. 'Open the ears of that Jewish God,' he told me. 'Open His ears, and those of my friends as well. And tell them I said "Good-bye" well-pleased.'

"I do not think my father feared death. I do know he conquered mortal fear more than once in his life. In that he was my inspiration. Last year he foresaw the impending struggle and felt the miraculous possibilities. His life prevented him from believing in miracles, but it also had taught him the power of hope. Hope, he told me, was the midwife of belief, and belief the key to remaking our reality.

"'Herzl was more than a romantic,' he said. 'When Herzl stated, "If the Jews will it, it is no dream," that was not delusion,' my father said. Rather, it was the same kind of faith, or will, that made the Torah so genuine it has transcended cultures and more than three millennia.

"My father also reminded me of Ben-Gurion's remark that Israel would not be secure until it had peace with its neighbors, ten million Jews and settled the Negev. 'B.G. had the right idea, but was out of order and off a bit on the details. We will be secure when we have six or seven million Jews and only a small Arab minority, settled as much of Samaria and Judea as we need and given the Arab states no alternative but to live in peace next door to, not actually with us.'

"He believed that the stage was set at last, not just for the proclamation of the resurrected Jewish state, but for its ultimate establishment as both a nation among the nations and as the Jewish State. An ordinary people would continue, as the God of history ordained, to do extraordinary things.

"Yehuda Tarbitsky did not approve of quoting rabbis, at least not often, blaming rabbinic Judaism in part for the stunted nature of diaspora Jewry, the twice fatal split between religion and Zionism. But even a good, lapsed agnostic kibbutznik could, and did agree with Rabbi Tarfon of Talmudic times: 'The day is short and the work heavy. It is not for you to complete the work, but neither are you free to desist from it.' That was the spirit in which my father lived his life. I don't know what Rabbi Tarfon said about enjoyment, but no doubt he had experience, being a Shabbat observer. Standing here, with the sea to our backs, the Carmel before us, it is clear we were not only meant to work in this place, to build this land and be built by it—for when has eretz Yisrael blossomed but when tended by its Jews?—but also that we were meant to enjoy it.

"When I was a student in America, I heard it said that 'in wilderness is the preservation of the world.' If that is so for the natural world, then in Judaism—in the vocation of the Jewish people—is the preservation and more, the redemption of the spiritual world. And of course, if the spiritual realm is not redeemed, the physical realm eventually dies as well. We are not aggressively seeking converts, but we do believe that 'From Zion shall go forth Torah, and the word of God from Jerusalem.'…

"'What is man, O Lord, that thou takes note of him? He is like the vine that rises in the morning, only to be cut down at night. But the memory of the righteous shall live and not die.' My father was not observant, but he most definitely was Jewish. A fighter for Israel, a founder of Nof Benjamin, an inspiration for Judah… a righteous man in his and any day. I know his memory will be for a blessing."

HaTikvah, that rare national anthem in the minor key, was sung with unashamed emotion. Not the politically correct, denatured version the ministry of education drafted in 1999 on the crest of the post-Zionist mania, but Inbar's original, the version that addressed "nefesh Yehudi," the Jewish soul and its eternal tie to the land of Zion and Jerusalem. Then, following the Jewish variant of an old Middle Eastern practice—placing coins or stones over the eyes of the departed—the mourners tossed handfuls of dirt and pebbles down onto the plain wooden coffin of Yehuda Tarbitsky.

The service over, they made their way slowly, in small groups, back toward the center of the kibbutz and the dining hall. A serious but not sorrowful reception with coffee, tea and wine, fruit, cheese and cakes awaited them. As they moved along the walks between the one and two-story buildings, including a few of the early red tile roofed apartments reassuringly unchanged by a half century of tumult, the trees and shrubs and a few lingering flowers lending a sense of place, fragments of conversation could be heard:

"All this religion, scriptural quotes from your husband. Quite a change from the old days. I'm not sure I approved," a friend said to Shoshana Tabor, who laughed.

"Me neither. But you know, when I hear it now, I finally feel it. I don't necessarily think it, or believe it—certainly not the way the haredim believe—but I do feel it. And I realize that feeling is something we missed before." And, she thought, what Ehud Kenaan and his comrades in the Peoples Progressive Party never allowed themselves to experience.

Aharon Tabor was talking with Professor Eshel, who had come to pay last respects to a friend and mentor. "Who would have thought it: the East Asians new colonialists in the Persian Gulf, with the Americans and Russians their protectors. Never in a hundred years…."

"And a real Kurdistan, at last, at Iraq's expense. Autonomous Christians in Lebanon, Copts equal if not autonomous in Egypt. Apparently justice is not impossible, only improbable," Tabor answered.

Felicia Sanchez Marcus had been staring at Sivan during the funeral. While her husband and the admiral talked—something they did often—she excused herself and went to the side of her new daughter-in-law. "Sivan," Felicia asked mischievously, "have you been putting on weight since the last pictures we received?"

"On the rations we get now?" Then she giggled. "I told Jeremy I ought not to wear this dress anymore. All right, you found me out. I'm nearly three months pregnant. Double rations!"

"Congratulations, daughter! And now it's your turn."

"My turn?"

"To congratulate me. I'm pregnant too! The doctor said I'm a very healthy forty-two-year-old."

"But Jonathan—my father-in-law—he's sixty!"

"Sixty-four, actually. But also quite healthy. As it says in Psalms, 'Planted in the house of the Lord, They shall flourish in the courts of our God. Even in old age they shall bring forth fruit, They shall be full of vigor and strength.'"

"Written by King David, right? A man with a lot of wives. Men never grow up, do they?" Sivan asked.

"The good ones actually do. But some only get older. The trick is leading them in the right direction. Some women can't, or won't, and some of us can, and do."

Inside the dining hall black crepe covered the chair Yehuda Tarbitsky habitually occupied so he could gaze out at his beloved shoreline, the dun-colored beach and the aquamarine waters of the Mediterranean. Nearby Fogerty talked with Jonathan Marcus.

"...and the knowledge of the Arabs, the Russians, even of the Europeans and Americans that we hold their major cities hostage may help ensure a pax Judah of sorts in our corner of the world. Certainly, no one seems to be rushing to dislodge us from our lands, or the Triple Alliance from its Persian Gulf stronghold, and that game's bigger than ours."

"Thank God," Marcus said, then changed the subject. "Did you see Jeri's broadcast? I thought she looked good, considering. And the way they photographed her, seated at that desk, minimized the effect of her being in a wheelchair. Jeremy tells me she's not expected to walk again."

"Maybe not, but she's as sharp, or sharper, than ever. Al-Masri might have done the Jews a favor in a way. Forcing her to prepare for the 'disputation' made her better prepared for the great assembly. And now that she and the children have been reunited, well, I don't think anything can throw her."

"That was peculiar, wasn't it?" Marcus asked. "To think that Hal Levi collaborated in his wife's kidnapping, even if al-Masri's people used the children's safety as a lever. Where is he, anyway? I mean, the Red Cross turned up the children in the prisoner exchange, what few prisoners were left alive. But Hal?"

"We've no idea," Fogerty said. "And even less about al-Masri. But I'm confident of one thing—if al-Masri's still breathing, we'll hear from him again."

"Yes," said Marcus, "I'm sure of it. But we'll know what to do; the first time he opens his mouth ought to be the last."

Rabbi Levi succeeded to the stature, if not the title, of chief rabbi. At the end of the War of Arab Unity the Ashkenazi and Sephardi chief rabbis had been executed shortly after Prime Minister Meir Sarid and Defense Minister Simon Tov. Al-Masri's ministry of Jewish affairs first had appointed an obscure, anti-Zionist haredi from the tiny Neturei Karta sect, but the fellow rarely ventured out in public and cast no shadow when he did. Many expected Bar Kochba Blum to be named the new chief rabbi after his heroic role in the reclamation of Jerusalem became known, but he gave the country a double shock: First, stating that he had been "tainted indelibly by warfare," he declined the job. Second, he endorsed Rabbi Levi, "an irreproachable model of the Jewish spiritual vocation," thus undercutting much of the resistance to a woman in the post.

Levi's proposed gathering was to begin the work of reconciling the three major branches of Judaism–Reform, Conservative and Orthodox–into one nation, one religious peoplehood if not one ritual practice. It also was to suggest to the constitutional convention ways to separate synagogue from state, to avoid the enfeebling entanglements of the old Israeli regime, without separating Judaism from society in the new Judah. While more than a few fervently Orthodox and secularized Reform and Conservative leaders refused to partici- pate, their general outlook–nation-less religiosity or soulless nationalism, let alone post-national universalism–had been so discredited by the events of the past decade that the bulk of their followers pushed the movements to participate.

In her broadcast, Rabbi Levi referred to the deadly clashes between religious and secular, which went all the way back to the beginning of the British Mandate and the struggle between extreme leftists in the Labor Zionist movement and the anti-Zionist Orthodox as well as the rightist followers of Jabotinsky. She noted their resumption during protests against the war in Lebanon in the early '80s, the assassination of Rabin in 1995, the scattered shooting between settlers and peace militants just before the War of Arab Unity, and the outright struggle between Magen Israel and the People's Progressive Party under autonomy. "Benjamin Franklin warned his colleagues at the start of the American Revolution that they must hang together or they most assuredly would hang separately," she said. "So it is with us, with the Jewish people now: we need a genuine unity based on our self-interest–not a contrived solidarity reached by papering over deep divisions but an organic healing of those divisions to restore a healthy whole, one refreshed by visions that are not so much competing as complementary, by energy from dif- ferent sources flowing toward the same direction." The overwhelming majority in Judah longed for the same thing.

During the fighting in Jerusalem, students from Blum's yeshiva, while wear- ing payyis and tsitsit, not only overran several anti-Zionist yeshivot but also, while adorned with kefiyahs and worry beads, shot up several meetings of the collabo- rationist Hebrew Canaanite underground. The decisiveness of Magen Israel's war within the war against the anti-Zionist Jewish left, and anti-Zionist orthodox right coupled with Rabbi Levi's resonant call for reconciliation, did much to marginal- ize any lingering Jewish opposition.

As for the great assembly itself, Rabbi Levi told her listeners, "there is prece- dent. In 1563, Rabbi Ya'acov BeRav of Safed tried to revive classic ordination according to the formula promulgated by Maimonides. And while the rabbis of Safed supported him, the rabbis of Jerusalem opposed. Nearly four centuries later, Rabbi Yehuda Leib Maimon, first minister of religion in the reborn Jewish state of Israel, again tried to revive unitary rabbinical ordination under Maimonides' formula. Neither he nor BeRav before him saw any fundamental obstacle, only those personal preferences that had hardened into tradition. Leib Maimon also proposed to both the new Israeli political leadership and the religious heads the revival of the Sanhedrin. Maimon noted that in the Mishne Torah Maimonides himself asserted that before the messiah could come, the Sanhedrin must be reconstituted—by human hands.

"But the divisions among the Orthodox parties in Israel, let alone among the Orthodox in diaspora and the rejection of the whole concept by the non-Orthodox proved too great. However, hindsight is golden. We see now that just as the Jewish state must have an elected leader, so to for the rabbis, all the rabbis who mean to re-forge Jewish peoplehood. Legitimate differences of opinion, based on our sacred texts, must be respected. But what lies outside the boundaries of those opinions also should be defined. Judaism is not infinitely elastic, it is not New Age bubble gum; the Torah is a sparkling gem that refracts light differently depending on the eyes of each reader—but it is not Silly Putty to be shaped at whim. The Sanhedrin's mission will not be to impose but rather to clarify.

"The assembly," Rabbi Levi continued, "is to bring Jewish practice into conformity with Jewish experience of the past 100 years. We will not try to restore that wholeness—however limited—that existed before the Enlightenment and Emancipation. We cannot, and in any case that unity was partly negative, enforced by external hostility. Judaism as a way of life and system of belief had lost ground in the freedom of the West which, ironically, Jewish ideas had helped call into being.

"We have yet to develop a credible, theologically consistent answer to the central question of where was God during the Holocaust. We have yet to deal openly, consistently with the idea of the ingathering as a new chapter of Torah, a new book of the Bible. We need to reemphasize the Torah as divine, the Talmud as inspired but subsidiary human commentary. Perhaps this is the way to real Torah Judaism and the way we can bring Reform and Conservativism back, and carry Orthodoxy forward, to avoid becoming two or more separation religions—as we nearly had done before the war—and to avoid becoming not a saving remnant but a living fossil, the Amish of the Middle East, for example. Our destiny is to be as innumerable as the stars, our message to be heard from Jerusalem outward over the entire world. Hillel famously asked, 'If I am not for myself, who will be for me? But if I am only for myself, what am I? And if not now, when?' In that spirit, let us start here, and let us start now.

"We Jews have longed for something—and pursued a score of false gods—for generations. Our persistent longing turns out to have been for an authentic religious revival. So," she added, "we will try, with good faith and goodwill, to find a broad and substantial consensus, based on tradition but incorporating our epic modern history. We must see to it that the tradition lives, positively, in the daily life of the people, speaking to our experience and aspirations, speaking of, to and from God, the God of Sinai, the source of ethical monotheism, Adonai who manifests Himself in history, who created mankind but expects us to be his partner in finishing, perfecting creation. We do not intend a post-rabbinic Judaism, although we have been perilously close to that, or the cop-out of post-denominational Judaisms—but rather neo-Torah Judaism, if you will—post-Talmud, post-exilic—for a people restored."

Marcus, speaking to Eshel at Tarbitsky's funeral, had noted that "so great is Jeri's status and so great is the people's desire for comity if not unity, that even a majority of the surviving disciples of the last free chief rabbis–who before would not even have bothered to scoff at the improbability of a woman chief rabbi or a new Sanhedrin–are supporting her call."

"Perhaps Jeri Levi will accomplish what Rabbi Maimon, even with Ben Gurion's ear, could not," Eshel replied.

* * *

Jerusalem (April 6, 2010)–David Ben-Melech had the oddest dream. Not only did he imagine that he was elected prime minister–which in fact had happened–or that all the embassies previously camped in Tel Aviv so as not to provoke the Muslims had moved to Jerusalem, but also that the United Nations itself had relocated to David's City. The Security Council vote had been unanimous, the General Assembly overwhelmingly in favor.

Ordinarily, he did not pay much attention to dreams. He had learned from one professor at university that they were "nothing more than random electrical discharges from nerves deep within a sleeper's brain," while another claimed that dreams were "the subconscious' abstract paintings of our deepest desires." In any case, his own–at least those he remembered–usually were quite mundane; the women all familiar and mostly clothed. But he too was aware of the old superstition and made sure to tell his wife, Pnina, before breakfast.

"Why would we want the U.N. in Jerusalem?" she laughed.

"Good question," he had replied. "Perhaps for the same reason President Andrew Jackson wanted the American Treasury next to the White House–to keep an eye on it."

He took a Sabbath afternoon walk from his apartment–restoration of the prime minister's official residence had not been completed so his family still waited to move–to the Old City. Outside the doorway to his building the old, bearded man, dressed all in white and holding an open prayer book, intoned from Hosea that "the number of the children of Israel shall be as the sand of the sea; and it will yet happen that, instead of saying to them, 'You are not my people,' what will be said is 'You are the sons of the living God.' Then shall the children of Judah and the children of Israel be gathered together, and select one leader, and return from exile."

"Do you want us to shoo him away?" one of his security guards asked.

"No, I kind of like the message, even if the messenger is a bit, ah, eccentric," Ben-Melech said. He had always wondered how one would be able to recognize the messiah and decided to err on the side of potentiality. Ben-Melech walked at a purposeful pace to the Temple Mount excavation. Ordinarily, teams of archaeologists from a dozen countries and their crews would be hosting debris from the earthquake-created trench. The sound of reconstruction of the Western Wall just below them would almost blot out the sound of their labor as workers set the war-razed Herodian stones back upon one another. Now, on Shabbat, the site was quiet, the destination of strollers. His guards fanned out around him, but even they began to enjoy themselves. The bright sunshine, the robust evidence of construction all around, the spontaneous applause when people recognized the prime minister—it was a day to cherish.

Complementing the historic restoration of the Kotel was the reconstruction of the abandoned Arab village, or neighborhood of Silwan—biblical Shiloach, still the site of King Hezekiah's well. Long a PLO stronghold, it now took on new life. Mid-rise apartment blocks, finished with the glistening Jerusalem limestone, were replacing the brown-brick and cement block houses of the Arabs. Many had been shattered by the earthquake, others damaged in the wars. Living in the new apartments would be not Jews but Christians, mostly fundamental Protestants from the United States and Western Europe. Whole congregations were immigrating, some demanding citizenship under the Law of a Return, claiming a "Jewishness" derived from the early church. Some announced their intention to "witness the recent acts of God" by converting to Judaism or, as some put it, "converting back to Judaism, the religion Jesus practiced." Others wanted to be on hand for what they were certain would be the imminent second coming of Christ. "Christian Zionists" were not just touring the Holy Land, they were coming in droves to live in it. A set of sticky problems for the ministry of religion, but one more welcome development for the ministry of absorption.

In the street young boys, children of the liberal San Francisco Chasidim, played an impromptu game of soccer. Their long side-curls danced as they chased the white-and-black ball through a pedestrian street in the rebuilt Jewish quarter of the Old City. From windows overlooking the plaza in front of the Western Wall reconstruction came the sound of prayers from older brothers and fathers in one of the reestablished yeshivot. Ben-Melech caught a phrase from Jeremiah: "I will gather the strays of my flock from all the countries to which I drove them, and will bring them back to their folds; and then they will be fruitful and increase." In the old Arab shuk the stalls of new Jewish merchants were shuttered for the Sabbath, but tomorrow would reopen for the trade of tourists from around the globe, in Jerusalem in wide-eyed wonderment to see for themselves the miracle of their time. Among them would be many from Japan, Korea and Taiwan. All about Ben-Melech the city thronged with life and pulsated with hope. All about him Jerusalem gleamed golden in the clear piercing light peculiar to the city the Talmud calls the center of the universe, the place where heaven and earth meet.

Total Jihad was designed by Tom Suzuki, Tom Suzuki, Inc.,
Fairfax, Virginia.
The cover design is also by Tom Suzuki.
The book was printed by Lightning Source, La Vergne, Tennessee.

The text is 9.5 on 12 Baskerville,
the display type is also Baskerville.

Printed in the United States
913500003B